RULE THE NIGHT

BLOOD LEGACY SERIES BOOK 6

ELISE HENNESSY

Flutterbye Trail Press
797 Sam Bass Road #2541
Round Rock, TX 78681

First edition

Editing by Red Loop Editing
Cover Design by FrostAlexis Arts
E-book Chapter Art by Real Life Design
Published by Flutterbye Trail Press

ISBN: 978-1-954582-02-6 (E-book)
ISBN: 978-1-954582-06-4 (Print)

Feedback: Encounter a problem with this book? Let us know at
elisehennessyauthor@gmail.com

Books by Elise Hennessy

Books in the Altare World

GRYPHON RIDER ACADEMY
Second Chance
Chosen
Storm Front
Wild Flight

ROYAL SPY INSTITUTE
The Crown Heist
Five & Chance

Also by Elise Hennessy

BLOOD LEGACY SERIES
Dream Walker
The Winter Key
Queen's Return
Court of Illusions
Shadow Dance
Rule the Night
Dhampir's Wish

Blood Curse
Blood Legacy: The Complete Series

Rule the Night

Blood Legacy Series Book 6

Elise Hennessy

Chapter 1
Jaromir

Sweetness tickled Jaromir's nose as a soft touch traced the ridge of his brow and then the curve of his dry lips. He recognized the humming tune flitting in and out of his ears. Fumbling for consciousness, he focused on the numb tingles in his fingertips and toes, sensation crackling unpleasantly over his chafing skin.

A bar of light slid through his slitted eyelids. White. Sunlight. He was in an infirmary, he realized. Someone was dangling a candy wrapped in bright paper over his face.

"Jaromir," a woman sang, her voice pitched gentle.

For a long moment, he wondered if he'd been caught in some feverish dream. It would explain the aches covering his whole body. Maybe he was still in New York, recovering after being bitten by a Fell Mad. Could it be that this whole expedition into Faerie was just a convoluted twist of his desires, born of his chance meeting with an exotic, unknowable dragon shifter?

He'd been alone for so long. It wouldn't surprise him if his mind had snagged on the first hints of affection from a stranger and spun up a story of their unlikely pairing. Him, a simple and old soul, and her, a free-spirited whirlwind.

Except Izell Firebrand was the one leaning over him, her fingertips brushing the side of his cheek. Her fae eyes were like white nebulae, shimmering with unshed tears as she breathed his name. This wasn't part of the fantasy, he thought. He never wanted to see her in pain.

He moved sluggishly, covering her hand with his, his skin tingling with the dry sensation of her scale texture. A laugh bubbled from her lips, little more than a relieved hiccup. "I'm so glad you're finally awake," she whispered.

She helped him move to a sitting position and fed him small sips of water until he was confident in his voice. "Izell...what happened?"

This wasn't New York. The infirmary was wholly unfamiliar and drenched with mild Faerie sunlight, some of which pooled harmlessly over one of his arms. It was brighter than usual because the wall opposite of them was mostly one solid sheet of undulating tarps trying to cover a massive hole with blackened edges.

Izell glanced over her shoulder to where he was staring. "Oh." Her mouth pressed into a sheepish line. "Ignore that."

"It's very difficult to overlook, lady fae."

Paper crackled as she unwrapped the candy and popped it into his mouth. He chewed obediently, savoring its sweet berry flavor as he pinned her with an expectant look. She blew out a sigh. "Fine. I made it."

"Why?"

"It's a long story."

He gestured to the bed. "I'm not going anywhere."

She covered his hand with hers, leaning in and breathing with quiet intensity, "Jaromir, you drank the blood of an angel. I was sure you were about to die."

For a moment, he blinked and flickered through the dregs of his memory. He had? He definitely had, but it was one drop diluted by a whole glass of water. At the time, he'd thought there was no way it could harm him in such trace amounts. Desperation to find his Gift again had made him think it was worth the risk.

Now, he was too numb to know if the Gift had returned or not. Izell looked him in the eye, her lips parting and then closing a few times as she struggled to shape her next words.

"You've been in a coma for weeks," she whispered. "But I didn't know it. I found out in the worst way possible."

She turned to retrieve another candy from a rolling table she'd perched by his bedside. She had a mountain of them heaped up beside a glossy book prominently featuring a man's naked chest on the cover. Jaromir couldn't help a fleeting smile amidst his concern.

"Tell me what happened," he coaxed.

As he chewed the next sweet, a chocolate this time, she deliberated. The distant pinpricks of stars in her eyes glimmered with thought. He admired her openly, because she didn't sit still often enough for him to simply...take her in. Izell was the most unique woman he knew, and that related to more than just her personality.

He'd never gotten to ask how much of her appearance was affected by her dragon. Some features were obvious—sandstone-colored scales covered her arms from elbows to fingertips, lending her a sharp ridge of spines along her forearms and wicked claws. She had a thin, scaly tail she tended to wind around her middle like a belt. She'd said once it was to avoid sitting on it, but Jaromir knew it was also to tame the most obvious tell to her various mercurial moods.

While most astral fae had night-dark skin and a silvery glitter of stars sprinkled over them, Izell's form was molded from gold. Her skin was a shade darker than her dragon scales and sparkled with brilliant stars like a living, polished statue. A loving hand had cast her face with high cheekbones and pouty, generous lips. Her fae ears formed sharp points sticking out of a tangled nest of stark white hair she'd piled and pinned haphazardly to the top of her head.

Now that he was looking more closely, he spotted the shadows haloing her eyes. She was as beautiful as ever...but she was also in absolute disarray.

"Did you meet a man by the name of Sondus Arus?" she finally asked. Her fangs flashed, another gift from her dragon side. A set of eight total, they transformed her face into a frightening grimace if she smiled too widely.

"Yes. He helped me get in touch with an angel," he said. The same one who'd given Jaromir a drop of his blood. The wingless astral fae, Sondus, had set up the meeting, stating that he'd wanted to help Jaromir recover from his disability.

Izell pinched her brow, a growl rumbling from her throat. "Sondus is a spy. After you fell unconscious, he impersonated you."

"Why?" He couldn't imagine he'd have any use, even to a fae spy.

"To have an opening to arrest and interrogate me."

Jaromir shook his head slowly. Why would...?

But, of course, his sluggish brain produced the reason right as she told him why. "Because of the demon spark inside of me, what remained of Jazrach. He figured it out and wanted to know why I was harboring a demon."

Not just any demon, but the one who'd twisted Lucia into a monster with just its spark lingering in her soul—the same terrible fate Izell was no doubt struggling from right at that moment, made all the worse because she'd discarded her stash of demon-suppressing herbs. He still didn't understand why she'd done that or why she'd shoved them into his hand right before disappearing through a portal.

"I wanted you to understand what was coming next." Her breath hissed through her fangs, coming quicker as she balled her fists. "And so, I explained myself to *him*."

For a fleeting moment, Jaromir was jealous of Sondus. Explanations from Izell were ephemeral and rare. It was why he kept very still, hoping she would unpack the details of everything again if he was just patient enough to wait for it.

Emotions flashed over Izell's face before she settled on a furious snarl. "The spark is gone, Jaromir." Smoke curled from between her teeth. "Sondus thought he was saving me, but in actuality, he has doomed us all."

Fear slithered through his gut. "What do you mean?"

"Let me tell you what you missed..."

Chapter 2
Izell

Izell, too, had woken up in an unfamiliar bed recently. After Sondus had knocked her out in the Sanctum, she'd sat up in the same infirmary and realized someone had clapped a set of nephilim chains on her wrists. Her magic was curtailed by the manacles, leaving her body heavy and exhausted.

A human man stood over her. "Ah, I apologize for waking you." He spoke with a pleasant smile. Her gaze flicked over his forgettable human features, made extra tan from an obvious love of sunshine, before settling on the writhing *thing* he was holding.

Ink-black tendrils snaked in a halo around his closed fist. They were pointed at her, pulsating and grasping. She realized she recognized this man—angel, actually—and had a sneaking suspicion about what was going on. If she'd had her magic, she'd grow her claws into talons and rake them over his arm so he'd release the creature and she could steal it back.

She lifted her wrists. Her arms trembled with effort.

All the while, the angel, Soren, exuded gentle rays of light from his fingertips. The writhing creature's struggles were dimming already. It made sense; it was only a spark of a demon, a tiny kernel of its soul. "I took this out of you," he said, taking a step back. The sharp tips of its tendrils drooped with a few dying jerks.

Izell breathed an "*ugh.*" The world spun from the simple

effort of turning onto her side, struggling with the simple task of pushing aside a sheet.

"I agree, it is disgusting. Did you know you had the spark of a corruption demon inside you? That's what this was. Luckily, I was able to remove it," Soren said. It crumbled in his hold, becoming a fine powder that sprinkled to the ground.

Dead. Izell watched it eddy to the ground, her insides turned to ice.

She lifted her gaze to Soren, staring without a blink. His cheer dimmed when she didn't react how he expected. Surely, someone anticipated violence from her, since she was clapped in nephilim chains. They weren't wrong.

She cleared her throat, testing her voice. It rasped more than usual, dropping into the lower registers. "Did I ask for you to remove it?"

"In this matter—"

"You just went ahead and did it," she interrupted.

A line appeared between his brows as he considered her. "It is my duty to protect the innocent from all demonic corruption."

"Innocent," she echoed with a scoff. "I *wanted* that spark, you inconsiderate fool. You...you..." Her whole form trembled, locked somewhere between fury and weakness from lingering drugs. Despair tickled her ribs, making it hard to breathe. Dark spots overtook her vision.

In a blink, she was lying back in bed, Soren's palm covering her forehead. She bared her teeth with a hiss, just menacing enough that he backed away. "Regardless of your reasons, I was unwilling to stand by and allow you to be corrupted by such an insidious demon." Conviction flashed in his eyes. "You are worth much more than that."

"I decide my worth, not you," she muttered, skewering him with a glare. She knew he would've destroyed the spark earlier had he known she was carrying it the last time they'd crossed paths. There was a good reason why she'd kept its existence a secret. Only two people had witnessed her bargaining with Lucia to take the spark in the first place.

It'd happened what felt like a lifetime ago, before Lucia's

death and transformation into a demon. The Sorceress had been chained up like a rabid dog in a New York warehouse, desperate to become herself again rather than continue down the path to madness spurred by the piece of Jazrach within her.

Taking it was part of a long play on Izell's part, one piece of many that she was putting into place to ensure Earth and Faerie alike were spared from an apocalyptical event. The spark was meant to fester in her until she could be considered a demon strong enough to empower the new Dark Eye of Worlds. She was going to sacrifice herself and, in doing so, save everyone else.

How was she going to save anyone without it?

"I'm sorry it worked out this way," Soren said.

"Me too. I'm so very sorry that millions are going to die because my plans just fell apart." Her voice lacked its usual bite. She let her eyes drift closed as it really sank in.

Thousands of years' worth of scrying and preparation, squandered. The only path to success she'd witnessed with her future sight, crushed out for good.

"We're all going to die," she croaked. "We're going to burn in Hell's fire because of you. I hope you're happy. I hope *Sondus* is happy. Meddling asshole." She had a lot more choice words for him when they next came face to face. Judging by the soft scuffle of paper somewhere else in the infirmary, she wouldn't have to wait long for that moment.

"I'm going to find something for the pain. You're not in your right mind," the angel said gently.

"*No!*" she snarled. Soren's footsteps halted as she struggled to sit up once more. "You will not drug me. It is my choice, and I refuse it."

Concern cloaked the man, but he nodded. "Very well. I honor your wishes in this regard." Instead of leaving, he drew up a chair. "Are you well enough to discuss Jaromir?"

A sharp comment was halfway to her tongue before she paused. She hadn't seen Jaromir in ages, too busy orchestrating the last few steps of her now-defunct plan. Well, she hadn't seen the *real* Jaromir in that long. She'd come to explain and say goodbye to the man she'd developed a fancy for, just to realize

Sondus had, at some time, replaced her dear, sad vampire prince.

Sondus's face flashed in her mind's eye. His features were slack with regret in the split second she'd revealed him before passing out in his arms. Fire stoked in her chest, fury cutting through the lingering drugs in her system and bringing new clarity.

"Where is Jaromir?" Her voice was deceptively quiet, while on the inside, she was ready to erupt.

Soren pointed to her right, where a dark curtain was drawn around one of the other beds. "Right over there. He is still resting, but I assure you he's showing signs of waking soon."

Izell could feel her jaw growing rigid. "Explain why he has to convalesce," she said from between her teeth.

The angel smiled, a gentle wave of light emanating from his expression. She recognized it for what it was, a trick of his nature to share calming magic. Her spine straightened with the hostility making her vision swim, sure that she was going to hate whatever he was trying to relax her for preemptively.

"I gave him a drop of my blood to reawaken his Gift," he said.

The tether on her control snapped. Eyes bulging, she raised her voice to a rasping shriek. "*What*! You did what!"

"There's no need to—"

"You fed him angel blood! Pure poison to a vampire!" She pointed an accusing claw at him. "You murdered him."

Soren shot to his feet as she peeled her sorry self from the bed at last. Her arms felt like they weighed hundreds of pounds, swaying uselessly in front of her. Still, the angel retreated in the face of her fury, his palms up in a placating gesture. She sensed a more aggressive wave of his magic flushing over her skin, drawing an aggrieved roar from her.

"He's okay. He's not dead. I promise," Soren said in a tone pitched to soothe. He shuffled back another step as Izell's lips drew away from her fangs.

"Did you put these chains on me?" she demanded. He must've. Anyone with half a brain should've expected this reaction. Angels were as unwelcome as demons in Faerie for exactly the reasons he'd proven—tromping on boundaries in the name of "duty," assuming their way was right without question. "Did Jaromir *ask* to be poisoned, or did you force it down his throat?"

Another person put himself between her and the focus of her ire. "Soren didn't do anything wrong," Sondus said.

"*You*," she hissed, her gaze narrowing to a red haze. She'd thought he was lingering in the room somewhere. He was no better than the angel, thinking to make judgments for her.

"Izell, I know this all looks bad—"

He ducked a clumsy swipe of her hands, the metal cuffs swooshing past his head.

"—Please let us explain."

"Your actions speak loud enough," she snarled.

"I took you here to save your life. I used Jaromir's cuffs on you," he said. This time, when she tried to hit him with the chains, he grabbed her wrists as her whole body swung with her momentum.

Stars above, she was still dizzy, still weak.

He took his opportunity to talk, his gaze earnest. "I asked him to give Jaromir his blood. *One drop* of blood. Izell, I'm sorry. Things have gotten out of hand. Now that we know what you were planning, we can help."

For a moment, all she did was stare at him. "You don't understand what's coming," she said to herself. "You've never seen a demon in your life."

"The stories are enough."

Her gaze sharpened into a scowl. "No. You have to see it for yourself. Maybe then you'll understand the depths of your foolishness."

She breathed a few words under her breath. Sondus had given her the one clue she needed to take back the upper hand—she knew these nephilim chains and the enchantment on them, including the emergency override command should they accidentally fall into the wrong hands.

With a metallic *click*, the shackles sprung open and clattered to the ground between them. Sondus glanced down, his lips parting in shock and then opening wider when her hand shot out and encircled his throat.

Magic poured back into her, but her newfound surge of strength came straight from her dragon side. Her dragon spirit, Queldian, awoke with a violent snort.

She didn't explain anything to Queldian. He woke up so rarely that they were both used to longer catch-up sessions when she was in quiet solitude. Tail lashing, she drew her dragon to the surface, feeling her body rapidly change. Scales covered her skin, bones popping and thickening to support her sudden growth into a full-grown fire dragon.

Sondus dangled in the circle of her talons, desperately trying to pry her scaly fingers from his neck and shoulders. His panicked glance went to Soren, who was at the door to the infirmary, calling for help.

"Don't worry, Sondus," she rumbled. "I'll show you *exactly* where you went wrong."

Chapter 3
Izell

Fae society revered dragons. The most powerful of their race were chosen by dragons as lifelong companions, but few understood the benefits to having a dragon familiar besides the obvious. Dragons were living, breathing fonts of magic, acting like a focus to magnify spells.

Izell hadn't needed an occultarus since becoming a shifter, as *she* became her own focus. She could point and shoot any spell she desired, a huge advantage to out-cast her fellows, who needed either an occultarus or complicated hand gestures for their spells.

With Sondus struggling in her grasp, all she had to do for her next spell was tap the back of his head with a claw. He had nearly no magic of his own, being a wingless fae, so he had no defenses as her magic sank into his mind. He went limp, his eyelids flickering.

Rushing footsteps and shouts approached from the hall, and she glanced that way with an irritated snort. With Sondus still caught in her grasp, she exhaled a gout of flame and melted the wall opposite of her. Charging through it, she scattered embers with the unfurling of her wings. Her nostrils flared as she took to the sky, filtering the smells of decay and chill from the golden-brown forest below. This had to be the Shifting Wood.

She roared, summoning a portal to slash open the sky before

her. Barreling through it, she left the shouting fae and the glowing outline of a flying angel behind.

Her attention turned to Sondus as they emerged from the other side of the portal and soared over an open expanse of glittering ocean. *"When I was young, I used to scry the future as far out as I could,"* she began. *"I would see the same thing way, way into the pathways of time: complete destruction. It became something of an obsession to me. What happened? And why did every vision always come to the same view of desolation?"*

The fae in her hold made a muffled sound, still addled by her magic. She figured it had had time to settle where it needed to, so she activated the second part of it, casting a memory-sharing spell with him. When she said she'd show him where he went wrong, she'd meant it in the most literal way possible.

"This is what I saw, Sondus."

As a side effect to the spell, she relived every moment with him. Her wings kept them aloft as her mind's eye went to a distant point.

Soon, the winter solstice would come, the day the Veil would fail and demons would be able to enter Earth and Faerie for the first time in centuries. Izell's vision sharpened to show a losing battle at Nyixa, where a demonic host would emerge. Coming to Earth was infinitely easier than climbing out of Faerie's hostile ground, so the little island would bear the brunt of the invasion at first.

"Without a suitably powerful demon already prepared for the ritual to create a new Dark Eye, the strongest of Earth's defenders die here, along with the thirteen people who own the Keys," she narrated. *"Then, they come for the Light Eye..."*

Faerie's giant orb of magic would be a brief setback for Hell's army since it contained concentrated angel magic. King Orin would detonate it as a last-ditch effort to eradicate the threat—it would be useless without a Dark Eye to help it tether the Veil between worlds.

"No," Sondus moaned.

They lingered on that moment, watching a giant column of brilliant magic explode into the horizon, taking the surrounding city with it. Orin would evacuate the area, but Faerie would lose its king in the blast.

She showed him what the demonic survivors would do, how the Lords of Hell would avoid the blast and go straight to slaughtering every fae they could.

"The gods. The angels...?" Sondus protested.

"There's a bitter truth you need to understand," she sighed. *"The angels will defend Earth first—it is their number one priority. And the gods... Every death will weaken them until this happens."*

Cyranos was first. His serpentine form was covered in countless burns, washed ashore from his ocean boiling around him.

Next, Raenith's white-hot glory guttered to embers as one of the Lords of Hell absorbed her heat.

Zalice was blown to shards. The air of Faerie would grow oppressive with decay.

But the sight she lingered on was Getana's dead form, the druidic green of her eyes faded, and her wooden body softened by decay. The moment she died, a winged demon with hellfire in his eyes would draw the souls of the Sanctum into himself, consuming billions of fallen and their magic to become a new kind of immortal. A self-made god.

"Do you need to see more?" she asked viciously. *"This is how every timeline ends. The demons destroy the rest of Faerie and rule what remains of Earth."*

"It can't be every timeline," Sondus whispered.

"It is!" she roared. *"We can't repel a demonic invasion. I saw one chance, one! I would carry the demon myself because Hell will not send up another powerful one before the next invasion."* Her fury wavered as emotions pressed in on all sides. With a flick of her claws, she dismissed the memory-sharing spell between them.

"You gave away your future sight," he replied, his voice growing stronger as he recovered. *"Seers are at their most accurate closest to an event."*

She snarled, scattering a mouthful of embers. *"Are you doubting what you've just seen?"*

"I have no doubt that was a future—"

She stopped listening, her wings slowing. Unpleasant tingles drew up one of her arms, sinking into a semi-familiar pattern under her scales. Turning her head toward it, she swallowed a new wave of trepidation. Sondus's panicked gaze darted between her and the arm she inspected.

Carefully, she shifted just that arm back to normal, peeling off the scales that marked her as a dragon shifter. Emblazoned against her skin in demonic runes was the mark of her pact with Lucia. Izell had taken Jazrach's spark in return for a favor from Lucia, and until she got her due, she would wear the evidence of their deal.

Unless Lucia died. The runes were vibrating at Izell in warning before abruptly stilling. The ink that formed them went dormant, as flat and magicless as an ordinary tattoo.

Izell cursed viciously. *"What? What is it?"* Sondus probed.

She shook out her arm, regaining full dragon features as she roared in denial. *"Lucia's dead,"* she groaned. *"But not fully. She has been returned to Hell."*

He waited, eyeing her like she was going to take a bite of him in the throes of her despair.

"Don't you see?" she snarled. *"There are two angels in Faerie."*

Sondus's brows drew together. She hissed impatiently. *"It means that Hell will send two new demons here. Two angels, two demons."*

"I'll alert my people?" he offered.

Shaking her head sharply, she inspected the ocean beneath them. They were almost to their destination, she thought, weaving a bubble of oxygen around them in anticipation. *"It doesn't matter now,"* she said bitterly.

She tucked her wings, diving toward the glimmering water below. Sondus screamed, dragged along for the ride as they scythed into the salty embrace of the ocean. She kicked her back legs, tail undulating like an eel as they rode their momentum deeper and deeper. Cold liquid seeped under her scales, but at least it couldn't steal her air as she sipped from the oxygen bubble sparingly. Sondus's hyperventilating was taking too much from it.

"Izell, please. I'm sorry," he pleaded.

She ignored him, pushing them ever onward until she spotted what she came for—a massive underwater dome of magic situated below a shelf of sparkling coral. The people of Adrun looked up and believed they were viewing the stars in all their glory when, in reality, their dark world was in complete exile.

"You have trespassed against me. If you want my secrets so badly, start looking in the place I've languished for three thousand years," she snapped.

She laid her claws on the barrier, creating a hole just wide enough to slide through. The magic was easy to enter but impossible to leave, sealing them both in the moment her tail flashed through. A salty rain of ocean water preceded their freefall into the dark world of Adrun. She roared her greeting to her old home, realizing this piece of land was tiny now that she'd seen the vastness of Faerie once more.

She took the shivering Sondus in a quick freefall, covering miles in minutes and zeroing in on the palace as it grew larger and larger on approach. *"Izell."* His mental voice was weak, his body likely struggling from the trauma it'd just survived.

"I want you to know that this isn't over," he whispered. *"Thank you for sharing what you planned, unwittingly or not. I can't help you if I don't know what you're going to do. No one can."*

She grunted, feeling less than charitable as she flared her wings wider for a landing. Maybe she should touch his face down first.

"We can make a new plan now. We will make it work."

"You're an idiot. I expected better of you," she replied. He had once been her most promising apprentice, who she'd practically adopted upon seeing the depths of his intelligence.

You don't need magic to make your mark in the world. Cunning will do just fine, she'd told him. Look where that had gotten her.

She landed on three feet, keeping his body from impacting the ground, then laid his sodden form on the cobblestones in front of the palace, snorting in derision all the while.

"Izell!"

Her head jerked up, realizing she had an audience on the front steps. Servants and highborn shifters alike were staring at her. Now that she was paying attention, there were still screams coming from the rest of the city as panic set in. Anything unexpected from the sky was taken as a portent of doom—if the magic above them sprung a leak, they'd drown, after all.

Standing in front of her court, hands on hips, was Queen Nyah. Her dress was soaked through, the pastel material clinging to the softening curve of her belly. Next to her, water dripped off Adrius's dark wings as he stared just like everyone else.

Izell paced closer to the royal couple, bending her neck to put her head level with theirs. "Prepare yourselves. Adrun will be pulled from Faerie's ocean in a matter of days," she said, watching their shocked faces light with excitement.

It was *supposed* to be joyous. If Izell still had the spark and the persistent whispers that came with it, she'd be happy too, knowing her people were free at last. Now, they had a month, if that, to enjoy Faerie's splendors.

She turned her snout to Nyah's belly bump, nosing it ever so gently. "Congratulations," she mumbled before drawing back.

"Where are you going?" Nyah murmured, tilting her head like the curious wolf spirit within her. "Come tell us about Faerie? We haven't seen you in months."

Izell huffed, in no mood to chitchat. She left just as abruptly as she came, finally alone to enjoy the solitude her dragon side craved. She made the familiar flight to her home, transforming back into herself in the relative privacy within.

Relative, because there was still a glowing portal to Earth in the middle of her living room. She tossed it a scowl on her way by, practically daring someone to come through while she was naked, her last set of clothing lying shredded where she'd first shifted.

"*Are you going to tell me what's going on now?*" Queldian spoke up the moment she was dressed, her weight dropped into her most comfortable chair.

Silence. She savored it for a moment. A part of her wondered if anyone was following her after that showing.

Then, she leaned her head back, sharing a glut of memories

with her dragon spirit. He'd last woken a few weeks ago, when she'd been writing a letter to the Trader to pass to the djinni Saniya. Queldian absorbed it all, rumbling thoughtfully.

"Interesting."

"That's all you have to say?" she sighed.

"You overreacted."

She snarled wordlessly.

"Fine. We'll talk about it when you're calmer."

Except they probably wouldn't, as he would be asleep by then. Sighing, she wrapped her arms around her middle, savoring the heat of her familiar's attention while she had it. He was an ancient dragon, just as old as her, enduring the ennui of time with sleep since he was a deceased spirit. Part of her worried that he would continue fading into dreamland until the only proof of his presence was his scales on her body.

"I would never leave you alone in this world," Queldian whispered, catching the direction of her thoughts.

Except he already was, with his long streaks of rest. Neither of them probed that thought, not when she heaved herself to her weary feet and stepped toward the portal. She slid a haphazard glamor over herself as she entered the human world, making herself look human too. In a blink, she was emerging into a cleaning closet and bursting out of it like she owned the place.

Coven Rehnquist's mansion hadn't changed at all. The too-bright lights hanging overhead drew an irritated hiss from her as her eyes narrowed to adjust to the influx of brightness. The scent of too many humans and vampires in one place hit her nostrils. Thankfully, it didn't take her long to find a vampire she recognized. Blonde and petite, the young Sorceress vampire was threading sparkling garland through the banister.

"Hey," Izell said sharply.

Violet startled, turning eyes the color of silver coins toward her. A tinge of gray touched her cheeks. "Oh, Izell! You're back?" She looked more closely at the fae, her brows drawn in concern.

"I'm here, aren't I?" Izell grumbled. "Do you have your box on you?"

"My...box?"

Despite her confusion, Violet patted over her person until she drew out her cell phone from a back pocket. "Yes, my box! I have it right here."

"Tell Armando"—her brow crinkled—"I have need of transportation."

She tapped her thumbs over the screen, nodding rapidly. "Is everything okay?" she asked, giving Izell another once-over.

She smiled with all her teeth. "Great. Never better."

Except her world was crumbling, and she had only just realized she'd blown a hole in the very same infirmary where Jaromir was resting.

"*Overreaction,*" Queldian supplied.

She finally agreed with him, the first brush of shame tickling her insides. In the face of her rage, she hadn't spared a thought for checking on Jaromir first. No, it'd been full speed revenge ahead. Who knew how he was faring for certain? Just the very thought of him hurt or worse had sent her into one of her blackest rages.

Her dragon flooded her with a wave of amusement. "*Yes, your friend. Just a friend and nothing more.*"

"*I'll strangle your ghostly hide,*" she grumbled.

"*Good luck. I'm holding my neck out for it right now.*"

She blew out a sigh.

Violet spoke up again, hearing that. "If things aren't actually great, can I help? I'm just taking a little break, promise. I've really come far with my magic."

"Got a greater demon in your back pocket?" she snarked.

"No?"

"Then just enjoy your break," Izell said with a scowl. She didn't express any more of her dark thoughts.

Thankfully, a *ding* on Violet's phone saved her from the younger woman's worry. "Armando's here," she reported.

Izell nodded to her, stalking out the front of the mansion. A little green wreath's red-painted bells tinkled when she slammed the door behind her. On the other side of the gates, a box-shaped monstrosity was parked, and leaning out the passenger's side window was a young Black woman, waving with a big smile. Armando honked the horn.

She slid into the backseat, her scowl remaining despite the cheer of the two people seated up front. The box hummed below her feet. She was sure this means of transportation had another name, but all she remembered was that humans moved around at high speeds in their boxes on wheels.

"Heyyyy, Izell. Nice to see you," said Charlotte, the resident dhampir. She and Armando turned in their seats, peering at her curiously and then exchanging a glance.

"Where we headed, *amica*?" he asked, rolling his words with a faint accent.

"Take me to the box store." She paused, realizing that wasn't very specific. Humans also shaped most of their stores like giant boxes, handling their processed food in boxes and then returning home to their cozy, box-shaped apartments.

Irritation scoured under Izell's skin. It was no one's fault but her own, because she itched to be in Faerie, not here. Her momentum was why she'd landed in this box with her two coven-appointed chauffeurs in the first place. Now, she floundered.

"I mean...the box that contains the book vendors," she clarified.

"You got it," Armando said with a smile. He drove them into New York traffic, silence settling over them all. Charlotte tapped away on her phone while Izell looked through the window, watching the night life of Earth scroll by. So many humans, all of them unknowing of the fate awaiting them.

She tried not to think about it, but the future was the only thing on her mind, weighing her body down more effectively than any set of nephilim chains.

Before she knew it, they were idling outside of the box store which sold books around the clock. "Thanks," she mumbled.

"We'll be right out here when you're done," Armando promised.

Izell nodded, heading inside and taking a deep breath. Ink and paper, plus the tang of coffee. Humans had so many books, such a huge selection from their modern printing technology and legions of authors all jockeying for shelf space. She filtered into the rows, searching for a specific section.

The moment she pulled a paperback off the shelf and saw her favorite human-invented trope, that of a bare man's chest, she burst into tears. If she'd been paying attention to herself, she wouldn't have been so surprised at the sudden rending of her emotions.

Jaromir had ingested angel blood. She hadn't checked on him, and he could be struggling for his life as she stood there sobbing over a human book.

He was *so* desperate for his Gift that he hadn't been willing to wait. He was supposed to have the Mending Key. There'd never been a question in her mind that he'd get his precious healing magic back when his time came.

That wasn't even the worst of it. Her careful plan was *wrong*. Jaromir hadn't fulfilled the task she'd set him on, even though she'd scried his success. She'd been seeing Sondus wearing Jaromir's face that whole time.

What else had she missed?

When had she messed up her own plan? Was it doomed from the start?

All she wanted was to keep things going, to extend this beautiful era of prosperity both humanity and fae-kind had enjoyed. She wanted a legacy; she wanted the end of her life to mean something. Just like her grandfather before her, Izell was ready to retire into death's embrace if it meant her name was immortalized forever.

Maybe this was the price of her hubris.

Izell froze a moment later, feeling the lingering static of a portal opening and closing nearby. She turned her head to the left as a pair of heels clomped over the store's cheap carpeting.

Though she looked like any other blonde woman, Izell recognized her as a fae immediately. While Izell slapped any random human features over herself when she walked around on Earth, the woman before her always wore the same glamor. "Hi, Izell," said Sorsha, eyeing her in obvious concern.

Indigo magic rested over Sorsha's irises, undoubtedly peeling Izell's glamor away to peek at the bedraggled dragon shifter underneath.

Scoffing, Izell spared her a glower. "You found me. Want an award?"

"Imagine my surprise to see one of my dear academy friends miraculously transported to Adrun," she replied, folding her hands over her middle. She was the picture of a composed diplomat.

"He deserved it," Izell muttered.

"I agree."

Izell raised a surprised brow.

"He trespassed against you, and you are fit to punish him however you please," Sorsha said. "Do I wish you'd been kinder? Of course."

She sneered. "There it is. You're here to chastise me on his behalf. What's the matter—is he too afraid of the human world to come tell me himself?"

A frown touched the other fae's lips. "Whatever you showed him put him in great distress. He's being tended to by the druids as we speak. What..." She drifted off, eyeing Izell. Her voice dropped to a gentler octave. "Why don't we return to Adrun? A little birdie told me it's about to be raised from the ocean."

"It is. I was the messenger," Izell grumbled.

"If anyone deserves to witness Adrun's first moments back in the sun, it's the woman who sacrificed herself to save the people within." Sorsha offered her hand. "Haven't you been waiting for this day for three thousand years?"

That, she had. While biding her time, preparing for the next threat, Izell had overlooked the fact her actions were already inked into the sands of time.

She'd also forgotten three thousand years of waiting for the sunrise over Adrun in her distress over Jaromir.

"Isn't that telling?" Queldian teased.

With a sigh, she took Sorsha's hand.

Chapter 4
Jaromir

"...And here you are, just fine," she finished with a shrug.

Jaromir sat back, reeling from the whiplash of her story. There were so many questions rattling around in his head. "So, Adrun has been raised from the ocean?"

"Yeah."

He blinked in disbelief at her bland tone. "The moment you've been waiting three thousand years for," he probed.

"It was fine, I guess. Maybe I spoiled it for myself, coming to Faerie without everyone else." She glanced down at her lap. "I also couldn't stop thinking about how short-lived everyone's joy will be."

"Izell—"

"You're probably wondering how everyone's doing. I didn't really talk to them," she continued like he wasn't even speaking. "When you're feeling up to it, we can go have a big reunion party or something."

"Izell," he repeated more firmly.

"Promise I won't be too much of a rain cloud. We have a month or so left, after all. Most everyone doesn't even know their soul is about to be consumed in fiery—"

He grabbed her elbow, shaking her. "Izell!"

"What!" she barked.

"Are you even listening to yourself?" he asked.

"Certainly. The words come out of my mouth, and I have to hear them too."

"This"—he gestured to encompass her—"is not the Izell I know."

Her lips thinned with displeasure, and for a split second, he was sure he was about to see her loosened temper firsthand. He rushed to explain before she could start sharpening her fangs in his hide. "The Izell I know doesn't give in to despair at the first setback." A soft growl rumbled from deep in her chest. "She's seen too much and watched others fail, so she knows how to succeed."

"There's no coming back from this. How do we even begin to fix it?" she muttered furiously.

He considered her tale again. She wasn't just upset about losing Jazrach's spark, but also the way it'd happened without her consent. In her shoes, he'd be angry too, but from an outsider's perspective, he wondered if her emotions were intertwining into a singular ball of negativity. "The problem is that we have no demon to sacrifice to power the Dark Eye?"

She spared a sharp nod.

"But Hell will be sending two demons to replace Lucia and Jazrach, if they haven't already," he continued.

"They will not be highly ranked demons," she sighed. "The problem is, Hell knows what we're up to. They know we need several things to create a new Dark Eye. The timing has to be perfect, we have to have all thirteen Keys, we have to recreate the ritual to accommodate a large group casting the same spell King Oberon did on his own...and we have to have a powerful demon to place in the new Dark Eye. If one—*one*—of those things is off, it won't work. We all die."

She stared into space, her eyes losing their luster. "Hell will not send up a demon powerful enough to fill the Dark Eye. And we don't have all the Keys yet anyway. We're fucked, Jaromir."

"It's not time to give up," he insisted.

A scowl twisted her fair features, but at least she turned her attention back to him. "Do you even know what that angel did to you?" she spat.

He leaned away from the hostility in her tone. Something told him he wouldn't be seeing Soren and Izell in the same room any time soon. It explained why the infirmary was whisper-silent around them.

She made a gesture, summoning up a circle of shimmering, golden light, the signature color of her magic. "See for yourself."

The magic solidified into a mirror. At first, he wondered if it was still filtering the color of her magic, because he was...different. He checked his arm, realizing he really did look tanner. The ghostly paleness that came with a sunless existence was replaced by a complexion that glowed with health.

He looked to the mirror again, leaning in. His fangs had receded, displaying a flat line of pearly whites as his reflection grimaced. "Are my eyes really...?"

"An angel's? Yes," she growled.

"No, a nephilim's." He'd seen the same sort of thing in Gwendolyn, but the shine looked more like the eyes of Nyah or Olivia. "An Alchemyst, maybe. What a breakthrough." A laugh of disbelief escaped his lips.

Still, he caught signs of wrinkles and a scattering of silver amongst the blond whiskers making a sad wisp of a beard along his jawline. His chin and cheekbones were sharper, giving his already lean face more definition. He hoped his immortality held despite losing some of the youthful glow of his Blood Prince level vampirism.

"Are you seriously happy about this?" Izell asked in disbelief.

His smile barely dimmed in the face of her incredulous look. "Yes, actually. I don't have to harm another being to exist anymore," he said.

No matter what he'd changed into, he no longer had to violate his doctor's oath to survive. The deeper that sank in, the more pleased he was with that basic fact. His nature had been a paradox, a strict balancing act between his savage thirst and more peaceful mindset.

Maybe it could be shared, used to spread around a different

kind of vampirism for others tired of the bloodlust. "This was one drop of blood! Can you imagine the breakthrough if we can replicate this for other vampires?"

Izell's lips quirked, but at least her aggression was dimming to the occasional twitch of her tail. "I'm not sure anyone else would survive the transition," she said slowly. "Soren and I have had a few *discussions* since I returned."

Jaromir assumed she meant "interrogations" from her emphasis.

"I think he should explain himself to you," she continued with a sniff, standing and stalking from the room. While he waited, he reached over and snagged a handful of candies, grunting from the effort of lifting his weight back onto the mound of pillows supporting his spine.

He chewed and considered what had to happen next once he was well enough to get out of this bed and back on track. Apparently, Sondus had finished his research for him, so that was one loose end tied up. He'd be damned if Izell left him behind again. When she recovered from her spiral of despair, he knew she'd patch together a new plan. This time, Jaromir would be there to keep her grounded.

Soren walked into the infirmary first, taking the seat Izell had vacated. The dragon shifter stood outside of striking range on the other side of the bed, her scaly arms crossed.

"Go on, tell him," she growled.

The tension between the two of them was thicker than the humidity after a rainstorm. Jaromir glanced left to right, reading their faces. It was Izell's hostility that made the hair on the back of his neck rise, while Soren's composure was perfect. If anything, he ignored Izell, which seemed to make it all the worse.

Jaromir had only met the angel once and recalled how easy it was to relax in his presence. Was that really some sort of magic? Izell had described it like waves of light coming from Soren's smile and voice.

"Good afternoon, Prince Jaromir. I'm glad to see you awake," Soren said, directing his smile his way. "I've been enjoying the companionship of your little research partner, Alaku. He's adamant in referring to you as a prince."

Jaromir softened at the news. Alaku was his research assistant at the library, being a young member of the lesser fae race that ran the entire Library of Faerie. The fact that Jaromir's title seemed so important had made the boy extra eager to please. "How is he?" Jaromir asked.

"Just fine. Using his library time to read a book for you, if I recall."

He shook his head. There was no need anymore, not when someone else had finished the required research. "I'll need to cut him loose so he can research something more practical for someone else."

Soren inclined his head in agreement. "I shared some of my mission here with Izell after our last...unfortunate interaction," he said carefully, earning a growl from the dragon shifter. "It was not by random chance that I offered my blood to you, Jaromir."

He felt his brow draw as the angel glanced down, tugging at his fingers. "Before I was permitted entry into Faerie, I was screened by the Goddess of Fire and entered a deal with her. I was to offer my blessing to the Blood Prince who yearned to be reunited with his magic. I told her that the light within me was too strong for a vampire to consume, but she was adamant that you would survive. When we first met, I realized why you would be fine. You may recall we discussed how Gifted vampires have distant angel ancestry?"

Jaromir worked his jaw. He did remember Soren's warm reception and the reveal that there was an angel somewhere in his bloodline. Not enough to be able to work with light magic, but just the tiniest of sparks to allow him the ability to heal instead.

"So, you only shared your blood because the goddess told you to?" he asked.

"It was much more forceful than a simple request, my friend!" Soren laughed, radiance forming across his back as he stood. He unfolded wings made of pure light and lifted his head, revealing the depthless pools of sunlight in his eyes. The effect spiraled into his clothing, lighting spiraling runes all the way down his robe. "My mission here is too important to jeopardize, so of course I agreed to her deal. But you should know what my blessing means for you, so behold my true form."

The light in Soren built further, igniting a burning wheel between his wings. It was nearly too bright to look at, but Jaromir tried anyway, awed by the circling disc of pure magic inscribed with thousands of tiny runes that resembled eyes from a distance. Brightness caressed the planes of his face, transforming it into something harsh and beautiful, as crisp as an artist's fantasy. In that moment, he was as inhuman as every description Jaromir had gotten of Jazrach's true form, mighty and radiant.

Izell put a word to it for him. "Archangel," she said, shading her face.

Soren bowed, his expression the picture of humility despite his obvious pervasive power. "The Archangel of Life, at your service."

Jaromir couldn't find his words until Soren dimmed his radiance. He blinked rapidly to chase away the bright arcs behind his eyelids. No wonder one drop of blood had been enough to lay him low—it'd come straight from an angel that powerful! "Incredible," he murmured.

"I did not only give you my blood, but my blessing." Soren was back to his plain appearance, though the brightness of his smile was telling. He hesitated, earning another irritated look from Izell. "Archangels are the ones that bless new souls when they are ready to earn their wings. If you were deceased, you would be an angel of life. But you are a living soul, so you now contain a nephilim's power."

Jaromir's lips parted with awe.

"You may know that vampirism twists magic in unexpected ways." Soren's expression turned apologetic. "I did not reignite your Gift. In fact, I believe you have gained the opposite: light that burns. You are the living equivalent of a battle angel, Jaromir. A nephilim filled with blazing light."

Just like that, it felt like the bottom dropped out of his world.

A warrior? Him?

That meant he was a nephilim like Gwendolyn, who used her

powers to smite the wicked. He shook his head in denial. "There must be some mistake. Surely you can teach me spells of healing light?" he beseeched. "I am a doctor."

"I'm sorry, my friend. I've been around battle angels since the dawn of time, and your light feels just like theirs."

On the inside, Jaromir screamed in denial. He stuck a fake smile on and let Soren excuse himself. Something cracked within him, but he didn't utter a peep until Izell read his expression and left the room to "let him rest."

Jaromir closed his eyes, expecting the call of agony in his heart would escape his lips at any moment. Sleep embraced him instead.

Chapter 5
Izell

THE NEXT TIME JAROMIR WOKE, SHE WAS THERE, READY
with a glass of water and the book she'd stolen from that box store.
He didn't say much, his unnervingly angelic eyes fixed somewhere in the middle distance.

She had the feeling he was mourning. Hope was a fleeting
feeling, replaced by the reality of what he'd become. Jaromir
wasn't a battle angel; anyone with eyes could see that. She
doubted he'd ever killed another. *Well,* she mused, *maybe a Fell.
But that would be all.*

While he processed the news, she read to him. It turned out
that she'd picked out a "sci-fi romance," as the cover's text
suggested.

She'd thought a colorblind person had made the original
cover, but it turned out that it didn't have a mistake on it. The
main male character was purple-skinned. *Purple!*

He'd abducted the female love interest for "probing."

Izell grinned when she realized how salacious that was. She
glanced up from the page to find Jaromir watching her, smiling to
himself.

"What?" she asked.

"Why do you read such things to me, lady fae?"

"The last book wasn't like this." She laughed at the memory
anyway, because she'd had time to be more careful with her selec-

tion. She'd picked a story with a gothic setting, featuring a swooning heroine and a brooding prince of darkness love interest who was a vampire obsessed with her "swan-like" neck.

Jaromir burst out laughing. "At least this new man has color. I can only hear about someone being described as white marble so many times before becoming self-conscious about my own complexion."

"You're more of a beige now, to be fair," she quipped.

Some of the cheer dimmed from his expression as he took another glance at himself, as if re-remembering. "I mean, why do you read me this sort of fiction?" He gestured to the paperback open in her hands.

She tapped her chin in consideration. It might dim his impression of her to know she'd established a similar ritual with a different man, but that was several lifetimes ago. Breathing a sigh, she said, "Let me tell you a story." She set the paperback aside. "A true story. You've met Keegan, right? My..." She counted on her fingers. "Great-great-great-great-great-grandson?"

Jaromir snorted, trying to disguise a laugh, the same reaction everyone had when she specified her relationship with her distant relative. "Yes, I've met him."

"He's the only family I have left to remind me of...*him*," she said more heavily. "My heartsong. I met him at the dawn of my life." Remembering that time of her existence was a challenge. She couldn't recall what her mate looked like anymore, but she liked to think she recognized a hint of him in Keegan. Especially when she antagonized him and earned his long-suffering looks.

She turned to Jaromir, who held an uneasy expression. She rarely opened the book of her life to this early chapter, back when she'd been just as much a foolish youth as the kids she advised and guided now. "I met him visiting my mother in a different place of healing—she was a doctor, you see. He was being held for a terrible magical disease, a curse from a blight fae. Because of the nature of it, he was bedridden and bored."

A wistful smile crossed her lips as she remembered the hazy shapes of that time. "I didn't realize he was my mate at first. His bored face caught my attention, and we got to talking. Eventually, I brought a book to read to him as he waited for his curse to wear off. He'd asked for me to pick out something interesting, so I opted for a romance."

"A romance, hmm?" Jaromir murmured.

"Yeah. And it was just as dirty as the modern ones I've been reading to you," she said. "Fae have been telling each other dirty stories longer than humans have existed."

He shook his head. "Why am I not surprised?"

"You shouldn't be. So, I guess you took me back to that time when I saw your bored face in Coven Rehnquist's infirmary," she admitted with a slow shrug. "You were my captive audience for candy and bad romance." She left it unsaid that she'd thought his sad, human-born features were endearing. Unlike the meatheads who made up the rest of the Blood Prince group, Jaromir's then-maroon eyes had been filled to the brim with deep thoughts and the kind of insights one didn't see often. She'd liked that he was a thinker rather than a fighter.

That, more than anything else, had reminded her of her long-lost mate. She hadn't tried as hard to remember him after meeting Jaromir.

"Hmm. How did you lose him?" he asked.

She made a sound low in her throat. "He was one of many casualties in the war between Seelie and Unseelie." Unlike Jaromir, he had been a fighter, but the profession was not a suitable match. A blade through the heart had ended him one day, leaving Izell alone.

Well, not so alone at the time. She'd still had Queldian. But with him asleep once more somewhere inside of her, she felt the loneliness of her mate's absence that much sharper in the moment.

"I'm sorry for your loss," Jaromir said.

She waved him off. "Please. I barely remember him. I just remember how he made me feel. There's been no one since."

"Really? No one?" he asked quietly with the kind of intro-spective look she recognized.

Did she have the energy in her to tell him how she felt? She'd already ridden the waves of those emotions once, just to realize she'd poured her heart out to the wrong man.

"I had hoped…" Hesitation stopped her. She was struck by the futility of the gesture when life as they knew it was about to end in a month or less.

Still, didn't Jaromir deserve to know how she felt? The *real* Jaromir, that is.

If Queldian were awake, he'd be razzing her so hard. She kept that in mind as she met Jaromir's gaze again. "If my life weren't forfeit, I would be pursuing you like a fox circles a henhouse. Relentlessly, in the dead of night, patiently waiting for any loosening of your defenses."

Several emotions passed over his features at the same time, settling on a certain sort of gloomy amusement. "Really, madam? I'm the hen in this analogy?"

"I would take it a step further if you weren't bedbound," she admitted.

"Please. Humor me."

"You could be the rooster if you'd let me in the henhouse." She waggled her brows. "I'd eat you right away."

He covered his eyes with one broad palm, cracking up. "Thank you. That is outstanding motivation to get out of this bed."

"Well, good. Get on with it, then," she quipped.

He shifted, cupping his hands together. A little sparkle of light appeared on his fingertips. "I know I should be more grateful for receiving an Archangel's blessing, but what am I going to do with magic designed to hurt others?"

"You hurt others with it," she said frankly, earning a surprised glance. She lifted a shoulder. "There's no sense in looking back. You have burning light, so burn with it. When you were a healer, you healed. If you want to continue that, you'll get out of this bed and let me introduce you to King Orin. He still wears the Mending Key and will give it to you if I ask."

There. She'd dangled the carrot on a stick. Hopefully, he'd chase it rather than let himself languish.

"He would really give it up without complaint?"

"Yes, you silly man," she sighed. "That's how this was supposed to go! You were supposed to figure out the spell, then I'd get the Mending Key for you. But Soren wedged himself in the middle of my plans."

"He didn't intend to ruin what you had planned."

She scoffed, rolling her eyes. Sure he did. He was an Archangel, the pinnacle of "I know better than you do."

Jaromir read her expression and reached for her. She laced her fingers with his, soaking in the gentle squeeze he gave her. "When you create a new plan, you *have* to share it with the rest of us." It felt like an uncomfortable echo as he added, "No one can help you if they don't know what's going on in that head of yours."

For someone who'd relied only on herself for so long, the reminder was a slow drip of unpleasantness. Yes, he was right. No, she didn't like it.

"This misunderstanding between you and Sondus wouldn't have happened had he known why you were carrying Jazrach's spark."

"Oh, I'm sure it would've. Just in another form. He'd have found a different excuse to force the spark out of me," she grumbled.

For the first time, she had to acknowledge that Sondus had behaved exactly as she expected. He'd sussed out a well-kept secret about her and acted as a caring former apprentice in removing her from danger. He probably felt he still owed her for saving his life. Very few greater fae survived having their wings removed, after all, let alone moved on to have fulfilling lives.

She'd made sure he had that. Maybe he hadn't felt he was betraying her at all, but helping her as she'd helped him.

"Let us in this time." Jaromir sounded close to pleading.

She met his earnest gaze, her fingers trembling with emotion she didn't dare show. "I know why you brought me and the others," Jaromir continued. "You wanted to help all of us by sending us on tasks that you could've done without issue."

"Yes," she admitted quietly. If she'd wanted to, she could've scried the location of every missing Key and gotten them without much trouble. Even the Flight Key, formerly held by Lord Zalice, could've been hers, but instead, she'd helped Sirius and Talina, even if she figured their love story ended slightly differently than she'd seen with her future sight. One of them had finally killed Lucia, after all.

"All of you have gotten a new start by now, except for you," she continued. "But the moment you have the Mending Key in hand, my plans for you are finished."

"Were," he corrected. "Wherever you go from here, I follow."

She arched an eyebrow even as warmth filled her chest. "Even into death?"

"Even there. Maybe when the time comes, I will save you." His nephilim-gold eyes glimmered with new conviction. "Besides, I need to let the fox into the henhouse at least once."

Chapter 6
Izell

JAROMIR DIDN'T GET UP RIGHT AWAY, BUT IT WASN'T FOR lack of trying. He recovered like he was a newly turned vampire, which was technically true of his changed nature. They were able to draw sparkling gold blood from him, proving that he was an Alchemyst, and it seemed like his body needed time to adjust to this new reality.

Days passed. While he rested, Izell plotted. She turned over variations of her original plan in her mind as she thumbed through page after page of Sondus's meticulous notes before stopping at the finished diagram blessed by the late King Oberon himself. They were *so close* to putting the pieces together and creating a new Dark Eye.

Jaromir was right. She couldn't give up now, especially when "close" still had a chance of becoming reality. They would figure out some workaround to their demon problem.

She glanced up, spotting Jaromir emerging from the showers, dressed smartly in a fae-cut tunic and soft khaki pants. He'd shaved his wispy little beard, hair still damp and spiky from his long scrub down.

"I'm ready," he said. There was barely a wobble to his steps. She'd take it.

"The servants will be glad to be rid of me. Maybe they can start fixing the wall," she said with a distinct lack of remorse.

With a flick of her claws, she had a portal open, the city of Summerhail reflected in its depths. Though she knew the way around the portal-jamming runes that decorated both the Library of Faerie and the Seelie Palace, having been one of the spell-casters who'd fashioned them in the first place, she set their location to a polite distance outside the palace.

Jaromir adjusted the collar around his neck. "And they're expecting us?"

She shrugged. "They will be the moment they see us."

"That's not..." He shook his head and went through the portal, leaving its surface rippling like water. She cast a look behind her, double-checking that she'd gotten all of their meager possessions. They were in a bag swung over her shoulder. Her traveling gear was in a different hidey-hole, and she was sure they'd need it all shortly.

The guards who stood at attention behind the palace's gates clenched their weapons the moment she appeared by Jaromir's side. She didn't bother hiding her dragon features. Fae carried deep grudges, assuming every *mort loci* had forfeited their bodies to spirits, animal or otherwise. It'd been a shameful, cursed existence in the past.

Except the shifters of Adrun had turned the practice on its head, using the spirits of their deceased familiars to make it impossible to be transformed into Fell. That was the kind of "*mort loci*" she'd seen for three thousand years. But these fae didn't have the same exposure to shifters yet.

"There goes another one," one of the guards muttered as she walked by, leading Jaromir into the spacious garden that marked the front courtyard of the palace.

"Shut up," the other one hissed. "That's Archfae Firebrand."

Izell turned a smile on them, baring all her fangs. "Don't worry, gentlemen. I don't bite."

The stares lining up on her back felt hostile as she kept walking. She had no doubt the other shifters who'd come here had received a similar reception.

"This was the part of Adrun's raising I was afraid of," she whispered to Jaromir. "Politics."

He frowned over at her. "You weren't kidding earlier when you mentioned *mort loci* are banished from fae society."

"Be prepared to witness some terrible culture shock," she sighed.

"Joy," he murmured.

She steered him past the long line of fae, greater and lesser alike, all waiting to petition their king or officials representing him. As far as she knew, Orin still wasn't seeing his people, but she knew for a fact that he'd finally left the Light Eye to attend to his other duties. The spell to remove the barrier over Adrun took both his and Kalimea's magic. Many generations ago, the Seelie King and Unseelie Queen of the time had stopped warring just long enough to agree to banish all the Fell in the first place, leaving the ability to reverse their work in the hands of their family members.

Of course, no one at the time had expected the two separate royal lines to agree to peace for all of Faerie and to unite in marriage. But Izell had witnessed it with her own eyes before she committed to saving the people of Adrun in exchange for three thousand years of darkness. It was a miracle both royals had survived this long.

She led Jaromir into the royal wing of the palace, ignoring the stares of palace staff and guardsmen alike. It was nearly as bad as being her true self amongst her vampire friends on Earth, but at least they stared because it was a shock for human-born to learn of the true existence of both fae and dragons in one go.

If she were a betting woman, she assumed Orin would be in his favorite parlor, listening as various advisors told him what he'd missed while tending to the Light Eye. That was where she led Jaromir, releasing a self-satisfied hum as she spotted four guards posted outside the door.

Two guards crisscrossed their weapons over the threshold when she moved to ignore them and open it. "No interruptions," one said. "Make an appointment."

She leveled a glare at him, infusing her voice with the smoke and gravel of her dragon's presence. "I don't make appointments."

On the other side of the door, a voice called faintly, "Bring her in!"

Izell grinned as that same guard opened the door for them. Orin knew to expect her, then. She walked in, not too surprised when she saw the faces at the table set just inside. This parlor abutted the royal rooms, full of comfortable and plush leather seating. The table could be lowered to accommodate cushions instead. The colorful pads Orin favored were currently lining the wall in a haphazard pile.

The man himself sat at the head of the table, smiling over the rim of his teacup. The porcelain was tiny in his mitt. It'd always tickled Izell that he'd married someone as small and vicious as Kalimea when he had the personality of a broad-shouldered marshmallow. He was a solar fae, pure and clean sunlight marking his pupil-less fae eyes. He wore a brilliant white suit with a stripe of navy across the breast and belt.

While his skin was the same yellow-orange of any solar fae's, his hair was a straight fall of silver, tied back from his face. Not even long hair could soften the handsome planes of his face, with the kind of fae beauty that would give a mortal a heart attack. His sharp features and blade-shaped ears were the results of generations of the finest breeding, but the white-hot flames that lined his back were from a blessing.

No solar fae had flaming, white-blue wings like Orin. They were a clear sign of favor from the only other creature of fire that burned so bright, Lady Raenith herself.

"Welcome back, Izell," he said warmly. "I'm pleasantly surprised you haven't barged into my bedchamber this time."

"Kindly never do that again," said the Unseelie Queen seated to his right hand, staring daggers through Izell for a moment before Orin laughed. Kalimea caught his mirth, twining her hand through Orin's. Her own sharp features relaxed in the halo of his light.

Izell would think it was cute if she hadn't scanned around to see who else was seated at this table. Her lips pressed to an irritated line to be face to face with *Archangel* Soren. Again! And beside him, dressed in a lord's royal indigo coat and ducking his head from her scrutiny, was Sondus, released from his punishment the moment Adrun was raised from the ocean.

"Isn't this a nice little meeting?" she asked through her teeth as she forced a smile. She liked the other four at the table, at least. Sorsha and Keegan had rejoined their mates. Theron's formerly untamed druid look was combed free of its feathers and twigs, his leather armor buffed. He'd scooted his chair closer to Sorsha's than decorum necessitated, his hand resting on the small of her back.

Meanwhile, Keegan and Ash were back to studiously pretending they weren't all over each other in private. Izell had no doubt that was partly due to her presence, so she draped herself behind Ash's chair and grinned at Keegan. "If it isn't my..." she paused for effect, tapping a claw to her chin. "How many greats—?"

"Five," he interrupted, fighting off an annoyed look. There it was, that little glimpse of a man she used to know.

"Great-great-great-great-great-grandson!" she proclaimed. "And his little circle of friends. Where's your dragon?"

"Right here." His crimson familiar lifted her head from the nest of cushions in the corner. Vidia blinked slowly at Izell in affection.

"Vidia," she cooed, elongating the dragon's name as she came over with arms outstretched. The dragon's rumble was practically a purr as she bowed her head for scratches behind the bony ridge of her scaled face. Izell turned back to the group. "This is Jaromir, by the way."

The former Blood Prince lifted his hand for an awkward wave, still standing a few feet from the meeting, where she'd left him.

"So, what's on the agenda today?" she asked casually, her gaze flashing to Sondus. "Getting briefed on how my most promising apprentice tricked me?"

A pause gripped the assembled fae. It was Kalimea who opted for the truth. "Yes, actually. He was to the point where a Lord of Hell slays Lady Getana and absorbs all the souls from the Sanctum."

"Oh, yes, the moment our utter and crushing defeat is secured," Izell said in a candy-sweet voice. Vidia reared back from her with a soft whine.

"I would appreciate it if you wouldn't publicly shame my spymaster," Orin said, waving a broad hand. "What's done is done. The future you showed him will not exist."

Izell didn't let her hackles rise. She nodded absently, taking the king's mild chastisement in stride. "You're right. Because you won't be detonating the Light Eye anymore." It was just a guess, but he nodded anyway.

"I was just bemoaning that Kalimea wiped out her little nest of demonologists," he said with a hint of humor. "We could empower one to summon the kind of demon you need."

"Good thing I was planning on doing that myself," she replied to dead silence and a set of stares.

"I was kidding, Izell," Orin sighed, touching fingertips to forehead.

She returned to Jaromir's side, crossing her arms. "A certain couple of someones in this room have taken exception to me not sharing my plans, so there you have it. We need a demon, so let's summon one."

Orin shook his head with a frown. "It takes a measure of black magic corruption to be capable of summoning a demon, even a low-level one. There's no recovering from twisting your soul in such a way."

"So? I'm going to be dead in a month either way," she said. As Keegan exchanged an alarmed glance with Ash and Theron muttered under his breath, she had the distinct feeling she was making this meeting too tense. Most of them didn't understand her original plan yet.

"Izell, may I speak with you privately?"

The last person she wanted to talk to was the one offering. Soren stood, offering his seat to Jaromir with a polite smile.

"I guess," she said reluctantly. Jaromir gave her a reassuring smile when she cast her concerned glance his way.

Well, nothing bad could befall him with a group like this, she thought. She followed Soren out of the parlor, her brows drawing to a scowl when he led her further into the palace.

"How are you today, Lady Izell?" he asked mildly.

"Sure am great to be in the presence of the man who ruined my plans without my consent and would do so again in a heartbeat if it fulfilled his angelic agenda," she snipped.

"Ouch," he said in that same calm tone. "I would find it admirable how you line your mouth with blades if the words weren't aimed at me."

"What do you want?" she asked flatly.

"Just a little heart to heart. Have you seen the new additions to the Light Eye?"

She hadn't, actually, and realized they were heading through the length of the palace to reach the courtyard built around the tool of power. They walked through a public area, drawing attention for different reasons, but the end result was a whole host of turning heads. Izell already wanted the anonymity of her glamor back.

The massive double doors that led to their destination were guarded by more armored Seelie, this time wearing the distinct markings of elite soldiers on their breastplates. A solar fae woman glanced between them and nodded to her fellows. They opened a crack between the doors for Soren and Izell.

She glanced around, emitting a pleased hum. More military elite patrolled the grounds, with a single armored fire dragon perched atop a newly erected stone fortification that encircled the inner courtyard. This was meant to be a place of peace and reflection, featuring the sound of lapping water and meandering, tiered paths. At the center of it all was the massive dome of the Light Eye, its dragon-forged glass surface covered in loops of fae runes.

"So, that's what he was doing," she said to herself. She felt eyes on her back as she circled the structure from a distance, reading the runes a patient hand had etched into the glass. They glowed orange, visible against the white light radiating from within.

"There are two spells here." She glanced to Soren, who

walked a pace behind her, hands laced behind his back. "The first one will make this whole thing explode."

"Apparently a foolhardy venture rather than a last-ditch defense," he said.

"Not apparently. No demon of high rank would get close to the Light Eye. As long as it shines, they wouldn't risk being burnt by its radiance. And this second spell..."

She squinted, reversing course to read the new ribbon of runes, which crossed counterclockwise around the Eye's dome.

Hmm. *Ingenious*, she thought. Rather than release all of the Eye's magic in one catastrophic moment, this spell could be focused through a smaller occultarus, turning a thin stream of light into a focused laser. Either Orin or an accomplished Archfae could turn the Light Eye into an effective defense.

"It's beautiful, isn't it?" Soren's voice pierced her calculations as she mused over the laser's force and width. She cast an annoyed glance back to the angel. His sunny smile gleamed with the tool's radiance bathing his face.

She couldn't help a thread of curiosity. "Was its creation a boon for you?"

"A boon, lady fae?" he asked mildly, his gold-tinged eyes turning toward her.

"As I recall, Archangel Cerindra was an Archangel of Life."

His face flickered with emotion, his tone thick. "Yes. My mentor, in fact. I have tried to fill her shoes ever since. Interestingly, this relates well to why I asked to speak with you privately.

"You see, amongst my people, sacrifice is considered the noblest endeavor. It is a beautiful act, to give so deeply of yourself so life goes on." Threads of sunlight wove around him as his wings unfurled, stretching to soak in more of the Eye's light. "I wonder, do you feel Cerindra's love as you stand here? Do you feel her the embrace of her magic?"

"Not as you do," she said, because she could tell they were having different experiences. The magic in the air was responding to his presence, glowing off him.

It reminded her of a different moment, when her grandfather's spirit had exploded into fragments of air. Just solid enough to hold, if only for a moment.

"Were you there when the Eyes were formed?" she asked.

"Yes."

"I was as well. But I was a youth, maybe ten years old. I don't remember much about the event, just that I didn't understand why my grandfather had to leave," she admitted.

"But now you understand."

"All too well."

"King Oberon's sacrifice changed the scope of the worlds we inhabit forever. He saved countless lives from knowing a war as vicious and unending as that which wages between angels and demons. I will strive the rest of eternity to touch as many lives for the good as he has." Soren sounded like he was deep in his own mind. It seemed like he was working up to why he really wanted to speak to her here.

"Don't go idolizing him now. He was flawed, as are we all," Izell replied. "The Dark Eye's destruction cinched it. We've lived on borrowed time, and soon, his deeds will fade, trampled under the machinery of war."

"You have lost your faith," he said quietly.

Her hackles rose to hear "faith" from an angel.

"Not in the religious sense," he rushed to add. "Perhaps it is more accurate to say that you have lost your *way*, your belief in anyone but yourself. I know of you, Izell. I've known of you for quite some time."

For her, the illusion of peace between them was fractured. Why was she listening to him spout off? She turned a look on him that could melt weaker wills.

Soren kept talking like he didn't notice. "I know of Spirit's Fall, when the closest living relative to King Oberon chose to exile herself. You were assumed dead on Faerie, so there was no question as to who ruled this land."

"How do you know about that?" she demanded.

His eyes twinkled. "In the same breath, you saved the people of Adrun. That was your life's sacrifice, and it created a thing of beauty. I haven't had a chance to see Adrun for myself, but I have heard of it. A place of life thriving against the odds, against the darkness. Because of Izell Firebrand."

She shifted uncomfortably, debating leaving him and his empty praise.

"I have an offer for you," he said, making her hesitate on turning her back until she heard it. "I will lay down my life to fuel the spell to create the new Dark Eye."

"Because you want to touch the lives of others for good?" she asked, immediately raising a skeptical eyebrow.

He smiled like the sun, sincerity pouring from every inch of him. "No one should have to sacrifice themselves twice. Besides, you have a love to live for, something brand new. I am old. I have lived, and died, and lived again, done everything in Heaven an angel should. Why should I continue when someone more ardent in their faith can replace me?"

Still, she doubted that he—or anyone else, for that matter— would see it through when they understood there was no way around being torn apart mind, body, soul, and magic for a greatest works spell. She scrutinized his words for any hint of an agenda.

"Why do you offer when I've lost my way, while you obvi- ously have never strayed from yours?" she murmured, at a loss for why he would even suggest such a thing.

"Because my death would be a sacrifice, and yours a travesty." He laid a hand on her shoulder. "Consider it, lady fae. You still have a little time."

She bit back a snappy reply. Maybe with time, she'd soften her answer, give in to that little voice in the back of her head that screamed that she should take his offer and *live*. But Oberon's blood ran in her veins.

Finishing what he started would be a fitting end to his legacy.

Chapter 7
Jaromir

The moment Izell and Soren left the room, the fae around the table turned toward Jaromir. It took him a confused pause to realize the attention was actually meant for Sondus next to him as the spymaster recovered from his cowed hunch.

"The other part of my report was to suggest we mobilize our forces to hunt down the two demons sent to replace Jazrach and Lucia, since neither of our angels plans on leaving," Sondus said.

The gray-skinned woman at Orin's side made a sour face. "And what good have either of them done for us?"

"Soren has been enchanting weapons with his angelic light so they can permanently kill demons, Your Majesty," he responded crisply.

"And I presume Gabriel is still sitting on his ass, drinking Lord Zalice's wine," she grumbled.

Jaromir raised a brow. That certainly didn't sound like the Gabriel he knew, as the man seemed more motivated by duty than ever now that he'd been returned to life and reunited with his wife.

"If I might ask..." He stiffened when every set of glowing fae eyes in the room turned toward him. "Does anyone here know how Lucia died?"

The news had been welcome but certainly a shock. The

literal devil that had plagued him and his friends was no more, and he wanted to hug the person who'd made it happen.

"You need to talk to Prince Sirius and his mate," said the Unseelie Queen. She smiled wide enough to show her fangs. "I'm sorry, but who are you? I've lost track of all the human-born Izell has let into Faerie."

Sorsha interjected with belated introductions. Jaromir cast a new glance toward Keegan and Ash in particular upon hearing their full titles. He knew Ash was the next in line for the Unseelie crown, but apparently, that made her husband Crown Prince for the other side.

"It's complicated," Keegan said frankly, meeting his eye. "But the royal couple had to name heirs."

"Who better to replace me than my lovely little sister?" Kalimea's voice was syrupy as she put an arm around a scowling Ash.

"Because I *so* want to be your heir," she grumbled.

"There's no one better for the task," Kalimea said, more sober as she righted in her seat. "Anyway, before we adjourn this meeting, I know why you were left here, Jaromir." She turned and held out her hand toward Orin. "Your ring, please."

The man put a mitt-like hand to his chest. "We're divorcing?" he gasped.

She rolled her eyes. "The other ring!"

"Oh, phew."

Jaromir's watched him remove a golden band from his index finger, the clear quartz stone glimmering as it caught the light. His breath held as it tumbled into her waiting palm.

"This is the man you were telling me about?" she asked, her flaming gaze fixed on Sorsha and then Sondus. Both of them nodded. She flicked the ring across the table, toward Jaromir.

The band flipped end over end. Jaromir fumbled to catch it, but used to his old reflexes, his hand swiped through empty air, and the ring tapped him on the forehead. He scooped up the Mending Key and placed it firmly on his finger. Tingling magic traveled from it through his body, suffusing his chest and palms most noticeably.

Jaromir could cry in this room of near strangers. His Gift! The ring hummed on the same frequency as his Gift, restoring his healing potential at last.

"I've kept that ring safe for ages." Orin spoke over the general chatter surrounding Sorsha. "But it has come to my attention that you are to be its new custodian if we want a chance at defeating what's to come."

He didn't want to offer it but forced the words out of his mouth anyway. "I shall return it when—"

Orin held up his hand. "No need. I give it to you freely to absolve Sorsha of her debt. Your healing magic is returned."

"Thank you," he murmured, glancing to the astral fae woman.

She smiled with a brilliant glitter of her stars. "No, thank *you*," she said.

"I regret to call an end to this meeting, but we all have important duties to attend to," Orin said, spreading his hands. The room stood when he did, and Jaromir blinked in surprise as the Seelie King unfolded to his full height. He thought he was a tall man, as he was a couple inches north of six feet, but Orin had him by half a head. Kalimea looked practically dainty at his side.

"Let me show you where your fellows are staying," Sorsha offered, showing Jaromir out with Sondus on his other side. The lanky druid, Theron, followed in her shadow.

"Izell was worried relations with the shifters wouldn't be going well," Jaromir ventured in the relative privacy of the hall. The fae steered him through several turns, enough that he knew he'd be lost without their help.

Sorsha flashed a sad smile up at him. "It's funny, we've now established permanent contact with Earth, a portal Seelie and Unseelie alike can go through. But they have to go to Adrun to access it, and very few have."

"I've seen a few reunions go well," Theron ventured.

"That's because they were druids. Your people don't care to discriminate against *mort loci* when they love animals so much in the first place," she said.

He shuddered. "Well, yeah. But I wouldn't want to share my body with one."

"It's not going well," Sondus said behind his hand as the other two fae started debating the pros and cons of being a shifter.

He gestured down the hall, where he saw a familiar woman with her hands propped on her hips. "...None of us want to hear it!" She leaned in toward a fae dressed in fine, draping layers, baring her teeth like a wolf. "For the last time, I am asking you to leave."

"I just want what's best for your people. It is unnatural—"

The fae man glanced over at the group arriving, his expression changing as Sorsha bustled ahead. "Archfae," he said with a respectful nod.

"Lord Forrester," she replied. "You are aware that His Majesty decreed that we are to treat Queen Nyah with the same respect as any visiting monarch?"

A bushy, white tail flipped behind Nyah in agitation as she leaned her weight back a step, her lips relaxing fractionally. A glittering crown topped her blonde head, plaits neatly braided to frame her heart-shaped face. Her golden eyes widened when she spotted Jaromir, scanning him head to toe.

"Yes, ma'am. But you must acknowledge that she and her people have committed a terrible crime against magic," the fae said, not to be perturbed.

Nyah's hackles raised anew.

"Lord Forrester," Sorsha repeated with firm authority. "The Adrunian shifters are a recognized class of lesser fae."

He huffed something that sounded like a curse and bade Sorsha farewell, stalking off with Nyah's glare burrowing into his back.

"Thanks, Sorsha. Would you all like to come in?" She gestured to the door behind her, her gaze flashing to Jaromir again. After their group filed in, she caught him in a hug. "It's so good to see a friendly face," she said.

"Hello again," he murmured, drawing back to take a closer look at her. She'd made the wolf tail disappear, most of her nephilim glow muted below a maternity dress that draped her shoulders to toes in fabric that shaded from crimson red up top to pale pink around her ankles. "Congratulations on your little one. But this stress can't be good for him or her."

"Don't know what I was expecting," she muttered, shooting a glare toward the closed door. "It's just an endless line of fae that have heard our survival story yet want to come tell me what an abomination I am. If they don't say it to me, well..."

His gaze followed where she gestured. A little fae girl with a furry, spotted tail was clinging to Adrius's shirt a few feet from where they stood. She sobbed uncontrollably despite his scaled hand gliding in soothing circles down her back.

It was surreal to see him again, as Jaromir had had mere days to get used to the dragon features covering his friend before Izell had whisked him off to Faerie. Adrius's dragon spirit, Zerenth, had claimed "half" of the man's body, leaving him with gleaming onyx wings and dark scales fading in with the unruly black mass of Adrius's hair. He'd shaved his beard off, skin still vampire pale under the dragon features. Angular, red-orange eyes were the finishing touch marking him as a hybrid.

At least they'd been given a richly appointed room in the palace, as spacious as a whole apartment, with an ajar door leading into what was undoubtedly a bed and bath. There was plenty of seating, enough for full meetings in comfort. Adrius and Nyah probably held a mini court here, based off how the chairs and sofas were already arranged in a loose circle.

"Our ambassador family was one incident from quitting." Nyah's lips quirked. "I don't blame them. In Adrun, we celebrated how little Nicola there found her spirit from a young age. We thought it was a sign of her strength. That man just said some ugly things that I don't think she'll ever forget."

"I'm sorry. Maybe things will improve with time?" he ventured. They would have to, he thought. Now that Adrun was a part of Faerie again, there was no other place for them.

"Maybe," she grumbled. "Come, tell me what's happening around here. We're so out of the loop. What's happened to your eyes? Actually, wait..."

At her request, Sorsha left the room with the crying girl. Jaromir sighed as he found a comfortable chair, knowing he'd be there a while with Adrius and Nyah both pinning him with curious looks.

"So, Izell gave us a little scare," Nyah began. "Is she...okay?"

Jaromir's lips quirked. "I believe she will be."

"That's not very promising," Adrius sighed. "Do you know where my brother is, by the way?"

He opened his mouth to reply when Sorsha re-entered the room, Neala behind her.

Now this is a reunion, he thought, looking around her redheaded bulk for the half-fae who'd caught her fancy. Sorsha closed the door, and Neala sat before he realized Cedric was a lyrebird, who perched on his mate's lap once she settled.

"Are you well?" Neala asked him in her new, melodic voice.

"Yes, thank you," he said, lifting his new Key with a genuine smile.

He didn't expect the little giggle from Nyah. "Sorry. I can't get over her voice," Nyah admitted. "Okay, Jaromir, I can't take it anymore. Now that we're all here, spill the beans. Why do you look different?"

The three fae turned curious looks toward him too. With a deep breath, Jaromir started his story from the top. "So, it turns out that Sorsha owed me a debt to repay saving her from a Fell Mad's bite, and Sondus tried to repay it..."

Chapter 8
Jaromir

With Sondus there to corroborate his story, plus Neala wanting to talk about the details of Lucia's attack at Kalimea's ball, they were all sitting there chatting well into the evening. Sorsha called for wine and opened the door to find Keegan and Ash standing there, holding two bottles each.

"Heard you were telling stories," Keegan said, sweeping inside to join the group. His dragon followed suit, accepting a bottle of wine after he removed the cork. She sat and cradled it in both her front paws.

"Have you all gotten to Sirius joining the circus yet?" Ash asked.

Jaromir searched her words for a trace of the lie before realizing she didn't have to lie when posing a question. He gave her a disbelieving look. Izell had mentioned that Adrius's anger-prone brother had found his match at last, but not *where* he'd found her.

"His act was showing off with his shapeshifting," Theron said, hooting and slapping his thigh when he earned an incredulous glance from Adrius.

"It was dancing, actually," Sondus put in.

"This sounds like something to hear from the horse's mouth," Adrius said.

"Maybe he hasn't finished Lord Zalice's trial." Ash cast a curious glance to Sorsha, who shrugged.

Another knock sounded at the door, revealing a servant with two more bottles of wine. She cast a sheepish glance over her shoulder as she delivered them and stepped aside to reveal Izell at the threshold. "There you lot are," the dragon shifter sighed.

Jaromir felt the silence that fell as she stalked into the room and sat next to him. "Well, what are you waiting for? Let me put on my best Chandra impression." She cleared her throat and announced, "Pour the wine!"

"Pour the wine!" Nyah echoed, passing out full glasses while she ended up cradling an ice water.

"Do *you* know where Sirius is?" Adrius asked, his voice full of frustration by this point.

Izell took a long drink from her wineglass. "Can't I get a break for a moment?" she sighed before sitting up from slouching into her cushioned chair. "Anyone have a piece of paper?"

Adrius stood and went rummaging through the next room. "I'm not inviting anyone but him and his mate," Izell told the assembled group. "I've had enough contact with angelkin for the rest of my existence."

"Is he with my parents?" Nyah asked, her attention sharpening immediately.

Izell smirked. "Yes. Do you really want to have a party with your parents around?" When the other woman shook her head rapidly, she snapped her sharp claws. "Didn't think so."

"Is everything okay?" Jaromir asked when Izell sprawled back in her chair again. She glanced over and offered her hand to hold, lacing her fingers with his after he closed the gap between them. A little shrug disturbed her shoulders, but all she really did was look at him like his face held all the answers to her problems.

He scooted his chair closer to hers, leaning over to try and steal a kiss.

"Found it," Adrius announced, coming up to Izell with a roll of parchment and a fountain pen. Izell's softening face morphed back into a scowl as she looked up at him.

"Write your brother a note," she instructed. "And I'll get it to him."

The other dragon shifter wandered away again, having Nyah

lean forward so he could write on her back. The dignified shifter queen's eyes sparkled with mirth as he dragged this out and tickled her.

Izell tugged on Jaromir's hand. "I believe you were about to kiss me," she stated, lifting her nose like a highborn lady. "You may proceed."

"Oh, may I?" he laughed. He sat back with a smile playing at his lips, knowing they were about to be interrupted again. Adrius was watching them with a hint of mischief on his features.

She took another deep drink of her glass. "Do I need to ask more nicely?" She slanted him a look that spoke to her inner desire, just a glimpse of dragon's fire amongst the nebulae that lived in her eyes.

"I suppose not," he said, feeling himself melt. He'd never told this woman no, and he wasn't about to start now. Leaning over, he met her lips halfway, tasting the wine on her breath.

Adrius announced loudly, "Okay, Izell, I have it!"

She parted from Jaromir with a low growl. "He'll be lucky if I don't shove him through a portal and leave him," she muttered.

"What was that?" Adrius asked. He smiled to show his fangs.

"You heard me, Zerenth," she replied, naming the onyx dragon within him. "Only you would tease me so." His smile was completely unrepentant.

Standing, she snatched the note from him and gestured, making a portal just wide enough for the hand she pushed through the magic. She fished around for a moment before pulling back.

"Hope he has the means to reply," she said absently, eyeing the portal as it remained suspended there.

After a minute, the parchment fluttered back out. She caught it and snickered. "We'd better get more wine," she remarked.

Waving her claws around, she closed the portal to open one big enough to accommodate a Blood Prince-sized person. Barreling through first wasn't Sirius, but a different vampire with a grin splitting his face. "Did I hear we're having a *party?*" Korin exclaimed. Theron hooted first, and his cheer was taken up by the tipsy ones amongst them.

Following in his rippling wake was Sirius, his eyes already rolling. He was arm in arm with a petite aether fae woman, her cloud-formed wings waggling behind her as her overlarge eyes beheld the size of the group.

With his back to his brother, Sirius spotted Jaromir first and pointed at him. "Where the fuck have you been?" he demanded.

"Reading," Izell interjected. "Something I'm sure you've never done."

Two things made it apparent that Sirius was different. The first was his altered appearance. No longer a hulking Fell Hunter, he was leaner, with eyes like bright rubies rather than Blood Prince maroon. He bore sharpened ears and two shadowy wings as ephemeral as most fae's.

He also didn't rise to Izell's bait, instead flashing a smile that crinkled the corners of his eyes. "That's fair," he replied.

Turning, Sirius and Adrius made eye contact. They were in a backslapping hug a moment later, leaving the aether fae to inspect Izell with a quirk to her pale lips. "Are you the fae who wrote in my journal?" she asked in a high, wispy voice. There was a subtle echo of power behind every word.

Izell spread her clawed hands. "Do you know any other dragon shifters?"

The other fae smiled shyly. "Thank you for your help."

Izell beckoned her over, dragging Jaromir to his feet. "This is Jaromir. I like him," she said by way of greeting. "Jaromir, this is Talina, a demigoddess."

He and Talina had the same choking reaction.

A touch of purple graced the fae's cheeks. "I think that's supposed to be a secret."

"Not with this group, it's not!" Izell slapped her back heartily.

Jaromir was just about to warn her when he felt the air shift, Sirius shooting daggers across the room when Talina stumbled. "She could smite me in two seconds, don't worry!" Izell called over to him, putting an arm around the smaller fae with a fanged smile.

"Please, this is supposed to be fun." Another person came through the portal before it collapsed, arriving in the nick of time.

She spoke like she'd seen the whole thing and opened her arms just as Izell released Talina to hug her instead.

Izell snuggled this unfamiliar vampire extra hard, only releasing her to frame her with her arms. "Everyone, look! It's adult Cossette!"

Jaromir's eyes bulged extra wide as a rustling followed. Neala beat everyone else to Cossette, embracing her next.

It's a miracle, he thought.

He'd studied the Ancient vampiress in front of him when she was stuck as a little girl, pushing the limits of his Gift trying to find a way to let her age. It was out of his control. But something had allowed her a change, and he caught the adult Cossette's joyful laughter as she flitted around, saying her hellos.

She hugged him near to last. "How?" he murmured.

She winked an albino-red eye. "Magic."

"Are you eating human food?" he asked a second later. She was a tall thing, but dangerously slim. Her white ringlets haloed a thin face, her skin so pale he could nearly count her veins.

Still, she flashed a reassuring smile. "I am, and I'll be fine. We need to talk, though..." she cast a glance over her shoulder, where Izell and Talina chatted more casually. Sondus hovered close by, hesitating in Izell's presence, though he looked eager to speak with Talina. Cossette nodded to herself before returning her attention to Jaromir. "Later."

"Later," he agreed. He finally took a sip of wine and let himself relax. Whatever hovered on the horizon, they could discuss it tomorrow. This evening was for all the friends he hadn't seen in ages and the stories he hadn't heard yet.

Because once Sirius had a couple glasses of wine in him, his retelling of his and Talina's journey was nearly too wild to believe. When Jaromir said as much in an aside to Izell, she flashed a tipsy smile.

"I have a new plan," she whispered back. "And it will be even crazier a journey. I hope you're ready."

"Totally ready," he replied, but only because he was drunk.

Chapter 9
Izell

Izell woke to a splitting headache as a perfectly executed rooster's crow echoed in her ears. She opened her eyes just a slit, grumbling at the pain that infiltrated her skull alongside the rush of sunlight.

An arm was draped over her waist, though, pulling her deeper into the embrace of the warmth behind her. "Mmm. Jaromir?" she mumbled.

"Wake up, everyone!" Cedric sounded like he was still speaking from his small lyrebird form. He said he was showing his shifter side "in solidarity," but the moment he crowed again, Izell's temper flared.

"I'll cock-a-doodle-doo you, insufferable little..." The fire wasn't there, though, as she held her head. *Ugh.* Too much wine.

"Sorry, madam. The only person who gets to cock-a-doodle-doo me is my mate," he replied from somewhere above her.

"Someone muzzle the rooster," complained Theron's voice.

Keegan's snide reply followed. "Thought you loved nature in all forms, brother."

Izell peered around slowly, realizing they were having a slumber party of sorts in Adrius and Nyah's room. She vaguely recalled the sober shifter queen helping lay her on her side, tucking a spare blanket around her. It was now tangled around her legs while a scaly crimson arm held her around the middle.

Vidia chuffed in her sleep. She had Izell snuggled to her like a teddy bear.

"Queen Kalimea is coming," Cedric twittered from his vantage perched on the top of a couch. He opened his beak to crow again when Neala's form threw a shadow over him, and she scooped him up.

She held the lyrebird to her face. "When I called you a chicken, I didn't mean like this," she sang in that musical voice of hers.

Cedric wiggled with glee. "But the queen is coming, and you all are still asleep," he sang back.

"How do you know?"

"Well, Nyah and I have actually left the room and stuff," he twittered.

Izell slowly worked her way out of Vidia's embrace. She doubted anyone else had drunk as much as her. And even if they had, most had their vampiric regeneration to assist with the very thing crippling her. Her thoughts returned sluggishly.

I should probably get presentable for Kalimea, she thought.

Looking at the wrinkled blouse she slept in, she shrugged to herself. *Nah.*

Instead, she went looking for Jaromir. He was kneeling beside one of the couches, his hands on Talina's calf, while Sirius looked on sleepily. "Your fae system isn't something I'm familiar with, but I don't sense any damage in your ankle," Jaromir was saying.

"Maybe I really healed it myself," she said, her cloudless eyes shimmering with wonder.

Sirius nudged the healer, jerking his head toward Izell. His golden eyes widened as he looked up at her. "Someone had too much wine." Jaromir flashed that gentle smile of his. There was a new confidence in his bearing as he stood and pressed warm fingertips to her temple. His skin buzzed with magic, vibrating against the pain in her skull until it started to lessen.

"You didn't need an angel's blessing after all. Just a Key," she sighed, closing her eyes as she soaked in his healing.

"Funny how things work out, hmm?" She could practically

feel his joy as he spoke. He was in his element, like he'd never lost his magic in the first place.

"Does it feel like your Gift?" she asked once he was finished. The worst of her hangover was gone, though the morning sunlight was still overbright as it streamed in from a pair of bay windows.

His teeth sparkled with angelic brightness. "Very similar, but much stronger."

"I'd hope it would be stronger. That ring should give you control of all aspects of healing," she remarked, taken by his expression.

Sirius put an arm around his mate, both of them exchanging a private look while she gazed on Jaromir like he was the only man in the room.

"Want to find some breakfast?" Talina whispered. She squealed a laugh when Sirius picked her up, leaving Izell to close the distance between her and Jaromir.

Running her claws gently over his shirt, she startled him when she grabbed a fistful of the material and dragged him into a kiss. His hands were just coming around her when Adrius appeared from seemingly nowhere. "Izell, I need a favor," he said.

She released Jaromir, panning a slow, flaming look toward the other dragon shifter. He hooked a scaly thumb over his shoulder. "Will you get the Queen of Faerie out of my room?"

Cedric apparently wasn't joking. Kalimea had slipped in silently, taking in the empty bottles of wine and scattered cushions where most of them had slept. She beckoned over a bedraggled Ash, throwing her arm around her taller sister.

"Did you have fun last night?" Kalimea asked. "Why wasn't I invited?"

"You weren't doing anything important," Ash replied.

The Unseelie Queen rolled her flaming eyes. "I was with my husband."

"Exactly," Izell interjected. "You were doing someone important."

Kalimea released a small snort. "Are we teenagers again, Archfae Firebrand?"

"Don't you know? When you get to a certain age, you become

young at heart," she replied. "I suppose you're here for something other than shaming us into have another party tonight."

She raised an auburn brow. "While that sounds like an outstanding idea, I was indeed here for..." She pointed to the side. "Sondus."

The spymaster was still rubbing sleep from his eyes but sat up alertly the moment he was singled out.

"Get yourself cleaned up, and report to your special room right away," Kalimea instructed. "You may come too, Izell and Jaromir. Something tells me we can't stop you anyway."

Izell flashed a proud smile. "Isn't that the truth," she murmured. She inspected the Unseelie Queen closer for any hint of what to expect, noting only a practiced, enigmatic mask she'd probably had to perfect from her time in court. Inclining her head, Kalimea left the room.

"So, what is Sondus's special room?" Theron mused. The group of fae were all on their feet by this point, casting curious glances as the spymaster rushed around in search for his shoes.

"Interrogation," he replied, muffled as he ducked to look under a couch.

"Figures," the druid replied. He glanced down, nudging something behind himself with his toes.

Sorsha followed where he was looking and sighed. "Quit it, Theo." She beckoned to Sondus to come retrieve his shoes.

"Hey, Kalimea knows I'm the only eternal teenager here," he replied, grinning.

Izell smiled to herself. She couldn't help but see the group of fae as they were as kids—three thousand years ago, before she'd gone to Adrun, she'd been teacher and mentor to them all. Sorsha, the last astral fae Sorceress of her generation. Keegan, her sullen brother figure with an uncanny ability to wield a sword like an extension of himself. Ash, the Unseelie Princess who'd desperately wanted to be as good and kind as her friends in the Astral Fae Academy. Theron, the lordling made humble by the untamed druidic nature hiding within him.

And Sondus...who turned his gaze her way now that he was ready to go. She took Jaromir's hand and followed in the spymaster's wake, remembering the broken young man who'd been smuggled back to the academy with his back still bleeding from his wing removal.

A youth she'd empowered, seeing an incredible mind held back from its potential just because he couldn't use magic like the rest of his race. The same man she'd left soaked and freezing in Adrun for the crime of trying to help her.

Remorse bit her in the side. Queldian was right; she *had* overreacted. Now Sondus would barely look at her.

"Before we see who I'm interrogating, I wanted to tell you something," he said, falling into step on her other side with his head bowed. "I had my contacts scour the magical markets in search of this. It's the last one you needed, right?"

He offered her a small box. Within, nestled into a bed of white velvet, was a ring set with a gleaming ruby of the purest red. Jaromir murmured in awe as she turned the whole box, scattering shards of scarlet light from its facets.

"The Summer Key," she said to herself, eyebrows raising. She'd thought she'd need to scry the location of the last gemstone, but here it was without any fuss.

"I sincerely apologize for damaging your plans to save us all." Sondus cleared his throat and gestured to the box. "This is my best attempt to help."

Izell shut it, cutting off the glitter of brilliant ruby sparks. "You want to help me?" she asked.

"Of course," he said immediately. "I only want what's good for Faerie. And what you showed me... I can't get it out of my head how horrible..."

Sondus only drifted off when she snagged his wrist. She forced his hand over, placing the box back into his grip. "If you truly wish to help, then you will wear it," she replied, waiting until he met her gaze. She let a hint of her dragon's fire fill her eyes. "Assist with the ceremony to create the Dark Eye anew. Then we are even, Sondus Arus."

The distant stars in his eyes seemed to dance as he considered her and her words, turning them over. He nodded. "I do not deserve such an easy forgiveness," he murmured.

"Implying anything to come will be easy," she remarked. They had reached a stairwell by this point. The steps descending into the earth were plain, leading into a cavernous maw of stone that lodged a modest prison block and interrogation rooms. Sondus placed the Summer Key on his right ring finger before straightening his spine, sliding on a merciless expression like placing a mask over his face.

Izell shuddered uncomfortably as she felt the dampening quality of iron. The cell bars were made of it, and the interrogation rooms were lined with a fine sheet of the debilitating metal, especially in the doors. It sapped her magic just from proximity. Sondus was unaffected and pulled out a key to let them into the first closed room.

King Orin glanced up and raised his hand in greeting.

Across the table from him and shackled with magic was the ugliest demon Izell had ever seen.

Chapter 10
Jaromir

A shriek echoed from the creature's maw as it noticed Jaromir. "No! Not an angel!" it screamed.

He stopped short, casting an alarmed look toward Izell.

"You told me no angel magic! You promised no death!" it continued, flopping within its restraints like a dying fish.

Izell heaved an exaggerated sigh. "We rushed over here for a servitor demon?" she asked with heavy scorn.

The creature couldn't have been human at any point, Jaromir reflected. Its features resembled skin melting down its face and turning a putrid shade of tar black. It didn't appear to have eyes, but instead a writhing host of tentacles to feel its way across the ground. Two huge, bat-like ears were cocked toward them, its mouth gaping open even when it wasn't shrieking.

"Good morning, all. Meet our new friend," Orin said calmly, gesturing toward it. "This particular demon has promised to tell us what it knows." He stood and backed up, letting Sondus take the seat across from it. He didn't quite lean against the wall, his flaming wings curving away from touching it.

Izell crossed the room to stand close to him. The moment Jaromir followed, the demon started to relax in its restraints too. "What is a servitor demon?" he whispered.

She scowled at the creature as Sondus began asking it basic questions. "The lowest level of demon in Hell," she replied.

"Some creatures spawn there naturally. Servitors, imps, even certain breeds of djinn. They're slaves, basically."

"Why would Hell send a servitor, of all things, in replacement to a greater demon?" Jaromir whispered.

Concern shaded her expression. "Servitors come first during war with Hell. They're meant to die. Their skin holds venom sacs, you see." She pointed out several bulges in its skin and tentacles where a green tinge was most apparent. "They poison water and grain stores when left unchecked. When killed, all their sacs explode, rendering a messy death for whomever dealt the final blow."

Orin whistled low. "Nasty creature," he murmured.

"Someone down below probably expected us to kill it," Jaromir said.

The Seelie King shook his head. "We won't be killing it. As awful as it is to look at, I suspect whatever would replace it would be much worse."

"There is a second demon. Two angels, two demons. Have your men caught it yet?" Izell asked him.

"No. All I can say is that we're on high alert for anything unusual," he replied. "I am hoping the two angels can locate it. Soren was the one to tip us off about this one."

They listened grimly as the interrogation continued. The servitor didn't know much but certainly shared a repetitious babble. Every once in a while, Jaromir noticed its ears stand upright and pan to exactly his location, and the demon would quake with fear.

It was a direct gift from the Lord of Envy, spawned from a poison pool in the bowels of Hell. Its goal was to render as much of Faerie's land as blighted and unusable as it could. Thankfully, it hadn't gotten very far before being apprehended and restrained in this room. If it'd been killed, there was a long line of servitors ready to replace it.

Apparently, the other demon hadn't been sent to Faerie yet. The Lords of Hell were fighting over what would be weak but effective to send before the looming invasion. Izell growled the moment it said "weak," her tail twitching in agitation.

"Well, that was informative," Orin sighed once the interrogation was done and they'd regrouped outside of the room. It was obvious Sondus wasn't going to get anything else from it, and its venom sacs made the creature impossible to torture.

"Well, it was a pleasure to spend a night here," Izell said, a note of finality in her voice, "but I really must be going."

Orin didn't seem surprised. "My resources are at your disposal."

"Where are we going?" Jaromir asked.

Sondus cracked his neck. "Indeed. Where are we going?" he echoed.

She scoffed and turned, scaling the stairs leading out of this dungeon. Jaromir dogged her steps, not about to take a dismissal this time. "You told me you had a new plan, Izell. What is it?" he pressed, watching her back tense up.

"Not so loud," she hissed.

She didn't speak until they were in a more private hall, heading back to the room they'd spent the night in. "I appreciate the 'we' you're trying to make, gentlemen, but only I can execute what comes next," she said over her shoulder.

Izell stopped in a shadowy nook before he could open his mouth to complain. She leaned against the wall, her expression drawn. "I promised to tell you what I was planning, so here it is," she sighed, lowering her voice so only he and Sondus could hear what she said. King Orin had chosen not to follow them.

"First things first, I will gather my new occultarus and seek the direct blessing of the four gods." She crossed her arms, staring daggers at them both like she was arming herself for a challenge. "And then I will do what my political rivals have been suggesting since I was a young lady. I'm going to Hell."

Horror flipped his heart. *Go to Hell? On her own?*

"Sounds like a party. Count me in," Sondus said after a shocked silence.

Izell drew a hand down her face. "No, you daft man. *I* am going," she said, stabbing a claw at her chest. "I am going to shake down Archangel Soren until he takes me, *alone*, because we need a greater demon, and Hell will not be sending one."

"Sounds like we're going to Hell, Jaromir. I'd pack some light clothes. It's sure to be a scorcher," Sondus said, clapping him on the shoulder.

"I'll bring plenty of water, too," Jaromir said, nodding slowly.

Izell bared her fangs with a low growl. "This is exactly why I work alone," she grumbled. "This grows more impossible the more people come along. Don't you see that?"

"Didn't you notice how that demon was afraid of me?" Jaromir interjected.

Sondus nodded. "We can both be assets to you. You have his light and healing prowess, plus my brains."

She took their measure, a low flame burning in the depths of her eyes. Whatever she saw must've convinced her, because she threw up her hands. "Fine. If you truly have a death wish, come right along."

"I'll get my affairs in order," Sondus said. He disappeared down the hall with swift steps.

Jaromir stroked his jaw. "Actually, there's something I need to do as well." He glanced to Izell, worried as ever that she'd bolt off without them in her desire to do everything herself. So, he invited her to go meet his little owl friend.

SAID OWL WAS ACTUALLY A TERRIX, A MEMBER OF A LESSER fae race wholly dedicated to the sanctity of knowledge. They ran the Library of Faerie, from head librarian down to the janitorial staff, and Jaromir had started feeling a kinship with one in particular.

He led Izell through a housing district, following the familiar twists and turns to Alaku's house. A dog's enthusiastic barking preceded the boy himself as he answered the door, tilting his head back and breaking into a wide smile. "Hi, Prince Jaromir! Is it time to get back to work?"

Sitting beside the boy's bare, talon-like feet was a puppy, her tail wagging enthusiastically. "Oh, you *did* keep her," Izell remarked.

Alaku's moon-like owl eyes turned toward her, his expression shading to a fearful cringe as he noticed her scaled arms. "Alaku, meet Izell. She's very nice," Jaromir said, ignoring her little snicker. "We've come to say goodbye."

"Does that mean you're finished with your research?" Alaku was his library-assigned research partner, someone who'd painstakingly worked through a giant tome to help Jaromir put his thumb on exactly what Izell needed him to discover.

"I'm afraid so. We're on to more dangerous tasks," Jaromir said. Hell was no place to take a young teen and a puppy, after all.

"Wait a second," Alaku said, darting back into his house.

Sofia, the puppy, padded forward and pawed at Izell's legs until she picked her up. The dragon shifter let Sofia lick her face. "It's not every day I find a tame dire wolf pup."

Jaromir blinked. "A what?"

"What?" Izell replied, scrunching her nose in confusion.

"What kind of puppy did you say she is?" he asked.

She was saved from replying when Alaku rushed back to them, holding an ancient tome by the spine while the pages flapped with every step. *A terrix librarian would be horrified,* Jaromir thought with an amused smile.

Alaku skidded to a halt, already pointing to a particular passage. "Read this!"

Jaromir took the book and smoothed the pages down, holding the book halfway between him and Izell when she leaned over to look too. The book was *The Legacy of Primal Magic*, the same one Alaku had been struggling with for weeks.

"Oh, interesting," Izell hummed.

"What am I reading?" Jaromir turned his gaze to Izell, who was nodding along as she speed-read the passage Alaku pointed out and turned the page. She placed the puppy down and took the book, holding it close to her face.

"Do you have this book checked out in your name, young man?" she asked Alaku, who nodded. "I need to borrow it. Don't worry, I will return it."

Alaku's gaze flashed to Jaromir, turning solemn. "If it will help you, take it," he said. "I always thought Prince Jaromir was doing something really important."

She winked. "Very much so. Do you know what's also imperative? Taking care of this pup." She thrust Sofia back into the boy's hold, and his face lit up. No matter what kind of puppy she was, she belonged to Alaku now, Jaromir thought.

He knelt down and hugged Alaku in farewell. "Promise you'll come visit when you're done being important?" the boy asked.

"Of course," Jaromir said, hoping he'd survive whatever the next step of Izell's plan entailed. He wanted to keep the world stable for youth like Alaku, who still had a life and a purpose ahead of them. He lingered for a moment to wish him well and then left Alaku and Sofia to continue on without him.

Izell turned away, her nose still buried in the book. She followed Jaromir without looking up, to the point where he held her elbow just in case.

"Are you aware that I am a primal fae, Jaromir?" she asked, sounding distracted.

"I don't even know what that means," he admitted. He assumed it was complicated.

And Izell's explanation certainly took him a few minutes to dissect. Being mostly made of magic, fae evolved from magical events rather than breeding favorable traits down to their limited offspring. The last and biggest event to change the fae was when King Oberon sacrificed himself and created the Eyes of Worlds. His dying breath had been a curse, splitting the greater fae race into Seelie and Unseelie.

Before this split, all fae reflected their base elements: earth, fire, water, and wind. She'd been a water fae before magically mutating to a Seelie astral fae.

"I may be the only fae still alive that used to be a primal fae," she finished. "And this book talks about the magic I learned in my youth like it is ancient history."

Jaromir bit his lip. Her gaze narrowed as she glanced at him askance.

"I know, I'm ancient history," she grumbled.

He held up his palms. "To be fair, I am as well."

She flipped her hand, returning to reading.

A few long minutes passed. She hummed to herself.

"So?" he prompted.

She shut the book with a sigh and tucked it under her elbow. "I need you to understand, Jaromir, why I have to be the sacrifice to create the new Dark Eye. It is my connection to primal magic." Sorrow swam in the nebulae in her eyes. "The passage just confirmed that this amount of magic can never be held by a Seelie or an Unseelie. My death will be the end of an era."

"Then you cannot die," Jaromir said quietly, stopping and turning toward her. He cupped her cheeks between his hands. In her face, he saw the ghosts of his past—countless loved ones who'd gone to war and never come back.

Souls he hadn't been able to save, no matter how skilled a healer he'd become.

"I can't stand by and let you do it. You channel the magic and let someone else give themselves, mind, body, soul, and magic," he said to her resistant expression.

"We must all let go of the past, Jaromir," she replied quietly.

More like he would never let go of her. He knew that as his fingers trembled. "No. What if this new Dark Eye is destroyed? There will not be another who can replace it."

She scowled. "Then the idiots who didn't learn from this comedy of folly we're stuck in deserve to die, don't they?"

He shook his head slowly. "There has to be another way, and I will find it. You will live, Izell Firebrand. I swear it on my blood and honor." Her eyes widened, recognizing a binding promise for a vampire. "I will not let you sacrifice yourself."

Multiple emotions flashed over her face before she put up her aggression like a shield, sparing him a sneer. "Because I'm so important and old?"

Jaromir took a breath, knowing what he felt and how it changed everything. Yet in that moment, he pulled an Izell. He didn't tell her that he planned to take her place, to lay down his life to save someone he felt deeply for.

He'd lived through Fell attacks, seen men die from horrific wounds he had no hope in healing. Thousands had drowned around him when Gwendolyn had sunk Nyixa. In the end, Jaromir hadn't been enough to keep their lives going. He'd tasted defeat and pain, sorrow and loss. Those feelings would be nothing compared to the agony of seeing Izell's bright spirit extinguish.

"Because I care for you," he answered, kissing the scowl off her face.

Chapter 11
Izell

She was still touching her lips hours later when she had Jaromir and Sondus before her. All of them had packed clothes and other supplies for what lay ahead, and she'd visited her stash of items to gather up the odd mix of human and Faerie-made tools she'd amassed in her travels.

I care for you. She kept repeating Jaromir's words in her head like a besotted teenager. Why did she have to find a man like him at the end of her life? Fate was a cruel mistress indeed.

"Ready?" she asked, panning her gaze to Sirius, Talina, and Cossette, who were coming with them for the first place Izell wanted to visit.

It was a shock to be face to face with Talina at last. The young lady was the spitting image of her father, the fearsome Lord of Storms, though she had exactly none of his severe, godly bearing. In fact, she was giggling over something Sirius had said, leaning her slight form against his side as she flashed him a smitten smile. He twirled a lock of her navy hair between his fingers and returned her gaze like she was the only woman in the room.

Izell rolled her eyes like she didn't want to be in Jaromir's embrace doing the exact same thing. "We're ready," Cossette answered for them.

Good enough. She flicked her claws, producing a portal for

everyone to head through. She dismissed it after going last, glancing around with a little tilt to her lips.

Lord Zalice had claimed this scenic bowl of paradise as his home since the dawn of Faerie, and it hadn't changed much. The bird-like shapes of skyriders circled overhead, a whole flock of them making a rare appearance. Untamed wind whipped overhead, stirring waves of grass and other bronzed greenery as their group walked toward the lone house built unassumingly at the corner of a pure lake.

Sondus hung back to walk by her side. "Is this really a god's home?" he asked in quiet awe.

She nodded absently. Most fae never came face to face with a god, but she knew for a fact that he'd met Raenith in person. "Surely it's not that big a surprise?"

"This isn't close proximity to a volcano. I would even say it's pleasant," he answered.

"It's not even the first nice godly home I've taken you to," she remarked.

Remorse clouded his expression. She held up a hand before he could apologize again. "You've taken your punishment, and I've forgiven you. I'd even venture to say that the Sanctum is my favorite place amongst the gods' homes. Count yourself fortunate that you've seen it."

Relief slanted through his shoulders. "Now I've seen every god's home, except for Cyranos's," he said, earning a snort of amusement from her.

"He is the most primal one, living in the arctic waters to the far north. Do you fancy freezing?"

"Not today, Lady Izell," he answered primly.

She smirked, turning toward the lone figure waiting for them right outside of the house. Sirius and Talina had slipped away during their little conversation, she noted. Cossette and Jaromir hung back so she could speak to the aether fae man waiting for them. She executed a proper courtly bow.

"It's been a while, Lord Zalice," she said, trying to keep the bitterness from her voice.

Dressed as finely as she remembered was the familiar face of Faerie's God of Wind, static crackling between his storm cloud wings. His eyes were filled to the brim with power, looking like jagged streaks of lightning just below the surface as he appraised her head to toe.

"You are displeased with me, Archfae Firebrand," he replied, his quiet voice holding the power of an untamed storm behind it.

Part of her had been expecting him to look straight through her. All four gods had different areas of expertise, and it just so happened that the Lord of Storms possessed nearly flawless foresight. Not only had he known they were visiting, he knew what she was about to say and many possible alternatives. Still, he clasped his hands over his middle and waited for her to speak.

A low growl rumbled in her throat. "Wouldn't you be, in my place?" she demanded.

Zalice slowly smiled. "I have missed your fire, Izell. For better or for worse, the best time for Adrun to be raised from the ocean is the timeline we are on."

She scowled, unable to help it. "Three thousand years of darkness. Can you imagine it, so lofty and free from your perch in the clouds?" Her fists clenched despite knowing she could never hope to fight the wind itself, nor the living manifestation of it standing before her.

"I was there with you every moment of every day." He spoke with ringing sincerity, no more able to lie than her. The concept of lies was anathema to the elements of magic, who operated on another level than mere mortals. Zalice tilted his head with a keen sparkle in his gaze, not unlike the skyrider form he was worshiped in. "Did you never wonder why you had breathable air in a bubble resting on the bottom of the ocean?"

She shrugged. "Magic."

"*My* magic. My siblings and I saw your struggles and helped where we could. You had my fresh air, Cyranos's clean water, Getana's blessing for a new Sanctum, and Raenith's hope in your hearts at the dawn of every dark day. We did not forsake you," Zalice promised. He stepped aside, motioning toward the open doorway. "Can I interest you in some tea or coffee?"

"Tea sounds great." She knew she couldn't argue with a literal god. Plus, she figured she knew what else he'd say if she pressed: it was done. They were where they were, and only the future mattered.

"You all are welcome in my parlor." He motioned for the group to go inside. Sondus had his head on a swivel as he beheld the perfectly average-looking home they passed through. If he looked too closely, he'd realize it was all one solid piece of wood, like it'd sprung from the ground fully formed and ready for a roof.

The parlor itself was modernized with comfortable seating and fresh furnishings. Already resting in a pair of chairs cushioned with navy velvet were two semi-familiar faces to Izell, the angel Gabriel and the elderly nephilim Gwendolyn. They were sipping tea together, and Gwendolyn threatened to slosh hers around as she gestured sharply. Her words were lost as they looked up at the same time in surprise.

Gwendolyn rose to her feet, limping toward Jaromir. "Good to see you again," he said, his expression creased with concern behind her back as they hugged. He held her shoulders afterward. "Do you mind if I give you a little checkup?"

"Your Gift is returned?" she asked, gasping with delight when he smiled and nodded. He helped her sit, starting to use his healing magic with his hand overlapping hers.

Sondus and Cossette went to sit somewhere comfortable. Izell turned her attention toward the powerful, crackling presence that moved to her side. "You know I'm not here for pleasantries," she said, reading Zalice's serious expression.

He handed her a cup of warm tea. "Indeed. This group will not miss you for an hour. The others are already waiting for us."

THE OTHERS, OF COURSE, BEING THE OTHER GODS. IN Zalice's private study, the goddesses Raenith and Getana were waiting for her in their fae forms. A golden orb rested on the solid desk in the middle of the small room, gleaming with potential.

"No Cyranos?" she asked upon entering and glancing around.

"He wants you to come to him," Raenith answered. She burned white-hot as always, her whole form consumed by flames in the shape of a buxom fae woman.

Izell scowled at no one in particular and sipped from her tea. It was one of her favorite flavors, a berry-filled green tea that practically vibrated on her tongue with its healthy potential. The leaves were grown by the Lady of Life, Izell knew, the only being that could infuse a drink with palpable goodness.

It was hard to be sour when the taste was so good. "Figures," she still grumbled.

"Nice to see you again, by the way," Raenith said more gently. She stood and moved to embrace Izell. Any normal person would panic when they felt the heat of the Goddess of Fire approaching them, but she knew better, sighing as she held the fiery woman.

A dragon's snort filled her mind. *"Mother?"* Queldian asked, stirring awake. Izell smiled with joy. All fire dragons referred to Raenith as their mother, even though her chosen form made it impossible for her to bear children. Queldian's presence quaked in delight as he saw the goddess through Izell's eyes.

"And hello to you too, Queldian," Raenith said, brushing the hair out of Izell's face with the impression of a tender smile radiating from her heat.

"Hello, Mother," he said through her lips. "We have so much to catch up on."

"Indeed." She released Izell, leaving a lingering impression of heat behind. A soft rumble rose from her throat, akin to a purr, all from Queldian rolling in the warmth of his old home.

"First, business," Izell sighed, having a seat in the chair they'd set up between the two goddesses. "I see you have my reverse-occultarus, for lack of a better name for it."

The three of them exchanged a significant glance.

"We've been referring to it as the god-occultarus. That is what it was originally for, yes?" Zalice's gaze gleamed with lightning.

Izell nodded. "Holding a portion of your power. It does not conduct magic, but absorbs it for use later. I paid quite dearly for this item." Her future sight, in fact, given to the Trader in exchange for him creating the most promising prototype that did the exact opposite of the orb-shaped tools Sorcerers relied on to magnify their magic.

She didn't need an occultarus to cast quick spells, not with Queldian's power at her fingertips, but she could still attune to this one and unleash any power it had absorbed when she needed it most. It was a vital tool for every task she had before her.

Including laying down her life.

"You all know I am not as powerful as King Oberon," she began. "I cannot channel the amount of raw power that he did, so I need to find it somewhere else. I need your help. You know above all others how imperative it is that we reestablish the Veil before angels and demons alike can come freely to our land. This time, it means your lives and, by extension, every life in Faerie."

Grim faces met hers. "I've seen the same future as you, and many more. We know what's at stake," Zalice replied.

"We have regrets that it's come to this," said Getana in a voice like rustling leaves. The miniature trees and vines that stood out of her back like bony wings shivered.

"Are you speaking of how you withdrew your blessing from my grandfather?" Izell asked, sharper than anyone else would dare to speak to a goddess.

Regret pinched between Getana's brows. "Indeed. We are not infallible. We never expected that we were doing anything other than expressing displeasure in Oberon's last choice as a living fae."

She was referring to his choice to select Jazrach to go into the Dark Eye when he had other, even stronger demons at his mercy. It was an emotional decision that made the Eyes unbalanced—the Light Eye containing its sacrificed Archangel more powerful than the Dark Eye and its lowly greater demon. For beings dedicated to maintaining the balance above all else, the discordance was enough to remove their blessings.

Izell understood this. She knew how they thought. However, had they smiled on Oberon just a few minutes more, Jazrach wouldn't have continued existing, biding its time within the Dark

Eye as its prison. It was clever enough to escape. Now, the sand in Izell's hourglass was running out, and bitterness lingered on her tongue toward the exalted ones she could trace this problem to.

"We made a mistake," Raenith said more directly. She rested a flaming hand over Izell's, drawing Queldian's happy rumble again.

"And since we understand all too well how we relate to the current crisis, we offer you our power and blessing freely. Rise, Izell Firebrand," Zalice intoned.

She got to her feet, her chin raised. The seer amongst the gods would be the first to acknowledge that she needed their help without any convoluted boons and deals. Zalice placed one hand on the golden occultarus, the other extended toward her.

"May the wind give you swift travels and lucky turns anywhere you step," he said. Electricity ran into the occultarus, and she braced as his blessing fell over her like the shroud of an incoming storm. It settled into her skin with fizzing potential, almost effervescent rather than painful like she was imagining.

She'd been blessed by Raenith before and knew it was temporary. The gods elevated their people to fulfill certain tasks. She was still lightheaded with the heady power that rolled inside of her as Zalice's lightning flowed into her potential for spellcasting.

"You'll find some extra from my daughter's ascension inside the god-occultarus. If you use up my lightning before it's time, I will replace it," he promised, standing back and releasing the golden orb. The only sign it now held a god's lightning was a gleam across its surface.

Of course, for Zalice to mention using his magic, she assumed he'd seen a likely future where she would need a boost in power.

Getana stood, placing her hand overtop the magical tool next and holding Izell's wrist. "May the earth's strength embolden you. Have no fear of death with the life of Faerie inside you," she said, solemn shades in her druidic green eyes.

Vines coiled from her fingertips, lashing Izell's skin. The earth's blessing was more forceful than the playful tingles of wind, or maybe the combination pushed the limits of Izell's potential. Sweat slicked down her back, and she stretched her limbs, filled with restless energy seeking some outlet.

Getana released her, just to reach up toward Izell's head. She ducked, closing her eyes as the goddess pressed a protective kiss against her forehead. "Good luck, dear," she said.

"See you soon," Izell replied, for she knew she would soon end up as another glimmer of energy in Getana's Sanctum home.

A knowing shimmer passed over the goddess's eyes as she inclined her head. "One way or another."

Raenith stepped up to give her blessing last. Izell tensed with dread, knowing exactly what to expect as the goddess threaded her burning fingers with Izell's. A thin barrier of magic prevented her from catching fire as well.

"You have me. We will be fine," Queldian assured her. He braced with her as Raenith's other arm lost its form, turning into a snaking channel of flame filling the occultarus.

"May my fire remind you that you are not alone in the dark nights ahead."

The heat over Izell's palm increased, turning to flames. Hot power transformed her veins to pure lava, coursing through her head to toe. Raenith's blessing was just as excruciating as she remembered, but Queldian armored her with a fire dragon's tolerance, making it more bearable.

Raenith's fire dimmed, coloring her yellow as she lent Izell her heat. When they parted, Izell bent over, clasping her knees and panting like she'd run for miles. "T-thank you," she managed to say. She was stronger than ever. Once she secured Cyranos's blessing, she'd practically be a demigoddess until her tasks were finished.

The Goddess of Fire rested a reformed hand on Izell's back. It felt cool in the wake of her magic. "I hope your blessings help you find your faith in us again."

She straightened, considering the deliberate wording. Here was one of few times she wished she could tell a lie. These three were familiar, old companions of an era long in her past, and...she truly had strayed from them. No longer were they the larger-than-life figures who could solve everything and anything that could trouble a fae.

They were gods, but they had weaknesses too. Not even they were infallible, and the danger on the horizon was beyond them. It was on her to go where they couldn't, but at least she would carry a piece of their power with her.

"I hope it does, too," she replied.

Chapter 12

Jaromir

Jaromir looked up from his work to realize Izell was gone and Cossette was holding two cups of tea.

"I'm going to delve a little deeper," he told Gwendolyn. He knew by now that there was no cure for old age, but she'd gained all the signs of elderly decline in the mere months since he'd seen her last.

The Mending Key had given his Gift back, but it was different when touched by the power in the ring. More powerful. He closed his eyes and felt his awareness fade into the spark of heat on his fingers. He eased aches and pains but also *saw* them. Sparks jumped in her joints, and a river of magic flowed through her, something he instinctively knew belonged within a different Key.

How interesting. He wanted to know what it was, and his magic told him. It was the power of life magic, the only thing keeping Gwendolyn alive rather than aging to the end of her accumulated vampire years. She may have shaken her vampirism by a miracle, but Nyah's gift kept her heart beating. Jaromir pressed his lips into a solemn line at the knowledge.

There's nothing else I can do.

His Gift had always made him a better doctor, informing him of certain things that no one could tell on a physical inspection.

But other times, it pulled back, recognizing a lost cause. He could make the other person comfortable, but that was all.

Gwendolyn's golden gaze met his own, acceptance already written in every line of her face. "It's okay, Jaromir. Why don't you pull up a seat and talk to us?"

"You would probably like to know why I'm a nephilim, hmm," he said, sheepish in the face of two people who had earned their light. He felt like a fraud by comparison.

"Actually, Soren and I are able to communicate across the distance between us. He's shared everything," Gabriel said. He was dressed in casual clothes, though they couldn't mute the glow from his skin as sunlight played over the side of his face. He'd returned to them looking like he was still in the prime of his life, and he'd maintained short, blond hair and a close shave just like the Gabriel who'd led the Fell Hunters some thousand years ago.

He was another person Jaromir felt he'd failed. While he knew he couldn't be everywhere at all times, Gabriel was murdered in their camp with few knowing it hadn't been a Fell to cut him down. Jaromir had carried the guilt of their commander's untimely death for quite some time and still felt its echo as he beheld the angel the man had become.

"I understand you are in need of training," Gabriel added, standing and clasping Jaromir's forearm like they were still old warriors.

"If I am not too old to learn new tricks," Jaromir answered. "However...shouldn't you be hunting the last demon?"

"Soren has it handled for now. There hasn't been a second one sent to Faerie yet. Hell's trying to keep us on our toes, I swear," he said.

Cossette spoke up while he considered that. "I'd like to borrow Jaromir before you take him for training."

"Of course, young lady," Gabriel answered.

She smiled and drew Jaromir outside, the two of them walking alongside the lake with tea in hand. It wasn't the first time Cossette mentioned wanting to talk to him, but she was quiet as she contemplated the waves that lapped at the pebbled shore.

She didn't have to wait too long for him to speak up. "How do I save Izell?"

A small sigh drifted from her. "The answer to that is simpler than you think." She turned her albino-red gaze toward him. Neither a giggly girl nor the solemn fortuneteller he expected, she wore a sense of knowing all the same. He wondered just how powerful her future sight had become and if she was in full control of it.

"You have to continue being you, Jaromir. That will save Izell."

He sighed, nodding in acceptance. "So, I have to take her place."

"Perhaps." She stopped and knelt, picking up a flat pebble and skipping it over the surface of the water. "Every action creates ripples. Your ripples are the ones to influence Izell most. In the end, it is you that will save her. But you will never expect how it happens until it's in front of you."

"What do you mean?" he asked quietly, watching the rings made with every skip radiate out. Some touched, while others were blown away from a stiff wind.

Cossette smiled to herself. "Don't you know the first rule of seer magic is that if you know specifics, you will miss your goal? You will overthink every step of the way until you fail. Just follow your heart when it comes to Izell. Besides, that's not why I wanted to talk to you."

He cocked an eyebrow. "Oh?"

"You're about to go to Hell," she said matter-of-factly.

"It's really happening, hmm." He hadn't truly thought Izell would figure out a way into Hell. But it was Izell. She was getting that powerful demon one way or another. "Is it truly safer for us to go extract a demon from Hell rather than summoning one?"

This was a matter he didn't understand. He'd never wanted to see a demon, not after Gwendolyn's descriptions of assisting her angelic father hunt them in her early years.

Cossette laughed without much humor. "Please. Neither of those things are *safe*. However, one path guarantees Izell's death, as it permanently stains her soul with evil. There's no coming back once you allow enough demonic magic in yourself to summon a greater demon. The other path is probably our only hope to see a pleasant future into eternity."

He considered for a few long moments. "Would a greater demon suffice for the new Dark Eye? Or do we need a stronger demon?"

"It would. You will have two options to take with you, either a ruler of Hell or a greater demon. Either would have the kind of power you need to tether the Veil once more. However, one of them would be better as your friend, and it's up to you to decide which one." She smiled when she saw his puzzled expression.

"Why would we want to be friends with a demon?"

"You'll see."

Really, he should've expected that answer.

"While you're there, you or Sondus should research what the demons call First and Second Realm," she suggested.

"What is...?" He didn't finish the sentence upon seeing the studious, blank look on her face. Right, she couldn't tell him. If Adrius were here, he'd say there was a *realm* of meaning behind her hints.

He heaved a heavy sigh. "Anything else?"

"Only things for Izell to hear." Cossette brightened as she spoke. "I can't wait to see what path you choose."

Her cheer struck him as odd in that moment, but he figured there would be answers aplenty the moment he was meant to know them. He wouldn't be like Lucia, who'd inevitably blundered her carefully scried plans every time.

Would he see Lucia again? He wondered if, against all odds, she was the "friend" Cossette mentioned. She was a miserable person and deserved her stay in Hell, but she was the only demon he could name.

"I believe you should learn some light magic while you can. Izell will want a piece of your time tonight," Cossette told him.

Cossette was, of course, correct. Jaromir could spend years under the combined tutelage of Gabriel and Gwendolyn, and he still wouldn't know everything his new nephilim side could do.

Unfortunately, Gabriel swore up and down that he couldn't talk about Hell, no matter how Jaromir asked. He decided not to mention why he was so curious, sure it would cause his group trouble in the long run if either of his tutors decided it was too dangerous for them to undertake their mission. If Cossette said it was their only hope, he wouldn't endanger it.

About an hour into summoning light in a god's parlor, he heard Izell's voice saying, "Are you looking into the magic? That's a great way of going blind, young man." She sounded tired but full of teasing energy.

"You're the only fae who'd ever call me young," Sondus replied dryly. Jaromir glanced up, realizing the spymaster had picked an inconspicuous spot to sit. He hadn't even realized they had an audience.

The sparkling orb between his hands snuffed out. He huffed in disappointment. Summoning raw power like that wasn't too difficult, but he still didn't like it. He was a doctor, sworn to do no harm.

Still, if he was about to go to Hell, he needed to know how to do a lot of harm. Hopefully, his conscious could withstand the weight of a new wave of death.

"You're in good spirits," he said to Izell, noticing she was smiling without her fangs.

"Queldian's awake," she replied. When he exchanged a curious glance with Gabriel, she supplied that that was the name of the sandstone-colored dragon spirit whose scales she wore as a shifter. She left them to go on a flight, just her and her dragon.

Sondus frowned when she left. "Think she's coming back?"

"Yes." It was Lord Zalice who answered, walking in and taking in the gathered faces. He breathed a soft, static-filled sigh. "Where is my daughter?"

There was a round of shrugs around the room. The god swept off to find her, and Jaromir returned to learning about his light, concentrating on cramming as much knowledge into this short time that he didn't notice the sun was setting. A savory smell wafted through his nostrils and drew him out enough to make him realize he had a much larger audience than before.

An unfamiliar fae woman was stirring a pot over an old-fashioned hearth, glancing over at him from the kitchen. She had stark white hair against skin the color of clean earth and unusual, sharp wings, while her eyes glowed with bright green magic.

Meanwhile, Talina was sitting cross-legged on the floor, cuddled up with a bird-like dragon who'd wrapped a slate-gray wing around her. Sirius sat close by, murmuring to a flash of pink in his palm. Blinking, Jaromir realized he was talking to a hummingbird, actually, and the tiny bird twittered back like they were deep in conversation.

"Done yet?" Izell asked, walking in again without any context. She looked him up and down. "Looks like you're done. Good. I smelled dinner."

"One of your favorites, if I recall," their new chef said. She had power behind her voice too.

Gwendolyn sat up, an eager smile crossing her face. "I'm getting spoiled in my old age, having a goddess prepare my meals."

Jaromir froze. *What?*

"A long life deserves respect, Lady Gwendolyn," the goddess answered airily.

"You get used to it," Gabriel said, noticing Jaromir's expression.

He realized this must be a daily occurrence for the group staying here. He shook his head slowly. "Does it not bother you to be around other deities?" he asked the angel curiously.

Gabriel lifted his shoulder. "They are not what I believe in, but I do not begrudge a completely different race for having faith that diverges from mine. That is not the love my God has taught me."

"Well said," Gwendolyn murmured. Jaromir nodded in agreement.

"Dinner," the goddess sang, summoning up the lot of them to

gather around the generous table Lord Zalice kept for company. He sat at the head of it, breaking bread with Talina and the goddess he learned was named Getana. The flaming goddess, Raenith, bracketed Izell with him and passed over her portion of meaty stew when the dragon shifter tore through hers with gusto.

Jaromir watched her go with an amused smile. It was a delicious meal, aromatic with herbs and thick with more meat than vegetables. He savored it and the company both, watching everyone interact.

Sirius was quizzing Cossette on what she'd do in various combat situations. Izell kept sneaking little touches on Raenith's arm, her tail swishing with deep contentment. Gabriel fed Gwendolyn a particularly large chunk of vegetable, the two of them having a chuckle over its rarity in the dish.

While Talina spoke with her father, her dragon, whom he learned was the skyrider Parax, kept snaking his head into her bowl, stealing bites when she wasn't looking. Getana noticed and muffled a laugh behind an elegant hand.

Family, Jaromir thought. As strange a group as they were, they laughed and carried on into the evening like the closest of family. He felt a little out of place until Zalice busted out some wine, and all eyes turned to Jaromir as he tried his first sip.

Electricity danced over his tongue, adding to the usual burn down his throat. He choked and recoiled, eyeing the deep red liquid until an arc of static danced over it. Izell laughed and slapped his back. "Wine made with *real lightning!*" she exclaimed.

"It's my specialty." Zalice smiled and toasted him.

Fae and their wine, he thought, shaking his head in amusement. He drank the rest of his glass slowly out of politeness, hoping to lessen the charge in it by swirling it about.

No luck there.

Izell was amongst the first to retire for the night, drawing him outside with only a jerk of her chin and a wink. He followed her readily, mesmerized by the sway of her hips and waggle in her tail. There was a new energy about her, like she'd tapped some hidden reservoir of confidence.

"They won't miss us for an evening," she said. With a single gesture, she pulled open a portal and backed through it while making a come-hither gesture.

How could he say no to an invitation like that? Simple. He didn't.

Chapter 13
Jaromir

HE RECOGNIZED THE DIM APARTMENT ON THE OTHER SIDE OF Izell's portal. She'd bought this little pad to give them a place to stay on the outskirts of Summerhail. Night after night of hard work had ended with him trudging inside and clapping twice to ignite the floating fairy lights that drifted in leisurely circles around each room.

Izell kept them extinguished, leaving her a glimmering silhouette from the loving caress of moonlight through one window. They stood a few feet apart. Her head took on a coy slant while he held his breath.

How many nights had he dreamed of this moment? To see this formidable woman let down her defenses and seek him out for a night alone.

He took a step toward her, and the perfect moment shattered. Her expression crumpled when he reached for her, tears filling her eyes. "Izell?" he breathed. His insides felt like they were filling with ice when he bundled her into his embrace and she sobbed into his chest.

"He's gone," she mumbled into his shirt, crumpling it between two fists.

He rubbed her back, careful of the wings of starshine that emitted sparks every time his fingers went through them. "Who?" he asked gently.

With a shaky breath, she stood straighter and swiped at her face. "My dragon," she sighed. "Queldian went back to sleep."

He puzzled over that. Surely she didn't want her familiar's spirit awake if they were going to have private time.

Her head thumped against his shoulder. "He went to sleep this afternoon, too, mid-flight. Raenith's presence can wake him, but..." Her throat worked, clicking in a dry swallow. "...he's dying, Jaromir."

Surely not, he thought. She'd been combined with her dragon spirit for at least three thousand years, if he understood her history correctly. Then again, he could hardly comprehend that length of time. Maybe shifter pairings weren't meant to exist as long as Izell had with Queldian.

Still, he coaxed her to sit on the only sofa in the modest apartment and drew her to his side. "How long has this been going on?" he asked.

He treated her concerns like an injury, asking questions until he felt he understood. She was shaken that her dragon spirit was taking longer and deeper rests within her. His heart ached to know she'd been carrying this silent burden, seeing Queldian's scales every day and not knowing if he would wake again or how long he'd stay.

"I'm sorry," he said when she finished explaining and rested against his shoulder with a forlorn sigh. He laced their fingers together, drawing on the Mending Key to give him a glimpse into her body.

Izell stiffened with a low growl but didn't draw away.

Closing his eyes, he tried to make sense of the images the Key showed him as it warmed on his finger. The Gift was a matter of speeding up already existing healing processes in vampires, but now he was sure the Mending Key was not vampire magic, but fae. And this particular fae's systems were bogglingly complex.

"Are you done pawing at my insides yet?" Izell grumbled. He released her, gazing into the nebulae sparkling in her eyes. Sitting back, she shook her head. "Were you trying to *see* my troubles?"

His brows drew at her tone. "Not literally."

At first, her answer was a little disbelieving laugh. "Oh,

Jaromir. I've heard so much about your vaunted healing hands, and here you are, making a rookie mistake."

The first roll of heat bubbled in his chest. "I've healed countless people and saved even more from the brink of death."

"No doubt." She gave his hand a squeeze, her lips turning up. "But you just got my kind of magic, and I would bet good money you've never successfully healed a fae of anything bigger than a headache. I doubt you'll find anything, but try again and do what I say."

He closed his eyes, still stirred up but not about to argue and point out that he'd taken her hangover just this morning. Images of nonsense passed before his closed eyelids as the Key went to work. "Try not to see. Or hear, or feel, for that matter," Izell instructed. "Healing magic is a sixth sense. It flows to where it's needed most."

"How do I use it, then?" He tried to nip his frustration as he forced himself not to look at what was right before him. The ring cooled, going dormant once more.

She took him through an exercise where he learned that he had a certain amount of magic within himself and the Mending Key, like a well of energy that slowly refilled once used. He could expend a few drops of it to check Izell's systems—the more magic he used, the faster it would be. If her body absorbed his magic, she was healthy and didn't need anything else. But if she had, for example, a broken bone, his magic would return to him and communicate the specifics of her wound. Location, severity, and how much more energy he'd need to expend to fix it.

"This is much different than the Gift," he muttered, wondering if he'd been using his Gift the hard way this whole time or if the Key changed everything for him.

"Congratulations on becoming a proper healer," she replied.

They'd see about that. He sent a pulse of magic through her, noticing the way she twitched. It must not be a pleasant sensation. After a few minutes, she shrugged. "Guess I'm healthy."

"I had to try," he said, feeling his shoulders sink. He'd been blessed with the most powerful shard of fae healing magic, yet he still couldn't help someone he cared deeply for. What kind of doctor did that make him?

Izell cupped his cheek, drawing him in for a short kiss. "I knew you would. Thank you, Jaromir." Her warm palm caressed him through his wrinkled shirt.

Who knew how long they sat, gazing into each other's eyes? He wished he could peer into her clever head just as easily as his magic could check her for injuries.

"You're my rock, you know that?" she said finally. "Steady and strong, holding my burdens when they grow too heavy to bear. I keep thinking that I wish we'd met earlier, but..."

He held his breath. But what? Did she regret relying on him so much?

While he worried, Izell was already straddling his lap, pushing his shoulders back into the couch. "But I've realized I'm wasting the time we do have," she finished. Her fingers fisted in his hair as their mouths tangled. This wasn't some chaste, stolen moment in the library's stacks, nor the teasing brush of her lips when in company with friends.

They kissed like he'd only dreamed about. Tongues tangling, her fangs grazing. She growled when he took her by the elbows and rolled so she was beneath him on the couch. An eager gleam lit up her eyes when he didn't shy away from the aggressive sound.

He'd learned Izell over time, discovering that she was more bark than bite. That prickly exterior was just a defense. She cared more about those around her than she'd ever admit to. Her even suggesting she needed him was as dear as if she'd declared her love then and there.

Their first time was as frantic as their kiss. She still acted like they were stealing only a moment together, and that just wouldn't do. He carried her to the bedroom afterward, laying her on the soft covers to make love with the proper worship of her feminine form. In her gaze, he saw something incredible, just a glimpse of her softer side as she finally relaxed, finally surrendered to their passion.

They lay together afterward, sharing softer kisses. Her hair was a tangled, white halo by moonlight, skin shimmering with sweat. He'd never seen such an alluring creature. "Again," she demanded softly.

She didn't let him get much sleep that night.

Izell fell asleep before he did, wearing a satisfied smile and little else. Jaromir practically glowed with contentment when he settled next to her, only to receive a jolt along his palm the moment he slung an arm around her hip.

His magic? The tiny pulse he'd sent into her, looking for an injury to heal. He'd assumed it was gone, yet it tingled against his skin for a moment before delivering its message. It'd delved into her soul, just to get confused that she had two souls within her. One was vibrant with health, while the other was faded, tired.

That's what Jaromir suspected from Izell's description of her familiar's sleeping patterns. What he didn't expect was what he could do to fix it.

He didn't speak to his magic, per se, nor did he fully understand how he directed it. But Queldian needed every ounce of his healing magic, and that's what Jaromir gave, down to the last drop of energy in the well within the Mending Key. He rested his hand on Izell's hip. The ring sparkled, heating to a brand against his skin. It gave the last bit of itself before going dim, and the flow of magic naturally turned to glimmering light.

Jaromir jerked away, afraid of hurting her with his burning nephilim light. The burst of brightness made sparkles glimmer all over her, but she didn't stir except for a soft snore. He released a tense breath, not sure how he'd explain his nephilim magic activating when he tried to heal Queldian. He drew the covers over them both, hoping by morning that she'd wake to a pleasant surprise: an active dragon spirit.

Chapter 14

Izell

Izell woke up sore in all the right places. Her tail swished in contentment even after a rushed shower. Jaromir was still out cold despite her banging around in the adjoining bathroom, and she grinned toward the bed, pondering how best to wake him.

Sadly, they couldn't stay here much longer. Time was of the essence when they didn't know how long they'd be visiting Hell—and if they'd survive the trip.

"Why don't you ask the albino seer?"

Why not indeed? That was a good idea.

Izell froze a moment later. The voice was so natural, a part of her, but it hadn't been her thoughts. *"Queldian?"* She poked about her head, feeling the dragon awake and active in the back of her mind. He hadn't been such a steady and strong presence in ages. Lifetimes, even.

"Surprise," he rumbled deeply, some of the sound leaking from her physical throat. Jaromir woke up to her clutching her cheeks and trying not to turn into a sobbing mess as Queldian shared that he'd absorbed a huge wave of healing magic while she'd been asleep.

It had to be Jaromir's work. The moment he sat up, she pulled the mass of him and the sheets up into an effusive hug. "You woke

Queldian. No, you healed him!" she exclaimed, laughing with Jaromir as they tangled in the bedding.

"Is this my cue to look away?" her dragon teased.

She paused with her hand already behind Jaromir's neck, their lips just beginning to brush. *Damn it.* They didn't have time for this, much as she wanted to give him a proper thank you. She ducked to kiss his neck instead, drawing a soft moan. "I want you, Jaromir. But we have to go visit Cyranos today."

"Can Cyranos wait a few minutes?" He tried to draw her back to his lips. She pulled up to nibble on his ear instead, with his grip growing more insistent around her shoulders.

"Maybe a couple minutes," she conceded.

Her "thank you" took at least an hour, plus a shower together. Now that she'd gotten Jaromir out of his clothes, she didn't really want him to put them back on.

It was with great reluctance that she got dressed and opened a portal to Zalice's private home. She started to sweat, as they'd donned thick wool and furs for a location much colder than Zalice's mountaintop. The God of Wind himself waited on the front porch, seated in a rocking chair with a mug of tea. He flashed the kind of knowing look that instantly irritated her.

"Good morning, Izell," he said.

"Yeah, yeah. It's good when I say it is," she growled.

His smile only widened. "And good morning to you too, Queldian," the god continued.

She let her dragon speak for himself. "It's a pleasure to see you again, Lord of Storms," he answered through her mouth, adopting a lower register. They'd long decided this was how to differentiate who was speaking, back when Queldian had been an active presence that still wished to converse with her friends.

Zalice greeted Jaromir too, perfectly at ease. "The two angelkin have left to contain a second demon scouted not far from here. Do not let it concern you," he said. "Sondus is packed and ready to go, but you should speak with Cossette first."

She nodded her thanks and breezed inside. The murmur of masculine voices faded behind her as Jaromir asked after Gabriel and Gwendolyn. It was, perhaps, a setback that he had barely trained his new magic.

She spotted Sondus sitting on the stairs, a packed bag beside him. His expression was set in a tense line.

Cossette wasn't very far either. She was serving herself a light breakfast of fruit and yogurt, only glancing up to flash Izell the same kind of perceptive smile as Zalice a few minutes prior.

"Seers," Izell sighed, plucking a slice of orange off Cossette's plate and popping it into her mouth. It wasn't meat like her dragon craved, but it'd do. "Always knowing what you're up to and why you're finally happy for the first time in ages."

"I wouldn't go that far." Cossette still giggled girlishly, but her cheeks lit like she knew exactly what Izell was referring to.

Izell rolled her eyes. "Tell me my future," she practically demanded.

Her curls tipped to the side as she considered. "You've experienced many important days in your life. Yesterday will rank amongst the highest." Cossette measured her words carefully, which meant they had some extra meaning. For the first time, Izell cursed that one of the strongest seers she knew was a vampire, who could lie and bend the truth outside of the rules of Seelie and Unseelie speech.

"I just wanted to tell you that I will take over on Earth in your absence," Cossette continued. "Everyone will be ready to fight when the day comes."

"Wouldn't expect anything less," Izell said.

Cossette bobbed her head. "That's all."

She raised a skeptical brow. "Really?"

"Oh, one more thing! You have to trust Jaromir like he's trusted you."

Implying she didn't already. Izell twisted her lip, trying to tamp down the pique that rose in her. She'd really expected more on the eve of a dangerous mission and an even more perilous magical ritual.

"Good luck, Izell." The seer caught her up in a hug.

"See you on the other side." She held Cossette for a few long moments. Her old plan had mostly come to fruition around her, despite missing the most important piece...the demon. Everyone she'd taken to Faerie had gotten what they'd most desperately desired. Cossette was an adult, ready and willing to be the kind of leader the Earth vampires needed.

The only person who didn't win in the end was Izell herself. If she was successful, she had to kiss Jaromir goodbye for the final time. Actually...she had to do that if they failed, too. The looming lose-lose situation made her heart's current preoccupation bittersweet. She was intimately aware that Jaromir had come in the house and spotted her, his shoes drifting in their direction.

"I packed you some food for the trip," Cossette continued, waving toward a sack perched on the countertop. "Though I'm sure you'll find enough water!"

Izell scoffed. Sure, they were going to meet with the God of Water, but most potable water in his personal domain was frozen solid.

"Just kidding, I packed water too," the seer said a moment later.

Izell breathed out some of her tension, deciding to keep in a barbed comment. "See you soon, hopefully. You know how to get back to Earth?"

She bobbed her head, bouncing her curls. "Lord Zalice will give me transport to Adrun, and I'll pass through Olivia's portal back to Earth. I'll be there by tomorrow."

Jaromir's hand molded to Izell's back as he said his goodbyes as well. By the time Izell secured their new supply of food and water, she turned to see Sondus nearly on top of them too, a light of eagerness in his otherwise starless eyes.

"I'm not running away without you," she grumbled, motioning for some space from both men. She started casting portals, setting the first to open up right in front of Lord Cyranos's home. It crumpled to dust a moment later.

She gritted out a curse. They didn't have time for these games, but clearly, the Lord of Waves wanted them to approach like petitioners rather than friends. It took her nine tries until she finally set the portal to a point outside of Cyranos's privacy barrier. She spread her hands, opening the portal wider. "Be *very* careful when you step through," she warned.

On the other side of the rip was an endless tundra. She let the two men pass through before nodding to Cossette in final farewell. The cold lashed unforgiving claws into her the moment she was through, a sheer wind blowing her fur-trimmed hood to flap behind her head.

"Good gods," Sondus muttered, hugging himself despite the warm clothing he was also dressed in.

"Welcome to the Path of Ice, the one and only way for us to visit Cyranos without completing an entire godly trial just to talk to him." Izell swept her arms out curtly. With Queldian awake and warm in her core, she could do this on her own.

But she wasn't going to be alone. The man she fancied and the guilty former apprentice by her side had made it clear they'd tackle everything with her from here on out. The freezing tundra stretching around them would be the most pleasant locale they'd see for a while.

She muttered uncharitable things about Cyranos as she wove spells for warmth over her two companions, knowing the god could probably hear her now that they were in his domain. If there was an answer, it came in a cutting gale which stirred the ice-encrusted grass and snow blooms around them.

"How long will we be out here?" Jaromir asked. The tension left his shoulders as her magic settled over him, weaving warm air in a bubble around his person. Lazy snowflakes melted within a few feet of him. *Good, that should keep him alive,* she thought.

"The longer we chitchat, the longer it'll be," she replied. She lifted her chilled nose to the air and caught her bearing. Queldian helped her locate the subtle and winding trail they were supposed to follow, which hid under a thin layer of ice.

"When will you tell them about the ice floes?" her dragon asked.

"That's the kind of thing that has to be seen to be believed," she snorted, fighting a scowl. Jaromir and Sondus followed her while she let her gaze pan over the flat, white-and-mint-green landscape

surrounding them. Any sunlight that struggled through a thin cover of clouds reflected back in her eyes twice as bright.

If it wasn't for the ivory snow blooms dotting the landscape, she would have no landmarks to mark their progress. The eighteen-petaled flowers were rare anywhere else, thriving only in places of extreme cold close to the natural lines of magic that ran through the land occupied by one of the Gods of Faerie. They walked past small clusters of the flowers, each one clenched into a tight bud.

The flowers grew in thicker clumps as Izell's small group ploughed on through the icy winds that pushed back at them. A shudder passed through the white buds, and Izell watched in shock as one close to her foot unfurled to display a tender, crystal-like stamen—and then it melted.

Izell drew up to her full height, immediately panning to take in their surroundings again.

"What is it?" Jaromir asked, doing the same.

Her nostrils flared, filling with the sting of cold. There was just a hint of something tickling at her nose. It smelled of flowers and iron and...

"*Sulfur,*" Queldian growled, the sound echoing in her throat too.

"Snow blooms melt when touched by most magics," she replied, snapping her fingers. The golden occultarus floated to her from the pouch she had secured at her waist. She'd attuned to it, so it should respond to her commands, but she hadn't expected to need it so soon. "And I smell *demon* magic."

A flash of movement had Izell whirling around in time to see a figure amass from a cloud of drifting shadows. It grabbed Sondus and slit his throat in one swift motion.

Chapter 15

Jaromir

An outraged roar from Izell deafened Jaromir as he stood there for a moment in shock. The figure behind him had appeared out of nowhere, a heavy cloak and shadowy magic obscuring any hint of the person's identity.

Sondus's eyes bulged as he tipped to the ground, pushed by the mystery figure. Izell lunged, lashing out with claws thickened into dragon talons. The cloaked person dropped to a crouch and barely avoided evisceration.

Jaromir didn't panic, though his heart beat fast enough to beat out of his chest. There was no time to second-guess. Light magic crackled through his palms as he drew on that doctor's calm to give him a steady aim. He threw a ball of angelic light at the cloaked figure, just for the person to calmly sheer through it with a swipe of their dagger. The weapon flew at him a moment later, embedding the blade into his outstretched hand. He pulled it free with a pained hiss.

"Thanks," a distinctly feminine voice drifted from the figure, who tugged off Sondus's glove and pocketed something along the way. The hood dropped from her head, revealing the flash of glowing amber eyes and a crown of four majestic horns for the brief time she stood still. She twisted, dodging a strike of lightning from Izell without even looking over her shoulder before running into the depths of the tundra.

"Get her! I'll help Sondus," Jaromir shouted. She called something back, but he was already falling to his knees by the prone form of the dark fae trying to draw breath with both hands fastened desperately around the wound on his neck.

The rise and fall of the other man's chest was already weak, and he'd lost a lot of blood, leaving a garish halo in the white-tinged ice below. Jaromir took a deep breath, riding out a spike of fear that he was already too late.

He was often too late.

As a healer for the Fell Hunters, he'd closed the eyes of countless brave men and women for the final time. Sometimes, Jaromir was not enough. That didn't stop desperate expressions like Sondus's from being imprinted on his memories forever.

Unbidden, he remembered many of those faces and the sounds of pain that escaped even the most fearless of souls as they face their mortal coil. Sondus choked, his desperate gaze fixed on Jaromir as he laid his hands on the man's chest.

I will not let him die. I will not fail him, Jaromir told himself.

He did as Izell had taught him, drawing on the well of magic within him and sending what he could into Sondus. But he had cinders—almost all of it had been poured into Izell to draw her dragon back to wakefulness.

It has to be enough, he thought. Every second echoed in the throb of his heart, filling his hearing alongside Sondus's sounds of agony.

It took moments for his magic to return and draw *hard* on what he had left. He physically jerked, dark spots drifting at the corners of his vision. His healing magic went dry as every drop fled into Sondus.

The fae's death grip slowly loosened, fingers falling away to reveal the swiftly mending wound. Skin stitched itself together, yet Jaromir had the distinct feeling his work wasn't done, even as Sondus drew a new gasp of air, breathing and coughing and *alive.* Jaromir backed away, kneeling in a fine crusting of snow and ice as the world tilted on its axis, back and forth in a blurry haze.

He's fine. He's alive, Jaromir thought. He lost his equilibrium, landing with his cheek in prickling snow as the dark spots engulfed his vision. He passed out with only one thing on his mind: *I wasn't too late.*

As gentle as his descent into darkness was, Jaromir woke with a sudden jerk, thinking something wasn't right. He was lying face down on a warm, uneven surface that rolled beneath him. The moment his eyes shot open, he saw sandstone-colored scales and felt the rumble of a deep voice vibrating under his cheek.

"I'm going to murder Cyranos," Izell was saying. Jaromir would recognize her acerbic tone anywhere, even hiding within the bass rumble of her dragon form.

"It's not wise to say such things aloud." Sondus sounded fine as well, Jaromir thought, carefully raising his head. The fae rode on Izell's back too, seated precariously between her folded wings while Jaromir was secured to the space between her shoulders and neck by a tight coil of rope.

Izell growled, twin curls of smoke leaking from her nostrils. One slitted eye turned over her shoulder, blooming out when it scanned Jaromir's face. "You're awake. Good."

She stopped long enough for Sondus to free him of the rope. He sat carefully with his legs dangling over her shoulders, holding one of her neck spines for support. "What happened?" he asked, holding his forehead through a dizzy fit.

He remembered healing Sondus with everything he had, just to come up with an empty feeling and unconsciousness. His magic had practically spoken to him, saying that he wasn't done healing the fae. "How are you feeling?" he asked on top of his first question.

Sondus did look gray around the edges, the rich purple undertones of his astral fae skin turned ashen from blood loss. Still, he smiled. "I am well. I owe you a life debt on top of everything else. It is likely I will never be able to repay you."

"It was nothing," Jaromir said immediately.

"Nonsense. I will carry this debt proudly until such day I can give you the same kind of precious gift."

"We have a problem, Jaromir." Izell cut through his thoughts and the argument he was building so this fae wouldn't feel such a crushing sense of obligation on his behalf. He turned a concerned gaze toward the dragon baring her teeth with lingering fury.

"I chased the demon long enough to see the hole she'd crawled out of. She went right back into it and closed it in my face." She loosed a frustrated growl.

"That's not the worst part of it," Sondus offered, his expression shading with grave lines. "She...took my Key." He laced his fingers, having forgone his gloves completely. The ruby ring was notably absent.

Still, Jaromir needed several long moments to let it sink in. With Sondus's life on the line, he hadn't given it a second thought, but the demon had stripped off his glove before she'd bolted.

"Shit," he muttered. They needed that Key and all the magic within it. It was as vital to creating a new Dark Eye as a demon's soul. There was no way this attack had been random chance.

But the fact that a demon had found them out here, so close to a god's domain, put ice in his veins.

"Agreed. That's not all," Sondus sighed. He closed his eyes. "I did significant research on a demon recently when Lucia was posing as her and trying to usurp the Unseelie Queen. Her name was Lilith, one of the Lords of Hell. A succubus with incredible beauty, two battleaxes, and..."

"Four horns," Izell supplied.

"Four horns. I saw her face when you attacked her, Jaromir. This was the *real* Lilith," Sondus said grimly. "But she didn't have wings like every sketch of her I could find."

"Does it matter?" the dragon snipped. "She had the face and the power."

Sondus frowned down at his fingers. "If you knew everything I know about Lilith, you'd understand why I hope it's not her, despite her face."

Izell's steps slowed. "It's a good thing we're already going to Hell."

She lowered herself to the ground, spreading out her wings to form two ramps off her back. Jaromir looked up to see that they'd reached the end of the tundra, the land abruptly cutting off to reveal deep blue water dotted with chunks of floating ice. The sun was setting behind the cloud cover, leaving the bobbing icebergs as the most distinctive sight.

Jaromir braced himself on Izell's side, wondering how they were going to cross the water without a boat. There weren't enough trees in the area to even form a proper raft for three people.

"These are the ice floes." Izell sounded weary as she sat back on her haunches. It was only then that Jaromir noticed she had their bags tied under her wings like she was an oversized beast of burden. "If we have Cyranos's favor, we will be able to continue."

Sondus muttered under his breath. Jaromir caught "...not so many insults..." before the words drifted away on a chill breeze.

"If we're lucky, we'll be in front of Cyranos before the moon rises," she continued. With a flick of her talons, three pieces of floating ice drifted toward them. "Follow my lead. I haven't done this with company before, but I assume a God of Faerie can test more than one of us at the same time."

Izell placed one of her feet firmly on the first piece of ice. It expanded to twice its size, allowing for her to take another step. The whole structure wobbled but held under the weight of her dragon form.

Jaromir and Sondus exchanged a glance and a shrug before following suit on the ice waiting for them. Magic tingled the soles of his feet when he was on his floating ice. It expanded at half the rate of the bridges forming for Izell and Sondus.

He eyed the sapphire waters lapping at the edge of his precarious bridge. If the God of Water decided he wasn't pleased with Jaromir for whatever reason, an errant wave could tip him into the freezing ocean.

Something cut through the water, reflecting off the meager light left before sundown. Jaromir caught sight of a slick, serpentine form breaching just yards away. "Who goes there?" The voice came from the teal head emerging between Izell and Sondus, inspecting them both with keen eyes in a scaled face.

Izell froze, leaning her head down as far as her long neck could reach. "Lyana?" she gasped.

The serpentine form slunk through the water, coiling up so the sea serpent could lift her head further out of the water. Each scale shone with an abalone-like finish, sure to be stunning in full daylight. She blew mist out of her nostrils, fins like white gossamer flapping around her head.

"Depends on whose asking," the serpent replied, her eyes narrowing to pinpoint slits.

Izell tilted her head before lifting a talon. "I'm Izell. This is my dragon form."

"This is my dragon form too." Despite her flexible form, the serpent was stiff and uncertain as she turned to eye Sondus and Jaromir. Both men had stopped to gape at her. With another snort, she returned her attention to the other dragon. "Your attempt to give me freedom came at a horrible cost, Izell."

Despite her lizard-like features, regret drew over Izell's face like a looming storm cloud. She sat, her snout still only a few feet from Lyana's. "I'm sorry," she murmured.

Jaromir had an idea of who Lyana was, though he'd never met her when she was possessed by Lucia. He just hoped that she didn't blame Izell for it.

The sea serpent let the moments slip by in tense silence, her gaze locked with Izell's. If they were wild animals rather than shifters, Jaromir would assume he was watching a dominance fight. He realized something had to be passing between them mentally.

Chapter 16
Izell

Lyana met Izell's eyes and spoke in her mind. *"I am the test for you to continue on. Lord Cyranos did not want to see you at all."*

"But you convinced him otherwise?" Izell asked, hopeful that she still had an ally with the fiercest God of Faerie.

Lyana's response was as frigid as the water she floated in. *"Something like that."*

That little kernel of hope sputtered. Once her joy at seeing Lyana whole and in control passed, she recognized the way the sea serpent coiled—like Izell was a threat, not a friend. There was no warmth in Lyana's reptilian eyes.

"Do you have any idea what that demon did to me?" she asked with quiet fury. *"While you bargained with her. While you stood back and did nothing."*

"I'm sorry. I did everything in my power—"

"No. You didn't."

Izell was struck mute before she could finish her sentence. Some Seelie part of her recognized she was about to lie and stopped her short.

"You had a pact with the demon." Lyana breathed a hiss aloud, a sound akin to boiling water.

Oh. Izell felt like the deepest fool, staring into the accusing pits of Lyana's eyes. Her deal with Lucia was something she'd discussed with the demon while she still possessed Lyana and used her body like a puppet. *"I was waiting for the right moment to use it. I planned to help you all along."*

Lyana scoffed. *"When?"*

"When the time was right. I didn't forget about you, and I hated seeing her use you." Izell spoke quickly, recognizing the desperate edge to her tone. She knew how it sounded, despite the truth that spilled from her.

She'd never intended for Lyana to get tied up with Lucia. It was another unexpected event her future sight hadn't warned her about. In freeing Lyana and telling her where to find Adrun, she'd accidentally condemned the sea serpent shifter to a brush with a fate worse than death. Facing her folly head-on filled her with regret that she hadn't been able to act on Lyana's behalf sooner.

"Right." Lyana's dry tone was like hearing a mirror of herself. *"Here comes your test, Izell Firebrand. Answer to my satisfaction, and you may proceed and speak with Lord Cyranos. Fail, and I will drown your companions."*

Izell took a dry swallow, glancing over at Jaromir. Both men stood like tense statues, watching the dragon stare-off silently. They probably knew there was something dire at stake here.

No matter what the test was, she'd put her claws through this beautiful sea serpent's throat before Lyana so much as looked at Jaromir with ill intent. The fact that they'd been friends briefly would not give her pause. She drew herself up, fixing a cool mask over her draconic features. *"I understand."*

"Tell me your plans. Why are you here to see the Lord of Waves? What do you intend?" Lyana prompted.

She couldn't help but chuckle. *"Do you have a few hours?"*

The serpent didn't so much as twitch from her threatening stare. *"I have until the end of my patience."*

"Then I shall tell you everything aloud so Sondus and Jaromir know why we're still here after sunset," she sighed.

"I am only listening to you."

"Fine."

Izell began to painstakingly explain her plan, ignoring Sondus when he tried to help her save her breath. She kept her gaze on

Lyana the whole while to avoid meeting anyone else's gaze by the finale—her death to complete the new Dark Eye.

Only one part was new. "I'm plan to sever one of Lilith's horns and put it through her skull for stealing the Summer Key," she growled.

Once she was done, silence drifted over the water. Both Sondus and Jaromir knew about her planned sacrifice, so she only earned a soft gasp from Lyana at the end.

"Let me get this straight," the sea serpent sighed aloud. "You plan on making an Archangel take you to Hell, where you will kill one of the strongest demons—one whose name my demon tormentor used as a front to scare the piss out of many Unseelie—and then you will kidnap a high-ranking demon to power the Dark Eye. And *if* you can escape Hell from there, you will lay down your life to make said artifact."

"I can't lie, now can I? You can always trust a Seelie," Izell replied.

"Why aren't you kidnapping Lilith for the Dark Eye?"

Izell glowered back toward the icy tundra. "She just got added to the plan a few hours ago."

"This plan won't work."

"I'll make it work," she answered in a low growl.

Silence was her response. She turned to see that Lyana had sunk into the depths. A spike of adrenaline hit her system as she scoured the water, terrified that the sea serpent would flash out to grab Jaromir in her jaws to drag him to the ocean's depths.

An arm reached out of the water, hoisting up a fae woman onto the ice platform Izell was balanced on. Icy water solidified around the fae, into a stiff, tube-like dress that was tastefully frosted in the proper places. Tilting her head to the side, Izell recognized some of Lyana's features...but she was something new.

No longer wearing her shifter side's scales, Lyana was instead crowned by deep indigo hair and a pair of wings made of pure, clear water. Izell fixated on those wings, feeling her eyes dilate with shock.

"You're not an astral fae anymore," she breathed.

"No." There was a soft echo behind the word. Lyana turned

away before Izell could get a good look at the elements swirling in her eyes. "Come. Lord Cyranos awaits." She lifted her hands and clapped once. The ice below their feet shuddered and merged, turning into an icy wonderland as it continued to grow into a proper bridge to cross the ocean.

"I passed your test, then?" Izell admired the bridge as it bore her weight, despite looking as delicate as carved ice. Dainty whorls formed handrails on either side of it. While her talons made it easy to navigate the slippery footing, Sondus immediately slipped and fell face first.

Jaromir helped him up, the two of them taking it slower. "I suppose you have," Lyana replied while Izell kept an eye on her companions.

Since she hadn't drowned the men as promised, Izell assumed that was a "yes, you passed," though her gaze was narrowed at the other woman's back and the curious sheen to her dark skin. She thought she might recognize what Lyana was now but felt the cold shoulder her words would land on if she asked how it happened.

Instead, she probed at a different topic hanging over them. "Will you take trespass against me?" she asked.

However Lyana answered would tell her a lot. Trespass was practically a fae law: an eye for an eye. Hurt a fae, and expect to be hurt back. But trespass was a controlled revenge, like how she'd punished Sondus, meant to be given with forgiveness to follow. If Lyana didn't want this, then she was unpredictable, as unknowable a quantity as the Lord of Waves himself.

"I am not sure it's worth it," Lyana sniffed. "But you owe me all the same."

Well, that's not a good sign, she thought. "Understood."

"*Into the viper's den,*" Queldian remarked.

Izell murmured her agreement. She'd thought Cyranos's summons were strangely hostile—surely the other gods had spoken to him about what she required and what was at stake. But Lyana, a shifter partnered with the last son of the Lord of Waves, may have colored events.

"*He may be ill,*" her dragon suggested.

"And why would that be? He is a god," she scoffed.

His amusement warred with the wariness she held within her. *"You don't see it."*

"See what?"

Queldian just laughed, retreating from her active mind.

"Queldian!" she protested. *"What is it?"*

"Have you done this before?" the quiet question came from Jaromir, who still kept Sondus steady as they crossed deeper into the ocean.

She shrugged to herself. Her dragon wasn't going anywhere, and he would eventually have to talk to her again. "Once. If I ever needed to visit Cyranos after that, he would allow me to portal to him directly."

"Why not now? It could've saved us a lot of aggravation." Was that anger she heard? She didn't know Jaromir was capable of even a bit of ire.

Sondus sighed. "It may be for the best, if we can manage to retrieve the Key. We know we have a mole in the palace now. Someone *very* close to the royal family, to know I had it in the first place."

Jaromir frowned. "How would they have known to find us here, though?"

"I don't know, but I *will* find out," the spymaster muttered.

The floating ice grew thicker on either side of their bridge. Izell knew they were close when she saw that many ice chunks were crowned by floating sculptures and works of art, all fashioned of the frozen element.

Cyranos's home had changed from an iceberg magically defying the odds in a tropical sea into the icy fortress looming ever closer. They were on the line of the border between Faerie and the hostile lands held by superstitious elves that were eternal enemies to fae and magic. Part of what kept elves out of Faerie was Cyranos's watchful eye and abundance of cold magic.

How long had the Lord of Waves enforced the laws and magic that kept elves from ever setting foot in Faerie? An uneasy feeling shuddered under Izell's scales. Cyranos was easily the most isolated of the four elemental gods.

His home was similar to what she remembered—a temple of glass-like ice built up from a massive iceberg. It glowed from within with shades of the aurora and the deep, dark ocean. Over the centuries, it'd evolved from a simple temple into a two-story castle bristling with spiked walls on all sides and no discernable entrance.

According to the rules of approaching a god, she was unable to fly, else they would've arrived a lot sooner. She still felt the magic weighing down her wings. "The entrance is underwater, isn't it?" she grumbled.

Lyana nodded. Any hostile actors would have to submerge themselves fully in Cyranos's element, Izell thought. A clever way to deter attackers—if anyone was actually looking to attack. It looked like a monument of paranoia to her.

"I'll form a tunnel for us," the sea serpent shifter said.

The bridge stopped several yards short of the bristling ice spikes. Lyana breathed an unfamiliar word of power and held out her hand, slowly drawing it back and up to shoulder-height. Ice crackled, a hollow cylinder of it breaching the surface of the ocean and connecting seamlessly to the bridge like a living, frosty worm. With a brittle sound masking a second muttered word, Lyana's magic rapidly formed a staircase leading underwater.

She led the way down. The two men exchanged a glance and then looked up at Izell. It was too narrow to fit her dragon form. A rush of nerves tickled her belly, but she still said, "Go on. I'll catch up with you."

Lyana could collapse this bridge and drown them while Izell shifted. She was well aware of the possibility even as she folded in on herself, their collected bags thumping to the ice as she regained two legs and a naked body covered in goosebumps. Dragon shifter or not, it was far too cold to be exposed. She fumbled through the bags until she found something warm to wear.

The other three waited for her in the tunnel. Jaromir had his face to one side of the ice, beckoning her over with a big smile. He pointed. A cluster of spotted seals was swimming by, some waving their front fins and slowing when they saw their audience.

Izell waved back. "They're selkies," she told Jaromir. "I didn't know anything lived this close to the Lord of Waves."

"He has offered them shelter," Lyana said. Her impatient tone had Izell straightening and passing off some of the bags across her shoulders to her companions. They continued down the tunnel, following a gentle bend before it rose toward a metallic hatch.

Rather than touch the door, their guide spoke a third word of power. The wheel cranked on its own, turning with the groan of heavy gears.

"She has an awful lot of magic, doesn't she?" Queldian suggested.

Izell tensed. He was right, and it was a key clue to a puzzle she felt was right in front of her face. Where had Lyana's magic come from? How had she changed into a different kind of fae—a relic of Izell's distant past?

As they climbed into the dreary bowels of Lord Cyranos's ice fortress, she studied Lyana with new intent. Finally, she remembered what Lyana's new appearance reminded her of. A primordial fae. She was a water fae, no longer held by the constraints of Seelie and Unseelie.

"Impossible." But the possibility wouldn't leave her head, so she called aloud, "Lyana."

The sea serpent shifter tensed, turning her head but not enough to catch more than a hint of her face. "What?"

He may be ill.

Queldian had caught something she hadn't. Why would a god be ill...unless he gave a huge amount of power to another person?

"Are you a demigoddess?" Izell asked.

Chapter 17
Jaromir

Waves will answer that."

Izell's shoulders lowered, her expression looking distinctly like relief to Jaromir. "Congratu—"

"Save it," Lyana snapped. She turned sharply and marched to a near staircase. The ice was patterned like tiles and damp, but it wasn't melting. With the dark ocean under them, Jaromir was glad of whatever magic held this impossible place together.

With a sigh, Izell followed in her wake. "We are not welcome here," she said over her shoulder. "Don't say a word until we're safe. I'll do the talking."

Jaromir nodded. "All right." She understood what was going on best, after all.

Sondus released a soft hum, stroking his chin thoughtfully. The spymaster didn't speak, though his dark gaze darted around, undoubtedly cataloguing their surroundings.

As far as Jaromir could tell, the fortress was completely empty. The icy walls were encrusted with frost and fine crystals, making it impossible to see into any of the rooms they passed. However, the air was sterile, free from the lingering scents that hung over any occupied space.

Jaromir marveled at the cold beauty around him as he noticed that the hand that had shaped the fortress had spent time making murals of furry frost. The magical lights that hung overhead danced in holders of ice cut like fine crystal. He didn't dare touch anything, afraid the heat of his fingertips would melt and ruin it, though the inside of the fortress felt pleasant despite the proximity of so much frozen water.

The hall emerged into a grand space that had Jaromir stopping short and staring. A peaked ceiling reached up both stories of the fortress, clearly claiming the center of the structure. Fairy lights frolicked on tiny wings, darting in the gaps between a massive chandelier formed entirely of multicolored ice sparkling like dazzling gemstones. Light absorbed into the dark ice lining the floor, making it not reflect into his eyes but concealing the pit until they walked right by it.

Below the chandelier was a hole that smelled of ocean water. It was wide enough for a creature even larger than Lyana's sea serpent form. A grate was pushed to the side, its black metal decorated with swirls of water and seafoam.

Jaromir swept his gaze from it to the throne that sat against the wall, currently unoccupied. It was nestled in a three-dimensional ice mural of sea life, mixing together creatures he recognized with others that he didn't: strange, toothy fish and beings that looked like they had human torsos fused to fish tails. Other figures were bipedal, with scales, fins, and the same bristling teeth as the sea life. The throne itself was a sculpture of a sea serpent, its coils forming steps up to a high seat graced by a real cushion—a pop of red—with the back formed of the serpent's head bending around to serve as an armrest. It was detailed down to the scale pattern, and Jaromir suppressed a shudder at the cold stare of the ice dragon.

A subtle splash was the only warning before the massive head of a real sea serpent breached the water behind them. Jaromir whipped around, his heart leaping to his throat. Undoubtedly, the creature was the Lord of Waves. He flicked out a tongue as thick as a tree trunk, inspecting them with a sapphire eye narrowed to a mere slit.

In the blink of an eye, the serpent's form shrank, replaced by an astral fae man floating from the water and dripping fractals of starlight from his fine but soaked tunic. With a brushing motion, every drop of wetness bounced off of him. "Let's get this over with," he said, his voice echoing softly with the hint of a bubbling stream.

Cyranos's fae form echoed Lyana's features. His skin was black as night, patterned with undertones of indigo and deep, oceanic blue. His wings were formed of stars, though, and more glittered over his skin like a scattering of tiny ice crystals. The snowy white hair that dropped past his pointed ears looked like it would melt from the warm touch of another, framing a face marked by sharp fae beauty. The god's lips were thinned with displeasure the moment his gaze fell upon Jaromir.

"Thank you for meeting with us, Lord Cyranos," Izell said, bowing formally. He and Sondus echoed the motion a moment later.

The god scowled. "If the fate of everything I love wasn't at stake, we wouldn't be meeting. Lyana has shared everything you said."

Jaromir breathed a soft sigh of relief, glad they didn't have to repeat the same hours-long explanation.

Cyranos crossed to Lyana's side, and Jaromir saw the woman's face clearly for the first time, recognizing the oceanic blue swirling in her fae eyes as the same sort of power coming from the god. The striking feature made them look closely related. He wouldn't be surprised if she truly was a demigoddess.

With a wave, Cyranos lifted water from the pit. It flew over and crystalized into five chairs. He lowered himself with a sigh, and Jaromir didn't miss how Lyana helped him down with an arm around his back. The rest of them sat, facing each other in a loose circle.

"Well?" The Lord of Waves turned his attention toward Izell. "State your purpose."

She glanced toward Jaromir, and he flashed a concerned look back, feeling the hostility from both of these fae.

Izell sat up straighter and pulled the golden occultarus from the pouch she'd reattached to her belt. "I have come to ask for your blessing. Your siblings have already lent their power to my cause, which is the recreation of the Dark Eye. I do not have the same level of magic as King Oberon, but with your help, I can borrow enough to complete the job."

Cyranos didn't blink. The hair lifted on the back of Jaromir's neck as he held this stare for several silent seconds. When he did speak, it was with quiet intensity. "You have some nerve asking me for anything, Izell Firebrand. Through your actions, you have tainted Faerie with the likes of vampires and hellspawn." Icy chill raked over Jaromir as his presence earned a glare from the god. "My Lyana was victimized by one such creature. I understand you had the means to force the demon from her but did not.

"Answer me one thing." He leaned forward, the swirls of water within his eyes darkening to a forbidding vortex. The whole fortress quaked as his fingers flexed into fists. "Why not?"

Izell paled and raised her hands defensively. "I...I needed that bargain I made with Lucia for something else."

"What could be more important?" he demanded.

She took a deep, shaking breath. One of the sculptures fell from the wall, shattering with a crash. Jaromir reached over, taking one of Izell's trembling hands in his own, hoping to give her something steady to rely on before this god shook his home apart in a rage.

"She was my backup demon. If I lost Jazrach for any reason, I could still call Lucia to my side and force her to go into the Dark Eye," Izell admitted with reluctance. Steam-like hisses drew from both of the water fae. "If she wasn't needed for that, she was still the one who possessed the Language Key for a millennium. I would've ordered her to participate in the ceremony and then pulled her from Lyana and destroyed her. But she didn't behave as I expected."

"No kidding," Lyana muttered bitterly.

"I should've known my plans were awry the moment she took over your body. It wasn't supposed to happen." Izell reached forward but hesitated, her fingers hovering in the space between them. "You were supposed to find Adrun and join the shifter people. Lucia was supposed to bide her time, not attempt to take the Unseelie throne or attack the Lord of Storms. In my visions, she was smart enough *not* to dangle her presence in front of Prince Sirius like fresh bait."

She swallowed, shoulders lifting under the icy stares of Cyranos and Lyana. "Had I known this was how it would go, I would've chosen a different path. And that's the Seelie truth," she said.

Lyana drew a sharp breath, turning her gaze to Cyranos. His fists unfolded, and the ice around them slowed its vibration. It was so quiet Jaromir could count the heartbeats thudding in his ears.

Cyranos let them sit there as he considered. Minutes passed, and Jaromir shivered as a nervous sweat froze along his back. He ended up noticing Sondus's knowing smile. The spymaster glanced his way and nodded.

"Your truth is a difficult one for me to hear," the Lord of Waves said at last. "But I suppose it has worked out for us up until this point. You have come to me seeking spare power for your quest and your...journey."

Izell nodded. "That's right."

His expression shifted from its severe scowl into a troubled frown. "I have none for you."

She drew in a gasp, though her attention flashed to Lyana.

"That's right. I gave it all to her," the god continued. "The demon burst from her soul in the most traumatic way possible. It was either make her a demigoddess...or allow her to pass in my arms."

"Stars above," Izell murmured.

Jaromir was glad to know the sea serpent shifter hadn't died because of Lucia's cowardice. He just hoped there was some way for them to still get what they needed from the last elemental god.

"It will regenerate, with time. The exact thing we do not have."

"Implying Izell's angel friend can get her into Hell and back, too," Lyana added with a skeptical raise of her brow.

Izell snorted. "Friend. Sure. He's an Archangel. I have no doubt he could retrieve our demon and our lost Key on his own."

"But you don't trust him?" she asked.

"No. So, I'm going to do it myself."

Lyana blinked once, slowly. "I have decided that you have trespassed against me, and in return, I demand you take me with you."

The scaly hand in Jaromir's hold flexed. Something like relief mixed with disbelief in her expression as Izell blurted, "*What?*"

"You're taking me to Hell," the sea serpent shifter stated.

Turning to Cyranos, Izell gestured toward her. "You're all right with this?"

Now that his show of power was over, Jaromir recognized the fatigue lining the pits under the god's eyes and the slope of his shoulders. "I assume she has a good reason," he said.

"The best. While you rest and consolidate your power, I'll make sure Izell's plan is a success." Lyana's smile was more a baring of her teeth. "*And* if we happen upon Lucia again in that blasted place, all the better."

Chapter 18
Jaromir

Jaromir woke, cold.

The crystalized walls glowed from the beacon of Cyranos's grand chandelier, even well down the hall from it, enclosed in a private room. He was just glad to see that the god kept his guest rooms furnished with warm blankets and real cushions. He tucked the extra sheets around a sleeping Izell as he rose.

There was little sense of time here without natural light. They could've been sleeping for hours or minutes, but it felt like the latter. Izell's worries felt like his own: the closer they came to the apocalypse, the worse the odds became in pulling off a victory. They didn't have all the Fell Keys anymore, or a powerful demon's soul, or even the blessing of all four gods. It felt like a giant hand was plucking off the corner pieces of the puzzle they were trying to assemble.

But one extra thing weighed on Jaromir as he shrugged on a warm set of clothes and left the sleeping fae. Pressure built up in the back of his head, urging him on. He hadn't told Izell about it, not wanting to add to her worries on the eve of their departure.

He remembered how his magic felt while healing Sondus. How he'd given every bit of it to save the fae's life, yet it wasn't enough. There was more to fix, and Jaromir thought it must be an illness or silent disability. He hadn't had the means to help him at the time, but now, he felt his magic renewed and ebbing around.

Searching for a person in need.

When Jaromir had his Gift, occasionally, it pushed him to wander. The magic sought out new faces because they might need him. The Gift wanted to be used, to spread good health and an end to illness.

When he thought about it that way, he saw the clear kernel of angelic magic within it.

He caught a hint of motion out of the corner of his eye. As far as he knew, it could only be one of three people, and he wanted to at least speak to all of them. Cyranos seemed injured—but Jaromir knew it was magical in nature rather than something physical that he could fix. The scope of it was mind-boggling, just imagining the level of fatigue a god experienced turning someone into a demigoddess off of a pure donation of power.

After he crossed the tunnel-like hall and emerging into the grand central room of the fortress, he breathed a sigh of relief. Touring alone was Sondus, still dressed in a fur-trimmed coat with his hands locked behind his back.

"Can you imagine the amount of magic that went into creating this place?" the fae asked without turning. His gaze was focused on the glistening likeness of a leaping dolphin surrounded by artful swirls of waves and sea foam.

"A godly amount, I presume," he replied.

"Shaping it, keeping it pristine and cold enough to be frozen while the air inside the palace is livable and warm. Incredible," Sondus murmured.

He moved on, admiring the next ice sculpture. There were plenty here to appreciate. Cyranos created and surrounded himself with the kind of delicate beauty that Jaromir didn't expect. Not from someone with the Lord of Waves' reputation.

"It is unstable. If he decided he didn't like it, all this ice would melt within days," the spymaster said. It was like he'd read Jaromir's mind. That was the changeable nature of water—and the instability of Cyranos. "We are blessed to catch this moment of beauty."

He nodded in agreement.

"What do you think of the conversation earlier?" Sondus

asked, his tone taking a reverent hush. "Do you see our God of Water differently now that you know he's fae? That he can be vulnerable too?"

They stood in companionable silence. Sondus didn't push, letting him think through all the revelations.

"I'm glad Izell handled it. I had the feeling Cyranos only tolerated my presence."

He sighed. "Mine as well." Jaromir glanced toward him in surprise, witnessing the uncertainty in his expression. "Without magic, I am worthless to the god of my element. He glared at you but didn't even spare me a glance."

"It's hard to be noticed, sitting next to Izell," he pointed out.

"It goes deeper than that." Sondus motioned to the center of the great hall, where the pit of water was now covered by the dark metal grate. "We are standing next to a font of great magic called the Heart of the Ocean. I used to dream about visiting it."

"Why was that?" Jaromir asked.

"My wings. Or lack thereof." His shoulders hunched. "I thought if there was any place I could reconnect to my magic, it would be here. Astral fae evolved from water fae...aquatic creatures that lived with selkies, sirens, and the like. But I'm here now, and I don't *feel* anything. The god of my element didn't even acknowledge me. I have dreamt for nothing."

Jaromir opened his mouth but thought better of it. With how casually Sondus spoke of his missing wings, it seemed like he had long accepted his disability and how it inhibited his magic. But this was new, raw. He'd reached the one place he hasn't visited that could've been his cure.

"Let me try to heal you," he blurted, earning a surprised glance.

"King Orin has attempted it with the Mending Key before." Sondus shook his head. "It is not a healable ailment. Wings aren't physical—they're magical. Mine were removed with spelled iron."

Jaromir's magic itched right under his skin, spreading like an unpleasant prickle. "Would another attempt hurt?" Because it might hurt him if he defied what his senses were telling him.

The fae regarded him skeptically. For someone of his age, it had to be hard to give yet another person the faith to try. "I suppose not," he said.

This had to be what his magic wanted to heal within Sondus. Jaromir had had his well of potential dry up upon mending the dire injury to the fae's neck, but enough time had passed that he felt he had regenerated enough magic to give it a shot. He placed his hand on Sondus's shoulder, taking a deep breath.

Releasing a pulse of magic, Jaromir pictured the same feeling as earlier, where there was more to be done to heal this fae. His magic echoed it as it bounced back.

Izell had told him that he wasn't supposed to *see* with his magic, but it displayed the problem before his mind's eye to communicate what needed to be done. "This way," he said in a daze, walking without really seeing. Instead, he inspected the sparking, unfamiliar internal injury. The sweep of spelled iron had severed and severely scarred what looked like an artery, though magic flowed into the barrier of sealed tissue rather than red blood cells.

Within his scars, a fragment of iron remained. Jaromir understood something: where there was iron, there was no fae magic. "Can you answer a few questions for me?" he asked the fae as he released his shoulder. He'd guided them blindly to stand on the grate. Ocean water lapped right beneath the ornate barrier.

"Hmm?"

"How often do fae survive having their wings removed?"

The spymaster worked his jaw. "Let me put it this way. I'm the only one that I know of, and it used to be a common punishment. It causes me pain to live, but I am alive and grateful for it."

Jaromir's skin itched. It felt like he was very close to some realization, centering on that shard of iron. "Why does removing a fae's wings result in fatality? Do your people know the scientific reason?"

If anyone knew all the details, it would be Sondus. He seemed to fight a leery expression. "You would need to understand fae anatomy. Though fae are *made* of magic, having too much power stored inside of us causes us to"—he popped his lips while making an exploding motion—"and wings are what regulate that. All greater fae literally burn off their extra, unused power. Without having that outlet, it causes the same kind of death as having too much power. There's literally nowhere else for it to go."

Jaromir nodded slowly, realizing now why Sondus was alive. His excess magic was pushing against that tiny piece of iron and getting neutralized in the process. No wonder the spymaster had nearly no magic at his disposal. "I know what part of the problem is...but the solution might kill you."

Sondus quirked his lips without humor after Jaromir explained what he knew. "A fleck of rust, perhaps. If you removed it, I would definitely die, but at least I wouldn't be in pain for a few hours."

Jaromir's eyes widened. "Are you so eager for momentary relief?"

Sondus drew breath to reply, but a scoff interrupted him. They looked around. The foreign sound seemed to come from nowhere, until Jaromir spotted one of the ice sculptures moving. A spotted fish turned to face them with its bulbous eyes. "Talk, talk, talk," grumbled Cyranos's voice.

The god transformed into his fae form, landing on his feet from a seven-foot drop. Jaromir closed his gaping mouth and bowed as Sondus scrambled to do the same. Cyranos waved away the formality, his scowl turned toward Jaromir. "Let me show you what to do so you'll let me sleep in peace."

Despite the sour expression on the god's face, his words filled Jaromir with hope. Sondus, too, smiled genuinely with a flash of bright teeth. "My brother's really pushing his luck, making me work with a vampire," Cyranos grumbled.

"Making you?" Jaromir echoed before remembering who he was talking to.

The fae god's lips thinned. "I owe a favor to my siblings. They took on debt to ensure Lyana survived and was returned to me, and so I will be assisting you with this task." He turned his attention to Sondus. "Once you understand what your magic can do, you will know why you were drawn in as my brother's pawn."

The smile fell from the spymaster's face, replaced by a wary mask. Before he could respond, Cyranos waved dismissively. "Many fae are caught in Zalice's schemes. It is the nature of a seer. He saw that your unbound abilities would be useful and made sure they would be released here."

"Esteemed Lord of Waves—" Sondus began hesitantly.

"Less talk," Cyranos barked. "You, place your hand on him." He gestured to Jaromir, who touched the fae's shoulder.

Nerves wiggled their way into his belly under the impatient gaze of the god. What scheme was Zalice running, and why was it coming up now? Jaromir said nothing, though, determined to restore his friend before he said anything to dissuade Cyranos's cooperation.

"Listen closely," the god warned. He started talking Jaromir through using the Mending Key for a complicated healing. Closing his eyes, Jaromir let his magic visualize the problem area again. He was to expend all of his healing magic to pull out the iron embedded into Sondus.

"It won't kill him, because your magic is coming next." There was a distinct sigh in Cyranos's tone. "You're probably wondering why this hasn't been healed before. Fae magic can't destroy iron, no matter how small and insignificant a piece it is. Your angel magic is going to do the job and reopen the channel of his magic."

"How do I make it do that?" Jaromir asked. He was already committed, his healing magic pouring into Sondus, numbing his insides for the pain Cyranos promised was coming.

He got the distinct impression of a shrug from the god. "Angelic magic isn't complicated. You have the hurting kind—it will get rid of the iron and open up the scar tissue where it was embedded."

A thought whirled through his head. "Would it do that if it was healing light?"

"No," came the grumbled reply. "Focus."

Jaromir tried to put it aside in his mind for the moment. He realized Cyranos had not answered his original question as his healing magic dripped dry and light warmed his palm. The light followed in the wake of what he'd done before, forming an arrow that scorched right where Sondus needed it. Jaromir's awareness of the injury faded as the fae gasped, bending double to clutch his knees.

The scent of blood hit his nostrils. Sondus wavered and slipped sideways, out cold by the time Jaromir caught his weight. "Did it work?" he asked the Lord of Waves, who watched with an aloof expression.

Cyranos nodded. "The cycle of debt is complete."

Shaking his head, Jaromir didn't mince words. "Is Sondus healed? Will he be okay?"

"Better than okay. What, did you expect wings to burst from his back right away?" he scoffed. "He will be important to you all, I guess." He turned to leave.

"Wait." Jaromir shuffled Sondus's weight to rest more comfortably against his shoulder. The Lord of Waves paused, back still turned. "When you called him your brother's pawn..."

Cyranos sighed, a world of weariness carried upon it.

"Is it related to...? The Archangel, Soren, said the price of his admission was a deal with Lady Raenith, that he would give me his blood. Did she do that because she knew this moment was happening?"

He turned around, his sapphire-blue eyes swirling with churning water. "You do have a brain in there, hmm, human-born," he remarked. "I'm impressed, so I will explain before you walk away assuming foul play or any other negative thing your vampire mind might concoct. Yes, those events are related. The four powers that rule Faerie aren't as separate as they might seem. This boy"—he jerked his chin toward Sondus—"was dealt a kindness today. You may say that I helped him."

Jaromir was leery to agree, seeing some of what Cyranos was trying to explain. "But to get to this moment, Raenith had to arrange for your...angelic transformation," the god continued with poorly disguised contempt. "Getana bargained with Zalice's heir to spare Lyana's life, and Zalice himself set up the opportunity to save her. Which bent my will to agree to help, and thus, this moment. Spare your gratitude, and give it to my brother. He arranged for Sondus to regain his magic to help you with your coming mission. I'm sure he has more plotting afoot to assist you further. As long as you act in the good of Faerie, you shall have the Lord of Storms' support."

Jaromir understood how powerful Zalice's future sight had to be, since he'd also heard Sirius talk about the coincidences that'd led to him stabilizing Talina's demigoddess-level power. It was a good thing they had the Lord of Storms on their side.

However, that wasn't the only thing on his mind. "I appreciate this. But I give my gratitude to you, Lord of Waves," he said, inclining his head formally since he couldn't bow.

Cyranos continued talking like he hadn't heard a word. "Your friend will wake in a day or so. See that he lies on his front. You both have disturbed my rest enough, so I will be off."

"Have a good night."

The god scoffed, but as he turned away, Jaromir swore his lips formed a fleeting smile.

Chapter 19
Izell

"Now what?" Izell asked flatly, staring at Sondus's prone form. Filaments of starry light were beginning to shine up from his back. She'd helped take him through a portal to the one place where he would get the highest quality of care. His infirmary secreted in the Shifting Wood—the same place this whole mess had started. Several nurses were lined up at the doorway, waiting for her to step away.

Somewhere along the line, she'd gained a reputation. Her, violent? *Nah.*

"Can you take us to the Library of Faerie?" Jaromir suggested.

Shrugging, she formed the portal with a flick of her claws. He went through, leaving her to make eye contact with the water fae who'd come along to make sure Izell would fulfill her promise. Lyana was in the process of drawing up a stool. "I'll stay and care for him. You will be back?"

"I swear it." Izell felt the flash of magic behind the words, another promise now looming over her.

The side of Lyana's lip lifted. "See you later."

Izell gratefully stepped into her portal, emerging into the dry comfort deep in the stacks of the Library of Faerie. She dismissed the rip in reality and inhaled the scent of ink and aged parchment, plus the subtle musk of her man. He pulled her into a deep kiss, pressing her back against the end of a wooden bookshelf.

She smiled against his lips, reminded of their first kiss, also in a private nook of this library. At the time, she'd shown her interest by smooshing her lips against his clueless face. "If this was what you wanted, why didn't we go back to the apartment?" she asked when they parted for air.

She'd passed out last night, embraced by his warmth, just to find out that he'd slipped out and healed Sondus's wings in an apparent miracle. He'd told her offhandedly when she woke, like he hadn't done something impossible while she wasn't looking.

Her humble, slightly less clueless human-born. If only they could just be locked together in a room for a few months. She had a few dozen things she wanted to try with him... *"Gods, get a room,"* Queldian protested, laughing.

"I'm trying!"

"Lock me out of it, too," he joked.

She muffled a snicker as Jaromir said, "I actually have a reason for being here."

"Oh, do you now?" She walked her fingers up his bicep, hoping that reason was her. But he'd put on his serious face, so she figured she might as well help him so she could get a piece of him later.

"If we're really doing this, we should know what we're getting into," he said, taking her in search of a librarian he knew. She nearly choked when he shared that it was Zizi, who was in charge of the rare and arcane texts section...and also Sondus's wife.

"Run it by me again. *Zizi* married *him?*" she pressed, tittering like a schoolgirl.

He raised a brow. "Is this scandalous or something?"

"Back in my very short-lived days as an instructor, there was a young lady terrix by that name who bemoaned Sondus constantly. *'He's hopeless and dull. How did he ever pass the entrance exams?'*" She mimicked in a higher voice. "She was getting a small stipend to tutor underclassmen and was assigned him."

"They must've found some common ground. Opposites do attract." He gave her hand a squeeze, flashing a fond smile that made her insides feel warm.

He led her to the reception desk, manned by a tan-feathered terrix with oversized, gray eyes magnified behind horn-rimmed glasses. Her lips pursed into a surprised "o" when her gaze fell on Izell's undisguised dragon features.

"Hi, kiddo." Izell waved, pretending it hadn't been three thousand years since she'd last seen the owl-like lesser fae. Zizi waved back slowly, blinking off her daze. "You got any books about demons?"

AFTER COMBING THROUGH THE RESTRICTED SECTIONS, they'd found five books that seemed serious and accurate rather than full of hearsay or an author's political fiction about what Hell *might* be like. They took their reading back to her apartment, sitting together to glean what they could about the journey ahead.

It started with them sitting across from each other at the round kitchen table. She cast a levitating spell on her seat and slowly inched it around as Jaromir worked, book in one hand, pen in the other. She took a few notes...scooted closer...jotted down a couple more. Soon, she was next to him, and he glanced up, startling at her proximity.

She winked and made her book float next so she could rest her hand on his thigh, leaving it warm with the impression of her scaled palm. Part of her wondered how deeply his self-control ran. He'd picked out an important, perhaps vital, task for them to accomplish while Sondus slept off his healing. Yet here she was, pondering how best to crawl into his lap from this angle.

He laced his fingers with hers, stilling her teasing as he turned his amused golden gaze away from his own book. "Are you trying to give me a hint, madam?"

She grinned, unrepentant. "Want to take a break?"

In answer, he lifted her hand to his lips, teasing the sensitive gaps between her scales. He smiled around her fingers, his interest kindling like a slow burn she'd needed to poke a few times. "Hmm."

"Mmhmm?" she made it sound like a hopeful question.

He set his pen aside and lifted her by the hips until she was straddling his lap. "We'll take the edge off, then go back to work. How's that sound?" He trailed his lips to her neck, kissing like they had all day and more. Methodical, a lover. *A keeper,* she thought.

Too bad she was impatient and her edge resembled a cliff from how pent up she'd become over the years. She'd started drawing the tunic off his shoulders when his hands caught hers, pulling them away.

"I don't want our break to be over that quick," he teased. He took his time covering her with kisses until she squirmed with need. Yet she didn't break his loose hold on her wrists or protest when he switched them around to press her into the table instead.

She ended up losing her clothes first, with his lips greeting each new scale and inch of flesh as it was revealed. He flashed a knowing look as he hovered somewhere above her navel. "I just realized something." His warm breath drew prickles over her skin.

"That you shouldn't stop when you've got me like this?" She dipped her chin downward, raising a brow.

"Something no one else knows about you." Those sinful lips skimmed in the right direction as he released a low chuckle.

"Don't tell. Let your tongue put in some work," she demanded.

"In good time." He drew back, standing over her with a grin splitting his face. Propping herself up on her elbows, she waited impatiently for him to return to her.

But he didn't, waiting for something as well. "Excuse me, you should be ravishing me right now," she said.

He got down on his knees and did just what she wanted. At her urging, they tried several unclaimed pieces of furniture, and she didn't hear a word more about what he'd discovered until they lay together in the bed hours later. Really, she was waiting for him to recover, drawing little patterns on his bare chest as he caught his breath.

"Casting a spell to get me going again?" he teased, watching her with hooded eyelids. A sated half-smile softened the angles of his face.

"If it were that easy, we'd never stop," she replied with a hint of her usual tartness.

His expression shifted in amusement, looking like he was in on some secret joke. "I like this side of you," he whispered.

"When I'm naked? I prefer it myself," she quipped.

He shook his head, tugging on a lock of her hair. "No, don't go doing that. I like seeing your armor down. No sharp words, no angry looks." He gave her a long, lingering kiss, his gaze liquid gold as he regarded her relaxed expression. "Like that."

She realized what he was trying to say. "The freshly pleasured side of me."

"If that's the only time I see you relax, then yes. You don't have to put your defenses up around me." He cupped her hand between both of his. "I like it when you smile. *Really* smile. I feel like I might be the only man in the world who knows who you are when you're not Archfae Izell Firebrand."

"*That's* your big secret?" she asked in disbelief.

He shrugged, tucking her into the line of his body with tender care. He stroked her hair like she was a delicate woman, not a fearsome dragon shifter, and it was enough to make her toes curl. "Not necessarily," he murmured. "I can't put it into words. But I like just being a man and woman together, where I'm not a Blood Prince and you're not one of the eldest fae alive."

She considered the unguarded affection in his eyes. It really was for her, and her alone. "Curse the fates for giving me someone perfect at the end of my life." Wetness swam into her vision, and she was sure she'd just ruined the moment by bringing in the specter that hung over her.

Instead, he wiped away her tears and kept a cheeky tone. "I'm perfect, hmm?"

She sniffed, huffing a laugh. "For me...I think," she said slowly. But she was a Seelie, bound to her words as truth, and she'd spoken one of her deepest thoughts aloud. Jaromir was mate material. Her feelings for him just kept delving further into her heart until she found herself wishing he was at least part fae so they could have something beyond the physical.

"Jaromir, I...I know I am difficult. I used to trust more, give more of myself to others. In my long life, I've learned it's a mistake to open up to the wrong person," she admitted, glad to see understanding in his gaze. Because she was just realizing she hadn't exposed any vulnerability to another at any point she could remember. Far, far back, before the Fell, maybe before her first mate passed away.

It was a wonder Jaromir had seen her guard drop. This man from another world held her heart in his open palm. Maybe he would notice it for the rare treasure it was. "I understand. But I hope you know that you can always open up to me," he replied, laying a tender kiss on her lips.

"I know." And left unsaid was all the other things he was already earning from her, least of all her growing affection for him. In her heart of hearts, as he held her so tenderly, she wished she had more time.

Chapter 20
Izell

The only way they got anything done was with her leaving Jaromir to read while she tracked down Soren that evening. Her glowing mood quickly dropped as she went back to the palace and considered what she would be asking.

It was time she requested the world of the angel she'd done nothing to ingratiate herself with.

My death would be a sacrifice, and yours a travesty.

Did he still believe his words? Would he stand by his earlier offer to lay down his life for the new Dark Eye?

Maybe she could still have time with Jaromir if she allowed an angel to save the day instead. It would hurt her pride, but at least she'd be alive.

"What will you do if he says no?" Queldian asked, breathing her fears to life.

"I don't know," she answered honestly. If no other person stepped forward, she would have to proceed like nothing had changed and bid Jaromir's gentle love goodbye. She didn't kid herself. It was her plan all along, and Soren probably wanted to cling to life just as much as anyone else.

She found the Archangel watching the sunset while bathing in the ambient aura of the Light Eye. His smile was full of peace and calming light as he turned toward her. "Ah, hello again, Izell."

"Hi," she said gruffly, sliding onto the stone bench next to him. She eyed the burning angelic runes half-revealed on the hem of his robe and asked a question that'd been plaguing her, even if it wasn't what she was here for. "Why do you hide the fact that you're an Archangel?"

"Right to the point, hmm." He chuckled and returned his gaze to the horizon lit with warm oranges and reds as the sun bid its farewell to another day. "What purpose would it serve to tell everyone my rank? I do not want admiration or respect if I haven't earned it through a genuine interaction. Remember that I'm technically deceased, Izell. My desires do not follow the patterns you're used to."

"How angelic of you," she muttered.

He didn't reply for a few long moments. "The sunsets are lovely in your land. I have really enjoyed the change of perspective here. When was the last time you slowed down and watched one?"

Izell drew in a tart reply and instead viewed the sunset with him. Some of the longest minutes of her existence passed as she practically burst out of her skin to ask if his offer was still valid. Yet she had to admit that it was a pretty sight and one she hadn't done more than glance at in the limited time she'd been freed of Adrun's eternal darkness.

"What can I do for you this evening?" Soren offered as the sky dotted with the first stars.

"Two things," she sighed. "I need you to take me and a small group to Hell."

She witnessed a rare frown from the Archangel of Life. "Why?" he asked in disbelief.

"Long story. Can you do it?"

He softened his tone and expression in understanding. "Is this about the greater demon you're requiring?"

She leaned in. *"Can you do it?"*

A spark of irritation lit his gaze, there and gone in a blink. "I can, but I need a *very* good reason, because I risk losing my wings at such a blatantly malicious act."

"It's not malicious if we ask for it," she scoffed. "By the way, yes, it's for the greater demon. And...another problem too."

Soren listened with growing horror as she described how Lilith had attacked them and stolen the Summer Key before disappearing into Hell with it. The one thing she left out was how she thought she'd seen Sondus secure Lilith's discarded dagger in his things during the scramble that followed. Surely the Archangel would want it destroyed, and she wanted to study it if it was still intact.

"This news troubles me," Soren stated, yet he'd regained his mild composure somewhere in the middle of her explanation. He flashed a smile full of calming angelic magic. "I will see that you have your artifact returned, as she has violated the law."

She rebuffed the aura coming from his sparkling teeth and glowered. "No, I intend to go down there and make her eat her pretty little horns. We'll drag her up and place her the Dark Eye."

"You can't," he practically blurted.

"With your help getting down there...sure I can." She flashed her own teeth in a fang-filled grin.

He scrubbed at his face, releasing a weary sigh. "I know you are powerful, but you have never met someone like her in serious combat. Lilith will destroy you, Izell. I cannot allow it to happen."

Izell felt the clawing of despair at her lungs as he spoke. *Stupid, righteous angel.* If he decided he knew best and that his best was not assisting her, she had no way into Hell.

"If you swear to keep it secret, I will tell you more," he said.

She considered it. "I will share it with the group accompanying me to Hell."

Soren's lips pinched. "Fine. If you go to Hell, you may share it with them."

"Then I swear to keep what you're about to say a secret."

The weight of her promise settled on her. Another deal, now several rested on her shoulders. It wasn't the best situation for a fae.

He lowered his voice, pitching it for privacy. "Lilith is what we call an Original. She was created with the founding of Heaven, one of many angels molded into being without existing as a mortal human before. The Originals were empowered beings and retain that energy to this day, though there are far fewer of them. They're the only angels with physical wings."

She rolled her eyes. "The woman who attacked us didn't have wings."

Sorrow shadowed the Archangel's face. "Tragically, she was tricked and trapped in Hell. She didn't *want* to be a demon, but she grew very good at it, to the point that she occupies the entire Realm of Lust, the first true layer of Hell. My point is that her status as an Original should chill you to the bone. You may know the name of another infamous fallen angel: Lucifer. They have similar abilities and knowledge...but he retained his wings."

"You say that like the wings mean something," she remarked.

"And you prove another reason why you should not be charging off to Hell. Wings mean everything to demons. The only way to tell if one is a greater demon on sight is whether or not they have wings. They need them to launch assaults on Heaven."

She nodded slowly. Jazrach had had wings, and they'd long known it to be a greater demon. "But wingless Lilith is still so powerful I should shake in my boots."

"Yes. But since she broke our laws, we can still get the Summer Key returned and a punishment metered upon her for attacking you," he said, as serious as she'd ever seen him.

Still, she shook her head. "Please. She took advantage of you and Gabriel being here. I bet she will weasel out of punishment. I just wish I knew how she knew where to find us."

"Energy signatures. Originals can sense them."

Hopefully he was right, because the idea that they'd had a mole communicating with demons of Lilith's station was frightening.

"Escort us, then. Help us get the Summer Key and a greater demon. I don't trust...that your angel friends can get it done in time." Gods, that was close call. He didn't seem to notice her quick save from telling him how she really felt about him.

"You're asking the wrong angel." Soren wore his regret openly. "I am not a fighter. I will never be authorized to enter Hell personally."

"But I *can* go there. We're researching Hell now. With your knowledge, we can be prepared for what's ahead and get it done before the winter solstice." She leaned forward earnestly. "How fast does your bureaucracy actually work?"

"What you are planning is reckless. Suicidal, even," he answered quietly. And in dodging her question, she figured she'd found the weak point to his argument. His angel buddies couldn't get the job done in the tiny window of time they had left.

Izell and her group could. As long as they had a solid understanding of what they were up against.

"Any chance is better than nothing. All risks are worth calculating. Please, help us," she beseeched.

His glowing eyes flashed over her posture, and he drew a heavy breath. "There's one more thing to consider. We would have to go to Heaven first, and then your group will take the pathway down to Hell. My job here is done. I have blessed an entire army's worth of fae weaponry. If I leave, I will not be able to return."

Icy sweat dripped down her back as she realized where he was going with this. "In that case, Izell, I cannot sacrifice myself for your Dark Eye. Are you okay with that?" he asked.

She realized he must've known the other reason she came here to speak with him. Her throat closed up on a quick response. Of course she couldn't have it both ways. Time didn't slow down just because she'd fallen in love.

There was only one way forward. So, with a heavy heart, she said, "I'm okay with that."

Yet she wondered if she'd somehow broken her Seelie curse and lied.

Chapter 21
Jaromir

Sondus laid out several pages of hand-written research across his office table, clucking his tongue. It was early morning, the air still full of the singing of night insects and the occasional *whoop* of some unfamiliar hunting creature. It had barely been a full day, and Jaromir hadn't slept.

The gist of what he had heard from Izell's conversation with Soren was good: the angel could take them to Heaven, supply them with information, and show them the way into Hell. But it couldn't all be sunshine and hugs, not with the faraway look swirling in Izell's silvery eyes.

"There are contradictions in this information. It seems none know the full truth about demons," Sondus was saying, shuffling the notes to the side. He eyed the stack of books they'd "borrowed" from the Library of Faerie before standing and turning to scan the titles on the personal bookshelf taking up the office's back wall.

This was the first time Jaromir had gotten to see Spymaster Sondus at work within the safety of the Shifting Wood. The small but cozy office was meticulously clean and ordered, and the lacquered desk had several small hills of paperwork, plus a misshapen mountain of unopened correspondence waiting for attention. Sondus had shoved half of it to the ground in frustration to have space to work with. A single lamp provided comfortably dim light, as the windows were covered by thick drapes.

With Sondus's back to them, Jaromir openly inspected his progress. One starry wing was completely formed, the other still jagged shards of starry frost mixed with dark matter. Jaromir was quietly pleased with the results, recognizing that the small signs of tension and pain in the lines of the fae's body were gone.

When Sondus pulled the book he wanted and returned to his plush, high-backed chair, he leaned back fully rather than sit with ramrod posture. His skin shimmered with extra stars, slowly winking into existence as his magic built up.

"This is the most accurate text I have on the matter," he said, showing them the spine of the extra book.

"Demonic summoning?" Izell read aloud, raising a brow.

He shrugged and opened it, flipping rapidly to a specific page. "I've investigated several occult organizations. Know your enemy and all. Ah, here it is. According to this source, there are eight levels of Hell, not seven." His eyes darted rapidly over the text.

Lyana shifted uncomfortably as he read. They'd shoehorned a chair into the room for her, and her legs were practically curled underneath it so they could all cram in together. "When Lucia was using my body, we came across a scholar who'd spent his life studying any remnants of demonic literature. I remember him mentioning that we know a fraction of anything about demons. Lucia wasn't all that interested in this stuff, either. She just wanted the rituals that would get her more power." Her lip lifted in disgust.

"It's the price we pay for locking ourselves away from them for a thousand years," Izell said, waving a dismissive hand. "We have to trust that Soren wants us to succeed and will tell us what we need to know."

"Then why did you insist I do some skimming for you?" Sondus asked over the ridge of the open book.

She gave an exaggerated shrug. "Would you walk onto a battlefield naked if you had armor at home?"

"I see that I'm the armor in this analogy." A smile quirked the spymaster's lips as he sped-read. At least, Jaromir assumed he was reading, even though he leafed through the pages rapidly.

He knew that wasn't the only reason Izell had jumped at the opportunity to see Sondus right away. "Can you test his magic now?" he asked, eager to know why Cyranos had placed such emphasis on it.

The rapid flicking of the spymaster's star-flecked eyes paused, nerves stealing over his expression when Izell nodded. "I have a good idea of what I possess," he admitted, presenting his wrist.

Izell told Jaromir, "We've always known he has strong Mind-aligned magic, because he could still make weak illusions without wings." Her hands moved as she spoke, weaving an intricate spell of floating runes over Sondus's wrist. Smacking them between her palms, she then spread her hands to show a fine web of magic stretching between her skin.

Though he looked over her shoulder, he didn't know the significance of the purple-tinged symbols written in the magic. Izell exchanged a glance with Lyana instead.

Sondus's signature white teeth stood out in a nervous grimace. "Well?"

Muttering a soft curse, Izell nodded. "It's unmistakable. You're mono-talented in Mind magic."

His breath caught. "How...powerful?"

Jaromir realized none of these fae were celebrating the news when Izell revealed he had the capacity to be *very* powerful. Sondus watched the two Sorceresses like they'd lash out at any moment, while their expressions were more speculative. Lyana, in particular, had her distrustful mask back in place.

Jaromir tried to cut through the thick pause by saying, "Congratulations. It must be a relief to know what sort of magic you wield."

Sondus dropped his gaze, sucking in a pained breath. "It's not really a surprise. I hoped it might not be the case, actually," he murmured. "Will you bind me, Izell?"

"Not yet."

Lyana released a soft hiss. "At least an oath of loyalty."

Izell scattered white hair with a sharp shake of her head. "An unbound Mindbender will be an incredible asset in Hell."

The water fae pinned her with a powerful glare. "If I may speak with you outside?" Both of them had taken up aggressive postures and bared teeth, echoing their inner dragon forms.

"Sure," Izell snarled, standing and brushing by her forcefully.

The moment both men were alone, Sondus withdrew a palm-sized item from a drawer and opened it to reveal a mirror. He murmured into it, and Jaromir picked up that he was asking his people to listen in and report if the two women actually came to blows.

The spymaster glanced up and made eye contact. "Not going to go out there too?"

"I've been around my share of aggressive people, men and women alike. Sometimes, a disagreement has to be resolved by a quick fight." Jaromir shrugged. He'd felt the tension shimmering between the two women from the moment Lyana had "tested" Izell.

"That's the last thing I'd expect you to say. Please tell me you're not afraid of me now as well."

Jaromir tasted that word on his tongue: *afraid*. He suspected there was some nuance here he was missing. "You haven't changed now that you've grown wings. Why should I fear you?"

The fae pressed his lips together, the picture of reluctance. "Most mono-talented fae don't have official names like *Mindbender*. Fae-kind in general see Mind-aligned magic as the most dangerous, so most Mindbenders are either executed immediately or bound by an oath to serve the Crown and never use certain aspects of their power."

Jaromir muttered a curse of his own. Everyone's reactions suddenly made crystal-clear sense. "You already serve your Crown willingly. Surely that doesn't have to change," he said.

Sondus shot a bitter look at the closed door when they heard the muffled sound of Lyana's raised voice. "This changes everything. Those that know about it will second-guess me. They'll wonder if I've taken a peek at their thoughts or manipulated their emotions just from a glance and find moments where they're *sure* I have. I will either be forced into a loyalty oath or the business end of a sword. It's just a matter of time."

He let his head fall into his hands. "I always knew it was possible, but it also puts my accomplishments into question as well."

Jaromir put a comforting palm on his shoulder. "The past is the past," he said, using his firm doctor's tone. "The world isn't ending because you're a Mindbender. But it might end if you go off despairing about it and seek out a binding oath."

The fae went rigid, undoubtedly turning over Jaromir's words more carefully. He realized the signs of Sondus's gift were there all along—his quick, clever mind, especially, always thinking harder than everyone else. "What do you mean?" he asked quietly.

"I mean that you're an asset to us just as you are. Your healing was no coincidence, and you being a Mindbender is nowhere in Izell's original plan. We're working off your gods' plans now."

Sondus dropped his hands, nodding slowly. "I thought the gods didn't care about me. Turns out I'm just a pawn in something far bigger than all of us." He wet his lips, his eyes practically sparking as they flickered with rapid thoughts. "Even a pawn can be useful when placed where it's most needed. But enough of this. I have not thanked you as you deserve, Jaromir. It would seem I have a life debt—"

They both turned toward the door as it opened, the hinges creaking slowly. The two dragon shifters came in and took their seats again, both looking unharmed from their shouting match. Izell smiled, and Sondus echoed it hesitantly. "Ah, welcome back. I was about to tell Jaromir that I wanted to make you all a promise to satisfy any worries that I might use my abilities against you."

"It can't hurt, but it's not necessary," Izell replied, glaring Lyana's way. "We have come to an understanding."

Sondus turned toward Lyana. "Still, I promise not to use my powers against you without your knowledge or against your will. I also promise that I will use every ounce of my new powers to help us fulfill our mission. Surely that will work for now?"

The sea serpent shifter spared a curt nod. Even if she didn't seem happy, Jaromir had the feeling she wouldn't complain again.

"Wish we had forever to prepare, but we head to Heaven today at noon. Think you can pack the useful books for later?" Izell asked.

"I'll have them read by then," Sondus promised instead.

"Wonderful." She spoke like he hadn't just volunteered to read thousands of pages in a matter of hours. "Jaromir and I need to get some rest." She took a hold of his hand and flashed him a look full of meaning. His skin heated, sure they weren't about to get much sleep.

JAROMIR WAS RIGHT. IZELL DIDN'T TELL HIM WHAT WAS bothering her, but he could guess from a list of issues that could be on her mind. He provided the support she wanted, which was all physical. No words, just hands and lips, skin to skin and scales. Izell held him in those quiet moments, gazing into his eyes like she was in danger of forgetting them.

When the sun was well into its path climbing the sky, she sighed and finally breathed his name. There was a world of emotion in that one word, enough to splinter his insides. She worked her throat with a dry swallow. "If we don't survive what comes next, I just wanted you to know..." She took a hard breath, tears pricking her eyes. "I wish you were a fae. If I could choose a new mate, it would be you."

Those words caught him so off guard he didn't know how to respond. Memories flickered behind his eyes, as ephemeral and difficult to grasp as feathers in a breeze. He'd done his best not to think of *her*, but now, he couldn't deny it. "I..." He took a hitching breath, trying not to embrace the panic making his heart gallop.

Izell smiled uncertainly, there and physical and *real*. If anyone could figure out how to make them mates, it was her. All he had to do was to say he felt the same.

"Do you still plan to leave at the end of all this?" he asked instead.

The hopeful light in her nebulous eyes faded.

"Izell." He cupped her cheek, knowing she needed to hear this now, before things progressed any further between them.

Words stuck in his throat, all hard edges. He muffled a cough into his shoulder, trying to break up that feeling before she closed herself off. "I feel very strongly for you too," he began. It felt like he was back in a clinic, assessing their relationship on the doctor's table. Too impersonal. "I just... There was another."

Her eyes narrowed to draconic slits. "A long time ago," he added, watching her relax and nod. "I see a lot of you in her, just like I suspect you see some of your old mate in me."

Trying to spare her the details wasn't working for him, so he realized it was time to open the book of his past. Jaromir was used to these details not mattering; very few people remembered he had a mate, as quick and doomed a relationship that it was. "I joined the Fell Hunters toward the end of their campaign. As a mortal, I was a traveling doctor, shared amongst several remote villages. The Fell came and consumed one while I was heading toward it."

He tried to block out one of his oldest memories. "All I found were bones and then the angry vampires who'd been too late to save my people. They pressed me into service for them, and I became one of their only Gifted healers. Death tolls from the battles that followed were, they said, a lot lower than in the past."

But he'd still closed the eyes of countless vampires he'd been too late to save. Old, bitter regret stained the back of his mouth. "I worked so hard I didn't notice her at first. Raisa the Ravenous, one of the best Fell Hunters there was. She only came by my tent after taking a vicious wound that needed stitching. She took off her helm and..." He sucked in a gasp, remembering what a sight she'd been, even smeared with dirt and blood post-battle. Built like a bear, Raisa had had fierce, ruby eyes standing out from a sunken face. She'd always worn a crown of braids, dozens of raven-hued plaits complementing her olive complexion.

She didn't eat human food, relying on Fell blood for her bulk and incredible levels of strength but also left with a constant, niggling hunger she'd never quite shaken. Now that Jaromir pictured her, he knew she fit the same category of all the other Fell Hunters who'd inevitably succumbed in battle. Fighting was her calling, her reason for being.

"Well, Raisa was my lifemate. We didn't really understand the phenomenon then, not until Adrius and Nyah started talking openly about their connection," he continued. "But she and I forged a mating bond before them."

Izell frowned, searching his features. "How long were you mated for?"

"Months at most. I can't recall the exact time anymore," he admitted, rubbing at a pang in his chest. "Raisa was a fierce personality and my first love. She led, and I followed, but ultimately, we had different jobs. When she fell in battle, I *felt* it, the way her death vibrated our bond to shreds. I...wasn't there when it happened. I was running triage to keep our wounded alive."

Izell's hand covered his as he fought off the swell of his grief and fury. Why hadn't he been there for her? Why hadn't he been enough?

"You have to understand, Izell...I've seen more people die than I've saved," he admitted on a whisper. "I buried my first mate."

Her eyes spilled over as she nodded again. "I wouldn't ask you to bury me too."

"Because you have a plan to live?" Now it was his turn to try to find some hope in their situation, something to cling to. Cossette said there was a way. Actually, she'd directly told him, *"You have to continue being you, Jaromir. That will save Izell."* Except he could already see he wasn't enough, just like he hadn't been for his first mate.

She was silent for a long time, leaning into his touch as he cleared the moisture from her cheeks. That she had no quick answer was telling. "I don't know anymore. But I don't want to hurt you and become another story of a love you lost too soon."

He sighed, shaking his head. He hated this situation, knowing it may be the last time he and Izell could talk freely. Regardless of how things ended, she was a story entwined within his own, a lover he stood on the precipice of losing in the name of the greater good, just like Raisa. Fate was a cruel mistress to only give him a taste of what he could have.

They lay in silence until it became apparent they were running out of time before the others would be meeting them here in Izell's apartment. They broke apart to get ready, and Jaromir made sure to take an extra cold shower.

Chapter 22
Cossette

Cossette returned to her old territory in New York, exhausted. Fae and their politics were even more of a headache than the vampire squabbles she'd seen. It didn't help that she knew she had limited time, so she'd traveled as fast as she could across Faerie and Adrun to arrive in this chilly, late autumn evening.

The sun will hurt again. Hide your hair and eyes, she thought as she trudged along the sidewalk, dodging errant splashes of slush thrown up by passing cars. She'd bundled her tall, slim adult form with warm clothes and had her hood drawn up. A light glamor darkened her hair and eyes so no one who met her gaze noticed she was albino.

Not that she saw anything but shadowed figures around her, lost as she was to the fog of her future sight. Possibilities and chance encounters occupied her mind's eye in full, living color, pouring into her senses to leave reality a muted echo of itself.

After working with Lord Zalice, who helped her understand and shape her gift so it didn't fully overwhelm her, she knew what needed to be done. He was handling events in Faerie, Izell in Hell. Now, it was Cossette that had to finish a set of required tasks to keep their vampire allies moving in the right direction.

She carefully climbed a set of stone stairs before coming to herself and glancing around. This building was nowhere near as tall and daunting as she remembered. "Get used to it," she told herself. This was the first of many places in her territory she'd be visiting—and all of them would logically seem smaller. She'd picked one of the most sizable first, the insides renovated to be a massive training complex for her coven's fighters.

They used the most successful method to deter curious mortals: a permanently locked door with a huge "NO SOLICIT-ING" sign out front. Cossette waved her hand, unlocking a set of heavy deadbolts with the force of her mind. The steel-plated door swung inward, to darkness.

She pushed the hood off her head, releasing her glamor as soon as she closed the door and re-engaged its deadbolts. Even to her vampiric hearing, the sound of gunshots was muffled as her people practiced in the underground range. As she walked the darkened hallway, she picked up the tenor of men's voices. Glass cases lined either wall, full of old trophies that'd lost their meaning.

Although, not completely. As a seer, she could still hear the distant roar of cheering crowds and screaming teenagers, each statue and plaque soaked with residual, joyful memories.

Focus. She pinched her wrist. She was here for a reason, and it wasn't to admire old accomplishments that weren't even hers.

There were familiar faces at the end of the hall, watching her from the shadows. She knew the two, though they didn't know her, watching with eyes narrowed in distrust. Times were obviously different if her two fighters didn't immediately threaten her for being a stranger approaching a sacred coven space.

"I am here to speak with Alex Rehnquist." She used their shared mother tongue, French, and practically felt their eyes moving over her white curls and ghostly pale skin, mismatched on a new stature that put her nearly at their height.

They would glance to each other and wonder if they were hallucinating. But ultimately, they wouldn't believe she was Ancient Cossette Deveaux, cursed to exist in the body of a child for eternity. The kind of magical miracle she'd experienced just didn't happen. At least, not on Earth.

She waited and was rewarded a few seconds later when they exchanged a look and a shrug. "It is urgent," she added.

They let her in, and she could practically feel their thoughts as they made platitudes and stared at her back when she walked in. "We're just letting anyone in now, aren't we?" one whispered.

"Not our problem."

She snickered, though her mirth only lasted for a few paces. She would never have camaraderie back with those two coven-mates, nor any of the others. The compound was teeming with vampires of all covens now, and her people trained new recruits alongside vampires from the other covens of rank. She stopped and peered through a window, watching men and women practice hand-to-hand techniques under the watchful eye of an old friend.

The room they used was part of a repurposed gym, with pads layered over long strips of lacquered wood flooring. She felt the trainer's gaze flash to her before she'd moved to unlatch the door and approach him. Cold crept over her in the wake of Julian's regard, his icy blue eyes glowing with restrained magic. He was no different than before her journey: close-cropped blond hair and a towering physique barely restrained with his signature black clothing.

One thing stung, though. The way no recognition flared in his expression, and his hooded brow lowered when she boldly strode past a pair of fighters still sparring. "Can I help you?" he asked in barely restrained disapproval. Most of his trainees had stopped practicing to listen in.

"*Oui.*" This conversation could easily crash and burn, but thankfully, she'd seen at least a dozen different things she could say and what his reaction would be. She wavered between two responses while a light furrow appeared between his eyebrows.

"This is not the reception I expected." She was still speaking French, a tongue they shared despite being immigrants from different parts of Europe. "Don't you remember how I helped you in your darkest hour, Mister Fairfax?"

Julian's jaw dropped, gaping openly through giving her another once-over. He turned his attention on his trainees, snapping for them to return to practicing. With shouts and grunts taking up the air once more, he drew her aside and gazed into her face until they both looked away in discomfort.

"Cossette?" All the weight of his disbelief weighed down that one whispered word.

"*Oui.* I am who I was meant to be," she answered.

A split second later, he surprised her, circumventing her carefully viewed path of the future by swooping her up into a bone-crushing hug. She released a surprised wheeze, though just as quickly, the rare show of affection was done. Still, he smiled for joy, and in the expression was an echo of his mate's eternal cheer. "Congratulations. So, you have returned?" His cool gaze raked the empty air behind her, like he expected Izell to burst in at any moment.

"Only me. I have an urgent message for Alex." She spread her palms apologetically. "Can you take me to him?"

He could get her past several vampires who would otherwise stop and question her as a stranger in the heart of this operation. She already knew that he'd either say he needed to stay and train his group or do as she needed. Lips thinning in contemplation, the ease of his manner faded to the same guarded formality she'd seen as an Ancient child. It was like he suddenly remembered she was still centuries his senior. "Of course, I'll take you to him right away." He went to his trainees to exchange a few quick words.

Cossette worried her bottom lip between her teeth. She knew what to expect amongst the people here, but a little part of her hadn't wanted to be right. Vampire-kind didn't often change overnight. So, while she wore a different face, she was the same venerated Ancient whose name was on the list of rules the New York covens followed...else the consequences were enforced by her wrath.

If she wanted, she could reclaim her seat at the table as the strongest and eldest vampire in New York. She'd seen a clear future where she did.

But is that what I want?

For the first time, Cossette saw her old world as an outsider. She let Julian lead her further into her old compound, watching curious faces turn her way and familiar features shade with distrust. It was a relief when they entered a back room and climbed a set of stairs leading to the specialized catwalks installed so each training area could be observed from above.

The metal platform they climbed onto was big enough for two people side by side, with thin arm rails installed as a formality for a race of preternatural creatures who could survive the fall with no permanent damage. She found Alex pacing over an empty training room.

His boots stilled with his back to her, a growl drifting through the air. She only caught a hint of his aura, but the force of age and vampiric strength rolling off him was like walking into a sudden inferno.

Alex had gotten a lot stronger when she wasn't looking. *Being mated to one of the only Sorceress vampires must've given him a boost,* Cossette thought. He turned, nostrils flaring. Shock ate up the deep evergreen of his eyes, pupils dilating quickly under the influence of his inner beast. She knew that Alex was the one person here who would recognize her instantly.

His aura reeled back so quickly she shivered. "Cossette, is that you?" he asked, a trace of English primness weaving into his inflection. The dark waves of his hair were longer than she remembered, tousled into a state of disarray. For the first time, she noticed just how attractive her old friend was, and it stole her words for a moment.

Alex's features always reminded her of the beast he carried within him—an animal both clever and feral, with narrow cheekbones and a full mouth that tended to pull up to one side first for crooked smiles. He wore fatigue well, the shadow of a beard filling the line of his jaw and the first hint of dark half-moons making an appearance under his lashes. Like Julian, he wore black combat equipment. Unlike the other vampire, though, he still had the insignia of Coven Rehnquist stitched to the shoulders of his jacket: a yellow lion's head, his preferred shapeshift form.

She beamed. "You caught me."

His reaction was a subdued echo of Julian's, coming forward to clasp her hands. He gave her a smile that was warm, nearly fatherly. They'd navigated vampiric social norms together, an unlikely partnership that played on their strengths. She had power but obvious immaturity, so he was her savvy adult friend, helping her navigate complex interpersonal situations in exchange for the protection from her massive, loyal coven. His hodgepodge coven of immigrants and misfits stayed below notice and was allowed to grow. A win-win.

Things were about to change irrevocably, and it wasn't just because she was an adult in appearance. Part of her job tonight was to warn and prepare him for the years ahead.

"Words can't express how happy I am for you," he was saying, drawing her back from the edge of a peek into his future. "So, Faerie. It is real?"

Julian smirked. "Ever the skeptic."

Alex rolled his eyes. "Just a year ago, we didn't have fairies and demons prancing around, Bloodhound."

Cossette couldn't help a laugh, a girlish *tee hee* escaping her lips. She hoped they didn't notice. *How mortifying.* The last thing she wanted was to remind them of a child.

"Right, Faerie," she rushed to say. "It's definitely real. I wish you could've been there... It's the most beautiful place I've ever seen."

"Matches the people?" Julian ventured.

"Definitely." New York was drab by comparison. Sadly, so were her own folk. Humans just didn't come in as many colors and varieties as the fae people, greater or lesser.

Taking a deep breath, she met the expectant looks of both men. "I came back to share a few things." So much to say that she didn't know where to start, even after puzzling over it and her visions for days.

She plucked out the most minor to share first. "Well...you should know that Bryant Collins died a few days ago."

Most would expect them to rejoice at the news. She knew that Collins had harassed their coven for hundreds of years in a misguided effort to end Alex's bloodline. Yet Alex cursed quietly and asked, "Who killed him?"

"Lucia."

Julian's hands balled into fists, a pulse of cold flowing from him. "Goddamn it," Alex hissed.

"She's dead too," she added.

The anger level between them spiked, so she told the whole story as succinctly as she could. How Lucia had attempted to slay Sirius and use his soul to steal a god's power. She'd overplayed her hand, succeeding in enslaving and accidentally killing Collins instead. Lucia finally met her end soon after.

Julian tipped his head in contemplation before kissing his fingertips. "*Bellissimo.*"

"Could've sworn you've talked my ear off about killing her yourself," Alex remarked. His gaze was faraway, lips tugging toward a frown.

"She died in the most perfect way." Julian's face split into a huge grin. "Alone, with no more allies to sacrifice in her stead. Now, she will burn in Hell where she belongs."

"Okay, fine, that's pretty *bellissimo.*" He purposefully botched the pronunciation to make Julian cringe. "And she dragged Collins down to the pits with her."

"Actually—" Cossette cut herself off, realizing his true location may not be received well. "Well, you probably want to hear his last words."

On the precipice of making it to Heaven, Collins had made the choice to go to Purgatory instead and help the souls of his fallen coven members and wife make it to the pearly gates. "*There is no guarantee that we will get to Heaven, but I will not go there without them.*"

Only Sirius had witnessed it, yet she knew what transpired through her visions. In the same breath, Collins had added, "*My only regret is that I never got to apologize to Alex Rehnquist.*"

When Alex heard this from her, his pupils narrowed to animal slits. He bowed his head to hide his reaction. "He murdered my first mate. Chased us across the New World, recruited mortals to hunt us too," he muttered, the words meant for Julian, who nodded and sneered. "But in his last moments, he regretted it."

Julian's express was stony. "Does that change what he did?"

"Of course not. But I'm too bloody tired to hate anything else right now. There's one less enemy in New York, and I'm glad for that." Shrugging, Alex turned back to her. "What else did we miss?"

"Well, it's time to mobilize and get your forces to the ruins of Nyixa," she said, feeling her expression shade to deadly seriousness, the same face she always made when proclaiming an absolute truth from her future sight. Both of them tensed, recognizing it instantly. "The demonic invasion will come early."

Horror shaded over Alex's face. "How long do we have?" he breathed.

"Three days," she answered. If Izell was successful, they would be fighting in a mere blink of time.

Alex turned to Julian, who nodded. "I'll get that started," he said, leaving when she nodded as well.

"One more thing," she said, halting Alex from following. He raised a brow, likely wondering what else she could possibly heap on top of the rest.

A smile graced her face, showing that it wasn't nearly as bad as the approaching apocalypse. "*When* we survive what's to come, things have to change in New York. I can already tell you've done a great job of holding everyone together. That needs to continue, as long as it takes."

"I agree."

"I can think of no better person to keep that going than you, Alex," she said.

His eyes narrowed, lips moving to soundlessly taste *"keep that going."* "What do you mean? You're still the mastermind of the Accords and the only Ancient with a coven here."

Heart beating out of her chest, she finally admitted what'd been weighing her down from the moment she saw her people training alongside his. "I won't be returning to my coven after the coming battle. I will tell my deputy the news and have him prepare. As of right now, there is no Coven Deveaux." His gasp sealed the finality of the words. "You are now the eldest vampire in New York, with the biggest coven. I pass the responsibility of my coven mates and Accords onto you."

"Cossette—" he protested.

She continued speaking, "I hope you remember what it felt like to be the leader of a few rogues in a big, hostile city. You now have the power to change New York for the better."

Just like that, it felt like a huge burden had lifted from her shoulders. Soon, she would be *free* and able to return to beautiful Faerie, where she could strap a sword to her waist and make new friends who'd never seen her as a cursed child. She could travel and go where she was needed most, finally able to fully control the direction of her life.

Alex worked his jaw. "I..." He shook his head. "It sounds like you've made up your mind. You know this is not something that can be undone, though, if you miss what you used to have?"

"I won't miss it." She smiled with all the serenity hiding in her soul, shining like the hope hanging on her horizon. She may visit her old friends someday, when the memory of her old self faded. But she had her eyes turned to the future now. Her seer abilities didn't extend to Hell, but she knew she would only have what she yearned for if Izell succeeded down there in the days to come.

Chapter 23

Izell

Soren had them all lie out comfortably, as he would be transporting their souls and anything of value they wanted to bring, like weapons, armor, and supplies.

Izell was too worn out to question why their bodies weren't part of this too, but Sondus asked anyway.

"Only souls exist in Heaven and Hell," Soren explained. He was in the midst of painting unfamiliar angelic marks on the apartment floor with his fingers, leaving behind glowing imprints in the wake of his fingertips. "As for the items, I can have you bring them because I have the power to. Dead souls don't usually have the strength to carry anything but a copy of the clothes on their back when they pass away."

"Fascinating." Sondus's eyes glittered extra bright as he turned over this information. "How long can we be out of our bodies like this?"

The angel put a few finishing touches on the floor, bowing his head to the task. "Years. It looks like a coma, but if your soul meets its end in Hell, your body will perish as well."

All four of them shifted uncomfortably at that fact. A glint of apprehension lit Lyana's eyes, the sapphire water within them swirling faster under the surface. She was stretched on the floor, arms crossed over her chest. Sondus rested beside her. Despite their conversation earlier, Jaromir had still opted to hold Izell as they reclined together on the couch, waiting for the magic that would rip their souls into another reality.

She hadn't meant to unearth some of his most painful memories but could see by his expression that he was lost somewhere in the middle of them even now. Izell should've assumed that a vampire who'd reached Ancient age had already met and lost a lifemate. But the sorrow woven into his words was what had her drop the "mate" word going forward.

"When she fell in battle, I felt it, the way her death vibrated our bond to shreds."

Gods above. How could she ever yearn to complete a connection with him when she knew how all this ended? It was the peak of selfishness to even consider binding them together for such a short time. She could pull some strings and have one of the gods give them fatecross marks, but she wouldn't think on those lines again. She loved him too much to inflict such pain on him for a moment of connection.

And it *was* love. Maybe she'd tell him that realization, but not while his past was still open like a raw wound.

"Ready?" Soren's voice cut through her reverie, and she breathed a regret-filled sigh. She probably wouldn't have another chance to get Jaromir alone again anyway. Just another missed opportunity.

When they all replied to the affirmative, the angel lifted his palms, coming alive with his Archangelic light. His form began to waver like a heat mirage while his magical runes glowed brighter and brighter until Izell's world was white-hot energy. Her body went limp, eyes rolling closed to leave darkness behind.

Her soul didn't have any senses to communicate what the trip was like. It felt like succumbing to the precipice of sleep and waking up sprawled in an unfamiliar dream. She sat up, her skin tingling strangely as she took a quick glance around. Open, blue skies scrolled overhead, and she was sitting securely on a chunk of floating island. She could see the edge of green grass fading into what was undoubtedly a drop into the abyss waiting underneath Heaven.

A familiar groan sounded, but she could hardly believe her

eyes when she recognized the fire dragon starting to stir next to her. He was a mound of shifting sandstone scales glittering in the sunlight. Lifting his head, his eyelid slid up, followed by a transparent membrane to protect eyes as brilliant as molten gold.

Izell's heart stopped in that moment. She forgot to breathe.

A feminine cry interrupted her shock. They broke eye contact to see Lyana launching herself at a teal sea serpent coiled several yards away, her arms hardly encircling half of his stout neck.

"Queldian?" Izell managed to whisper, turning back to her dragon. She reached out to stroke his gilded snout, just to pause and stare at the black skin and blunt, ordinary fingernails attached to her hand. The old pact she'd made with Lucia was still there, the demonic markings gone dull with the demon's death even here.

He scooted closer while she inspected herself in astonishment, discovering that she was as dark as any other astral fae, with clusters of golden-tinged stars shining from her as an outward sign of her Archfae status. He took advantage of her preoccupation to lick her cheek in a great slurp and butt her chest gently with a head as broad as her shoulders.

She slipped her fingers up the proud ridges of his horns, finding his pointed ears hiding under them and scratching behind them like she remembered him liking. A deep rumble of satisfaction vibrated under her as he angled his head. *Yes, definitely Queldian.* But how?

"I missed you," the dragon murmured.

"You were with me this whole time," she replied just as quietly. She kept scratching his ears and wept for joy to have this moment, only to hiccup a few giggles when he leaned in to clean her face.

"It's not the same. Couldn't snuggle you when you needed it or smack you when you also needed that," he rumbled.

She wanted to say that she, as a dignified Archfae, did not *snuggle*, when he lifted his head. Jaromir stood nearby, admiring the dragon's shimmering scales. His arms were clasped before him as he waited, ever the polite one. Izell gestured him over enthusiastically. "He doesn't bite."

Queldian snorted. "Such a lie." Still, he nuzzled Jaromir's hands while Izell made introductions. Her old dragon greeted her human-born love like he was her mate, even allowing Jaromir to touch his face scales and the bony ridge of horns sweeping back from his forehead. Either Queldian approved of him or was going soft at long last.

"Ah, I see my surprise is well-received," Soren said, approaching her other side. Past him, she could see Lyana speaking to Sondus, her serpent's looming presence coiled behind her.

"What, exactly, happened?" Izell asked. Much as she hated surprises, this one was more than welcome.

He walked with her as she crossed toward Lyana, wondering how exactly they were going to hide two dragons in the depths of Hell. Maybe it wasn't such a convenient surprise after all, especially since a sea serpent required water. Lyana's dragon was twenty feet of *obvious* and *out of place*.

"Your body contained two souls. So, in the process of taking your soul out of its body, your dragon came along. It happened to Adrius and his dragon each time he died as well," Soren said, beaming.

"Too bad they will have to say here," she replied.

They were close enough that the sea serpent's attention turned their way, his white gossamer fins flipping along his back. "Why would we need to stay?" he asked. Like most dragons, he was large enough to have a voice like an earthquake, deep and booming. He hissed in inflection, tongue flicking out on the "*ssstay*."

She raised a brow and gestured to his whole self, coiled links of teal scales with an abalone-like shine in the light of day.

He flicked Lyana an amused look. "Do you think my mother was a serpent?"

Izell tilted her head in consideration. She'd never met Lyana's sea serpent in life, just knew *of* him and his brother, both sons of Cyranos. "If you're asking, the answer is obviously no."

The fins bracketing his face flapped before he was consumed by a rapid change made of crackling bones and shifting scales. He shrank down, and down, growing limbs in the process. Izell assumed she was about to see an astral fae and then came to the conclusion she should stop assuming anything when the shifting stopped.

"There." He flexed spindly fingers tipped with razor-sharp fins. "Much better. But am I still a demigod?"

Izell's brow furrowed as she filtered the last echoes of his bass voice, searching for that telltale echo that marked the kin of the gods.

"I don't think so, especially since I still have it," Lyana answered. She balanced an orb of water over her palm, turning it to ice within moments. It spun there, suspended and waiting, an anomaly created without a word of power, just the focus of her mind.

"Hmm." The creature that used to be a sea serpent frowned. He cut a broad-shouldered silhouette next to Lyana, his musculature only softened by a coating of sharp-tipped, teal scales. Izell could see the contour of his abdominal muscles as gentle waves in the scales, plus an obvious V-line, courtesy of the sash of fabric barely covering the family jewels. With a swimmer's thick thighs and broad, webbed feet, he was sure to be deadly in the water, but at least he could walk in this form.

"Are you part hythian?" Izell named the race of lesser sea fae who had vast nations hidden in the depths of Faerie's oceans. The water hid those people from the ravages of the Fell, and as far as Izell knew, they'd never resurfaced since that dark chapter of Faerie's history.

His lips pulled back, revealing a half moon of razor-sharp teeth, not unlike the uneven triangles lining a shark's mouth. "That's right. Prince Sissaron Waveborn, at your service." He tipped his head regally, inspecting her with keen eyes as blue and slitted as his serpent form's. Izell could see the resemblance to both sides of his family, with the hythian short, shark-like snout, plus his serpent scales. A short tail swung behind him, marked by a pointed fin for quick maneuvers. He was unique enough to be an oddity on the level she was at as a shifter.

"You've been holding out on me," she said, directing this to Lyana, who eyed him like seeing an apparition. The water fae startled, an indigo blush over her cheeks. "How did you get a man like this as your familiar?"

Sissaron flashed a sharp smile. "Maybe she was my familiar." He held Lyana's gaze for long enough that Izell swore she saw literal sparks.

Uh-huh. His familiar. She wondered how maddening it was for them to share the same body.

"It wasn't like that," Lyana protested.

The hythian turned back to Izell with a shrug. "As you can see, I can accompany you to Hell without a problem. It is your dragon that will be the concern."

She bristled immediately. "If you're going, Queldian is going. I will accept nothing less."

Before he could reply, Sondus cleared his throat. Izell felt her gaze pulled to him and recognized it for what it was. While Lyana was concerned about having an unbound Mindbender with them, especially one with no training, Izell knew him well enough to figure he'd memorized everything a Mindbender could *potentially* do. That was just how Sondus worked.

"Might I remind you all that we planned to have four people go to Hell, not six?" he asked, and it was, for a moment, the most reasonable piece of logic Izell had ever heard. The bigger the operation, the more likely they were to get caught. Especially Queldian, who would have to wear a two-legged illusion. She didn't think he would know how to function even pretending to be fae.

There was a pause in her mind, where she waited for Queldian to pitch in his two cents. But there was only silence. They had no familiar bond, nor were they linked as two souls sharing the same body. She rubbed at a sudden pang of sadness zinging through her chest in the empty space where her dragon used to be. He may have padded over to stand next to her, but he felt absent in the one way that'd made them so close.

"Plans can be changed. We don't even know how this is going to go," Sissaron said. "We've placed our hopes on the Archangel and, by extension, your new Mindbender powers."

So, Sissaron had been active and listening in Lyana's mind. Izell wondered what his opinion of recent events was, having been crammed into the same awful situation as Lucia's puppet.

Sondus nodded. "Back to work, then." He exchanged a glance with the Archangel in question, who offered his palm. As soon as Sondus took his hand, they both disappeared. They already knew that Soren was giving the spymaster a much-frowned-upon visit to Heaven's great repository of books.

She crossed her arms in the lull that followed, coming to terms with just how much trust they had put on the shoulders of the man who'd double-crossed her "for the good of Faerie" not too long ago.

"I'm going for a walk," she muttered, patting Queldian's shoulder. She only wanted her dragon's presence, itching to leave behind the heap of nerves pinging around inside of her.

She walked him out of earshot and then a few paces more, stopping to admire the blue bowl of cloudless sky that Soren's island was suspended within. "Well, what is it?" Queldian rumbled, noticing something in her bearing or simply knowing her too well.

Izell blew out a sigh. "What if we can't trust anyone around us?" A long life had taught her one thing: someone was always waiting with a knife behind their back. She'd needed to look into Sissaron's eyes to understand she only trusted three people on this island: Jaromir, Queldian, and herself. "It's not too late to go our own way. Now that we're in Heaven, we can find our own way into Hell."

A muffled *thump* sounded behind her. She turned, ready to strike out, when she realized her dragon had flopped onto his side. He gestured with his claws, and she lay down like he wanted, letting him rest his heavy arm over her to draw her into his warm belly.

He snuggled her like she was the small spoon, like nothing had ever changed between them. For a beautiful moment, Izell felt millennia younger, just a girl taking comfort from her dragon's sheer presence.

When he spoke, he sounded like the little voice that hid in the back of her subconscious, whispering that it was okay to have events moving outside of her control. "We're in too deep to assume those around us will act against our mission. Do you think anyone here truly wants the apocalypse?"

"No," she said in a small voice.

"We're in Heaven. Let's try to have a little faith." At her snort, he added, "And a good plan."

Now that was something she could get behind.

Chapter 24

Jaromir

That evening, they gathered on Soren's patio with sweet tea and Sondus's copious notes. Jaromir had napped the day away and later learned that Izell and Queldian had wandered off to do the same. He now sat next to her on a wooden bench, with her dragon's head resting in his lap while she stroked his neck. Queldian emitted low rumbles that shook Jaromir's bones.

"Here's what I'm thinking," Sondus began. He had one book with him, its spine edged with gilt. It was passed around, open to a set of diagrams which showed Hell and its planes.

Jaromir took a long time with them, trying to wrap his mind around how this worked. Hell was separated into slices of land stacked on top of each other like plates, eight in total. The very top layer was the coolest, open to the sky and thus Heaven above it. The other layers were all marked with one of the seven sins, with Lust being the topmost and Pride being the bottom, a location flooded with magma and hellfire.

With layers of solid earth between one plane and the next, they were nearly independent except for a single tunnel in each that led to a knot of pathways labeled "The Labyrinth."

"We are very lucky, because we're going to Lust, the easiest plane to reach. Demons have access to teleporters, and part of their magic abilities includes ways to phase through solid rock, so they fight each other without a problem and leave the Labyrinth to be an elaborate trap for sinners that try to escape Hell," Sondus said to a nod from Soren. The Archangel sat in grim silence, his signature smile nowhere to be seen.

"Before you wonder, I have a means for you to move as a group between levels." Soren opened his palm, revealing a glass disc and a square, leather holder for it. "I'm not meant to have this, but maybe Michael will forgive me for borrowing it."

"Michael, like—" Jaromir began in shock.

Soren sighed and handed him the disc. "It would help greatly if you didn't ask questions. Just take it, and make sure it comes back in one piece." The clear glass was heavier than expected, pushing Jaromir's hand into the table. It had a small hole in the center, perfect for fitting a finger through to hold it without smudging the surface.

Jaromir placed the disc back into its holder for the moment, listening as Sondus gave them a breakdown of what to expect. First, lust demons were either lithe and beautiful creatures like Lilith herself, or huge brutes with spiked knuckles. They would encounter serving-class demons like imps and others, but those were seen on each level of Hell. Plus the damned souls, who, on Lust, were kept in pens separate from the living areas of the demons and the grand palace where Lilith lived.

"Keep in mind that the demons you meet started as human souls. Anything added in their demonic transition is a sign of power. Note tails, the number of horns, and especially wings in the demons you face," Soren warned. "The most powerful demons have feathered wings. They're former angels, Originals."

Heads nodded around the table.

"Lilith, as an Original, can sense our energy signatures. I looked into that too," Sondus said. "Our goal should be to avoid her and search her chambers for the missing Key."

Lyana raised a brow. "And if she has it on her finger?"

"I will attempt to use my mental influence to convince her to take it off so we can steal it. If that doesn't work...it will be a fight. She'll sense us through any glamor we make." He turned back to the diagram of Lust while Jaromir's stomach roiled. It seemed like there was no way to avoid the coming showdown with the demon who'd ambushed them so easily.

"But I believe we should glamor ourselves as a group of imps. We would be less likely to stand out if we took this path..." He started pointing out where the demonic servants had a hovel on the outskirts of the palace.

"We still haven't figured out how Queldian will be coming with us," Sissaron interrupted.

The dragon in question snorted hot air over Jaromir's arm. "I spent all this time in a two-legged body. Don't you think I know how to pretend to be a two-leg at this point?"

"Do you?" The scaled man frowned.

"I do. I will not be left behind," he growled.

"As I was saying," Sondus interjected. "We will take our imp forms into the palace and start searching from there. If we split into two groups of three, that should make us seem like a normal group of servants. I will keep us connected mentally so we can coordinate. Anyone object to this plan?"

While Jaromir thought that was the best they could do without seeing the place for themselves, he did speak up with another concern. "What about the greater demon?"

"I say we hogtie and kidnap the first winged demon we find," Izell muttered.

Sondus gestured to her. "Basically that. I was thinking we could ambush a winged demon once we have the Summer Key in our possession."

"How rare are greater demons?" Jaromir glanced to the Archangel for this question. "What ranks are there?"

Just like earlier, it didn't seem like Soren wanted to disclose this information. But it was vital to their mission, so Jaromir watched him wrestle with it and eventually share what they needed to know. "Greater demons are about a one-in-ten occurrence. The only demons stronger than them are the Originals and the Lords of Hell, which are one per plane, except for the top level, which is just a receiving area. Any other demons are the foot soldiers and torturers, all the same rank. Imps and servitors and other naturally occurring creatures are considered the lowest on the pecking order."

"But a demon can evolve to be stronger, right?" Sondus prompted.

The Archangel grimaced. "If they consume enough soul energy, yes. A lesser creature can become an ordinary demon, or an ordinary demon can sprout wings and attain greater status. It is not very common. The Lords of Hell prefer to keep any excess energy to themselves."

Jaromir nodded, feeling his heartbeat throb in his ears as a wary silence fell over the group. They had a plan, and they had nightfall, when it was less likely for them to encounter any demons while infiltrating Lilith's palace. It was time to take the plunge and go to the last place any sane group would head to willingly.

Soren's lips pinched as he gestured for the glass disc. "We consider this a means for invasion. No corner of Hell is safe from it, and it can activate any teleporters you encounter in Hell. Since you are going in blind, I suggest you pick the least populated areas to teleport to and keep a copy of our maps of each plane. You never know, you might need to visit more than just Lust."

He showed off how to use it, holding the disc on one finger and spinning it. White sparks drifted upward as it activated. Anyone touching the person holding the disc would be teleported along with the user, and it responded to the whims of the one holding it.

Just as dangerous as any Fell Key, Jaromir thought. Those, too, could be picked up and used with no experience, despite the devastating amounts of magic they held. It was also their only ticket out of Hell once they went down there, so it was worth its weight in precious gemstones.

Izell sat up, patting her dragon's neck until he lifted his head. "Let's go," she sighed.

"One last thing," Soren said. The Archangel turned to Sissaron. "I wanted to offer you weapons and something more... comfortable to wear."

Sissaron glanced down at the scrap of fabric around his hips. "This is fine."

"I must insist."

Though Sissaron smirked, he let the Archangel talk him into a visit to something he only referred to as "the Vault." Spinning the disc on his finger, Soren had them all touch his arms and teleported them there. Just like with the transition from his body to Heaven, Jaromir blinked and was in another place. No vertigo, just a vague sensation that he was moving when his senses told him he was standing still.

"Surely this will make us a beacon amongst demons," Jaromir remarked to Izell as they stood side by side in a plain room filled with racks of various weapons. Each carried the distinctive crystalline-and-gold motif that he'd come to associate with angels. Soren led Sissaron further into the Vault to get fitted for armor, while the rest browsed what was on offer.

"I have a feeling we will be, no matter what," she whispered back. She drifted toward the sleek shape of a white rifle painted with golden, angelic sigils. "You should take this."

He balked even as she pushed the weapon into his hands, followed by a box of ammunition. "I don't know how to use it," he protested.

"You point and shoot. Isn't that easy?" Her hips swayed like she still had a tail as she inspected the rows of weaponry. With her golden occultarus bobbing behind her, it wasn't like she needed a weapon. Except Jaromir assumed these armaments were steeped in magic, capable of sending any demon to their eternal end.

While her back was turned, he re-racked the rifle and went in the opposite direction, passing Sondus strapping as many daggers as possible to his person. He smiled sheepishly when Jaromir raised a brow. "What's that?" he murmured, pointing toward a hilt peeking out of the spymaster's pants leg. It was dark compared to the crystal blades around them, with a polished ruby hilt—a weapon he recognized a split second before Sondus jerked his clothing over it.

"Figured Lilith would want it back. I intended to give it pointy-end first," the fae whispered.

Jaromir released a concerned hum.

"Can't have too many daggers, right?"

"Right." Jaromir shrugged, leaving it at that. He kept looking until he found his weapon of choice hanging on a small hook.

Sondus snorted. "Taking up carpentry?"

For he'd picked up a hammer, its crystal head about the width of two thumbs. When he swung it, the crystal released a dull hum and left a ribbon of light in its wake. He hooked it to his belt with a nod of satisfaction.

"It's perfect. I used to have one for self-defense against the Fell." And his old friends would tease him about the size of his weapon then, too.

"If you say so," the spymaster replied skeptically. He practiced a glamor on Jaromir while they waited, shrinking him considerably and coloring his skin redder than a sunburn. Sondus muttered to himself as he tinkered with the illusion to get it to his exact specifications.

Sissaron emerged a few minutes later with a fluid prowl that reminded Jaromir of a hunting predator, wearing an ivory tunic belted at the waist and a sturdy pair of dark-washed pants. Two short swords were fastened to his hips. He stopped short, eyes narrowing. "What is that hideous thing?"

"That's Jaromir," Sondus replied innocently.

"Is it that bad?" The voice that came from his lips was high-pitched, as pleasant as claws raking across his ears.

Sondus winced. "That's just my guess as to what an imp sounds like. The books describe their voices as chatters and screeches, but we can adjust when we hear a real imp."

Shaking his head, Sissaron pointed to Queldian. "Him next."

As the spymaster went over to give the dragon a copy of the imp illusion, Jaromir had to wonder if there was some rivalry afoot between the two because of their species. The dragons had been at odds the moment they'd arrived in Heaven. He silently rooted for Queldian as he tottered on two feet, inspecting the clawed toes he was now working with.

Now he could see why Sissaron had called him hideous. The imp illusion was about three feet tall and sported a smile that stretched literally from ear to ear. It wouldn't be so bad if it had nostrils, but without them, the creature had to have a permanent opening somewhere in its gap-toothed mouth to breathe. With squinty eyes and bat-like ears, maybe they weren't meant to see well.

Queldian began to walk more confidently, a hiss escaping his mouth with the flick of a forked tongue. "See? Just fine," he said in an imp's screech.

"May the gods protect my eardrums," Sissaron grunted. Before long, they were a gaggle of six imps, the only difference between them being horn lengths and the strategic placement of open wounds or old scars.

Jaromir knew it was done well when Soren walked in, stopping short. The angel's hands glowed with light until Sondus pulled down his illusion, smiling and waving. Putting a hand to his chest, Soren breathed out in relief. "Looks like you're ready to fit in," he said. "Go with my blessing. I pray for a swift, successful mission."

You and me both, Jaromir thought. He hopped forward to accept the disc that would teleport them to Hell and spun it on his fingertip.

Chapter 25

Izell

There was a flaw in all this, and she saw it the moment they appeared in a shadowy corner of what she hoped was the Lust level of Hell.

They had no idea where they were.

Smoke shrouded the sky in place of clouds, and the air hung stale with no wind to speak of. Jaromir had probably gotten them close to the palace, but in the murk, she couldn't see further than a few feet in front of her face. And she'd thought Adrun was dark! There was a difference between eternal night and the smog-filled atmosphere they'd entered.

At least she understood why her imp illusion had such big ears and no nostrils. The lingering smell of sulfur and something sickly sweet assaulted her nose under the glamor, and she fought off a gag.

"I hear real imps. That way." Queldian pointed to their left. She shrugged, starting to head in that direction. Maybe they could infiltrate amongst these creatures and get led right to the palace. She had every intention of going straight to Lilith, wherever the Queen of Lust might be, hit her with a sleeping spell, and drag her back to Heaven. Demon and Key all in one neat package. They could be done in hours.

"Gods, that smell," she muttered. While she knew Hell was a

place of punishment, it didn't have to punish her nose with the added odor of offal as they approached the screeching tones of a pack of real imps.

A roll of smoke parted, revealing a brick-red imp with one horn curled an extra foot up from its head. The other had been lopped off by a clumsy hand, leaving a lumpy scar in the patch of missing skull over its brow.

"Lazies!" it screeched, facing them with its bat-like ears cocked forward. Izell could tell it didn't sense them with its eyes, which were glazed and sunken from disuse.

Still, she startled back at the sudden scream of its tone. She hadn't sensed it until they were right on top of it. Who knew what else lurked nearby, hidden by smoke and odor?

"Lazies help with feast. Now!" Orange-red flames licked its palms, illuminating a many-legged silhouette of a small legion of stick-like imps hauling a limp corpse. It was shaped like a cow, with at least four horns too many.

"*Smells like a farm nearby,*" Sondus commented in her head. Since his voice carried a dull echo, she figured he had connected a thread of Mind magic so they could all communicate mentally.

"*Where do you think the feast is?*" Lyana asked. She was the first to move to the corpse, adding herself to the group hefting it.

"*A place we need to be. Don't try too hard, by the way, it seems these imps are pretty weak,*" Izell remarked. She supported the head by one horn so it wouldn't drag in the dirt. The moment the dragons helped too, the load lifted, and she held her breath, hoping none of these little demons noticed.

The taskmaster imp extinguished its flames, muttering about "Lazies these days..." But the last ounce of its energy illuminated the creature's three sets of eyes and sharpened teeth: cow-shaped, but definitely not a cow.

They trundled the cow-thing through the dark, listening to the real imps hiss and chatter their jaws. Reluctantly, she started making the same noises past a growing headache. "*They'd better be feasting in the palace,*" she muttered to her group.

"*Logically, that's the only place that could host a feast here,*" Sondus said.

"If most of the demons of rank are attending..." She drifted off, biting her lip. *"We can search the palace, but getting a greater demon will be a significant challenge."*

"We could wait in Lilith's chambers for her to return," Lyana said.

Izell tilted her head before nodding to herself. *"We could still get her and the Key if she's wearing it."* Chances were good the Queen of Lust wouldn't let it out of her sight.

Her sight wavered when she tried to look ahead. As someone used to the enhanced sight of her dragon familiar, her natural vision seemed watery and weak. She missed the strength and surety that she held as a dragon shifter; however, she would never trade away the glimpse she'd gotten of her deceased familiar.

She could feel a faint connection with him even now, a steady presence who radiated confidence in whatever he saw ahead of them. Sensing the direction of her thoughts, he shared it with the group. *"We're almost to the palace. It's...not very large."*

"I would call it a castle," Sissaron snipped.

"We don't need semantics right now," Queldian growled back.

Izell rolled her eyes. *"Really? Cut that out. We're on the same team,"* she snapped at them both.

"Sorry," her dragon muttered. *"Anyway, we're going toward a side entrance. Do you smell that?"*

Yeah, she sure did. She thought her nose was deadened, but the new smell he meant washed over her a few moments later. Something savory. Roasted meat and spices blended to a siren's call to her stomach.

A beacon appeared amongst the shadows above them. The imps groaned as they heaved their cargo up a flight of stairs, passing the threshold into the palace and between two lit torches. Sconces burned against plain stone corridors at regular intervals, a relief for Izell's strained eyes.

The smell of food was coming from straight ahead. It was like they'd walked from Hell into the average castle's kitchen, except a scantily clad lady demon was stirring a jumbo pot of stew over a reddish fire. Another succubus watched them place the cow-creature on a low table, sharpening two butcher knives with a grin splitting her beautiful face. She spoke to the imps in a low, hissing language immediately translated by the magic hanging over Izell.

"That should be enough. You're dismissed." She started butchering the delivery without sparing them another glance.

Izell coordinated with her group as the gaggle of imps went chattering out of the kitchen. While they turned right, heading back into the shadowy night, she cast a spell to create six copies of their imp disguises to go with them. She watched them go for a split second, her heart leaping to her throat. Imps were so sound-dependent, and illusions just didn't have the same presence as a real body.

The others were already heading the other direction, and she followed in a quiet shuffle of feet. *"Well, we have no alibi if we're caught. Blind creatures can't serve as guards or waiters,"* she remarked.

"I have something up my sleeve," Sondus promised.

She had an opportunity to see what he meant as they rounded a corner and picked up the sound of hooves clopping on the stone floor. A demon headed straight for them, nearly human save for a pair of inch-long horns sprouting from his forehead, a ruddy complexion, and the hooves announcing him several yards away. He was the most clothed demon they'd seen yet, wearing a button-down and slacks.

He should've seen them, but his gaze remained forward, clip-clopping his way toward the kitchen. Izell wiped a cold sweat from her forehead. Of course, their Mindbender could make them beyond notice, but in that split second, she'd wondered if Sondus had the power and experience to pull off such a maneu-ver. *"Come on. More are coming,"* he said, leading the way.

The flames lining the walls were placed at more regular inter-vals as they hustled. Izell picked up the susurration of many voices nearby as they passed a pair of succubi, one dressed in black lace that barely covered her breasts and the cleft between her thighs, while the other sported a professional getup like the incubus before her. They'd tucked serving trays into their armpits and gossiped amiably on the way by, paying the cluster of imps underfoot no mind.

They skirted the open set of double doors leading to the feast itself, ducking not to risk any chance of looking in and having a demon look back. *"Time to split up,"* she said the moment they emerged into a central room with hallways splitting off of it like a spider web. They needed to cover as much of this place as they could while the feast was ongoing.

Queldian turned his head first, snorting out a sound of distress. *"We need cover. Now!"*

It was too late. By the time she realized what was going on, a strip of leather wrapped her arms to her torso. She cursed her slow, non-shifter reflexes as her imp illusion dangled before the eyes of a demon man who drew her up to full height. She didn't dare look back, just in case her group was still retreating, instead staring daggers into the incubus who'd caught her.

"Well, well. What do we have here?" He spoke like the softest of caresses, eyeing her from amber eyes set in pools of darkness for sclera. Full lips parted, showing sharpened teeth. He had the face of an angel, framed by artfully tousled black hair and a pair of horns curling back from his forehead to circle his ears. He wore no shirt, just a pair of low-slung pants. Maybe *angel* was an accurate word for him when she noticed the feathered wings folded neatly to his back.

Oh, fuck. An Original. And she'd blundered right into him.

The leather around her arms tightened as his expression tightened with displeasure. "What are you? I'll have you writhing on the ground if you don't reveal yourself this second." A second strip of leather appeared in her periphery, and she realized it had a barbed tip dripping a clear fluid.

Chains clinked, ice crystalizing out of nowhere to lasso this demon just like he'd done to Izell. He released her with a grunt of pain, her illusion dropping to the ground. From this vantage, she saw that what she thought was leather was actually a pair of thin tails coiling up with a third one attached to this Original demon. His handsome face turned feral as he hissed at Lyana. Her illusioned imp hands glowed teal, fae runes of magic dancing at her fingertips.

"I know that smell. Fae magic," he growled, wiggling his shoulders under the binding chains tightening down to restrain his arms and wings together. A second set of ice bound his ankles.

Lyana grinned, displaying miles of jagged imp fangs. "Looks like we have our demon."

He drew breath and loosed a scream pitched like a dog whistle. Izell throat punched him to make it stop, and as he choked, she realized they had a huge problem. All sounds of mirth and conversation from the great hall had stopped, silence accompanying the ringing in her ears.

"Take him. Run!" Izell said urgently, gesturing Sissaron over. The sea serpent scooped the demon over his shoulder like a sack of potatoes, holding his three whipcord tails by their base so they couldn't sting him with their mystery poison. Lyana conjured a ball of ice and stuffed it into the demon's mouth, using a little extra magic to make it too big for him to spit out.

They chose a corridor at random and ran. As the demon's head bounced over Sissaron's shoulder, his expression relaxed, his gaze meeting Izell's. He made a distinctive orgasm face around his icy gag.

Ugh. She should've expected nothing less from an incubus.

"Are we going back to Heaven with him?" Jaromir asked. The question felt aimed at her, and she hesitated on answering. Her kneejerk reaction was to say yes. They could sacrifice him for the Dark Eye spell.

But such a powerful demon disappearing in the heart of Lilith's operation meant infiltrating it a second time would be that much harder. *"No, we have to salvage this, and fast. No queen would investigate a sound like that herself."*

"What?" Sondus blurted, sounding shocked.

"Let's find her chambers, and if there is no Key there, we can decide whether or not we leave," she said, slowing her tread. The hallway had several guards searching for the Original now, taxing Sondus's powers of deflection to their limits.

"This way." Queldian's nostrils flared, guiding them further

into the maze of corridors, though he took them with surety to an iron-studded door like many they'd passed. *"We scented her earlier, remember?"* he prompted her as she flashed a skeptical look at it.

So they had. She nodded, feeling robbed of yet another sense. It didn't help that her next spell had to be made with both hands, rather than the indolent flick of her fingers that she was used to as a shifter. The lock clicked from within, allowing them to open the door and duck inside.

Sondus collapsed, their illusions falling with him as he panted on his side. "You did a great job," she assured him after making sure it was just magical exertion making his stars dull. He'd be fine with a short rest.

She was more than aware that the demon was inspecting them all, speaking something muffled by his gag. Sissaron dropped him to the ground with a grunt. "That *thing* was aroused this whole time," he muttered.

The demon winked back.

"Ignore him," she said, but not before she made her own binding spell to tie the creature's three tails into a complicated knot. He wouldn't be stinging anyone.

Her gaze turned to the rooms around them, surprise making her jaw go slack. This first room had modern human furnishings. Flicking a light switch, she illuminated hardwood flooring and a pool of water bubbling on its own. Coven Rehnquist's mansion had something like it called a "jacuzzi," which she only remembered because she'd thought it was an unusual word.

The others were already spreading out, except for Jaromir, who was taking Sondus's vitals and murmuring over him in a low voice. She couldn't help but notice the incubus snickering as he watched her walk by, annoyance creeping over her skin. What was so damn funny? His little alarm had ruined their element of surprise.

A *click* sounded behind her. Walking through the door, key in hand, was none other than Lilith herself. She stopped dead, face to face with Izell, before she started to grin.

Izell threw a quick lightning bolt. And...the demoness caught the spell and held it crackling in her palm. She inspected it like a particular curious kind of insect.

"Never in a thousand years would I expect you to come down here," Lilith said, still smiling. She flashed her fingers, where the Summer Key's brilliant ruby glowed. "I'm *so* happy to see you."

Chapter 26
Jaromir

Izell bristled with menace, her fingers already flying through another spell as Lilith crushed the lightning in her palm until sparks rained down from between her fingers.

"Your sleeping spell won't work on me," the Queen of Lust droned, raising a brow as Queldian came charging back into the room. "Why don't we have a conversation? I don't want to kill your precious dragon spirit today."

Jaromir exchanged a glance with Sondus as the buzzing of magic in the air faded. Even Izell seemed uncertain, letting her spell go for a moment. Lilith wasn't dressed for a fight, and there was no way a weapon could be hiding on her person. A tube of form-fitting black leather lifted her breasts, baring most of her toned midriff and plenty of cleavage. A lacy strap fitted to her hips, holding two panels of emerald silk to hide her modesty but leaving miles of peach-toned skin exposed all the way down to her cloven hooves.

"Or any of the rest of you, for that matter," she added, slowly lifting her hands to expose her palms. Her single whip-like tail closed the door behind her, the barbed end flipping the lock. Her smile only widened when Queldian glanced to Izell and his charging steps turned into a weary shuffle.

"Talk, then," Izell barked.

"Now, now. You sneak into my home, tie up my favorite plaything, and at this moment, hide two more souls in my bedroom. Is that a great way to start?" Lilith said smoothly. She glided by them, her hooves soundless on the hardwood.

Jaromir stood, carefully letting Sondus up too. Both of them looked to Izell, whose head was cocked and lips thin.

"As far as I can tell, she's legitimately happy to see us," she answered their looks. Confusion lined her swirling, white eyes, the only thing about her complexion that remained unchanged now that she and Queldian had separated. "I don't use my empathy virtue...much. But that's what I sense."

Lilith's hands were melting the chains and gag keeping the other Original contained. With her back to them, Jaromir spotted two angry red lines where she'd once had wings too. "You're a weakling, Rosier," she was saying as he shook off the magic.

"You love it," he answered in a low purr.

She smacked the back of his head, earning a laugh. "Go get my meal. I left it behind saving your sorry ass," she snorted.

"Yes, my queen." He popped to his hooves with a jaunty salute before leaving. Jaromir could've sworn he just watched the incubus walk *through* the stone next to the door. He scrubbed his eyes, but the door remained locked, and the demon really was gone.

"Now, let's get more comfortable," Lilith sighed. She didn't walk; she sauntered, her hips and tail swinging with the motion as she moved into the next room without a glance back at them. Like any ruler, she simply expected to be followed.

"We have to get out of here," Sondus hissed. "She's going to get a weapon and bathe in our blood."

Jaromir went first, his fingertips glittering with light magic. They found a richly appointed living room and Lilith seated on a velvet couch by the door, her hooves propped up on a plush footstool.

"As amusing as that would be, blood is terrible for the complexion," she said without looking up. Her fingers were laced behind her thick head of strawberry blonde hair, lips turned up. "Besides, my weapons of choice are on the wall. You'll know if I go for them."

She jerked her chin forward, toward a pair of cleavers resting on heavy hooks above her fireplace. Wood crackled pleasantly in the silence that followed as uneasy looks abounded. Jaromir didn't feel like the demoness was menacing them, just waiting and amused at the uncertainty she'd stirred in them.

"I must insist you make yourselves comfortable. And for your two bonus friends to come out too. Six of you, hmm? I expected just as many angels."

As she spoke, Sissaron peered out from another adjoining room to see what was going on. Jaromir had a seat first, with Sondus following, while Izell leaned against a wall with her arms crossed and a scowl firmly in place. Lilith gestured lazily. "Yes, you. And the lady too. Aren't your souls interesting? A dead demigod and a living one. Nothing funny now, or I finish what I started with your Mindbender." Her amber eyes flashed to Sondus. Just like with the other Original, the color glowed out of a sea of shadows. "How *did* you survive, by the way?"

Sondus set his lips, jaw so tight his teeth had to be sparking.

Lilith shrugged. Slow footsteps approached, first Sissaron, then Lyana behind him, shooting disbelieving looks toward Izell. The mental bridge between them all had fallen at some point, so Jaromir could only read the betrayal on their expressions. Hopefully, Izell was on to something, because he'd seen Lilith when she was out for blood. He'd be dead before he could activate Soren's disc to get them to safety. Sissaron sat within striking range of Lilith, a hand inches from the pommel of one sword. Lyana stood behind his seat.

"There. Isn't this cozy?" The Queen of Lust grinned, baring a mouth full of delicate fangs. "What interesting guests. I'm just dying to know how many of the angels' precious laws you've broken to be here right now. But you're not here to talk. I stole your precious ring so *someone* would come hear me out. I sensed the power of your souls like a beacon in Faerie, and it's an answer to my every wish that you came yourselves."

Jaromir rubbed an uneasy feeling creeping over his skin, trailing goosebumps in its wake. She'd nearly murdered Sondus and stolen the Summer Key so they'd come have a chat with her? She was either delusional or desperate, he thought.

"Of course, no angel would dare come look me in the eye." She breathed a scoff, turning her unsettling amber gaze into Jaromir's nephilim eyes instead. She stared, challenging him to break away first. "You came back for your property yourselves. This is the best possible scenario, because I have yet to meet an angel with the balls to do what I require."

Izell snorted. "Which is what, exactly?"

"As you clearly already know, the Veil between my existence and yours thins by the moment." Lilith sat back, lacing her legs together. "War is coming."

No one moved as Izell bit her lip, physically restraining one of her usual comments.

"Want to know how many angelic emissaries have come down here for some diplomacy?" She breathed a chuckle. "*None.* Seven different levels of Hell, seven different rulers, yet we're assumed to be a collective of evil. Isn't that right?" The pointed question was aimed at Jaromir.

He had no idea how to answer that, save for a simple, "Yes." Because all along, they'd assumed Hell, as in all of it, was about to invade and overwhelm Earth and Faerie.

"Humph. So, why attempt to speak with us, right?" she snarked. "Your enemies are the alliance of the bottom three: Wrath, Envy, and Pride. And *my* enemy is Pride himself, Lucifer. If you want your ring back, I propose we come to an agreement."

Jaromir felt his face go slack with shock. His every imagining of their trip to Hell ended with either Lilith dead by their hands or avoided completely. He hadn't expected her to seem halfway reasonable, but the impending bargain she was to offer seemed exactly a demon's power play. She held the cards here just by having the Summer Key glimmering on her finger.

Izell raised a skeptical brow. "Are you saying you don't want to invade Earth?"

Six sets of eyes skewered the lounging Queen of Lust. She smirked and waved to their surroundings. "I don't. What's on

Earth that isn't here? My mastery of soul shaping means I live in comfort. No one messes with me. *Except* Lucifer."

Jaromir could practically feel the disbelief rolling off of Izell, knowing exactly what her scrunched-up expression meant. "Do tell," she said tartly.

The amusement fell off Lilith's face, shadows gathering in the hollows of her face. She was terrifying and heart-stoppingly gorgeous in the same breath as she bared her teeth on a low growl. "Then I will be frank. Lucifer will invade your worlds and slaughter your people until only souls remain for him to feast upon. He will destroy Faerie, and then he will pluck the feathers off any angel who attempts to defend Earth from the same fate. But *I*, one of the independent leaders of Hell, don't want this to happen any more than you do.

"Many eons ago, Lucifer cut my wings off and left my battered body in Lust. He does not deserve to taste the souls in your goddess-blessed Sanctum. He should never breathe the fresh air outside of his captivity here, deep in the bowels of the universe's asshole. I will make sure of it, and you lot will help. Are you listening now?" she hissed.

"I'm still waiting to hear how exactly you expect us to help." Izell just raised a brow in the face of the demon's anger.

A moment later, a man's voice rang out from the entranceway. "Yoo-hoo! Lily dear," Rosier crooned.

Her shoulders relaxed a fraction. "In here," she called back.

The incubus came in with a tray of food and a glass topped to the brim with amber liquid. "Oh, I'm missing something juicy, aren't I?" Now that he had the opportunity to speak, his voice held an effeminate touch, though his wink was aimed at Lyana as he squeezed in at Lilith's side.

Rosier seemed like what Jaromir would expect from a freshly fallen angel. His skin was ashen, the extremities a darker, nearly burnt color. Every delicate feather lining his tucked wings was white with blackened ends, curled from a brush with extreme heat.

"Don't run your mouth, Rosier," Lilith muttered as she

aggressively worked a knife and fork into a cold steak, shoving a cut square into her mouth.

He smirked, propping his chin on a hand as he turned his attention to Lyana. "What's your name, beautiful? Tie men up often?" he purred.

"I'll castrate you myself," Lilith interjected.

The incubus pouted. "You're no fun. Don't worry, beautiful. It grows back."

"Leave the lady alone," Jaromir said. The look Rosier shot him was pure acid, but Jaromir already thought the incubus was disgusting. If Lilith wasn't going to send him away, he wasn't afraid to lock horns with a demon.

Rosier grinned a moment later. "Don't worry, nephilim. I swing both ways."

"*Anyway,*" Lilith said pointedly. The incubus rolled his eyes and licked his lips in Jaromir's direction, eyeing him like a piece of meat while the Queen of Lust turned her attention toward Izell. "I wanted to propose a deal of mutual benefit. The defenses around Pride have tightened such that we can barely sneak in and get a sniff of their plans. But we know enough. Lucifer had developed a new kind of weapon." She jerked her chin toward Sondus, who stared at her stonily. "Well? Pull out the dagger. I sense it on you. I don't want the damn thing back."

At Izell's nod, he reached into his boot, slowly withdrawing the black-metal weapon with its ruby pommel. Neither demon made a move toward it, Rosier going as far as to cross his arms as Lilith busied herself with another bite of steak.

"We call that a soul-stealing weapon. They're very new, and only your enemies have them at present," Lilith said, pointing a single claw at the ruby. "Had you died earlier, Mindbender, your soul would be trapped in there."

"Lovely," Sondus said flatly.

"Good thing one of your companions saved you, hmm? But one piddling dagger doesn't represent the might of Lucifer's cache. They are the edge his army has over yours." She lifted her shoulders in an exaggerated shrug. "Wouldn't it be such a shame if something happened to them?"

"The greatest shame," Rosier echoed.

"And since I cannot personally go there and set the explosives, why not my new friends, who are already down here to salvage their little ritual?" she continued, gesturing with her fork. "Destroy those weapons, and do us both a favor. Deal?" she flashed her teeth at Izell.

Izell sighed. "And in return?"

"You get your ring back, of course." Lilith turned her hand to make it catch the lights overhead. "Plus the assured knowledge that your people won't have their souls trapped and consumed by the weapons you destroy. Isn't that a good deal?"

"I think it's an excellent deal," Rosier purred.

"Rosier," she deadpanned.

"Yes, Your Most Dignified Majesty?"

"No one asked."

He rolled his eyes, stealing her drink to take a long sip.

"I'll even sweeten the deal, if you think you can handle a second task," Lilith said, ignoring him. "Bring me Lucifer's weapon, and I'll risk my limited fighting force in helping you."

Izell wasn't the only one who tensed at the offer. "How so?" she asked, forcing a guarded expression back on her face.

"Well, they're going to attack you regardless when the Veil fails." Lilith shrugged again. "If you give me his weapon, I will attack his army from behind. Now, isn't that an even better deal?"

Rosier's cheeks darkened as he restrained himself from answering.

Izell frowned. "This wasn't your original plan?"

"Why, no. I was going to have your people fight his and destroy the stragglers later." By Lilith's expression, it was all the same to her. "But I'm also of the impression that Hell is better off with no meddling. We don't belong on Earth or Faerie just as much as you don't belong here."

Jaromir nodded slowly. No one had truly had up-to-date information to share with them to help on this mission due to how closed off Hell was. It made him wonder where angels and demons met each other in combat, but that wasn't important at the moment.

"Can we have a moment alone to discuss?" Izell said.

"No," she replied crisply. "Decide now. I'm not moving, and you're not leaving until I know if we're allies or not."

Sissaron cleared his throat. "In summary, you are offering us two deals. The first is that you will return the Summer Key if we go down to Pride and destroy Lucifer's cache of soul-stealing weaponry. And the second is if we steal his personal weapon and give it to you, you'll help us during the fighting to come."

"That is what I said, yes."

"I, for one, would like to know about his weapon before we pledge anything," the scaled fae said.

Sondus spoke up next, "And I would like a guide who knows where these weapons are, plus the explosives you mentioned. We will not be fodder for a task we can't complete."

"All fair requests." She inclined her head toward Sissaron first. "His weapon is the original soul-stealing one, a corrupted Archangel's sword he's named Soulcleaver. If it's not on his person, it's in his bedroom in the heart of his personal chambers. It's the weapon that stole my wings, and I would love to shove it through his heart, but I understand if you cannot manage to take it. The cache is the more important target anyway."

Her attention went to Sondus next. "And you may have my explosives, plus the service of my best spy." She patted Rosier's thigh. "This man right here."

Jaromir barely restrained a sound of denial. Couldn't it be anyone but that incubus? Rosier posed proudly for more than one reason, a grin fixed on his face. "We're going to blow shit up!" he exclaimed.

Izell's disbelieving gaze flashed between the two demons. "Hey, don't look at me like that. I really am the best," Rosier protested. "Only Her Marvelous Majesty is a stronger lust demon than me."

"I...am prepared to agree to both deals," Izell said slowly, waiting for dissent amongst the group. Though Jaromir didn't like it, he didn't complain. If this was what they had to do to cripple the looming apocalypse, he would do it with a smile on his face.

Maybe if they were successful, it would change the doom and gloom Izell had witnessed in their immediate future.

His fae lover repeated both deals, adding a clause at the end that he thought was quite necessary. If any of this turned out to be a lie or betrayal, their agreement was completely null and void. Lilith agreed and finally stood, offering her hand. When Izell, expression conflicted, took it and shook, a burst of magic echoed between them. New lines inked into Izell's skin on her formerly unmarked hand and forearm, demonic runes burning to cherry-red life like a long stretch of jagged wounds that detailed the terms of their two deals. A twin of the same deal appeared on Lilith's flesh.

The moment they released their handshake, the new deal settled into what looked like red ink. Lilith rubbed her new marks, smiling to herself. "Yes, very good," she murmured. "All right, my new allies, it's late, and you lot must be tired. Rosier will show you to guest rooms."

Jaromir reared back in surprise. Rooms, here? He doubted he'd catch a moment of sleep, no matter his status as a "new ally."

Izell must've been thinking down the same lines. "That won't be—"

"I must insist," Lilith interrupted. "Souls tire easily here. Part of Hell's charm. Go sleep. Otherwise, you'll regret it with Lucifer and his lot breathing down your exhausted neck."

Rosier stood, flashing a smile full of charm. "How many rooms do we need? And whose bed needs me to warm it, hmm?" He waggled his brows.

Lilith scrubbed her face. "Forget it. I'll show you to your rooms. If you'll step into the hall, I have an incubus to tie up first." Rosier's face lit up, and Jaromir wasn't the only one leaving in haste.

Chapter 27

Izell

"This is made of magic too." Izell flung a throw pillow over her shoulder. "And this!"

"Is it safe to say everything is magic?" Jaromir asked from behind her. When she turned, she saw that he'd caught every piece of stray bedding she'd tossed aside in her inspection of their new room.

"I've never seen anything like this, Jaromir," she replied, thumping to the bed. The plush sheets absorbed her, far too soft for anything she'd assumed she'd find in Hell.

He rearranged their pillows and the heavy comforter she'd stripped off, lifting her by the hips to pull it under her. "Aren't *you* made of magic?" he asked.

"That's completely different. This"—she shook a lacy doily—"is made from a tiny piece of someone's soul. As is this bed. As is the electricity in the walls. And the rugs on the floor. And..." She waved toward a still-steaming platter of food a scantily clad server had brought them. "That's not. But it was prepared in a kitchen made with soul energy."

He glanced that way. "So, it's safe to eat the food?"

"I don't know. I wouldn't." She didn't know if their souls needed sustenance, but her rumbling belly told her the answer was yes.

Jaromir gave the bowls a longing glance but didn't head over to eat anything either.

"It's Hell. I didn't think any comfort lived here," he admitted, sitting next to her instead. She leaned against his side when he placed an arm around her hips. "Are you implying that someone's soul was stripped into pieces and turned into all the things in this room?"

"Gods, no. At least, I hope not," she muttered. "My understanding of things down here is that souls come in with excess energy, and it can be harvested to transform any soul into a demon or be used as a power source. Naturally, we don't know everything about the process or how soul energy is used." She gestured to their surroundings.

Their guest room was a suite with many of the amenities they'd noticed in Lilith's chambers. It was, Izell had to admit, eerie to see her expectations subverted in such a way. These demons didn't live in stone huts, eating human skins, like she'd expected. At least not on the Lust level. They didn't have poison pools and servitor demons like the blight creature they'd caught and interrogated in Faerie.

The group had split between three rooms. Even now, she could sense Queldian's amusement, as he'd been placed in a room with Sondus. Their spymaster was the only one who'd wanted to keep a demon around. To ask questions, of course. Apparently, *many* questions. Her dragon fed her any tidbits of useful information gleaned from this.

"It seems useful," Jaromir ventured. "Maybe angels do the same thing. There are even less resources high in the sky, rather than deep in the earth."

Her reply was stolen on a long, jaw-cracking yawn. Shaking her head, she stood, dragging herself before the mirror she'd spotted as part of the en suite bathroom. *Holy gods above,* she looked awful. No, that wasn't the right descriptor. Strange. Different. She hadn't stopped to view herself as the astral fae revealed when Queldian's scales were pulled away.

It wasn't that she hated her old appearance. It just wasn't her anymore. She'd been half-dragon, an oddity, for so long that it was normal to her to have scales and claws, plus a tail that always seemed to show her true feelings. That version of her was strong and in control, while her true self was...weak.

She'd been on a collision course with this realization from the moment she'd been tricked by Sondus and had Jazrach's demonic essence stolen from her. She was neither strong nor in control anymore. In this place of demons and unfamiliar soul magic, she was now a living pawn in the ongoing war between Lilith and her dire enemy, Lucifer. Worse still, she'd dragged others along for the ride.

No, they dragged themselves along, she thought, casting a glance back at Jaromir, who was now reclining on the mountain of pillows he'd heaped on his side of the bed.

She looked back at her reflection, loosing a sigh. With her days numbered and her hours rationed, she was truly standing before a mirror moping? She flicked her fingers through an illusion spell, casting a new glamor over herself. It coated her head to toe in golden dust before scales replaced the pacts marking both her arms and a tail slowly uncoiled. At first, her tail flicked in agitation before she inspected herself anew in the mirror and gave an approving nod.

If it helped so much to be a dragon shifter, then she'd be a dragon shifter. She felt more confident already.

Jaromir sat up, blinking at her. She showed her fangs in a smile and sauntered over. "I missed it," she said simply.

As she straddled his hips and leaned down to steal a kiss, he replied, "I missed this. But I also didn't think we'd have another moment alone down here."

"Let's make the most of it." She was already finding the little buttons on his shirt, working them free one at a time. He watched her with eyes shining like liquid gold, soot marks staining one cheek from their time outside. Wetting her thumb, she brushed the ash away, and he leaned into the simple caress.

No matter what happened next, no one could take this moment away from her. Jaromir didn't look at her like she was an oddity or weak. He cupped her face and drew her close, and she lost herself in him. He was her world while they entwined in the most intimate of dances.

Lilith had implied that their souls would tire easily here in Hell, and Izell felt it after a couple short hours in Jaromir's arms. She sprawled out atop him, his shoulder the most comfortable pillow in the room. Her heart felt full, the cracks mended by Jaromir's presence. It became something she couldn't deny and also couldn't keep to herself.

Yet just this once, he beat her to the punch. "I love you, you crazy fae," he whispered over her hair. He tilted her head up to press a kiss to her slack lips, a proud smile crossing his face at her reaction.

"I'm losing my edge. I was just about to say... I mean..." she stammered. "I love you too."

He smoothed a hand down her back, still looking all too pleased with himself. As un-Jaromir as it was for him to be smug, when he said, "I've known for a while. Just thought you needed to hear it back," it was delivered with his quiet perception. She released a soft laugh, on the verge of tears. But it felt like she cried in front of him far too much, so this time, she tamped it back with effort.

"I also think you handled Lilith well. None of us were expecting what we found down here, and I think you saved us from certain death by making a deal with her," he continued.

While she soaked in his words, she also frowned to herself. "You don't think she's playing us?"

"It's foolish to trust a demon...but you seemed to find something in her that was trustworthy?"

Her empathy. Izell had all five virtues but barely used them except for the future sight she'd given away. When she was part dragon, she didn't really care what others around her were feeling, so she'd let it wither to a husk that occasionally whispered its insight to her. She'd sensed a hint of sincerity from Lilith, that she really *was* happy to see their group in her personal quarters.

"Indeed. I believe if we are useful to Lilith, she is willing to work with us. By crippling Lucifer, we also help her, and something tells me we're about to deal a blow to him that she's wanted for a long time." She tilted her head thoughtfully. "However, I will be glad when the Veil is back in place, to lock Lilith and the rest of the merry band of demons here forever. An ally today can be an enemy tomorrow."

"Tomorrow, still an ally. Much as I don't want to work with Rosier." He sighed, lying back into his pillows.

She scoffed. "I'll handle Rosier. He has to have some useful talents, as an Original."

"Like flirting?" he grumbled. "He'd better not try with you. I swear I'll punch him."

Izell settled atop him again, getting comfortable while hiding a pleased grin. Seems she was rubbing off on him at last. "Such violence."

He opened and closed his mouth a couple times, his turn to be flustered.

"It's pretty hot. Show me your possessive side," she said with a wink.

He snuggled her to his chest. "Sleep first. I'm sure you'll see it tomorrow." Something told her she'd see many new things tomorrow in the Pride level of Hell. But a possessive Jaromir was the only thing she *wanted* to see.

Chapter 28
Gwendolyn

The pits and valleys of Gwendolyn's long life were full of wasted time. She had gained the patience to wait but not to waste away doing so. While she'd joined a caravan of fae and shifters heading back to Earth, she'd busied her time prepping herbs and other ingredients for her daughter's potions, should they be needed. It gave her purpose, and she found her own meaning from that.

Her powers were needed. Cossette had set the alarm—they had to move vast quantities of people and equipment within days. The albino Ancient herself met Gwendolyn at Coven Rehnquist's manor headquarters, helping her both time and place her portals. While her shaking, thin hands had struggled with the task of stripping leaves and crushing stems, they channeled the power of the Portal Key without so much as a quiver.

"Will it really be two days?" she asked Cossette as they watched the newest team carrying sheets of dragon-forged glass between two portals she kept open with either hand.

The Ancient kept her hands in her pockets, a sense of peace about her fine-boned face and solemn, red eyes. "For better or worse, it will all be over two nights from now. You and I will both need to be there to make sure the new Dark Eye is made successfully."

"Of course," she murmured. They'd talked in depth about the coming ritual and the sacrifice that would need to be made to successfully lock a demon's essence into the giant ball of dragon-forged glass that would assemble around it. Turned out, everything except the glass was a decoration created by the fae generations ago. The symbols of magic, the beautiful base and supports that allowed the Eye to spin and create portals with the power to pierce the Veil, all of it optional.

All they needed was a prison, a sacrifice, and a demon, so they worked toward assembling those things together.

"Nyah will be arriving soon. Why don't you take a break?" Cossette offered.

She couldn't help but brighten at the news. Any word of her precious daughter did just that, even months after their miraculous reunion. "How long can you spare me?" she asked, already forming ideas.

Cossette shrugged. "Once we get all of the glass transported to Nyixa, I think you could have the rest of the night. There's no place for anyone to sleep over there, so we'll need you to save your magic anyway."

She nodded, seeing the wisdom of that. The covens were finding places to host the fae and shifters willing to help them fight. The night of, she'd be making portals left and right to transport everyone to Nyixa in time. She knew the numbers and tried not to let them frighten her—more help would be coming, as the Unseelie army would be arriving straight from Faerie, and the warrior angels would rain down from above.

"Then let's finish up, and I'll see you tomorrow," Gwendolyn said.

Cossette nodded, rocking back on her heels. "I think you'll find the details of the ritual fascinating. We're really in a golden age of understanding fae magic and where we fit in it."

"All I care about is that it's successful." She'd lived too long protecting a delicate balance to see it smashed by a demonic invasion.

The albino Ancient smiled to herself. "And I see about four different variations on success in our future."

"How many times do you see failure?"

It was perfectly timed for Cossette to glance over and gesture. "Ah, there's our last batch of shifters." Emerging from the portal linking to the manor was Adrius in all his scaled glory, escorting Nyah on his arm.

Her girl glowed with health and a vibrancy only held during pregnancy. She rested a hand over the swell of her belly as she squinted around. Her golden nephilim eyes landed on Gwendolyn, and she rushed forward, the two of them entangling in a hug.

"Hello, Mother. You beat us here." Nyah giggled, drawing back to look her over. The same concern as always pinched her brow, because the ravages of time had not lessened Gwendolyn's burden since the last time their paths crossed.

No one said it aloud, but it was whispered behind hands, passed from ear to ear. Nyah had to understand it, like everyone else. Without vampirism, Gwendolyn's body struggled. Still, she smiled and patted her daughter's cheek, if only to get that expression to leave.

"I'm just the portal person today. Let me get your group to their temporary housing..." She drifted off to count upward of twenty people, with many faces she recognized as shifter nobility in attendance. Coordinating with Cossette, they found room for them elsewhere in Coven Rehnquist's now-massive territory and gave them a portal there, leaving Adrius and Nyah their guest room here in the manor.

"That's everything?" she confirmed with the Ancient.

"Yup. Go have fun!"

Gwendolyn turned an eager look her daughter's way. Adrius was in the process of dragging their luggage up the stairs, giving them a moment alone. "Would you like to see some of New York before you retire for the day?" she invited.

Her daughter's face brightened. "I've been meaning to! Do you think anyone would miss us for a little bit?"

"Better than wasting time waiting," Gwendolyn answered honestly. She'd rather have a distraction to keep her thoughts away from the looming battle, as there was little left to do except micromanage people and resources.

But she had a more fun idea, and for Gwendolyn, "fun" was usually an elusive concept.

"Are you hungry?" she asked.

Within minutes, they were bundled up against the cold, and she was making a personal-sized portal to take them to her favorite pizzeria. They emerged in the shadows between two buildings, where no one would suspect two women had just appeared out of nowhere. "I think it's absolutely criminal your people did not have pizza in Adrun," she announced.

Nyah flashed a smile, her nostrils flaring when they walked inside and were caressed by the scent of warm pizza sauce and oregano. "Ooh, this place smells heavenly," she said quietly.

"I couldn't let you live without it." Gwendolyn waved to the pair of vampires who ran this shop twenty-four-seven, slinging pies for customers of all sorts. They didn't even give Nyah a second glance when she approached the glass still wearing her crown, which Gwendolyn had overlooked.

She spoke quietly as she explained the toppings on the pre-prepared slices while the vampire workers busied themselves with prepping and firing new orders. They were probably listening... Maybe they'd even met people before that didn't know what pizza was. Nyah wasn't self-conscious until Gwendolyn worked the crown off her head and tossed it into a small portal she hid under the counter.

A muffled "ouch" sounded from Adrius on the other side, prompting them to giggle together as Gwendolyn closed it quickly.

They ate together, overlooking a quiet night, watching a few mortals walk by a streetlight right outside the window. By unspoken agreement, they didn't talk about demons, or Faerie, or anything else relating to their crazy adventures. They were just a mother and daughter sharing a meal together.

How Nyah's face shone the moment she tasted pizza for the first time! "This is so greasy it can't be healthy," she said, delighted.

Gwendolyn laughed. "That's why mortals like it so much."

"The world's changed so much," Nyah said after a few more bites. She glanced down at her belly. "I know my son will grow up with all of this being completely normal. Cars, electricity... sunlight." Her lips quirked with humor. "Pizza. I hope wherever Adrius and I settle, we have 'shopping centers' and quality schools to fulfill his every need."

"I'm sure you both will make the best place for him," Gwendolyn replied.

Nyah blushed, the apples of her cheeks dusting with gold. "Aww. I hope so. Have I told you that I think we've finally agreed on his name?"

"No, do tell."

"Gabriel Raphael Fabron." A glimmer of light flashed from her smile. "I wanted to honor Father, and Adrius really wanted to do something nice for Sirius, so we borrowed his middle name."

The corners of Gwendolyn's eyes stung, and she covered her mouth with her fingertips.

"Do you like it?" Nyah asked more hesitantly, seeing that reaction.

"Of course, sweet girl. I love it. As will your father when he hears the news," she said. Gabriel was a hero's name and more than fitting as a namesake for the future Prince of Adrun. "And Sirius...if he doesn't already know."

"Oh, he knows." She rolled her eyes with a fond smile. "He didn't like it at first, but he was just being humble. He and Talina already volunteered to be the godparents too, but I don't know..."

Her lips quirked as she pushed away her empty plate. "I was hoping to ask Izell."

Gwendolyn cleared her throat. They were uncomfortably close to talking about the future and the uncertainty to come. "There's something else I want to show you," she said.

She'd gotten so used to Faerie's bright autumn that she'd nearly forgotten it was December on Earth, and this time of year meant decorations and light displays on around the clock. They drew their scarves up, and Gwendolyn buttoned up her heavy coat, determined to show her how Christmas was celebrated by modern mortals.

It was a beautiful night with her only daughter, a glimmer of brightness against the darkness of what lay ahead of them. Gwendolyn didn't let her thoughts taint any moment of it, even though she... Well, she wasn't ready to give voice to a new idea yet, lest it get affected by her family's good intentions.

Chapter 29
Izell

Sondus changed the illusion over her again. Rosier clicked his tongue. "You aren't even going to fool their imps," he scoffed.

Izell shot an impatient glance toward Jaromir, who was busy eyeing the basket of muffins Rosier had brought them to snack on. Except no one was eating. Lining the couch next to her love were Lyana and Sissaron, his arm slung over her shoulders while she fought off another yawn. Queldian sat on the floor close to Jaromir, his head resting on the man's knee as he watched the demon in the room with unerring intensity.

"How is it possible Lust has two types of demons and Pride has *sixteen*?" Sondus asked, tossing up his hands. This was the fourth he'd tried before Rosier got too impatient and steered him toward a different illusion that was "much easier" than the last.

"That's just how it is, hot stuff," Rosier purred. "We can try something else, and if you get it right, I will—"

"No," Sondus replied sharply.

"—be very happy with you," the incubus finished.

Sondus shifted uncomfortably. "I, ah, would like to finish with this one. It's not as ugly as the rest," he said. Izell hadn't seen him flustered like this in a while and smiled to herself under the monstrous glamor laid over her skin.

"Well, what do you expect? Not everyone can look as beautiful as a lust demon." Rosier stroked his jaw and neck, giving the fae bedroom eyes. Sondus studiously tried not to look his way.

Izell felt the subtle shifts happening within the glamor as he tinkered with it. They were currently making her a demon of plunder, a lithe beast with an extra pair of arms and jagged spikes lining her spine. Since this was apparently a rare sub-type of Pride demons, representing souls that had violently stolen what didn't belong to them in life, she would be the only one wearing this glamor.

She would've assumed this type of demon lived in Greed, but it turned out Pride intercepted the most powerful souls of all seven deadly sins. It explained a lot...though neither Lilith nor Rosier would admit that they were having their resources choked by the most powerful Lord of Hell, who could make power grabs of the sort.

Suitably uglied up, though, she stood to the side and watched as Rosier guided Sondus through a different glamor, this one applied to Queldian. "Lucifer likes to keep mixed groups of soldiers," the incubus explained. "Each type of demon has a specific strength and weakness and has a higher chance of nailing the fears of any enemies they encounter."

"Great. What will be expected of us?" Izell asked, posing with hands on hips. All four of her illusioned arms made the same motion. *Weird,* she thought. She practiced moving them independently so she wouldn't be caught as an imposter.

"Just look ugly, dearie. We'll be walking right through their camp in broad—well, daylight is your word for it." He chuckled and lifted a shoulder. "Pride has these rivers of lava everywhere, so there's no night to speak of down there."

"What is this great plan you apparently have?" Izell asked, crossing both sets of illusioned arms.

Rosier's smile turned wicked. "Simple but effective. Once we all look the part, myself included, we will become just a few more demons gearing up for war. Lucifer's artificers are stockpiling the weapons right now after making sure they work as intended. It's heavily guarded, but we're setting charges on a long timer. It's not rocket science.

"We've noticed that the weapons store souls in the red crystals. We didn't get to steal more than a couple, but each time we damaged the crystals even a little bit, the magic leaked out of them...and they also shatter themselves further. So, our goal is to create enough of a disruption to crack those crystals. We're lucky they're prototypes, and unstable ones at that."

"You're sure you weren't allowed to steal defective crystals?" Sissaron interrupted.

Rosier clicked his tongue. "I wasn't *allowed* to do anything. I take things from Pride all the time. It's my talent. If I didn't want you to know that I was here, you wouldn't see me."

Sissaron made a sound of disbelief, and that's when the incubus disappeared. A confused murmur drifted from Izell's throat.

"Don't touch me," the scaled man hissed, pushing at the air in front of him. Rosier rippled back into existence, his head thrown back on a laugh where he stood inches from the couch.

"Soul interference. Only another Original can sense it," the incubus said, lifting his chin. "But to any little souls, I can be completely invisible. I prefer, however, to go unheard." His hooves clopped on the hardwood flooring as he crossed back to Sondus's side before even that sound disappeared.

Izell nodded in understanding. No wonder he'd been able to sneak up on them. She'd thought Rosier had to have some talent, as he didn't seem to be much of a fighter. Why be big and bulky when one could become invisible at will? He could be deadly without trying.

"So, you could go set these charges and destroy these weapons yourself," Sissaron stated, his expression tightening to a severe line. "Yet you and your mistress insisted on including us."

Rosier's grin didn't fade. "Let's get something straight. I said another Original can sense my tricks, and Pride has the biggest collection of Originals with their own scary soul manipulations. I've always gotten caught within a couple hours. However!" He held up a finger before pointing it at Sondus. "Combine my soul interference with this guy's mind, and that's where we're deadly. He overcomes my weakness by distracting their minds, and I make sure they don't sense that most of your souls are both alive *and* fae."

She didn't miss the flicker of disgust the incubus shot Jaromir.

"As I was saying, once we set the charges, we can set them to explode when we're well away from the cache. I happen to know where the crystals are manufactured, and it's in the palace. If you don't want them replacing what we destroy, we can hit that location next. Easy as tossing a bomb inside and shutting the door," Rosier said.

Izell set her teeth. While he had a point about more soul-stealing weapons being made, they hadn't agreed to hit a second place, and she doubted it would be as easy as he suggested.

"And after *that*, we can be assured that Lucifer himself will grab Soulcleaver and take a gander outside, looking for us trouble-makers." The incubus stroked his bottom lip, obviously proud of his plan and the mayhem he wanted to cause. "We go to his chambers, cast the strongest spells we have to evade notice, and wait. He'll eventually come back and put the sword down, and that's when we disappear with it."

Jaromir was the first to speak up with a hesitant, "I don't know about that."

"We have to at least try," the incubus scoffed. "You don't want me to tell Her Incomparable Majesty that you chickened out of even trying to get Soulcleaver, do you?"

"Even Lilith acknowledged it's unlikely we'll be unable to get it. It's hopeful wishing on her part," Jaromir argued. "A stretch goal, you could say."

Rosier's amber eyes flared with unearthly light, his fangs bared as he hissed, "Look, nephilim, this is the first time I've ever had a chance at holding Soulcleaver. You have no idea what it'd mean to her if we put it in her hands."

"I agree with Jaromir," Izell said loudly. "We have to see the situation first and decide from there. If the choice is between even one of our lives or Soulcleaver, I will pick the life every time."

Heads nodded around the room until Rosier drew himself back up, tails flicking behind him. "Fine. But there is my plan. I'll give you the exact space to drop us into Pride." He gestured to the square of fabric on Jaromir's hip, which held the glass teleporter.

"I'm taking us down there?" Jaromir asked, eyes widening.

"You all got your explosives and a guide," Rosier sniffed. "We're using your invasion device."

Jaromir's teeth set on edge, and his gaze found Izell's, raising an eyebrow with meaning. *Are you sure we trust this guy?* was written clearly on his expression.

"What you're saying is you have no teleporters that link Lust and Pride," Izell said, drawing the incubus's attention back to her. "Just how long have you been at war?"

Rosier stroked his lip, quickly transitioning back to coy as he eyed her. Not much to see, really, with the demon glamor, unless he could see beneath it to her soul. "Ever consider being a demon? You're sharp. And Lust is the best level to belong to," he purred.

"That doesn't answer my question," she said in a low voice. She toyed with a lock of her hair; anyone but Jaromir would suspect she was flirting back.

He rolled his eyes, apparently not buying it. "Lucifer used to own all of Hell. He's the leader of the Originals, but one by one, the Archdemons have died and been replaced by Lords or Ladies of Hell who are more interested in carving out their own slice of anti-paradise. Pride lost its hold on Lust the moment Lilith chopped off Asmodeus's head and mounted it on her throne. It's been war ever since. We're talking thousands of years or three moments. There's not much difference down here. Time passes like cold molasses anyway." He murmured that last part with a touch of bitterness.

"And for the record, we disabled the teleporters to make Pride demons climb all the way up here if they want their necks chopped by glorious Queen Lilith. If I want to go down there, I use the tunnels." He rolled his eyes. "*So* annoying. Are we done with this history lesson? We have shit to blow up."

"Just a couple more illusions," Sondus muttered.

"Oh, right. Let's do a corruption one ne—"

"No!" shouted half the room, startling the incubus.

"No more corruption demons," Izell muttered.

Rosier recovered quickly, at least. "Ooh, this sounds like a juicy story. Why don't you spill?" he cooed.

He coordinated with Sondus to give Lyana a demonic illusion next—thankfully not a corruption demon.

"Do the names Jazrach or Lucia mean anything to you?" Izell asked.

"Actually, yes. Jazrach got smashed into atoms and turned into your precious Dark Eye."

"Atoms?" Queldian whispered to Jaromir, who shrugged.

"C'mon. Basic science? No?" Rosier laughed at their expense. "I guess not everyone can get knowledge the demon way."

She pondered whether to ask what "the demon way" was and decided against it.

Rosier clicked his tongue. "That guy was a mess. Got into Heaven and had his wings plucked off by one of the Archdemons. He was real pretty before he started growing mouths all over. Could've been an incubus, but alas, he thought whispering was more fun. Who am I to judge? Lilith let me lick her toes last night. That's my kind of fun—"

"What about Lucia?" Lyana interrupted. Her illusioned demon face was inflexible, but Izell caught the distinct note of interest in the question.

His smile turned sly. "Why? What's she to you? Give a guy some gossip."

Her hands balled into fists. "She's the bitch who used me like a puppet in her bid to take over Faerie. I *know* she's down here somewhere. Do you know where?"

Rosier wet his lips. "Gods, that's hot. Revenge is my favorite kink. How much is this information worth to you?"

"Lyana," Izell said warily.

The other woman didn't even flinch. "I'll get the sword if you help me make her suffer."

"Is that a deal?" the incubus purred.

Izell stepped forward. "Listen to yourself right now."

Lyana only looked at one other person in the room, her gaze on Sissaron's determined face. "It's a deal," she said.

They didn't shake hands, but a single rune sizzled into being on the back of Rosier and Lyana's hands. Izell hissed, seeing red. How could Lyana have stumbled into such an easy trap? She hadn't agreed to this just for herself—she'd dragged the whole team into it just to keep her safe. No one but Rosier truly looked happy in that moment as the weight of the deal settled in.

"Well, well." Rosier grinned. "We all felt it when Lucia's soul fell into Hell. It was big and bold, ancient and *vibrant* with power. Any demon worth more than half a damn wanted a piece of her, but her sins were so great she fell all the way to Pride without stopping. Lucifer himself made the deal to shoot her right back into her body." He traced a path downward slowly with his finger as he spoke before rocketing it back up.

"So, of course, we felt it the *second* time she died and fell, again, all the way to Pride. You're in luck, fae babe. We were going right to your obsession all along."

Izell cursed Lyana under her breath.

Chapter 30
Jaromir

Before they left to Pride, Sondus slowly wove their mental connection, starting with Jaromir, Izell, and Queldian. The moment Izell confirmed who was on the link with her, she burst out with, *"Let's just make this as hard as possible!"* Fury lived in her demonic illusion's eyes, centered on the water fae pointedly ignoring everyone but Sissaron.

"The second deal is worth securing," Sondus said, putting his palms up.

"Please. Did you really think we were about to taunt Lucifer and give Lilith a stable weapon able to steal souls?" Izell snarled.

"We will have to now," Jaromir said. He wasn't much happier than Izell, but he saw that they were cornered by the wording of Lyana's deal.

Actually...

He breathed a sigh of relief. *"She never specified which sword."*

She'd said, "the sword," and that was all the ambiguity in the world when it came to a deal. Izell herself had taught him that, since fae lived and died by their deals.

Izell didn't relax, her expression fixed in fury. *"She may not have said Soulcleaver, but we have to at least try to get it, lest he decide to go invisible and slit our throats for tricking him. Gods damned Lyana. I knew we shouldn't have brought her here."*

They stood in awkward silence until Sondus added Sissaron and Lyana to their mental link, followed by Rosier. *"It'll be okay,"* Queldian said neutrally, going over to brush against Izell.

"Well, isn't this the neatest thing," the incubus said in their minds a moment later. *"I'll go get the explosives, then off we go!"*

The moment he was gone, Izell rounded on Lyana. "Cyranos will have our asses if you get yourself killed. What were you thinking?" she asked between clenched teeth.

Meanwhile, Rosier chattered away on their mental link. Jaromir could see why Lilith kept telling him to shut up.

Lyana stepped up into her face. "Let me worry about myself. Besides"—she yanked Izell's arm up, exposing the dormant deal beneath as she stripped away the glamor over it—"you owe me one."

Izell pulled out of her hold. "I owed you when you demanded to come down here. *That* was the trespass I agreed to pay. *That* is how we've made ourselves even. How dare you make a deal that endangers all of us!"

Magic crackled between them, drawing goosebumps up Jaromir's arms. He jumped to his feet, putting himself between the two women before one of them lashed out. "Ladies, please." Static rose from Izell's form, while crackles of ice coated Lyana's fists. "We've all suffered because of Lucia. It's only natural to want revenge for what she's done."

"That's right," Lyana hissed, leaning around him to stab a finger at Izell.

"However, our mission is much bigger than any one of us." He wished he had Soren's command of calming magic at this moment as he watched Lyana draw herself up. "We have to be prepared to let Lucia live on down here if punishing her interferes with our mission. Can you do that?"

Lyana wouldn't meet his eye, so he looked toward Sissaron. He may be a deceased dragon spirit, but he'd experienced demonic possession alongside Lyana. If anyone understood her pride the most, it was him. His expression was resigned rather than furious, acknowledging the silent question in Jaromir's look with a nod.

"Revenge is hollow, Lennie," the sea serpent said. "You can't keep blaming Izell for what happened to us. Eventually, you have to acknowledge that it was bad timing that Lucia found us and decided you would make a good host."

"You too, huh?" Lyana said under her breath. Pain brimmed in her expressive fae eyes. "It's done. What Lucia did to me, I mean, and the deal. You can't stop it now, none of you can. I will have my revenge, and we will have our advantage when Hell comes knocking." She took a step away, turning her back pointedly on the whole group.

Izell crossed her arms and ground her teeth. She leaned into Jaromir's hold when he put his arms around her. Silence fell over their group as the moments ticked by.

"*Hello? Is this magic working?*" Rosier interrupted. No one had been replying to his mindless chatter.

"*We can hear you,*" Sondus sighed.

The incubus burst into the room, carrying four wooden boxes that stacked up over his head. "Got 'em!" he exclaimed.

The top box wobbled the most as he walked in balancing his precarious load. He tossed them to the ground unceremoniously, leaving Jaromir just enough time to shout in alarm.

Nothing exploded.

Rosier laughed heartily. "Got you! Don't worry, this shit doesn't go off unless it's exposed to a soul flame." He flicked his finger against his thumb, lighting a single flame that burned an eerie white-gray on the tip of a claw. "It's condensed soul matter, very unstable under the right circumstances. If the concussion doesn't shatter their soul weapons, then the influx of all this combusting matter will. Questions?"

He waited half a second. "Of course you have questions, but we don't have time for more interrogation. Let's go." He beckoned to Jaromir, slinging an arm over his shoulders when he parted from Izell. "Hey, buddy. I brought you a map so you know exactly where to drop us."

In his distraction over the explosives, Jaromir was just realizing that Rosier had finally found a shirt to cover his lean chest. Out of its breast pocket, the incubus pulled out a square of aged paper and unfolded it. Jaggedly torn out of a book, it read "Pride" in a cursive script at the top. The Pride level of Hell was vaguely rectangular, sloping downward toward a vast lake of liquid fire. What looked like rivers were actually, he assumed, endless lava flows.

"Are these...homes?" Jaromir asked in disbelief. The seat of Lucifer's power, his palace, appeared to be surrounded by them.

Rosier clicked his tongue. "Yeah. He has enough excess soul energy to power a whole village. Isn't that insane?"

He had the distinct feeling that he and the incubus had different definitions of how "insane" that was.

"I mean, he regularly ashes sinners to gather up their energy quickly. We use more humane methods," Rosier continued.

"I don't want to know any more about it," Jaromir muttered.

The incubus chuckled, pointing out an area that looked like empty plains. "Here's where we're going. Pride's army has an encampment here, and at its heart are the weapons. We're going to be semi-invisible between our combined mind and soul magic, plus those unsightly illusions you're wearing. Remember, the goal is to set the charges without detection. I'll flick the soul flame, and we head to the palace from there. I'll make sure the explosives give us maybe ten minutes."

"Sounds too simple," Jaromir murmured. But if they pulled it off, it would change the tide of the coming battle. He had to think this was the moment they curtailed the coming apocalypse if their infighting didn't ruin it.

Ignoring him, the incubus pointed a claw toward an area south of the plains, where the lava rivers began in earnest. "Not even Lucifer's best scouts will expect us to show up from this direction. Think you can teleport us here?"

When they'd come to Lust, Jaromir had only had a map, much like this. They'd ended up in the place he intended for them to go, yet they hadn't known it due to the oppressive smoke hanging over everything. "I'm confident I can get us there. And the visibility is better?"

Rosier rolled his eyes. "Stinks like an asshole, but yes. Lava literally everywhere."

Jaromir reluctantly pulled out the glass disc, which glimmered the moment he fit his finger through its hollow center. As unpleasant as he found Rosier, he knew the Pride level was a new level of hostile. He looked around at the faces coming in to touch his arms so they could be caught by the teleportation magic.

Well, he imagined their faces. His team looked like a pack of demons, but he knew Izell was still furious and terrified in equal proportions under her glamor. Queldian rumbled and pressed against her for comfort. Sondus's fingers trembled ever so slightly, his magic already taxing him to maintain their monstrous illusions.

Rosier laced his fingers through Jaromir's with a taunting wink while Lyana and Sissaron claimed their places at the same time. He wished he could speak with Lyana privately, seeing how her pain was an open wound she was letting fester. She didn't meet anyone's eye, not even Sissaron's as he placed a webbed hand on her shoulder and murmured into her ear.

Taking a deep breath, Jaromir focused on the Pride level and the place on the map that Rosier had pointed out. *Not into the lava,* he thought as the disc warmed, starting to spin on his finger of its own volition. *But a place where we won't be seen.*

For a heart-stopping moment, Jaromir ceased to exist. Darkness closed in like a blink, and just as quickly, his nostrils filled with the stench of concentrated sulfur.

Close by, Izell made a distinct gagging noise.

"Kinky," the incubus laughed.

"Don't make me hurt you," she muttered back. Jaromir rubbed his eyes, seeing that they were all present and standing over a lip of obsidian-colored rock. Several yards below rolled orange-red magma. Superheated steam curled up from its hissing surface, washing over them until they moved toward more solid ground.

Rosier mock-pouted. *"Aw, here I thought we were becoming friends."*

Jaromir resisted scoffing at that, his gaze continuing to rove and take in their surroundings. The glow off of the lava illuminated the fact that they were in a giant cave of sorts, smoke curling around stalactites thirty yards overhead like the teeth of a looming maw. He wondered if Lust would've looked similar if they'd had better lighting.

"This way, lovelies. No time like the present." Rosier turned and marched them away from the lava river. As he walked, a shimmer surrounded him like a heat mirage before jumping to the others one by one. In return, Sondus changed Rosier's appearance until he appeared to be a wingless incubus with a different face.

The ground sloped up as they walked. Jaromir picked up the sound of clashing weapons and hooting voices. His hand flashed to the hilt of his light-infused hammer, but he recognized a moment later that they were approaching a war encampment, where such things were not uncommon.

There were no fences or other demarcation to show they'd entered a camp. Just a winged demon standing guard, his many eyes roving over the plains and sky like he expected an attack at any moment. Despite that, none of his eight eyes fixed on their group as they walked right by him.

It's too simple, Jaromir thought uneasily. He kept his gaze on Rosier, expecting some trouble at any moment.

Chapter 31
Izell

Demons. Demons everywhere.

Izell struggled to act normal, since the whole plan hinged on them fitting in and evading notice. Sweat formed on her brow and dripped down her back from both the ambient heat of this lava-tinged plain and the exertion of holding up the illusions of the group. She and Lyana were both pitching in their magic to help Sondus, giving their Mindbender more breathing room to save his magic for when they needed it most.

Surrounding them was only one piece of the army set to invade soon. Izell figured there were several camps just like it, each with a cache of weapons—but perhaps Rosier's information was right and this was the real stockpile of soul-stealing weaponry.

"*How many weapons should we be expecting?*" she asked, realizing this was a vital question they'd missed asking earlier.

"*Less than you would expect,*" Rosier answered.

Her eyes narrowed. What was that supposed to mean?

He caught a glance of her scowling face. "*Far as we can tell, they're difficult to make. Like with any valuable weaponry, they're for the best fighters first,*" he continued. "*Which means as many of your people as possible will have their souls stolen unless we're successful.*" Though he had a point, she bristled at his sharp tone.

"We're not getting cold feet. She was just asking a question," Queldian said for her.

They slowed as a female voice bellowed for attention. The bustle of a busy camp came to a halt as eyes turned and feet shuffled toward a demoness sporting leathery bat wings and tarnished bronze armor she must've stripped from an angel. Unlike many of the demons they'd met, her skin was bone-white, but what really caught Izell's attention was the huge ruby affixed to the hilt of a black-steel sword she held over her head.

Several demons muttered "commander's call" as they gathered around her. *"Perfect. Let's give them the slip,"* Rosier said, walking the other direction as the growing crowd of demons.

Sondus groaned quietly. It couldn't be easy to divert the eyes of dozens from them as they went against the flow and away from the bellowing voice. Izell's heart flickered faster when she realized the demoness was beginning to instruct her people on the different kinds of Unseelie they'd be fighting.

She wanted to listen in further, but this moment really was perfect. With a good portion of the fighters distracted, they were able to cover more ground, weaving through a densely packed tent city covering miles of dusky, barren rock. They passed by a roaring flame with a hanging cauldron stirred by a stout creature. Its many eyes fastened on them.

Izell tensed until it looked back toward its task, poking a bubble that surfaced from the thick glop it tended. It wasn't the only stray demon they nearly tripped over. Packs of cackling imps drifted through the tent city, their attentive bat-like ears picking up the group's presence. Despite having Rosier's soul magic and Sondus's mind manipulations, they weren't invisible.

She was coated in nervous sweat by the time they spotted a building in the middle of all this. Winged figures stood on the flat roof. *"Go time. Lucifer's spared one of his Original lackeys for this,"* Rosier said, rubbing his hands together with a big, bloodlusting grin.

As they crept closer, Izell saw that one of the two demons keeping lookout on the roof had feathered wings. The other resembled a gargoyle, its stooped body composed of pockmarked stone. A third demon patrolled the immediate area, its purplish skin immediately recognizable by the slitted mouths crossing its arms and wings like open wounds.

"Corruption demon," she hissed.

If it was anything like Jazrach, it would sense their deepest secrets and use them against them. Dark mist rolled from the creature as it lumbered by, lapping against Rosier's cloak. It lifted its head, turning a face riddled with black veins in their direction. Curses rolled through the mind link as it pointed, shooting black mist over them. Sensing their weaknesses...and true identities.

Rosier shot into motion first. *"Fuck. Kill it. It's going to sound the alarm."*

He drew a pair of daggers from his sleeves, shooting one into the creature's throat as the rest of the group followed suit. It went down with a gurgle, the *thump* of its body hitting the ground as loud as an earthquake.

"You there!" shouted a gravelly voice from the building's roof. The gargoyle pointed a carved claw directly at the incubus twisting the knife to make sure the corruption demon wouldn't utter a peep of what it'd sensed.

Rosier righted himself, flicking black blood from his glove. "Me? You didn't see me," he said, staring the other demon in the eye.

"You didn't see him," Sondus echoed, staring directly at the gargoyle and the angel-like Original who was starting to draw the weapon strung over his shoulder. Magic hummed in the air between them.

The gargoyle's face started to go slack. Izell breathed a sigh of relief.

Then, the Original shoved his companion, scowling down at them with fire visibly flickering over his burnt-black wings. "Nice try, *Rosier*. You're dead, whore!" Nearly faster than the eye could track, he leapt from the roof and unsheathed a broadsword made of black metal. Its sharp edge caught fire, turning into an inferno as the Original slammed it to the rock where Rosier had been standing.

Scrambling, the gargoyle picked up a curved horn from the

rooftop. Izell aimed a crack of lightning at him as he put the mouthpiece to his lips. He grinned, not to be deterred by the element crackling harmlessly over his stone skin. He sounded the alarm, shaking the stone around them with the horn's deep resonance.

"Set the charges! I'll handle these guys," Rosier ordered.

He didn't have to tell Izell twice. She rushed to the building's door, which was padlocked with heavy, black chains. The gargoyle dropped to the stone in front of her, towering at nearly eight feet tall even with the slump in his shoulders. His eager grin turned to shock as Sissaron barreled over, lifting his form with a labored grunt and tossing him away.

Izell whispered words of power over the padlock, summoning shafts of colored magic to enter the lock and jiggle its inner workings. She didn't dare look over her shoulder, even though she could hear the Original screaming in outrage and the crackle of ice as Lyana assisted in fighting off the gargoyle.

Queldian stood behind her, his real form exposed so Jaromir could start unloading the crates they'd tied to her dragon's back for transport. Rosier had taught them all how to set the explosive charges, but she couldn't remember a damn thing as she frantically pulled on the lock until her magic snapped it open. Chains fell, and she yanked on the ring handle of the door, discovering that it was much thicker than expected. The walls and roof as well. Though the building stood at a decent height for the average person, inside, she had to stoop for a four-foot-high clearance.

"You go inside. Set the charges," she ordered Jaromir, trading places with him. She busted the crates open, sending wood shards everywhere in her haste to remove the bricks of explosive material inside. Each left an oily coating on her palms, goosebumps creeping up her arms at the sensation. Jaromir ducked inside, leaving behind long fuses as close to the doorway as he could.

They were running out of time. Wings approached rapidly, ahead of a dust cloud of running demons.

"We need your fire, Rosier!" she shouted. *"Light the explosives!"*

No response came. They'd set out two crates worth of explosives, and Izell chucked one of the intact ones after it for good measure. She whipped her head around, discovering that Sissaron and Lyana had frozen the gargoyle in a tomb of thick ice, while Rosier and the Original he'd been fighting were circling in the sky. Except as she watched, a flash of flame preceded Rosier's plummet toward the ground.

Queldian chuffed, gone before she even had the thought. He stretched out his long neck, taking flight in a flash of sandstone scales. It wasn't until she glanced to her side that she realized Jaromir had gone with him.

"*Where's Sondus?*" Lyana asked.

Izell realized he'd been lost in the melee but found their Mindbender slumped on the ground, a burnt wound cauterizing the side of his head. His heart was still beating ever so faintly at his wrist. "*Hey, demigoddess. Help me,*" she snapped.

"*The flying demons are here,*" Sissaron reported. Izell could hear the beating of their wings and realized they needed a miracle.

She retrieved the golden occultarus from its pouch at her belt. It crackled with energy as she reached inside for the essence of the gods. The moment three of the four gods had blessed her felt like an eternity ago, but the blessing of Zalice leapt to life the instant her magic called his from the occultarus.

His crackling voice echoed in her ears. "*We are with you, Izell.*" Wind roared from the occultarus, taking a life of its own that she just pointed in the right direction. It assumed the dark gray shadow of a skyrider with wings outspread, its scream the shriek of gale-force winds. Izell spotted the white-skinned demoness a split second before she was swatted through the air like a meddlesome fly. Tents went airborne as the force of Zalice's magic narrowed to a funnel of air that kept their enemies at bay for the precious time they needed.

Sondus's voice was a hazy murmur behind her. Izell felt the chill of Lyana's magic as she worked a healing spell on him. While not as strong as Jaromir's attentions would've been, she knew she could trust the other Sorceress to take care of him as she focused her attentions on maintaining the wind.

Except Zalice's influence drew her to close her eyes and look at something else with her magical senses. As she channeled her spell, she witnessed Queldian making a crash landing with Jaromir and an unconscious Rosier on his back. The incubus rolled to the dusty ground, splaying like a broken doll.

"I've seen this moment often. It has been my only glimpse of Hell," Zalice's voice narrated. She knew the God of Wind could only see things under his domain, and Hell didn't qualify. *Except* she was channeling his magic as he spoke and as Jaromir jumped to the ground and began applying glowing hands to the incubus's side.

Queldian reared up with a roar, taking a swipe at the Original fallen angel as he moved to land close by. He rolled to the ground a few yards away, circling as the sandstone-colored fire dragon mantled his wings over the two men he protected in a clear warning sign.

"Don't worry. They don't need you this moment. Look at Jaromir," the god instructed. *"And see why we made sure your mate borrowed a nephilim's power."*

Chapter 32

Jaromir

His magic reported back instantly. They could heal Rosier, but it would take everything he had. There would be nothing left if another person was wounded.

He heard the wind and the shouts of alarm from demonic throats. It had to be Izell's work. Taking a deep breath, Jaromir knew he had no choice.

He poured every bit of healing energy from the Mending Key into Rosier. Shattered bones stirred, reconstructing themselves in the incubus's wings and side. Torn muscles stitched themselves together, blood regenerating, skin sealing. The next time Rosier breathed, he took in a hard gasp as consciousness returned to him in one painful jolt.

Glowing amber eyes, surrounded by their sea of black sclera, fixed on him. Rosier's slack face shaded with surprise. Here they were, face to face, a demon and a nephilim. Sworn enemies.

Then Jaromir's magic continued to surge, as it had with each healing he'd done since gaining his Key. Where healing magic ended, light replaced it, trying to pour into Rosier like a river of molten light.

Rosier jerked away with a soft hiss through sharpened teeth. Hostility replaced gratitude, hands balling into fists, while Jaromir put his own up defensively. The incubus read his expression and stance, relaxing. "You're not really a nephilim. I didn't realize it, but now I see it clearly in your soul," he said quietly. "I don't want your gift, Jaromir. My destiny is down here, with my queen."

He watched Rosier root around before he pulled two additional daggers from the sheaths on his thighs. Standing, the incubus limped out from behind Queldian's protective stance. The fallen angel they faced dripped blood from several unseen wounds, fire dancing over the point of his weapon as he took in his three opponents.

"Round two, then," he remarked, leaping into motion. His massive sword descended toward Jaromir in a flash of flames, just to be knocked off course as Queldian's fanged maw closed around his ankle and crunched. Flames splashed harmlessly over the dragon's scales while the Original screamed.

Rosier leapt into motion, slicing new flesh wounds into the other demon. Jaromir reviewed his limited understanding of offensive light magic, hesitating. When Sondus was attacked out of nowhere, there was no room for second-guessing. Yet with Rosier's words still ringing in his ears, he wondered what exactly the incubus meant by him "not really" being a nephilim.

Either way, he recognized that if they were going to have a chance at surviving to see another night, he had to fight. They had to defeat this fallen angel before Izell's wind tunnel died down. He unslung the hammer from his belt, charging forward and swinging it when there was an opening between the three bodies in motion.

The hammer sang as it swung through the air, impacting the fallen angel where his armor already sported a bloody gash at the shoulder. Jaromir cringed as he heard metal crush bones and bruise flesh, knowing down to the detail what he'd done to the other man. Except veins of light erupted from the angel-forged hammer, sinking into the new wound.

The next swing of the broadsword was meant for Jaromir, its flames kissing his skin with searing heat and leaving a blazing line to cleave him shoulder to hip. Only his quick reflexes stopped the wound from being too deep, though golden blood still sizzled, and his natural healing frantically kicked in to keep him alive.

As Jaromir hunched over, clutching his wound, he watched the arm he'd struck go limp. The Original's massive weapon was too heavy to lift in time as Rosier buried one of his daggers into his skull in a killing blow. "Fucker," the incubus muttered, kicking the corpse.

"Are you okay?" Queldian murmured, immediately turning to nose Jaromir.

He nodded slowly, trembling as he felt the worst of it seal together. Without healing magic, it would take time, but he was fortunate the Original's flaming weapon had cauterized the cut. "Go light the explosives. They're ready," he muttered to Rosier, who immediately took wing to make it happen.

Queldian kneeled, moving carefully to carry Jaromir to meet the rest of their group midway. One crate of explosives drifted behind Izell, aloft from her magic, while Sondus wavered on his feet, sporting a patch of ashen skin across the side of his head.

"We have to go," Jaromir said, seeing that the only uninjured one among them was Izell, who stood apart from them, still channeling her wind spell. It was petering off, a clear sign of urgency.

"Not until we get Lucia." More than one incredulous look shot toward Lyana, who crossed her arms. "Sorry, guys. That was the deal."

"*Your* deal," Queldian rumbled. "So, *you* stay and get that damn sword."

"Guys, we don't have to fight," Sondus slurred. "We can get the sword later."

"There won't be a later. You and I both know it," Lyana snapped.

The air changed. Jaromir glanced up, realizing it was the end of the wind spell. He drew the glowing disc from its pocket and began to spin it. "That man has a concussion," he told Lyana curtly, pointing toward Sondus. "My healing magic is spent. *And* Izell has used up a priceless blessing to buy us time. I'm going back to Lust."

Sparks rose from the disc, illuminating Lyana's stubborn expression. Still, she put her hand on Queldian, as did the rest of the group. Izell ran over, sending up a skid of dust as her hand landed on the dragon's flank. They gestured over Rosier as the incubus shouted his success and flew away from the set charges. "Go, go, go!" the demon screamed. Jaromir pictured his loaned room in Lilith's palace, remembering how Izell had picked it apart and sussed out that every piece of it was made of pure soul magic.

He locked onto that location and urged the disc to take them there. He felt a jerk under his skin, pulled in one direction, before that feeling snapped him back into his body. They hadn't moved.

"Give it to me," Rosier shouted, making a grab for the disc. Dazed, Jaromir held out his finger, and the demon grabbed it and spun it. The darkness of a teleport seized him the next moment, spitting them out in an unfamiliar room lit from above by bright globes of hellfire.

Jaromir caught his bearings just in time to watch Rosier use their element of surprise to bury his blades in the backs of two guards. "Get them," he ordered, gesturing toward a trio of wingless demons who were just starting to back away.

They were in a workroom, and Jaromir immediately recognized the ruby-like gems these demons were either cutting, polishing, or testing. He gaped, betrayal worming in his chest as he turned a furious glance back at the incubus polishing blood off the teleporter disc.

Rosier offered it back casually. "Why are we still in Pride?" Jaromir demanded as he slammed it back into its padded pocket.

The incubus shrugged. "There's a way to jam teleporters. Since there was no way back to Lust, I decided to continue the mission rather than let us get chewed up by Lucifer's army."

Jaromir didn't believe that for a moment. "Did *you* jam the teleporter?" he accused.

"Whoa there." Rosier chuckled, sidestepping him. He flicked his bloody daggers through his fingers as he headed for the three demons who struggled against the icy manacles Lyana had locked them in. "Don't worry, *nephilim*. I owe you a life debt. Why would I endanger it?"

Without a moment of hesitation, he slew the three demons. "Nice work, keeping some explosives. Let's blow up this operation and see to Soulcleaver," he said to Izell.

As he reached for the floating crate, she pushed it to float away from him. "Let's get something straight first." She squared up to him, fury blazing off of her. "Where are we?"

"The basement of Lucifer's humble abode," the incubus answered.

"And you think we're going to get to his personal quarters with our Mindbender concussed?" she demanded.

"You can make illusions too, can you not?" he scoffed, trying to step around her. She matched the motion.

As they squared off, Lyana caught her bottom lip between her teeth and glanced to her sea serpent. Jaromir wished they still had a mind link, but that simple spell had unraveled again somewhere around the time Sondus had gotten his head wound. He watched her expression shade before she burst out, "I take back my deal with you! Lucia is not worth it. We have to go back to Lust."

The incubus stilled, turning his unsettling gaze her way. A slow smirk crossed his face, and he casually raised one of his blades, licking a dribble of blood from its flat side. The look he gave her blazed with clear lust. Next to her, Sissaron tensed, flashing his shark-like teeth with a furious hiss. "I'm afraid I have to decline. A deal is a deal," Rosier purred. "What kind of fae are you, to try to back out of one?"

Ice crackled over her fists. "We have to go back."

"And the longer we wait here arguing, the more likely it is that Lucifer returns to his quarters before we get there. Do you want to face him, or just steal his sword?" The incubus canted his head, taking a closer look around. "Oh, look at you lot, so cross with me! Try to kill me, and I'll blow up that crate of goodies you brought along—we'll all die together. Is that what you want?"

"You *did* jam the teleporter," Jaromir breathed. He knew the single-minded determination that'd gripped Rosier. The incubus would do anything to get this sword for his mistress, including getting them all killed.

"And I won't unjam it until you lot help me." Rosier's three tails snapped as he turned a grin Jaromir's way. "So, how about it? Get those disguises on before sweet cheeks and I go without you."

"She's not going anywhere with you," Sissaron hissed.

"I said *the sword* in our agreement, not Soulcleaver. So, here's a sword. Now, let's go." Lyana shoved one of Sissaron's angel-forged blades toward Rosier.

The incubus stared at the gilded handle and then back at her, all hints of humor vanishing from his bearing. Fury made his amber eyes living flames. He spoke in a low tone more frightening than any outburst. "No matter what clever agreement you think you made, you're still stuck down here, and I'm the only demon in Pride willing to help your sorry asses escape. You've *lost*. Now quit wasting fucking time and come with me, or stay in this room and die. Your fucking choice."

A clatter sounded behind them. Jaromir turned, watching Izell scoop up an armful of rough-cut rubies. She went and dumped it on a central desk, where several were already heaped. She turned when she realized everyone's eyes were on her. "Do what the demon says," she told them before her shimmering gaze lifted to Rosier's. "But you're going to wish Jaromir had let you die when I'm through with you."

Rosier managed a smirk as she scooped up more gems. Slowly, Sondus and Lyana peeled away from the confrontation to follow suit. "Can't wait to see you try," the incubus purred.

"I'll help," Sissaron murmured to Izell. Soon, everyone was pitching in to make a mini-mountain of rubies and setting up explosives around them. There would be no more soul-stealing weapons with the rubies destroyed and the crafters dead.

Rosier didn't light the fuses until everyone was covered in new, patchy, demonic illusions. Without Sondus pitching in, Izell and Lyana just had to do the best that they could in recreating his perfect disguises.

"Good enough," Rosier finally said, rolling his eyes. They had five minutes to get away from the coming explosion, so they moved after the incubus quickly as he slunk into the hall and glanced left to right. His soul magic was still crackling over them, making it that much easier to walk by a pair of guards who patrolled the hall like nothing was amiss with the laboratory doors closed.

With no mind link, they were completely at the incubus's

mercy as he led them to a stairwell and followed its spiral up several stories. He couldn't explain exactly where they were going, but Jaromir had the feeling they were heading to the very top of the palace. Lucifer must like overseeing his domain.

Jaromir practically carried Sondus up the stairs, just making sure the spymaster didn't lag behind. Whoever had gotten him back on his feet hadn't done a great job at it, he thought. But there was no time to regret letting go of all his healing magic, not even with Rosier's betrayal. The only thing they could do was hope they could steal away Lucifer's sword without any more trouble.

He felt the muffled *boom* of their diversion, followed by shouts of alarm from several mouths. They went flooding down the stairwell, taxing Rosier's magic. Thankfully, no Original was amongst the demons responding to the explosion.

Rosier kept them climbing until they emerged into a lavish entry hall complete with electric lights, just like with Lilith's palace. Giant panes of glass gave the illusion of this massive room being open to the air, but they kept the smoke and sulfur stench out. Jaromir's gaze flashed to the pair of guards patrolling across the marble floor. Dressed in impeccable suits, they bore no visible weapons and chatted casually despite the explosion that'd occurred elsewhere.

He would've assumed they were harmless, except both bore the burnt feathers of Original fallen angels.

Rosier smirked as he turned and gestured. "Help me kill them."

The incubus had the element of surprise as he rushed forward and leapt onto the woman's back, ending her life with a stab of his blade. The other Original flared out his wings, scream-ing. Flames leapt up his arms, but it was Sissaron who killed him with an efficient sweep of his angel-forged sword. The body sizzled, consumed rapidly by angelic light.

Rosier dusted off his hands. "Easy. No real security means Lucifer's not in yet," he said. He tried the knob of an elaborately decorated door, opening it soundlessly.

"And he will have Soulcleaver with him," Izell sighed. They

filed into Lucifer's quarters, which were already fully illuminated by electric lights.

"We hide and wait, just like we planned," Rosier answered. He gestured to Sissaron. "Go ash that bitch real quick. We don't want him noticing something's wrong."

Sissaron muttered in another language which didn't translate, even with the translation magic over Jaromir's ears. It sounded like cursing, though. His blade set the demon woman ablaze, and any ash that remained disappeared, as it had with the first Original Sissaron had killed. That done, Rosier closed the door after them and strode with purpose through several rooms full of every comfort Jaromir could imagine. He was just waiting to stumble upon a harem of scantily clad women to finish it off.

Instead, they found the bedroom, a study of red. Crimson wallpaper, maroon sheets draping a bed big enough to support ten people at once, and dried blood. He'd thought it was comfortable, except...

They'd found a woman, but it wasn't what he'd expected by a long shot. She had to hang by a pair of manacles that just barely kept her toes from scraping the floor. Two rags barely covered her modesty, and open wounds crisscrossed her abdomen. The smell rolling off of her suggested infection taking deep root. She might've had wings once, but they were cut at the second joint with the membranes removed, two sad stumps sticking from her shoulder blades.

With her head bowed, her face was shrouded in dull, black hair. Rosier ignored her, pointing to a pair of hooks over the bed. "It's not here after all. But good news." He smirked toward Lyana, gesturing to the half-dead creature hanging there. "Here's Lucia."

The demon stirred with a low moan, one eye too swollen to open. The other flicked a silver iris around before it fixed on Jaromir.

"Help," Lucia croaked. "Help me. Please."

Chapter 33
Izell

THE MOMENT SHE SET HER EYES ON LUCIA'S BROKEN FORM, the old pact tingled on Izell's arm. Under her illusion, the ink flared with new life, ready to be invoked.

"To turn back the hands of time and be myself again. I would give anything," Lucia had offered when she was whole and proud. It was the terms of their deal, that Lucia owed Izell an open-ended "anything." The pact had been made when she still bore a kernel of corruption, the meddlesome spark of Jazrach's soul that'd driven her further and further to depravity.

It'd pushed her to this moment, where she hung like a prize side of meat in Lucifer's personal quarters. Now, she had nothing. Hostility blazed from Lyana and Sissaron alike, but neither moved to take the pound of flesh they deserved. Izell understood all too well. She met Lyana's water-filled eyes, recognizing the pity there.

"He...he promised," Lucia said with effort.

"Save your strength." Jaromir didn't approach, but his tone softened in the face of her obvious suffering.

The limp mop of her hair shifted as she shook her head. "I am bound. This...is my soul's home," she wheezed. "Master... promised...said I was special. Strong." She coughed up red spittle.

Izell turned to Lyana, raising a brow. "Can we go now?" she asked quietly.

Rosier wouldn't let them leave without Soulcleaver, but Lyana seemed to understand what she meant. "No. Not yet." She drew one of Sissaron's angel-forged blades, approaching Lucia with it.

No one moved as she drew her arm back, aiming the tip at the demoness's heart. Lucia lifted her head, expression scrunching. "I see how it is. This...is the help you offer," she breathed.

Voices rose from somewhere close by. Lucia breathed a hiss through dry lips. "He's coming," she whispered.

"Over here," Rosier said, gesturing urgently for her to sheathe the glowing sword. It hummed quietly in Lyana's hand before she rushed to hand it back to Sissaron. They followed Rosier into the en suite bathroom, where, as a collective, they laid their strongest concealment spells down. Rosier's soul magic mixed with what mind influence Sondus could summon up while she and Lyana wove illusions to make their still bodies look like the bathroom behind them.

She imagined all the different ways she would murder Rosier for putting them in this situation to give herself the motivation to make the best illusion of her life. A winged man strode into the room as she got to the third technique. Her mind stilled.

He was a beautiful creature dressed in black battle armor, though his helmet was tucked under his elbow, giving a front-row view to his expression. Clean-shaven, he had a strong jawline and a cleft in line with his cupid's bow. Sinfully full lips dipped in a frown as he surveyed the room. Her heart leapt as she prayed to her elemental gods that he didn't sense anything amiss.

There was no mistaking him as anyone but Lucifer. Not because of his good looks, nor the blue irises surrounded by black sclera in his unsettling gaze, but the pure black wings trailing behind him looked the worst burnt of all the Original fallen angels she'd met. He was otherwise free of demonic features. No horns, no tails, and regular-shaped feet encased in his boots. "You're sure Adela and Epios were left to guard?" he asked someone behind him in the kind of smooth tenor that could melt any woman's heart.

"Yes, sire," answered a crisp, male voice.

"They can't be far. Get the guards combing over every last room in the palace," Lucifer ordered. Several boots snapped, and silence followed as they left the devil himself alone in the same room as Izell's hiding group.

He strode to Lucia, brushing his fingertips over her cheek. "Hello, my little failure. I see you're awake," he cooed to her like she was a coveted pet.

Something prodded Izell in the back. She carefully turned to see Jaromir patting the pocket with the disc, giving a meaningful look at Rosier. The incubus was busy licking his bottom lip, naked glee and anticipation in his expression. He had his daggers out, poised to leap the moment they were discovered. And she had no doubt that they'd be revealed soon, with how Sondus wavered and struggled to keep his eyes open.

Rosier glanced over and smirked, shaking his head no. She wasn't too surprised. He had more riding on this retrieval than they did, else he wouldn't be forcing them into helping him. Lucifer wore a sword on his hip, and while it didn't seem anything special sheathed, she had no doubt it was the coveted Soulcleaver.

"M-Master," Lucia croaked.

"You have something to say?" He dug his thumb into her cheek, drawing out a stifled cry.

"Master. I can...I can still be useful," she whispered.

She's going to sell us out, Izell thought grimly. She still had the blessings from Raenith and Getana in reserve—perhaps she could burn this whole palace down and throw Rosier in the bonfire for good measure.

"The intruders... They are here...right behind you," Lucia continued, biting out every word with wheezing determination.

Rosier crept forward, grinning.

And Lucifer laughed, taking Lucia's chin between his finger and thumb. "I know. Perhaps you can still prove your worth," he purred. A pulse of magic passed between them. With a snap of his fingers, the manacles holding her sprang open. Her limp body landed in a heap while he spun on his heel, an inferno of white-gray soul flame erupting from his palm and blazing directly at their hiding spot.

Rosier leapt into motion, scissoring through the fire with his blades cutting an X pattern. The embers rained to the floor harmlessly. "If it isn't Rosier. So nice to see you again," Lucifer drawled.

The incubus snarled and lunged, just to get a boot to the gut. Lucifer shook him off like waving away a pest.

The devil lifted his hand, and the room morphed around them. Walls crumpled, amenities vanished, all of them turning into small balls of energy, which zoomed to burn above his palm in a white-gray orb. What used to be his quarters formed a tunnel of dark volcanic rock.

He grinned as Izell and those able to fight revealed themselves around her. Jaromir glowed with his nephilim light, while Sissaron had both of his angel-forged blades drawn. Lyana bristled with icy magic, her fingers glowing brightly with a demigoddess's potential. Queldian maneuvered for space, smoke curling from his maw. Only Sondus held back, clutching his head, his skin ashy pale and coated in a sheen of sweat.

"Your souls are too powerful to hide. Worth this...expenditure," Lucifer said, unruffled by the force of hostility in front of him. He tipped his hand, the orb of soul magic bouncing into Lucia's body. She seized as it permeated her.

Izell raised her fingers, casting a quick stunning spell. Magic flew, and steel flashed as Sissaron rushed forward first, aiming to behead their opponent with his blades crossed. Lucifer had his own weapon out and up to parry in a flurry of sparks, his handsome face bland, like he often kicked massive half-hythian men into the path of spells aimed at him. Sissaron took the stunning spell, falling to the ground in a clatter of weaponry.

"Surely that's not the best you can do," Lucifer scoffed. He caught Queldian's horn mid-charge next, taking a bath in dragon fire as he swung with the dragon's momentum and threw him into the stone wall with such force that it broke. Queldian plummeted out of sight. Izell stifled a scream, knowing she had to focus on the danger before her.

Lucifer's wings and armor burned with flames crackling over his form without damaging him. They cast a red glow over his pristine teeth as he grinned. "Want to see a *real* magic trick, little fae?" His fingers formed claws as he gestured at Rosier, who was just getting to his feet. Soul energy ripped from the incubus, and he collapsed with a choked cry.

That energy sped toward them, forming a second, much larger volley of white flames. Lyana shouted a word of power, holding up a thick shell of ice, arms trembling as the fire melted her quick defenses little by little.

Izell hadn't realized just how outmatched they'd be. Despair had her combing all her magical knowledge, seeking some answer. Her golden occultarus bobbed in the corner of her eye, glowing with a halo, flames of its own. But these were kissed by blue. When Izell reached out to touch the tool, Raenith's blessing activated, flowing liquid power over her until she burned like Lucifer did, but with the white-hot energy of the Lady of Passion.

"I gave you power so you can use it," Raenith's voice chastised. Time seemed to slow as this new boost of potential let her see what made the soul flames burn. With a slash of her hand, they extinguished, and Lyana's ice shield crumpled a moment later.

She assumed a battle stance, occultarus in one hand, flames of the hottest blue in the other. Her senses sharpened enough to hear Queldian climbing back into the room and Jaromir moving around the edge, trying to get out of this corner they were backed into.

All of Lucifer's attention was focused on her, a gleam of interest there. He fought like he had no equal, but had he ever come face to face with someone invested in Raenith's full fury?

"Take heart, Izell. You know you can win." The goddess's presence set fire to her doubts until only inspiration remained. *"Your friends put their faith in you. And what is faith if not the courage to believe against all odds?"*

Izell believed. She took a deep, steadying breath. And then she attacked, not with fire—Lucifer was obviously immune to flames—but with a blast of super-chilled wind. She sucked all the heat in the room into herself as she bowled the devil over, sliding those pristine black wings in the dirt. She stepped over Lucia's writhing body, barely noticing the whispers of a corruption demon that slid away from her ears.

Her senses picked up Lucia standing, flexing her magic. "Deal with them. I want this one for myself," Lucifer ordered as he flipped to his feet and brandished Soulcleaver at Izell.

"As you wish, Master," Lucia stated woodenly. Her voice rasped like she'd gargled with ashes.

Izell trusted that her friends could take on one fallen Sorceress. She focused all her attention at the dark figure before her. Soul flames danced on his weapon, revealing twin lines of runes—first gold down the crystal-forged blade and then a second set beneath them, written backward in gray-black ink.

She reached toward the floor, calling to the lava rock forged of the hottest flames. Even down here, it responded to the call of a fire goddess, leaping to form a staff of rock that steamed with heat. "*En garde,*" she stated, her voice echoing with Raenith's power.

Metal clashed against rock. Each time he struck her weapon, it gave a bit, donating rapidly cooling crust along the sharpened edge. Lucifer noticed and scowled, shooting soul flame in her face as he stepped back.

The flames stopped an inch from Izell's skin, snapping harmlessly. With the power of Raenith behind her, the heat felt refreshing, adding itself to her power. Steam lifted from her, coating her in a heat mirage.

Lucifer used a burst of soul flame to melt the cooling rock off his weapon before it could harden. He smiled broadly. "At last, a challenge," he said.

He struck out with a whirl of shadows while her weapon oozed back together. Lines of pain opened up along her arms where they drew blood like the strike of several whips. She touched her occultarus, sending a wave of biting frost to chill his demonic heat and force him back another step.

"*A Firebrand will never wield the cold well,*" Raenith stated as an icicle flew past her, embedding itself through Lucifer's wing. The goddess was right, but a demigoddess of water was made for such a task.

Lyana stepped up next to Izell, nodding as their gazes met. "This is your opportunity to kill Lucia," Izell stated.

"You need me more," she answered.

"Do you two need a room?" Lucifer cut in. Shadows wrapped around his form, stinking of whispers and rot. She recognized a corruption demon's signature before he used it to lash out at their minds.

Fire crackled in her ears, while blood wept from Lyana's. The demigoddess dropped to her knees, the teal magic extinguishing from her palms. Whispers coiled around them both as Lucifer advanced, flames burning brighter in the absence of the demigoddess's chill.

He was ready this time, only feinting a thrust as Izell lifted her staff. "How curious. Her soul burns with more magic, yet it's snuffed that much easier." He clenched his free hand, and Lyana's lips parted in a silent scream.

Izell knew she'd watch helplessly as Lyana died unless she acted fast. There was only one thing she *could* do, which was to shoot the golden occultarus to nestle in the other fae's palm. Raenith's warm presence vanished from her mind, and she released the staff before it could maim her non-blessed hands.

Lyana stopped screaming. Her eyes cracked open, just for her to drop the golden orb in horror at what she saw.

Izell's body jerked, her senses slow in the wake of giving away her blessing. She observed the length of crystal blade that was thrust through her heart.

But before she died, she called on her last blessing. Blackness swept into her vision, painted in increasingly dark shades of emerald.

Chapter 34
Jaromir

While Izell and Lucifer exchanged blows, Lucia got to her feet. The last of the damage to her body was rapidly healing, bruises on her face fading while she bared jagged fangs with a soft hiss.

"Deal with them. I want this one for myself," Lucifer ordered.

The rings of silver in Lucia's eyes gleamed, though she spoke without emotion. "As you wish, Master."

Her hand raised, lightning cracking toward where Jaromir was standing. He brandished his hammer, light glowing in a warm halo around him. Ice crackled beside him as Lyana posed, icicles at the ready. Sissaron twitched on the ground, still stuck in whatever spell he'd taken by accident, while Rosier was splayed in a heap, out cold from Lucifer's maneuver.

"Go help Izell," he said to Lyana out of the corner of his mouth. Maybe if he could speak with Lucia, he could get her to see some reason.

However, he didn't expect Lyana to nod and shoot a wave of wintery air at Lucia, knocking her off balance long enough for her to slip by her and aim one of her prepared icicles at Lucifer instead.

"Lucia...can we talk?" he invited, holding his arms out at his sides.

"What is there to talk about?" she spat back. Many whispering voices surrounded her as she shook a coating of ice off her arm. Her eyes were vulnerable within her ruined face, black veins just under the surface of her skin. Now that her wings had grown back, he realized she had developed a corruption demon's signature set of mouths all along the leathery lengths. The skin on her arms was just starting to purple. Maybe it took time for the flesh to deform more.

"You don't really want to kill us. You wanted help... I want to offer you help." He spoke as quickly as he could. They didn't need another enemy as strong as Lucia right now, not while the woman who held his beating heart dueled the devil right behind her.

Lucia pursed her lips before a fist of whispering shadows wrapped around his torso and tightened down. "Master will free me, if only I wasn't a failure," she muttered. Her fingers flew through a spell. A sharpened spike of stone leapt from the rubble of the ruined wall, and she took aim for his heart. "Have the same mercy you would offer m—"

A sandstone-scaled blur slammed her to the ground. Queldian's head and torso bled freely, and one wing was askew, but he'd survived his fall to growl like distant thunder as his claws held the Sorceress down.

Her many mouths emitted a piercing shriek as that sharpened spike reversed course, embedding deep in the soft flesh where the dragon's neck and shoulder met. Jaromir uttered a helpless noise, watching blood gush around the weapon.

His fingers tightened around the grip of his hammer. It hummed a comforting tune against the backdrop of screams and crackling flames around him. Lucia stood, just to have him seize her wrist. Her demonic flesh sizzled from his nephilim light, and her Adam's apple bobbed from the barest press of cold crystal against her neck.

"After everything you did, we were still going to give your mercy." He barely recognized the fury in his own voice or the way his sight swam as he pinned her to a section of intact wall.

"I...I'm sorry. I had no choice." She still spoke with no emotion, her silver eyes as flat as any snake's. He expected a forked tongue to flick out from between her dried lips at any moment.

She'd always had a choice, but before he could swing the hammer, she twisted and swiped his cheek with her free hand's claws. He released her on instinct, knowing his mistake a moment later when electricity shook every nerve in his body. The ground rushed up to meet him, still smoking and twitching.

Her bare feet stopped at the corner of his eye as he struggled to control his spasming muscles. "When I give him your soul, all will be well," Lucia said tonelessly. Hot magic formed above him.

"Jaromir," someone whispered. Forgotten and propped in a corner, Sondus could barely lift his head. But he'd managed to draw a weapon from its sheath and slide it across the rocky ground. The ruby glinted in the light of the spell Lucia charged.

He knew what he had to do. His shaking fingers wrapped around the hilt, and he jabbed Lucia's foot with the dark blade. Shrieking, she dropped her spell, and Jaromir rolled away, his side kissed by a surge of fire. Agony danced around his vision in white-hot stars, but he batted away the worst of it and stood.

Lucia was already casting a new spell. He already knew the one weakness to spell casters without an occultarus—anything more complicated than a bolt of lightning was slow and easy to fumble. He ducked another wash of heat and surged forward blindly, burying the blade deep in her chest.

Blood streamed from the corner of her mouth. "Jaromir," she whimpered. But she was a soul, and the dagger was designed to steal and store souls. Her form melted in the blink of an eye, sucked through the black blade and funneled to its glittering ruby. It vibrated rhythmically, like two fists smacking it from the inside.

Jaromir released a pained wheeze. She'd burnt him worse than he expected, and his regeneration struggled to mend the worst of it. "Hold...on to this...for me," he managed, dropping the dagger into Sondus's waiting palms.

He turned to Queldian, who bled out around the spike in his neck. The massive dragon could barely lift his hand as Jaromir knelt, placing his hand on the massive, plate-like scales below his horns. Closing his eyes, he reached into the Mending Key.

A single drop of magic greeted him, dancing emerald green in his mind's eye. It wavered and extended, the motion typical of any liquid under pressure. But it seemed to question him—did he really want to use it now, to save the soul of a dragon who'd already died long ago?

He pressed that drop of healing into Queldian without regrets. The dragon was loyal and strong, and his soul didn't deserve to die in the bowels of Hell. When he opened his eyes, the stone missile had slid free from the dragon's neck, replaced by a circle of healing flesh. He breathed a little easier; Izell would be relieved to know her dragon had survived.

A blast of emerald green rocked him backward, but he caught himself on the unconscious dragon's horn, dread filling his chest at what he could make out. Lucifer's sword was thrust clean through Izell's chest, and the explosion of green was centered in the impact point.

He rushed forward, uncaring that a wound like that was a near-instant death. His hand landed on Izell's shoulder as he called on his magic again. The dry well of the Mending Key taunted him even as nephilim light answered his anguished internal scream. Izell's body began to sag against him.

"She was a good opponent. I'll gladly feast on her soul," Lucifer said, his gaze on the blade and its pulsing gray runes. *Soulcleaver.* Stealing his love's soul away even as he desperately searched himself for a miracle. Her body—just a soul down here in Hell—was sucked into the blade.

All he had was light. Burning, blazing, blinding light. He lashed out, not at Lucifer, but at the blade itself, erupting with hot brilliance. No one could have Izell's life, nor her soul.

Sword and devil alike took shelter from the radiance exploding from his every pore. He caught the golden orb that floated into his hand like acknowledging a new owner. Vines raced up his arm, and a presence washed over his mind. Time slowed, as did his pain.

"Life and death were never Izell's specialties. I grant you my power in her stead."

"Lady Getana?" he whispered.

"You are surrounded by death, young man. From life, death. And from death..."

"Life," he echoed her. Suddenly, he could sense the life force of everyone in the room, including the devil, who hid behind a shield of soul magic he'd erected against the onslaught of Jaromir's radiance. The sword he held pulsed with the life it'd taken, the soul of the woman he loved.

He didn't think; he just reached out. With Getana's might behind him, he seized Izell's soul and tugged. Soulcleaver broke Lucifer's shield of magic, tugging him closer and closer by the hilt he refused to release. The blade's twin lines of runes pulsed haphazardly, one row responding to Jaromir's nephilim side, the other to Getana's borrowed might.

It gave up and shattered into a thousand glittering pieces.

Izell's soul came free, shooting free and taking form on the ground. She glanced around, holding her head.

Taking one look at the blade-less hilt he held, Lucifer tossed it aside and spat in Jaromir's direction. "I will torture you soul for a thousand eternities for that, nephilim!" Hellfire flared in his eye sockets, fangs growing and gnashing.

Jaromir silently asked Getana what else her magic could do. In response, the palace shook. The whole thing was rock—the walls, the floors, everything. Soul magic had made amenities and food, giving it the illusion of a comfortable place in the midst of tortured souls and endless plains of nothingness.

With a twist of his hand, he attacked the foundation, turning rock to powder in an instant. The power that thrummed through him guttered from the effort, consuming nearly all of the blessing. But the damage was done. He could hear roaring, falling rock from there.

Lucifer tilted his head a split second before the floor buckled. He shot to his wings while Jaromir swept up Izell and the hilt of Soulcleaver, jerking his head toward Lyana. The demigoddess stared at him, her water-filled eyes taking up most of her face with her naked awe.

He had just enough of Getana's power over life to shoot magic toward his fallen companions. What had been Lucifer's bedroom caved inward, sliding Sondus and the occupied soul blade toward a swift plummet. The spymaster took the donation of magic to recover from his concussion, rolling to take Lyana's hand.

Queldian stumbled toward them, also disoriented from his sudden recovery. Rosier sheathed his daggers. "Whatever the fuck you did, I'm sad I missed it," he stated.

"Shut your mouth and hold on," Jaromir snapped. He wasn't glowing anymore. It felt like all of his magic had abandoned him as Getana's blessing faded. His limbs felt a hundred pounds heavier, but he still drew out the teleporting disc as the floor wobbled one last, violent time.

That blasted incubus had better not *block this,* he thought, spinning the disc.

"Leaving so soon?" Lucifer's dark magic lashed out at him as he pictured Lust. A whip of black energy smashed into the disc.

Then they were gone, landing in a heap in the comfortable room Lilith had lent them. Had it only been a night ago? He cracked open his weary eyes, taking in the blood-streaked faces of his friends...plus Rosier...and the comfortable silk pillows lying just a foot away, still where Izell had tossed them last night.

He breathed a sigh of relief, relaxing for the moment before the teleportation disc fell off his finger, broken into two uneven pieces.

Chapter 35
Jaromir

THE JAGGED PIECES OF CLEAR GLASS LOOKED COMICALLY small in his palms. Their lifeline to leaving Hell...gone.

"So, what'd I miss?" Rosier asked casually. Six sets of hostile eyes turned in his direction, and he raised his hands. "We're all alive, right? No need to be so angry-like."

"Izell died because you couldn't let your fool's errand go," Jaromir said in a low, furious voice. "And now we're *trapped* here."

Lyana gasped and pointed at the shards of glass he held. "We're trapped!" she echoed.

"But you *did* destroy Lucifer's palace," Rosier pointed out. "And you *did* get Soulcleaver..." He picked up the hilt, which sported a cracked piece of crystal at the pommel. "...Well, what's left of it."

"Count your moments, because you're dead, pretty boy," Izell hissed, making a grab for Sissaron's waist, just to come up empty. He lifted his webbed hands with a shrug, sporting two empty sheathes on his hips.

The door opened, and a different incubus peeked in. "Everything all right in here?" he asked, startling when he saw the group.

"Get Queen Lilith before I'm murdered by compliments!" Rosier fanned himself, then jumped to his hooves, rushing over. "No, wait, I'll get her!"

Jaromir just watched him go, shaking his head slowly. The fight seemed to drain out of him, leaving him an exhausted husk. Judging by the expressions of his friends, they weren't faring much better. It was nothing short of a miracle that they'd all survived and made it back to Lust. He had no doubt that Lucifer had been trying to break the disc to strand them in the collapsing palace alongside him.

Lyana wet her lips. "Before he comes back, I just want to apologize. I should've never gotten into any agreement with him." She looked Izell in the eye. "I put you all in danger, and if I can repay that, I will."

Izell breathed a tired sigh. "No more debt."

"Agreed. You've repaid your trespass against me...and then some." A shaky smile touched the demigoddess's face.

Sondus lifted his hand for attention. He'd regained much of his color, but Jaromir doubted he'd be pulling any Mindbender tricks out for a while. "There's the matter of Lucia." He lifted the dagger by the ruby, balancing it between his index and middle fingers.

The stone rang with a hollow *ping* as their attentions turned to it.

"She's in there?" Izell asked, taking up the dagger to hold the ruby close to her face.

Sondus hooked his thumb toward Jaromir. "Someone nailed her in the heart."

She turned an astonished look his way.

"She almost killed Queldian. I had to." Jaromir absently reached over to stroke the dragon's neck, earning a pleased rumble. Shifting around, his head was soon in Jaromir's lap, ears flicking for attention.

When he glanced up, he realized Izell was pointing at the weapon and then him, confirming silently with Sondus, who was nodding emphatically.

"Gods above," she muttered. "Perhaps it is a good time to tell you I didn't actually die. Soulcleaver... It's hard to explain. It... *captured* my soul? It wasn't painful—it was just a perspective shift. I saw everything from the safety of my crystal prison. So, it would follow that Lucia isn't dead either, just locked up in here." Her illusioned-on claw tapped the ruby, and Lucia *pinged* back.

"That explains why Lucifer thought he was going to eat your soul for dinner later," Jaromir muttered.

"Right. But!" She forced her face into a grimace of cheer. "You lovely people, guess what! We have our greater demon!"

No one had energy for much more than a round of smiles and nudges. Izell turned her attention to Lyana, clearing her throat. "That is, if that's what you want done with her soul." She lifted her arm, stripping away the illusion of scales to show the glimmering black symbols inked there. "I didn't use this to help you when I should have, so I want it to be your choice. Is this how you want me to use my pact with her?"

Lyana exchanged a glance with Sissaron. He gestured, his gaze warm on her excited expression. "Your choice, Lennie," he murmured.

The ruby *ping ping pinged.*

"Yes. I want you to use her to make the new Dark Eye." Lyana patted the vibrating crystal. "Let's do it right this time around so she never escapes."

"Beautiful." Izell passed the dagger back to Sondus, who secured it on his person. She stood and offered Jaromir a hand up, tilting her head toward the privacy of the bathroom. "Something you need to see," she said quietly while they walked the short distance in that direction. Electrical lights flickered on a pace before them, illuminating a porcelain tub he longed to soak in.

They stopped short of it, turning toward a mirror instead. Jaromir recoiled at the double of himself staring back. Covered in soot, his clothing hung off him in tatters. Blood, both golden and red, made its mark on him head to toe.

"While I channeled his magic, Lord Zalice told me something about your...light." Izell spoke quietly as she stripped fluffy, white towels from the bathroom. She dipped one under a rush of water from the sink and started wiping his face clean with tender strokes. "Look at your eyes."

Such a small detail he'd overlooked for the big picture. But now that she'd pointed them out, their glow seemed...duller. Shading toward the color of old, burnished gold.

"I'm not really a nephilim." He was only repeating what Rosier had said. "Right?"

"For the record, I don't care what you are, except 'mine,'" she began, but he heard her hesitation. "But apparently, no one can be *turned* into a nephilim. You have borrowed power, and it looks like breaking Soulcleaver took most of it."

He considered his face, checking his teeth next. Still dull. If he wasn't a nephilim, he supposed he wasn't an Alchemyst for much longer either. "Every time I exhaust the Mending Key, it feels like my magic wants to give away the light in me next. Rosier recognized it but didn't explain past 'I don't want your gift.'

"What happens when it's all gone, Izell? Do I become a human?" He didn't ask what else followed along with that thought... Would he rapidly age like Gwendolyn?

"I was assured that *wouldn't* be your fate," she replied. She finished cleaning his face, the soot-smeared towel hovering just off his cheek as she inspected every inch of his expression.

He caught her lips in a gentle kiss. She tasted a little like a campfire, all smoke and a hint of sweetness. In the relative privacy, he drew her close, content just to hold her as their lips parted. "Then...I can't wait to give away the rest," he whispered. "I never wanted to have violent magic."

She tucked her head in the crook of his neck. "It doesn't fit you," she agreed, muffling a massive yawn in his shoulder.

Their peaceful moment shattered when a door slammed, and Lilith's quiet voice greeted their friends in the other room. Jaromir sighed, dusting one last kiss on Izell's head, before returning with his share of the towels.

The Queen of Lust raised a brow as Lyana eagerly seized a few and poured cold water magic over them. They all wiped their faces free of dried blood, and Jaromir helped Izell with the task of cleaning Queldian's scales. "All right, whatever," she said to herself.

Rosier had not returned with her. *Coward,* Jaromir thought. At least she was dressed more today, wearing a bustier top and a full skirt split to show the creamy skin of one leg. Her strawberry-tinted hair was tied back from her face, holding up an elaborate, five-pronged crown.

"So...you lot look terrible. What happened? Rosier was completely depleted. He handed me this and passed out." She held up Soulcleaver's hilt.

"That's the sword you wanted," Izell supplied.

Lilith tapped a fingertip to the sharp sliver of crystal that used to be its blade. "It's maybe a third of Soulcleaver, and that's being generous."

Concealing an eye roll by turning away from her, Izell instead invited the group to draw straws for the duty of retelling their adventure. Jaromir waved her away and found a comfortable seat, soon joined by Izell and Queldian's warm bulk against his legs. The others pitched in occasionally, but he told the bulk of what happened down to the details.

Lilith listened intently, even naming the occasional demon they'd encountered, like the Original with the flaming broadsword who'd nearly killed Rosier. "Thank you for saving his life," she said with true sincerity.

He nodded, because there was obviously more between the two lust demons than simple attraction. It wasn't his business. But he still wished Rosier wasn't getting away with forcing them into harm's way with no repercussions.

He continued the story, aware of her keen amber gaze sharpening when he told the truth of Rosier's trick to get them into Lucifer's palace. Her lips formed a displeased line that dug deeper until he started talking about their fight with the devil himself.

"That reckless idiot," she muttered. "I told him the sword wasn't *that* important."

"Apparently, it was," Lyana snarked.

"Like you have room to talk. I smell the pact on you even now," the demoness snorted. "So, you were saying. Lucifer clearly sensed you hiding in his bathroom and harvested his rooms to reinvigorate Lucia's battered soul."

She didn't interrupt for the rest of the retelling, only taking up the two uneven pieces of glass that used to be their way out. Once he was done, she mused in silence for several long moments. Finally, she turned her attention to Izell, twisting her arm around. "I declare our pact complete." Light flared between them, the ink fading from their skin.

Lilith stripped off the Summer Key, tossing it to Sondus. "Don't burn yourself."

He flashed a grimace like she'd told a bad joke before juggling the ring between his hands like she'd handed him a hot coal.

The Queen of Lust got to her hooves, dusting invisible wrinkles from her skirt. "And as promised, my people will fight Lucifer's when the day comes. We'll chop their heads off from behind. Pride will fall, and Lucifer with it." She grinned viciously. "When the dust settles, I will rule this place of eternal night. Now, I will be taking my leave. There are preparations to make."

"Wait. What about our way out?" Izell gestured to the glass pieces, which she'd passed off to the side.

Lilith lifted her shoulder. "A shame. But not part of our agreement."

"*What?*" She leaned forward, breathing that single word with quiet intensity.

"It's not my problem. Oh, you're all free to stay." She spread her hands to encompass the room. "Maybe your Archangel will come find you, but probably not. We've been over how cowardly angels are."

More than one growl filled the air, but Lilith only smiled at that. "It's not so bad, for Hell. At least you have air conditioning. You can follow us up when the Veil rips open for good."

"It would be too late," Izell muttered.

"Besides, why be in such a hurry to leave? Two of your number are dead... This may be your last time to see their faces." In this, the Queen of Lust was deadly serious. She turned to leave in a swish of skirts.

Jaromir met Queldian's glimmering eyes, discovering twin pools of despair. He'd grown so attached to Izell's affectionate dragon. To think she'd carried him this whole time, only able to talk to him rather than hug his warm, scaly bulk when she needed him.

He had an idea. Gently pushing to his feet, he called, "Queen Lilith! May I walk with you?"

She turned back, raising an eyebrow. Izell hissed his name, shaking her head.

"Trust me," he murmured.

His love's expression was odd. Almost taken aback. Like she'd changed her mind that quickly, she waved him on.

Lilith hadn't exactly invited him along, but she waited to leave the room until they fell into step. She rested her hands primly over her middle as she walked down the hall, head held high and regal. "You wished to speak with me, or just walk?" she asked.

The worst thing she could say is no, he thought, steeling himself.

He wasn't sure where exactly to begin in his offer or if it would be enough. Even though Rosier and apparently Zalice understood the nature of his "not-nephilim" nature, no one was stopping to explain how it worked and in what way he could use it. His mysterious light was more of a mystery than a blessing, but he couldn't let Lilith know he viewed it that way.

"I wanted to ask if there's another way we can safely return to our bodies," he began.

She simply nodded, fixing him with those startling amber eyes.

"You may want something in return," he continued, feeling awkward when she ventured no answer.

"That is how Hell works. No information is truly free," she replied. "Because the moment I answer, you will want my help in making it happen. I have more pressing concerns than returning you lot to the surface."

Perfectly logical. He hoped he could appeal to this reason-driven side of her. "What if I could offer you something in return?"

Her expression remained flat. Bored, even. "I don't have time for games. Tell me what you think you have that interests me."

His heart nearly stilled as he hoped that he was right. "Queen Lilith...from the moment we became allies, there was one thing I knew I wanted to do for you. I wanted to restore your wings." Her top didn't hide the tops of the brutal scars that crossed her back in their place.

Her lips drew back from sharpened teeth. "Speak *very* carefully." Menace crept through the soft words.

Wings. It was the one thing powerful demons had in common...save for the Queen of Lust. But he knew for her, it was more than a status symbol. It was a visible sign of what she'd lost.

She was a fallen angel who hadn't chosen that fate. That's why she'd wanted Soulcleaver—the weapon that'd sealed her destiny. It was the next closest thing to killing the one who'd made her who she was.

"I used to have healing magic that could help a vampire heal any wound, including a missing limb. But I lost it. The spark vanished when I was bitten by a Fell Mad and briefly afflicted." He spoke quickly. She listened stiffly, but at least she *was* listening.

"I met Soren...Archangel Soren...later and learned that what I lost was a hint of angelic lineage," he continued. "He tried to replace what I lost with a drop of his blood, since it's a vampire thing to take the magic from the blood we drink."

"That won't work," she muttered.

"I know. It made me a nephilim, but it seems that's only temporary." He wondered if she'd noticed what Rosier had or if it wasn't so obvious to her demonic senses.

Yet she smiled nearly immediately. "I know. That's why I didn't kill you on sight." She shrugged indolently when he choked in surprise. "I'm glad I cut the Mindbender instead. If you'd died, things down here would've ended much differently. Isn't it interesting how much one decision changes?"

She chuckled at whatever she saw in his expression. "Sorry, you were saying? I assume this mini life story is going somewhere."

"Right." He gave himself a shake. "I don't have much light

left, but it seems like it was meant to be given, not kept. And I couldn't think of a better person to give it to."

"Than *me?*" She laughed. There it was, his worst-case scenario. He gritted his teeth while she paused, swiping under her eyes. The mirth faded from her bearing quickly. "Look at you —you're serious."

"I wouldn't have offered if I wasn't," he murmured.

"No, you're *sincere*. That's worse. You've spent so much time around Seelie that you're walking around as a giant poster boy of truth." She pointed an accusing claw at him. "You actually want to help me."

His gaze dipped to the red-painted nail and back to her face. "Is that...so bad?" Surely she knew he was desperate as well, but he had the feeling that was unremarkable to a demon.

Her pointing finger dipped into her hair, ruffling it as she stared over his shoulder. "I've seen the world when it was young. That is how old I am," she muttered. "But...I've never had anyone offer their light to me before. Not in thousands of years."

A new experience for her, he thought. He might be one of the only living souls to see Lilith ever get caught off guard.

"And if I accept, I don't know what will happen," she sighed. "But I'm willing to make a deal with you for the opportunity to try."

Chapter 36

Jaromir

Lilith rushed him off in another direction, muttering to herself. Most of her palace looked similar, with the ever-burning sconces and dark stone, the corridors narrow and doors lining each side at regular intervals. Jaromir assumed, when one was keeping a place stable and cool with magic, it had to be that way.

But the hall she rushed him to had one large opening, which she burst through. The scent of old paper and ink rushed over Jaromir. Déjà vu gripped him until he took a closer look around and noticed that the stone walls and bare, dustless floors.

Still, this library smelled like the Library of Faerie and had the same pseudo-endless depth of perfectly placed stacks full of books. It may not have the thick rugs and the expensive art that the fae bedecked their hallowed place of knowledge in, but he still understood the respect a group of demons had to have to maintain a library in the middle of Hell.

Giggles sounded around the corner, and he caught a glimpse of a pair of succubi sharing a padded chair. One held a book between them and whispered into her companion's ear before giving it a shameless nip. Heat rose to his cheeks, and he averted his gaze.

Lilith was watching him, her lips twitching. "Korsta. Attend me," she ordered.

The succubi parted, with the smaller of the two pouting and leaving the library. Korsta rose from the chair next, rolling to her cloven hooves with a soft simper. She sported a pair of short, leathery wings and wore a modern style of chunky, black glasses resting on the tip of her nose. Her breasts were dangerously close to being exposed from her white blouse, and a pair of black tights and a tiny skirt finished her look.

Jaromir felt himself grow even warmer. *Definitely* not the Library of Faerie.

"What can I help you with, Queen Lilith?" she purred, all while eyeing Jaromir like he was a tasty snack.

"I need my best book," Lilith said.

Korsta bobbed her head multiple times. "The very best. Of course. Right away." She rushed deeper into the library with the clopping of her hooves.

The Queen of Lust turned her attention back to him. "Most of these books were from Earth. Sinners retain many memories in their souls, which we can use to recreate the books they remember best."

He shifted, still of the mind that he didn't want to know exactly how demons extracted that information, along with the "soul energy" that seemed to power everything here.

"However, some are straight from an Original's mind, constructed with details of the worlds and its inhabitants. We have an incomplete Book of Names, an outdated Annals of Time, and most importantly, my best book. I traded for a real copy of this one. You wouldn't understand the price I paid to get my hands on it." She lifted her shoulders, pride in every word as she surveyed her mini domain of knowledge.

Korsta returned with the promised book, which was bound in soft leather. It was slim, maybe two hundred pages, and written in a language Jaromir couldn't make out. "I need a safe transference spell," Lilith murmured to her librarian, the two of them pouring over its pages and thumbing through them slowly.

"What's being transferred?" Korsta asked curiously.

She jerked her head toward Jaromir. "The rest of his light."

The librarian gasped quietly, lifting her gaze to eye him anew.

She squinted hard before nodding to herself. "But why? He doesn't have much, but…"

Trepidation swirled in his gut, but he didn't dare move away. If there was something to discuss here, he wanted to know exactly what was at stake.

"If there's a spell for us to detail exactly what we want the light to do to me, then it will be safe," Lilith insisted.

"Safe for you?" he asked.

"That's right. Your little gift would kill most demons," she said without looking up from her studying. "Maybe at full power, you could restore an Original so they could rejoin Heaven." She breathed a bitter laugh at the thought.

Korsta piped up. "More likely they burn up from the inside out, though."

Thinking back, Rosier had spoken like he'd be forced to leave Hell. *"I don't want your gift, Jaromir. My destiny is down here, with my queen."*

So, Lilith didn't want to die, nor return to Heaven. He figured it made sense. She had a little community down here and her revenge, plus an obvious hatred for angels. Yet it still seemed like she was smacking away a second chance at what she used to have.

"Ah. Here." Lilith's claw stabbed at a diagram. She and Korsta exchanged a glance and started reading through the spell, speaking in a guttural tongue that flowed over Jaromir's skin like clinging oil.

It might be safe for her, but was it safe for him? Was he making a terrible mistake, offering himself in the first place? Rosier had proven that they couldn't trust a demon, yet he trusted Lilith, just like Izell had chosen to.

The back of his neck itched. A voice tickled his awareness, coming into focus with a crackle of interference. *"Jaromir?"* It was Sondus.

"You should be resting," he answered in his firm doctor's tone.

"Give us some peace of mind, then. Where did you go?"

"Lilith's library. I'm getting us out of here," he said.

There was a pause, during which he imagined a pacing Izell

pelting Sondus with a dozen urgent questions. *"Izell insists we trust you. Review any deal you make extra carefully, okay?"*

Jaromir asked him to wait, because the two demonesses seemed ready to engage the spell they'd found. With a flick of her wrist, Lilith changed the ground beneath their hooves to a solid wooden slab. He approached the edge of it, watching as they placed the book to the side, open to a circular diagram, and got down on their hands and knees. The Queen of Lust created two sticks of white chalk and then they started copying the diagram onto the wood in bold strokes of white.

"You don't need to use blood?" he asked.

Lilith paused, doing a slow pan toward him with a clear *"Are you actually an idiot?"* look on her face.

"That's a stereotype," she grunted.

"Sorry." Guess blood was just a vampire thing; not that vampires needed to create complicated ritual circles anyway. Five feet in circumference, the circle contained a thick rope of runes that looped around to create a sideways figure-eight connecting two smaller circles that were left empty.

He leaned over, studying the markings more closely and realizing he recognized two distinct types. Demonic and angelic together, the little chalky symbols holding hands in some places and running parallel to each other in others.

Lilith started explaining as she worked. Chalking up the symbols would take time, and Korsta stopped assisting to call out runes to Lilith, who created them precisely. She worked on the outer circle, making an array of tiny runes around the inside and outside edges.

"Here's the deal I'm willing to offer you," she began. "Your participation in this ritual in exchange for me sending you and your five friends back to where you came from. The ritual will not harm you, but it will remove all traces of angelic light from you. And I will make the process of returning to your body safe as well. However, the ritual is one of equal exchange."

She scuffed out a rune and redrew it while Jaromir waited, listening intently. He still had a link to Sondus, so he shared every word she said with the fae. His companions would be better versed in turning over the wording of the deal to come for any flaws.

"Me giving you a way out of Hell is not an equal exchange once we activate this spell circle. I have to give you something else." Ice crept up his spine as she spoke, because what else did she have to give him? He didn't want to be an incubus or hold any demonic abilities, no matter how powerful they seemed.

"Would you accept a gift of knowledge?" she asked, giving him pause. "I can tell you things only an Original knows. Secrets of the cycle we occupy and why your two dragon friends are about to have a change of fortune."

"What do you mean?" he breathed.

Her amber eyes glinted as she finally glanced up from her work. "I want to make you dangerous, Jaromir. I want you to understand your place in the universe. Do you accept this as a fair trade for your magic?"

Meanwhile, Sondus was an insistent presence in his head. Secrets and knowledge, exactly what the spymaster wanted. But was it what *Jaromir* wanted? He tuned out the fae's voice until the connection faded. Ultimately, it was his decision and probably his secrets to carry.

"I think it sounds fair. My magic for your knowledge in the ritual, but the ritual in exchange for freedom from Hell," he stated slowly. "All of it done safely for all involved parties."

"Exactly. I'm fairly certain this will work." She got to her hooves, surveying the complicated arrangement. Korsta brought her the book, and they compared the chalk markings to what was on the page. With a nod, she dismissed both the librarian and book before turning to hold her hand out to Jaromir.

She repeated the agreement for a formal pact between them. His attention flashed to her fingers, which trembled with all the emotion she wasn't willing to express. There was no guarantee that she would gain her wings from this deal, but she was willing to part with a lot just for the attempt. That's why he shook her hand in the end and watched the markings crawling up his arm without concern.

He was going home. He just had to say goodbye to the

burning light within him and accept his lot in life. Without the Mending Key, he was an Ancient with no magic. *But that's okay,* he thought. Magic didn't set his worth. It'd taken him far too long to come to this conclusion, to get out of his infirmary bed and start changing the world again. He wasn't a sham wearing a magic ring. He was still a man of medicine and knowledge, and he had people relying on him.

Lilith showed him where to stand, both of them taking up positions facing each other within the smaller rings in the larger circle. She murmured, and the runes lit up, hellfire red next to gold, casting her face in contrast on either side.

He leaned forward and offered his hands, palms up. She mirrored the motion, her heated palms rested down overtop his. Eyes closing, darkness overtook him, though he didn't feel like he moved from his pose.

It was more like a dream, sudden motion and jumbles of color dancing behind his eyelids. He simultaneously was in a library in Hell, listening to the guttural spell escaping her lips, and sitting down somewhere comfortable.

The comfortable sensation solidified until it was the dominant sensation in his mind. He could still hear the spell distantly, but he opened his eyes to see an endless plain, waves of evergreen caressed by a gentle breeze. Impossibly blue sky rested overhead, along with clouds far closer than he'd ever seen. He was seated in the grass, a sensation of peace and harmony echoing in his chest.

Next to him sat Lilith, but not the succubus he knew. Barefoot and smiling, she wore a pure white dress that feathered away from her ankles and shoulders like flower petals. Wings of dove gray were spread out behind her, each filament kissed with silver. She was beautiful, but not in the impossible, sharp way he'd grown accustomed to. Free-flowing, blonde hair blew behind her, framing a soft, oval face marked by overlarge green eyes and a button-like nose.

Angel Lilith looked down at herself, lips quirking. "At the beginning of time, I was shaped into this form. My name was simply Lily, and my first job was to sing welcome to the newly minted souls of babes." She had a soft, lyrical voice. Exactly what he'd always suspected an angel was like.

"What happened to you?" he breathed. It was hard to compare her to the Lilith he knew, to know such purity had been defiled.

She smiled wistfully. "I trusted the wrong man. But I promised you secrets, not my sob story. Here it is. The one thing your favorite angel friends will never tell you.

"Angels and demons guard a sacred cycle, protecting it from each other while also perpetuating it. The life cycle of souls, Jaromir. Humans are unique in that they live twice. Have you ever considered that?"

She leaned back, admiring the sky while he thought about it. "Once as mortals, and once as an angel or demon?" he guessed.

"Indeed. But that is the simple version, once you add in potential. Some souls wither up and die immediately upon being sentenced to Hell, while others never leave the Fields of Paradise in Heaven to take angelic form. We consider those souls weak, but the cycle needs them. They are eventually recycled and returned to Earth. Their energy fuels the birth of new souls. Are you following me so far?"

"I believe so," he said.

"Every time an angel or a demon dies, their soul energy is recycled. It also goes to birth new souls. But the older either is, the more energy they put back into the cycle. In the end, we all die eventually. It is meant to be for the energy inside of us to continue life."

"Right, that makes sense. It's like magic. Nothing is ever lost— it just goes to a new vessel."

She smiled to herself. "I'm glad you mentioned magic, because that's where things get complicated. Humans are born without magic. Right?"

"Right."

"But angels and demons have magic. As do vampires," she said.

"Well, vampires get it from the fae. We vaguely follow their thirteen schools of magic," he pointed out.

"The presence of the fae and their connection to Earth is where I'm probably going to lose you," she warned. "Fae are made from magic, as are angels and demons. If you think of it from my perspective, they are a walking soul, because that's what my kind are. Humans have to die to get magic and become a walking soul, AKA an angel or a demon."

His brow furrowed, unsure of where this was going anymore.

"Think of it this way. Humans exist on Earth. Fae exist on Faerie. Think of the time before Oberon and his Eyes of Worlds. Earth was the first place life came into existence, but it is tethered to Faerie, the second place where life developed. We called this the First and Second Realm, because naturally, when a human died...their resulting reincarnation would be able to come and go from Faerie easily, the place of magic."

He put up his palms. "So, a human lived their first life on Earth and their second life on Faerie?"

She nodded. "Of a sort. Our homes were still Heaven and Hell, but we could engage in a process to go to and from Faerie and enjoy its peace. That was the golden age of existence, before too many of our souls ventured over to Faerie at the same time. We encountered each other and the fae enough that many had the idea to use them to fight in our war.

"It grew so bad that King Oberon created his Eyes of Worlds, and now, the human cycle is mostly separate from the fae cycle because of the Veil, which is a complicated sheet of magic that isolates Heaven and Hell together. Basically, they make a separate Realm now. I see the question on your face. Why is this important?"

"Well, yes," he admitted.

"The Veil has created a barrier in the nothingness between Realms. That place of darkness is composed of pure creation energy, donated to by Heaven, Hell, and the resting place of souls in Faerie, their great Sanctum. Let me give you an example on a smaller scale. Have you been through a portal before?"

"Of course."

"Have you ever wondered how it works?" She drew a line midair, leaving behind a glowing line mimicking one of the slashes in reality. "Crossing from one place to another is no easy task on your body. The magic snatches at the very molecules of your body and what's on your person, tearing them down in one place and building them back together in the other."

Immediate and incredible discomfort lifted goosebumps all over Jaromir's skin. "I could've gone my whole life without knowing that," he admitted.

She smirked, raising a brow. "Has a portal ever put you back together *wrong*? Magic doesn't make mistakes, unlike the souls that wield it. Portals do the same thing for you as the process for a demon or angel heading to Earth or Faerie does for them. To that end, have you ever wondered why the angels you've met have had a *physical* body? They've already died. They're souls."

He reached out and touched her hand. Her skin was soft, bone firm. As real as he was. "Another thing I haven't really thought about," he admitted.

"In the process of going to Earth or Faerie, our souls have to cross the creation magic between Realms. We are wrapped in potential like newborn babes, the shape of our souls creating a brand-new living body to occupy. If it wasn't for the droll Heaven-Hell Accords, an angel or demon could exist there as a breathing being, occupying the same niche as an immortal super-natural that vampires are blessed with." She smiled as realization finally crossed Jaromir's face.

"Are you sending us through the Veil?" he asked.

Lilith nodded again. "I created a rip in it by visiting you earlier. I can send you and your companions through it."

He felt that they were running out of time in this alternate reality. The light above was dimming, the wind slowing to let the air hang over them, charged with static. "It's the secret to true immortality, isn't it?" he asked, watching that glint in her eyes. Her expression all but confirmed it. "As long as a soul can go through the Veil, it can get a body. You're restoring Queldian and Sissaron to life!"

He blinked, and his reality shifted. His hands were now wrapped around Lilith's, gold and red light dimming to embers around them. Though her demonic features were unchanged, a pair of sizable, silvery wings were extended behind her to their full span. Her grip anchored him as fatigue had his limbs trembling. She held him up as she concluded the spell and the magic circle flared one last time. The runes were permanently branded into the wood in place of chalk.

"I got you," she murmured, catching his shoulders when he pitched forward. In a slow blink, she had him seated with his back against one of the stacks. She knelt before him, her fingertips sparking with white soul fire.

"Your wings," he breathed, lifting a shaking hand to touch the edge of one. She was the only fallen angel he'd seen with pristine feathers.

She placed a hot hand over his brow as he let those silvery filaments tickle his palm. His wavering vision came back into focus, heavy limbs feeling like she'd picked up some of the weight. A little laugh escaped him. To think a demon was *healing* him.

Once she was done, she took up his hands in hers. "You have given me a gift I can never repay, no matter the agreement we struck," she said, her smile tinged with sadness. "I know you made this deal out of desperation... Now that I've seen the depths of your soul, I feel like we could've been friends, and I have so very few of those."

He gave her hands a squeeze. "We can be friends." He'd seen a side of her he'd never expected of a demon and wondered how much of Lily remained within the formidable Queen of Lust.

"Well, friend." She tilted her head ever so slightly, considering. "Six souls barreling through the Veil in its weakened state will tear it to shreds. I suppose I will be seeing you in a couple days, at maximum."

"What—?"

She continued speaking over his protest. "Good luck. And tell Izell congratulations for me."

White soul magic glimmered in her hands, growing nearly unbearably hot where she held him. Darkness closed in, this time completely.

Chapter 37

Izell

The last thing Izell remembered was a winged Lilith bursting into their room, white flames surrounding her hands. A single touch from her had caused darkness before she woke groaning in her own very stiff body. She peeled open her eyes slowly, only able to vocalize a rattling moan. Everything hurt. She was far too old for this shit.

Jaromir had been successful, then. She was entwined with his still-sleeping form, right where they'd left Faerie. Peeling herself away from him slowly, she peered around through slitted lids. The little apartment where Archangel Soren had lifted their souls remained nearly identical.

Except someone had drawn up an extra chair where there hadn't been one previously and sat there, waiting. The air was still; Izell was clearly the first of them to wake from their ordeal in Hell. But *was* she awake? For the man who met her eye just a few feet away, seated on the wicker chair like it was the noblest of thrones, was her grandfather, Oberon.

He was obviously a spirit rather than a living man, his body translucent. The lines of his form were constructed of silvery light, but that face... No stone recreation could catch the hint of humor to the set of his lips, nor the wisdom that sparkled in his monochrome eyes. His ghost reminded her of what he'd looked like, for time had worn his memory clean in her mind until the name Oberon simply evoked a strange love-loss feeling in her heart of a beloved figure who'd left her long ago.

"Grandfather?" she breathed, trembling. This was no longer a joyful reunion. Any fae knew that ghosts were the worst thing to encounter, for they had refused the bliss of eternity with the gods for a reason. Usually revenge. And it was her fault he was awake in the first place; she'd been the one to call him back, after all.

"Peace, little one." His voice was a gentle wisp of sound. "I could not rest when I became aware of the danger you face."

Tears pricked the corners of her eyes. "I shall join you soon." Now that they'd successfully braved Hell and gained the Summer Key and a greater demon's soul, she had to face the executioner's axe. Soren was in Heaven, unable to sacrifice himself. It had to be Izell. It'd always been Izell's calling. And the sand in her hourglass was finally down to the last grains.

He didn't argue or give false hope, only studying her for a long moment before nodding in agreement. "I didn't want to leave either. But I couldn't stay, not when the difference meant the preservation of so many lives. You didn't understand that when you woke me with the false lover at your side. But now you do."

"I do," she agreed, wiping at her face. She paused, looking more closely at her unglamored hand. Dark skin and sparkling golden magic greeted her, free of scales.

"Enjoy the unexpected gifts first. When your group is ready, the gods are holding the rarest of events: an in-person Convocation of the Elements in the palace. You don't want to miss it," he said, his gentle voice starting to fade.

"Grandfather, wait," she protested, reaching for him as his ghostly body faded too, blowing away like specks of light.

He left her with the impression of warmth. "See you soon," he whispered like the barest breath of wind.

She closed her eyes to sob at the sudden rending pain of his loss *again*, only to experience the sensation of waking up for the second time with a single tear escaping the corner of her eye. So, she had been sleeping. And reality was still pain, but this time, it was accompanied by the snap of something in the couch beneath her and Jaromir's heavy weight.

The whole couch gave a groan before toppling onto its back, flinging her into something hard. "Ow," she groused, her eyes flying open.

Sandstone scales filled her vision. She jerked back, eyeing the whole bulk of an adult male dragon sprawled on his side, blinking sleepy golden eyes and looking around in utter bafflement. His scales were all buffed, shiny and new. A familiar bond snapped into place between them like he'd never left, like the terrible night a Fell slayed him had never happened. Her emotions were his, and his power was hers, melding them together in an unbreakable connection.

Breathing a friendly chuff, he bumped her forehead with the tip of his snout. She scratched his ears, the whole moment so surreal she figured she had to be stuck in yet another dream.

"We're awake," Queldian whispered, answering that thought.

"You're alive," she whispered back.

"No wonder everything hurts." He spoke her other thoughts, and she laughed, hugging him around the head and letting his rumble resonate through her whole body. Her joy reached a level where it was confused with every other emotion swirling in her heart until she was hiding shaking, ugly sobs between his horns.

A hand rested on her shoulder, unexpected. She glanced blearily over her shoulder to Jaromir, who had awoken as well. "Don't cry," he murmured. "It's a gift from Lilith."

Queldian shifted, licking the man clear across his face. "Thank you," he rumbled. "I can finally snuggle Izell again."

As he spoke, a squeal sounded. Izell groaned as she heaved herself onto her elbow, looking over the side of the toppled couch. Next to Lyana, a full-sized sea serpent was just starting to wake, his fins flapping in confusion as he looked around. *"Ronnie!"* the water fae exclaimed.

Izell wet her lips, casting a side glance at Jaromir, who lifted a brow. "She calls him Ronnie." She muffled a snicker. "They *have* to be a thing."

Sissaron shifted into humanoid form, his tattered angelic armor hanging off his body. Neither of them seemed to care as they embraced, lips locking a moment later. Izell grinned. *Called it.*

Sondus picked himself up from the floor, smiling as he watched this too. "Cyranos is going to be beside himself," he remarked. He ran a hand over his head, which was unmarred by the injury he'd sustained as a soul.

The words were like a dose of ice water. Cyranos. The gods! "There's a Convocation of the Elements we have to attend," she blurted, tripping over herself as she jumped to her feet. Jaromir caught her, and for the first time, she noticed the change in him.

The line of his cheekbones was softer, and a little more gray had woven into the yellow of his short hair. But his eyes...they were a normal brown, crinkled at the corners with laugh lines. He looked human, and her senses told her he was much diminished. Untouched by angelic power, even, and surviving the brush with it without any fangs or taste for blood. Not really a vampire anymore, then, but an immortal of...no magic.

"What happened?" she demanded.

He smiled, unbothered by this change within him. "I restored Lilith's wings with what remained of my light, and she made this happen." He gestured to their companions. "The process of returning to Faerie through the Veil brought Queldian and Sissaron back to life."

"Incredible," the sea serpent murmured.

Jaromir glanced to the side, brow furrowed in thought. "She also mentioned that our passage through the Veil would rip it further and that we'd be seeing her soon."

They all reacted in the same moment, becoming a crescendo of noise that had him lifting his hands. "Maybe we should freshen up and get going?" he suggested.

"No wonder the gods wanted a Convocation," Izell muttered. They had new haste to attend, but first, there was a round of quick rinses in the shower to clean off the smell of however many days they'd been laying around.

Izell turned the apartment over for clothing that would cover Sissaron's broad, half-hythian shoulders. Everyone had left some behind, but Jaromir's clothing was cut too slender, and she had the hardest time finding one of Sirius's cast-offs. Eventually, she found a white undershirt of his, which fit Sissaron snugly. It would have to do for now.

As soon as everyone was ready, there was a knock at the door. An astral fae man in palace livery stood there, looking confused when Izell glamored herself as her old half-dragon shifter appearance after opening the door. She realized no one would recognize her "true" self and had no desire for it to become known that she was no longer a shifter.

Shifter-fae relations were a far cry from the first issue on her mind, but she still supported her old shifter friends over any *mort loci* rhetoric currently seizing Faerie.

"Good evening, Lady Izell. A message for you," the servant said, passing her a scroll sealed with green wax stamped with King Orin's symbol. He bowed and took his leave quickly.

She broke the seal and scanned the note. Written in Orin's hand, it was a dashed-off notice that the gods had invaded his favorite dining spot in their fae forms and called a Convocation.

She couldn't help a smirk that he'd refer to it as an "invasion."

"I don't think we're late," she announced but still opened a portal for them to get as close to the palace as possible to make haste.

Jaromir was the last through, eyeing the rip in reality with a dry swallow. She nearly had to push him through. "Something wrong?" she asked quietly.

He shook his head, hiding his lips behind a hand. "Tell you later."

She accepted that since they were already passing the gates and earning nods from the guards. They were expected, with other palace servants leading them with haste into the underbelly of the Seelie Palace. While she appreciated the effort, she knew exactly the room they were heading to: Orin's favorite parlor.

Sure enough, they were ushered straight there. Eight of the military elite lined the wall, faces straight and serious. Izell wondered how many knew why they were called to guard duty.

Their entry made the parlor cramped. The table was usually set for a maximum of twelve. As she entered, Izell wondered if the gods' glowing was for show or if it was required for an official Convocation of the Elements, but the ambient lighting was overshadowed by the outline of each god radiant with their signature element. They sat at the four cardinal points of the table—two in the center of the seating, and two at either head of the table.

Sitting on either side of Raenith were King Orin and Queen Kalimea, while Talina sat at her father's right hand. That left five spots open, like they were expecting Izell's newly enlarged group.

Along the wall, cushions were laid out for a seated audience of other important faces. Sirius sat by the door with a hand on his knee, ready to leap at a moment's notice. Next to him, Neala leaned against Cedric, who was in his half-fae form again at last. Another massive Blood Prince sat with arms crossed and his back to a wall. Korin, she believed his name was. He met her gaze and flashed a wink.

Various dignitaries, such as the Archfae Council, were also in attendance. Izell's favorite quartet of former students was next, using Vidia's crimson bulk as a makeshift backrest. Theron and Sorsha were snuggled up tightly together. Ash was petting Vidia's neck while Keegan's starry gaze went unerringly to Queldian trotting in. His jaw dropped, and he pointed. At the same time, Sorsha gasped, her pointing finger aimed at Sondus.

The room was suddenly awash with noise, multiple voices exclaiming names or questions. In the middle of it all, Cyranos glanced up at the newcomers, his scowl fading and his jaw dropping open. He stood first, crossing to his son for a murmured conversation. Sissaron dwarfed his godly father, all the better to pull him in for a hug. For a moment, both of them glowed with navy-blue radiance.

"Please, have a seat," crackled Raenith's voice, cutting through the general noise. She'd caught the moment Theron was tugging at one of Sondus's wings, saying something that had the spymaster grinning. Behind them, Queldian had accidentally knocked Keegan down with an enthusiastic greeting and was now snout to snout with his growling familiar.

There was a shuffling as individuals parted, curious glances and bitten lips showing that this was just a brief interruption.

Sissaron and Lyana sat at either side of Cyranos. The God of Water wore a rare smile, beaming even, his watering eyes turning into fractals of crystal-like ice as he barely contained his joy. "Thank you," he whispered to Zalice, who tapped his chin before pointing to Getana, who, in turn, smiled and pointed to Raenith. "Fine. Thank you all."

"As you would do for me, brother," Zalice said, his voice a sigh of wind. He flashed a fond smile toward his daughter.

Izell took the seat next to Kalimea so Jaromir could sit beside her. That left Sondus with the last spot, between Sissaron and Talina. Of course, Queldian wouldn't be left out, so he wiggled into the space between hers and Jaromir's chairs, sitting up attentively and earning an ember-filled chuckle from the Goddess of Fire.

"We are all in attendance," Raenith intoned.

Getana nodded, drawing herself up. "Mind. Body. Soul. Magic," she recited.

"Fire, water, air, and earth. The sacred elements decided at the birth of the world," spoke the Goddess of Fire.

"We keep the balance to this day. Four are our number, and four attend this Convocation," Zalice said, glancing toward Cyranos. *"This time,"* whispered a soft wind.

The God of Water glared back. "So may it be," he grunted.

"We have called a Convocation of the Elements," they said together, in sync despite their varied expressions. Magic warped through the room, heavy like humidity. Jaromir shifted in discomfort, and a murmur sounded from the vampires behind them. Izell soaked in the same feeling, reveling silently in the power of her gods.

"Excuse me. Is it too late for one more?"

Izell exchanged a glance with Sondus, the only other soul who'd heard that voice. Softer, gentler than his ghost, as delicate as the hooves that crossed the room as he took form from pure magic. Oberon was a pure white prize stag made of fractals of light.

"Of course. Welcome, King Oberon," Getana said, holding out her hand. The stag took pride of place standing next to her, allowing a pat on his shoulder before he edged away, holding his impressive rack high and proud. In the wake of her words, the buzzing of voices rose, gasps sounding out.

"I return to advise and support only." His liquid eyes met hers across the table, and she swore he winked.

"Advice we shall need. The Veil has ripped wide open," Zalice said, speaking over the next wave of reactions. "Tonight is the last night we have to prepare. When the sun next sets over Earth, a full moon shall rise, and with it, the first demon shall break free from Hell and emerge on Nyixa. Accounting for the difference in time's passing between Faerie and Earth, we have less than a day to react."

"The Unseelie Army is mobilized and ready. We, too, will be breaking through to Earth for the first time since the Veil's creation," Kalimea said. Her eyes were focused on Oberon with burning intensity. If she could set him on fire with a look, he would spontaneously combust. "King Oberon shall see that the Unseelie he left behind have become friends to humanity."

"While my Seelie Army is at the ready to defend the Light Eye and repel any demonic invaders who reach Faerie," Orin echoed his wife.

"Our most pressing concern is the creation of the Dark Eye. Do we have everything?" Cyranos asked, his voice like a cutting edge of ice turned toward Izell.

She nodded to Sondus, letting him answer. "We have all the Keys and a demon too. Get a view of this," he said, unsheathing the demonic dagger and floating it to the center of the table.

Ping ping ping, the ruby pommel rang out.

"We successfully captured the Sorceress-turned-greater-demon, Lucia, within the magic of this weapon," he continued, gesturing toward it. Cyranos picked it up first, his breath blowing frost over the gemstone.

He passed it to Raenith, muttering, "Take it before I freeze her for her crimes."

"Don't give her the easy way out, brother," she whispered back.

Izell spoke up next. "I plan to use my pact with Lucia to force her into the ritual. For once, I believe we have everything in order, though we have a few Key-holders in attendance here who will need to make it to Nyixa."

The gods glanced amongst themselves. "Well, that's not exactly true, is it?" Getana asked, her rustling voice gentle.

Her confident smile started to fade. *What was that supposed to mean?* They had the Keys, the demon, and the sacrifice ready to power the spell. Then, she glanced to the golden occultarus just starting to bob over her shoulder and breathed a little sigh. "Oh, yes. We used your blessings and magic to make this all possible. I apologize, though each was necessary for us to survive the challenges of Hell."

"Magic can be replaced," said the Goddess of Earth. She waved her hands, conjuring an item made of fine fibers that wove together tightly at her command. When it was done, it floated over to settle before Izell. "But something else cannot be."

She lifted the corner of the fabric, unfolding it and recognizing the buttery softness, its soothing scent, and the bit of magic within it. It was Getana's favorite gift to expecting mothers who had earned her favor, a self-cleaning diaper.

All thoughts in her head ground to a sudden halt, her heartbeat flooding her ears. She didn't understand. Why did Getana give her a diaper? What help would this be when she was to sacrifice herself upon moonrise tomorrow?

"Congratulations, Izell," Raenith crackled with proud warmth.

Why...was she giving congratulations?

Her breathing quickened as she swung her gaze back to Getana. "No. No no *no*. I can't be... It's not possible..."

Jaromir's hand covered hers. She didn't dare look at him, not yet, trembles wracking her as the end of her plans teetered over an abyss.

"It's true. I sense in you the first sparks of life," Getana confirmed with a smile.

Izell clutched her head, seized by an instant, crushing headache.

"We called this Convocation in part to find another willing to sacrifice for the good of Faerie, for Izell is with child. The elements no longer recognize her as the one chosen to follow in Oberon's footsteps," Zalice said calmly. He might as well have knocked her from her chair with a stiff wind.

She launched from her chair, pointing at him. "You *knew* this was going to happen," she accused. Deathly silence closed in around her. The fae in the room knew she was putting herself above the seated gods, grounds for punishment. But she didn't care. She only saw Zalice's knowing smile, that same smug look he'd worn after her first night with Jaromir. "You've always known. How did you set me up?"

Talina's eyes were round as saucers. She gestured urgently for Izell to sit, for static was rising in the air, rolling from the Lord of Storms. "Set you up?" Zalice repeated quietly. "In nearly every timeline, we end up here."

She knew he wasn't about to smite her, not when the gods had gone out of their way to tell her of her pregnancy. "Sure, this happens. But what did you do before now to lead us here?" she demanded.

"Izell, please, it's a good thing." Now Jaromir was on his feet, blocking her view of the god who happened to be the strongest seer alive. He drew her into a hug, folding her shaking body to him. He whispered over her hair for her ears only, "You're just overreacting a little. You get to live. We...we're having a baby." It sounded like he was in shock as well. But like always, they processed things very differently.

"The only thing that changes per timeline is whether or not we tell you," Zalice said.

"Just one *huge* problem," she exclaimed. "Do you really think there's someone in this room just chomping at the bit to replace me?"

Despite her shouting, Zalice remained placid, other than the zip of electricity making small arcs through his darkened wings. He spoke a phrase of ancient fae-tongue, one that had no true translation, just this approximation: *what will be, will be.*

"Yes, Izell. Someone will replace you," he said.

"We love you," Raenith whispered in warm embers of sound. "You didn't really think we'd let you die, did you?"

She collapsed back into her seat, spent with her fading anger. She'd just started to come to terms with it, and now it felt like the decision was ripped away. A child was one of very few things to stop her in her tracks. But even now, she didn't hear anyone volunteering to sacrifice themselves for the spell, and that was terrifying.

Meeting Jaromir's gaze, she wondered how this looked to him. He was half of this equation too, yet the way it was revealed had sucked away the joy for both of them. Jaromir held her hand, but he looked lost, his gaze in her direction yet unfocused.

"Anyone who holds a Key is eligible to take Izell's place," Zalice continued. Stars above, that made it worse, she thought. There were only twelve candidates other than her, and fewer still were in this room.

Jaromir lifted his head. "I will do it. For Izell and our unborn child, I will sacrifice in her place."

Chapter 38
Izell

"No," she gasped. The room rocked, steady boards turning to jelly underfoot. Nothing in this world was stable, not with those damning words echoing in her ears.

Jaromir took her face in his hands, making her meet his steady gaze. His lips were moving, but she didn't hear anything, just the screaming of sudden tinnitus. The words "trust me" pursed his mouth, and she tried to shake her head.

No! She'd already trusted him, and he'd gone and sacrificed his nephilim light to get them out of Hell. Cossette had told her to trust him like he'd trusted her...and she had. Just how much faith did she have to match? Enough to let him go and fulfill the duty she'd always meant for herself?

Too upset to answer her own question, she just stared at him, numb, before rattling off some of the thoughts returning to her all at once, "I was ready for this. I had everything set up. Everyone that came with us, they got something special..." Except for herself, but she breathed a little wheeze of a laugh.

A baby. What kind of insanity was that? She was nearly five thousand years old, and here she was, about to have a baby. The gods couldn't lie, and Getana also never made a mistake recognizing when a woman was blessed with new life.

She'd had her last mate's baby, too, before he'd left her. Different circumstances, same ending. The exact same situation she'd been about to put Jaromir through—an untimely death of a mate. She'd thought he was strong enough to handle it, to find another someday. At the same time, she knew she wasn't that strong. She didn't have time to get used to the idea.

The gods were still talking, moving on from the most devastating moment of her life. Jaromir still held her, waiting patiently for her to come back enough to listen. "I have a plan," he whispered, perhaps sensing that she was finally ready. "Tell you later."

"When we don't have an audience?" she asked under her breath. And what an illustrious audience to witness her breakdown.

Jaromir nodded, holding her hand as he finally turned back to Cyranos, who was speaking.

"...ready to empower the golden occultarus with extra power, to ensure there are no mistakes with this new Dark Eye."

He gestured, and Izell's occultarus wavered, invisible forces playing tug-of-war with it. She reluctantly let it go, and it started spinning above the center of the table. Most of the power she'd stored within it had been unleashed while they were in Hell, leaving it an empty vessel ready for whatever the gods planned.

The air itself shifted, all of the magical potential of the four gods moving in harmony. Rather than offering a separate blessing to her, they gave their full might to the golden orb, wrapping it in multicolored bands of raw elemental magic so bright she had sunspots branded behind her eyelids. Either they were holding back on her before, or their magic regenerated faster than expected, but the process took several long minutes of constant input.

When they were done, the occultarus vibrated violently, jerking with a mind of its own. She held her breath. It was only a prototype, after all, the first of its kind created by a greedy but resourceful artisan.

Still trembling, it started floating toward her. She leaned back, imagining the explosion if it rejected the power contained within it. When it was uncomfortably close to her face, a shimmer gleamed over its surface, and it returned to orbiting her like nothing had happened.

She breathed a sigh of relief. "Thank you all," she said with stiff respect.

"Now, there is the matter of the ceremony itself. I would like to review it one more time," Oberon said.

There was some glancing around and rummaging before Zalice reached under the table and produced a battered journal from seemingly nowhere. He flipped it open and surveyed several diagrams in Jaromir's handwriting before it shifted to Sondus's notes made in his best forgery of the former's penmanship. Oberon padded over to look over the god's shoulder.

"What would you change?" the Lord of Storms asked. A pen shot from its holder into his hand.

They surveyed the diagram and the words without saying anything. *"Thirteen people holding thirteen Keys, plus a fourteenth casting the spell itself,"* Oberon said. *"I believe Izell's original plan was for her to be the spell caster."*

"That's right," she confirmed. "But it also hinged on Lucia working with us rather than being the sacrifice." She drew on the chain around her neck, revealing the half-melted ruin of the Language Key, the band Lucia had worn for her entire immortal existence. With her death, the still-intact gemstone had only just started responding to Izell.

She'd been saving her pact with Lucia to make the former Sorceress stand with them and create the new Dark Eye. But now, Izell would take her place with the Language Key.

"So, we don't have a spell caster, and the last line needs to be altered." Oberon nodded, meeting Zalice's eye. Something passed between them silently before the god crossed something out and began writing a new ending to the spell.

Though she'd been silent through all of this, Lyana stirred now and cleared her throat. "I volunteer as the new spell caster. I have nearly as much experience as Izell with speaking the old language. It's the least I can do to help..." She flashed a glance toward Izell that had her hackles raising. Pitying, apologetic, regretful, everything in Lyana in the wake of the events in Hell. She'd gotten everything back—her freedom, her long-lost mate, revenge—while Izell stood on the edge of losing Jaromir. How the tables had turned.

Oberon gestured to her with his rack. *"You are an excellent candidate for the job. Memorize this spell, and teach the last line to Jaromir."* While he spoke, Zalice passed her the notebook.

"I won't let you down," she promised.

In the ensuing pause, the gods waited patiently for anyone else to speak up. Their business was concluded, for better or for worse. All the pieces were set up... Now, all anyone had to do was their job, and they'd see if they survived the battle to come.

She had to admit that her carefully scried plan for the future looked nothing like the reality in front of her. She'd never assumed she'd successfully go to Hell and return or that she'd fall so deeply in love with a human-born man.

Yet here they were.

"This Convocation is at an end," Raenith finally said. Zalice stood first, blowing away on a breeze until the only evidence he'd been there was his pushed-out chair. Getana was next, though she burst into a cloud of dust and sparkles.

"Showoffs," Cyranos muttered, standing and remaining there. He made a portal and gestured for Sissaron and Lyana to accompany him.

When they were gone, Raenith signaled the true end to the Convocation by getting to her feet as well. Her white-hot gaze burned into Izell's cheek, but for the first time, she had trouble even looking at her patron goddess. "Would you and Jaromir accompany me?" she invited, gesturing toward another portal of her creation.

Jaromir shrugged, helping Izell to her feet. He offered his arm, no doubt feeling how unsteady her legs were. What felt like hundreds of eyes followed Izell's progress toward the portal, and she was filled with gratitude that she didn't have to talk to any of them with this easy escape.

The other side of the portal ended in...her apartment. Jaromir went over to try pushing the broken couch upright, but it sagged backward immediately, the broken legs no longer enough counterbalance to keep it from falling. The moment the portal closed behind her, Izell just watched him, numbness creeping back into her limbs.

"Did you need something?" she muttered to Raenith, who crackled in her superheated glory only a few feet away.

The goddess swept her up in a hug, pleasantly warm despite the flames her form was made of. Izell stuttered a complaint, but Raenith didn't let go, holding her past the uncomfortable stage until she was forced to accept this was happening. She rested her face in the fiery shoulder in front of her, soft sizzles the only sign that she began releasing the tight coil of grief within.

"I wanted to offer fatecross magic to you both so you can still experience a mating bond before tomorrow night," Raenith crackled.

In return, Izell sobbed harder.

"Will it work for us?" Jaromir asked. She barely felt the heat of his palm compared to Raenith, but he was there too, rubbing up and down her back in soothing circles. "I understand Sirius became part fae beforehand?"

"That's not a necessary part of the process. Only an epic love that crosses the line between fae and human-born," Raenith said.

Izell pulled from her, turning to embrace Jaromir instead. He crushed her to him, holding her like he never wanted to let go. Part of her just wanted to clutch the front of his shirt and sob, but she drew that in, sniffling and breathing in his scent, committing it to memory. "Epic is the right word for it. It survived Hell, Faerie, and even his infirmary bed," she said, forcing a watery laugh.

"Do you want to be mates?" he asked. Earlier, he hadn't wanted the same when it was her leaving. She knew it paralleled his lost love too closely. But now that he was the one leaving...she guessed it was on her now. Did she want to feel his mating bond for a day before he had to go?

She composed herself despite the great *crack* her heart experienced at the thought. One day was better than nothing. She'd take the pain if it meant their hearts were in sync for even that short a time. His eyes simmered with tenderness as he wiped her face with his thumbs, brimming with love and...confidence.

That's right, he had some sort of plan, something he only wanted her to hear.

"Even if it's just for a day, I want your mating bond," she said, hoping her expression similarly spoke to the depths of her feelings. "I love you, but I will hate myself forever that you have to be the one to go. It was meant to be my burden and sacrifice."

"It'll be okay," he murmured. "It is because of my love that I'm willing to do this for you. And...our child? Is it really possible...?" His hand rested over her flat belly.

"The gods are never wrong about such things," she replied. She laced her fingers with his, full of the same disbelief and hesitant joy. So much heartbreak lay ahead that she barely had a chance to consider celebrating.

Raenith cleared her throat politely. "Where would you like the marks? I will leave the moment it's done. Just know that you need to start traveling to Earth at daybreak. That will be perfect timing."

"Right. Daybreak," she nodded, considering for only a brief time. "I want my mark over my heart."

"Same," Jaromir echoed immediately.

The goddess flashed a smile, just a reddish line. It was uncertain what emotion she expressed, but she seemed happy for them from the tender warmth she exuded. "You won't feel a thing. I'll make the trigger something simple so you can enjoy it once I leave," she promised, stepping up to them.

Jaromir flinched when Raenith reached for them together, her fiery fingers dipping below his shirt like it wasn't even there. Izell felt her fingertips tracing a complicated pattern on her chest, sealed with a burst of heat, but it wasn't as painful as most blessings from the Goddess of Fire.

"See you soon." She smiled, bursting into a cloud of sparks and embers the next moment.

"Wait, what was the trigger phrase?" Izell called. But the goddess was already gone, her energy flickering out before anything could catch fire.

Jaromir caught her shoulders, hauling her into a kiss the next moment. They met in a tangle of lips and tongue and teeth, a desperate duel to make their mark before it was too late. Yet he pulled back before it could go much further, saying, "Finally. That was unbearable."

"You could've kissed me at any time," she quipped.

"No. I knew it'd be suspicious if I took you aside and explained earlier, but...I don't intend to die tomorrow."

She blinked, dumbfounded. He was completely serious, though, determination written clearly on his face. It was sexy, she had to admit, to see him so sure of himself at last. But... "This is a greatest work spell, Jaromir. You know what that means. You just agreed to sacrifice yourself, mind, body, soul, and magic."

"King Oberon's soul survived," he pointed out.

"Well, yes," she said slowly. "It doesn't *destroy* a soul to cast a greatest works spell. The sacrifice just means you die pouring all your energy to fuel it."

"So, my soul will live on," he said.

Her brow furrowed. "But you'll be *dead*. That's the whole point."

"Then I'll come back." He said it like it was just a brief trip, a vacation for his soul. "I learned something from Lilith that I don't intend to share with anyone but you. Sissaron and Queldian came back because of this secret, and I intend to as well."

He gently steered her to the bedroom, and she collapsed in the downy sheets. With effort, she flipped onto her back. "Please, do explain." She was trying not to hold onto any hope, but they had already seen a miracle in motion for the two *very* dead dragons coming back to life.

Laying out next to her, Jaromir told her everything. He spoke of soul cycles and energy until her eyes felt like they were crossing, and then he blew her mind. Just like Lilith had done with him, apparently.

"I don't know how long I'll have to be there or even where I'll go—"

She put a finger to his lips. "You're going to Heaven. I have no doubt."

He kissed the pad of her finger. "—but I intend to find a loophole and come back. I'll sneak out. No one will be the wiser. I will return to you, no matter what it takes."

"Even if it means a demon gets released from Hell?" That's how it worked now; one escaped demon meant one hunting angel. But she'd never heard of an angel getting hunted by a demon for escaping.

"I don't intend to get caught," he murmured. "Which means I need to learn the rules first and what can be tracked. It'll take a little time."

She smiled, curling herself into his side. "To think the great and righteous Jaromir intends to break heavenly rules for me." She didn't think it would work with a reinforced Veil being slammed into place the moment they created the new Dark Eye with his sacrifice, but she didn't mention it. Not when he was so confident. For once, nothing was going to stop Jaromir from getting what *he* wanted, and that was her.

He offered her the kind of hope that was impossible if she were the one to go. With his human-born soul, he'd live on. Maybe he'd even come back, utilizing the secret of true immortality.

"Of course I will. I would do anything for you." He stroked her cheek tenderly. "I love you, Izell."

Something sizzled quietly, and he grunted, touching his chest. She gasped, exclaiming, "I love you too!" A corresponding hiss bubbled from where Raenith had marked her, but more importantly, a feeling was offered to her. A mating bond, a bridge between their species offered from magic but no less real or necessary.

The moment she accepted, it tugged into place, linking them permanently, deeper than the flesh. He was her mate in all ways. Their emotions joined, along with the steady beat of their hearts in sync. Love mingled with a deep pool of her unspoken reservations and his fear and uncertainty hiding underneath his conviction.

"It might work, and that's all that matters right now," she said, speaking to that medley of doubt before it could fester, fed by them both. "I'll take any hope. Because, well..."

She didn't want to raise a child alone, not again. The babe deserved to know how incredible their father was. Jaromir echoed warmth back to her along their bond, melting away any lingering negativity.

It would be okay; there was hope. But she still spent the night with him like it was their last, because there were no guarantees in life or death like having the man in her arms.

Chapter 39
Jaromir

INEVITABLY, THEIR LAST NIGHT TOGETHER HAD TO END. He didn't catch a wink of rest, but ended up holding Izell while the sky slowly washed with shades of pink and orange at the break of a new day. She was truly exhausted after her emotional explosion during the Convocation, but he understood why the gods had done that to her.

If there weren't witnesses, Izell might've tried to throw herself into the spell anyway. He knew how important she viewed the sacrifice and how billions of souls relied on what they were about to do. So, he was infinitely grateful that Oberon had rewritten the most important line of the spell—the very end—and whispered the words into Jaromir's mind. Izell physically couldn't complete it without the right line.

He wasn't sure what his future truly held, but he knew he'd move Heaven and Hell to return to her. If he couldn't escape Heaven...he had a very powerful friend in Hell now who was willing to break rules no angel dreamed of challenging. There was a chance he would succeed, and he hitched his fortune to that chance, that he could be both a savior and a father, a sacrifice and also a mate to the most beautiful, passionate woman he'd had a chance to love.

He waited until the first hint of sunlight on the horizon before stirring Izell's star-flecked hair, pressing kisses to her face until she grumbled awake and peered at him blearily. Emotions stirred along their bond. Her heart leapt at the sight of him, until panic took hold as well. "Gods! I fell asleep," she gasped.

"You needed it," he said, stealing a slow kiss now that she was awake. They shared a regret-filled sigh, knowing what the rising sun meant.

She held him tightly. "Why didn't we meet earlier? When we could have night after night together, with nothing urgent to wake us?" she murmured.

"I'm just grateful we met," he said, brushing a kiss over her nose. She scrunched it with a soft giggle. "If this is truly the end, then know I am grateful for the adventure you brought me on. So much better than sitting in a library while everyone else risks their lives."

Sunlight hit her eyes, sending off fractals of rainbow light. He wondered how she could be any prettier, but everything about her that was different and fae was beautiful in a way he'd never seen in a vampire woman. Izell was truly it for him: his reason for being and his reason for continuing. The old Jaromir would've given up the moment he woke up from Hell and realized he had no magic left, save for the Mending Key. But his worth wasn't hinged on how "useful" he felt anymore.

Izell's face softened. He loved seeing her let down her guard and express what she really felt under that armor of scales and sharp words. "I'm grateful for the time we've had, too," she said. Her fingers pressed to the mark on his chest, right above his heart. It was like a tattoo, a brand of flames. "I'd still lock you in a library to keep you out of danger."

He felt an unexpected blush, remembering the librarian in Lust. "As long as you're dressed for the part, you can lock me in a library." He winked.

She snuggled in closer to his chest. "I'll wear whatever you want. Just come back, okay?" she murmured, hiding her expression against his skin. He drew her up to kiss her instead, not letting her keep anything a secret, not anymore. Mates shared everything, and so he took her pain, sharing the burden of fear for what was to come.

"It'll be okay," he murmured. He repeated that mantra even after they dressed and gathered what they would need. Since the angelic hammer had survived the trip, he strapped it to his belt. Izell donned flexible pants and pocketed a few trinkets to help the potency of her spells.

Instead of making a portal then and there, she opened the apartment's door and let in her sandstone-colored dragon. Queldian rumbled with displeasure at being left outside, padding straight to Jaromir and butting his chest hard enough to stagger him. "I knew you two would be mates," he said. "I've been calling it since Izell told me about you."

"Have you?" Jaromir laughed. He scratched the dragon behind his ears, smiling when he earned a more pleased noise from him.

Queldian pushed his head into Jaromir's shirt and whispered, "Yes. Don't leave her now, okay?"

"Not for long," he promised.

"Let's go, boys," Izell called, standing before a portal now that they were all together. "Hope you're ready for some vertigo. It's at least four portals between here and Nyixa."

He turned green around the edges at the thought but went through the first one without too much complaint. They emerged in front of a small house surrounded by dark greenery of an untamed forest. A bramble of ruby roses curled under one of the house's windows, and Izell spared it a glare before turning to him. "This was my house in Adrun, before Olivia put a permanent portal in my living room."

He laughed. "How'd that happen?"

"You know, just a regular night, having tea with my good friend Nyah when a portal appears out of nowhere. Olivia reaches through, grabs Nyah, and the rest is history," she said with a vague wave. She shaded her eyes and looked around and up at the towering trees. "It's...weird to be back here. This is the first time Adrun has had sun in so long. I wonder how the druids are coping."

"Surely this makes their jobs easier," Queldian said.

Izell gave herself a shake. "Right, who cares right now

anyway? Let's go." Her house was unlocked, so she strode straight inside and through a perfectly oval portal waiting right off the entranceway. The other side was Earth, he knew. A musty cellar that contained yet another portal, plus an albino seer waiting for them with her back propped against the wall.

Her eyes were unfocused and cloudy when Jaromir first spotted her, but soon, she snapped back to herself and startled. "Oh, hello! It's that timeline. You're already here," Cossette said. "Well, no time to waste. You're the last."

"The last of what?" Izell asked, eyes narrowing in suspicion.

"The last stragglers to Nyixa. Gwendolyn's through this portal." She gestured to one half-hidden behind some fallen shelving. It quivered, unlike the permanent one between New York and Adrun that they'd just passed through. Without concern, Cossette used it and gestured for them to follow.

As promised, elderly Gwendolyn stood close by once he became aware of his new surroundings. He rubbed a rush of goosebumps from his arms. "I hate portals," he muttered. Knowing him, he'd find the first portal that didn't put him back together properly.

They were in Coven Rehnquist's mansion, where only a few lights were on. There was no sound save for what came from their little group. "Hello, Cossette. This is it, then?" Gwendolyn smiled her way.

"Yes. They're just in time," the seer answered. At his curious glance, she added, "The sun set not long ago. We just moved our vampires and other photosensitive friends to Nyixa to await the moon's rise."

With a gesture, Gwendolyn opened yet another portal. Jaromir's gut lurched at the sight, but he went through it. He was needed, after all. Witnessing the gleam of white stone, he recognized Nyixa right away, but not the ruin it'd become. There were no buildings and, more importantly, no impossibly massive palace that gleamed like moonstone, its spires scraping the sky.

The first Dark Eye's explosion had destroyed it, toppling it into uneven chunks of stone that covered a good portion of the island from his vantage. His allies hadn't bothered trying to clear it, but it was obvious they'd still been busy. They'd emerged next to where the Dark Eye used to stand, as the dark blast mark was underfoot, the ground crystalized with the force of its detonation. Someone had hauled in massive stone blocks to create a circle to show where the new Eye would be built, alongside the massive sheets of dragon-forged glass and stacks of metal to re-create the cradle that'd held it.

The other Key holders were already standing nearby, talking quietly with Lyana. Jaromir left them for a moment, walking away with Izell to view the empty plain where there'd once been houses and an open-air market. The stone framework of those buildings was either crumpled to dust or removed, creating the perfect staging ground for a battle to come.

"They will first emerge on the other side of the island," Cossette said, pointing into the distance. A mingled host of shifters and vampires was getting into place between that area and where the Dark Eye would be reconstructed in the center of the island. "We've rigged the area with land mines and a few magical goodies, but most will fall into Hell before they do any damage to the invading demons."

"How many should we expect?" Izell asked, coming up on Jaromir's other side.

The seer's mouth formed a tense line. "Too many. But at least there won't be any soul-stealing weapons to worry about."

"That's something," the fae muttered. "We can only start the spell when the moon rises. Unfortunate timing."

Jaromir took a few steps away, inhaling the salt blown in on a stiff breeze. If his eyes didn't deceive him, a slithering teal shape was slicing through the distant waves. A head emerged, fins flapping up a fine mist. It was Sissaron, cutting a deceptively slow path around the island. Jaromir smiled to himself, grateful they had someone to stop any demons who thought they could swim away from the island.

"Beautiful, isn't it?" Gwendolyn's voice startled him. She released a rusty laugh, moving carefully with the assistance of her cane.

"There is much beauty in Faerie I wish we could experience here," he answered, turning his attention back to the sky. Purple touched it here, the sun gone even while it'd just risen over Faerie. It was surreal. "Do you know how much time we have?"

"A couple hours. We should get into position soon," she answered, turning toward the palace's ruin. "But I can't help but reminisce on us landing on these shores for the first time. Do you remember?"

The better question was, how could he forget? That blood-stained night where Fell and Fell Hunter had thrown themselves at each other in a grand melee where there were no winners, only death. They were amongst only a handful of souls who'd survived that night. Jaromir breathed out a slow breath, blocking out his mind's eye before he could remember the aftermath. "If we aren't careful, the same thing will happen here," he answered. It sounded like they didn't have the numbers to hold the demons at bay for long—not until the Unseelie and reinforcements from Heaven arrived. Neither was coming until they saw the first ugly face emerge from Hell.

"I understand the spell is neither quick nor painless," she said. "Is it true we are losing Izell tonight?" She turned watery blue eyes his way, keen despite her outward age.

He shook his head. "No, she cannot finish the spell after all. I will be doing it in her place," he said, finding it harder to speak the words aloud to someone who hadn't attended the Convocation yesterday. It would be an awful shock to his friends if they weren't warned, though.

"So, what Cossette saw was true?" Gwendolyn spoke in a hush. "She said she'd seen a great meeting of the fae gods and their strongest champions. That Izell...is with child?"

He was still proud, despite the circumstances. "That's right."

"She saw it through the eyes of the seer god, Zalice," she continued.

"The whole thing?" He knew the two had grown close in their brief association, but not *that* close.

"Mmm, I believe so. Izell didn't take the news well, she shared. And a glowing stag the gods called Oberon suggested a change to the ritual?" It felt like she was probing now, but he nodded all the same.

"Zalice, Oberon, and I are the only ones who know how to close the spell," he said. But if Cossette was watching at the right place, she would've seen the Lord of Storms write down the words.

Gwendolyn nodded. "Of course. It's important that nothing gets in the way of it." She reached out, clasping his hand in hers. "I will miss you, old friend."

"I will miss you too," he sighed, giving her hand a squeeze. Her skin was dry and paper-thin, aging even in the short time since he'd seen her last. If this kept up, she wouldn't have much time until she was knocking on Heaven's pearly gates.

"Would you like something to drink?" She pulled her hand free and gestured, creating a portal just big enough for her hand. After a quick rummage, she produced a bottle of water like modern mortals drank.

He took it so he wouldn't seem rude, since she'd already risked having her hand in that portal. "Thank you," he said, turning the cap. It gave without the crackle of a seal.

They walked back to where the other Key holders were already in place, standing in a large circle around a base of metal already placed carefully where the first Dark Eye had been.

"There you are," Lyana said, pointing out the two empty places in the circle, which happened to be either side of Neala with her Mind Key. Jaromir smiled when he was placed between her and Izell.

"Just a reminder, I will be reciting the spell as quickly as possible, but the various elements of the Dark Eye will need time to slot together," Lyana said, gesturing to the piles of metal and glass. "You will be holding hands in a perfect circle while this occurs, and the spell will draw on the Keys, then the golden occultarus, followed by our demonic sacrifice"—she lifted the demonic dagger—"and finally, the one who will lay down their life to seal this spell as their greatest work. Questions?"

"I'll know my cue?" he asked.

She didn't quite meet his eye as she nodded. "You'll see it."

"Got it," he sighed, taking a long draught from his bottle of water. It was cold and crisp, a small comfort for the nerves burning in his stomach.

From his research, he already understood most of what was about to happen, especially on the technical level. They were standing in a particular order, grouped by how their schools of magic related. First was Shield and Sword, represented by Adrius and Cossette. Beside them was Night and Day; Olivia chewed on her lip and shifted restlessly, while Gabriel waited stoically with his hands behind his back, watching the sky as it darkened and the stars sparkled to life.

The seasons were next, and it seemed Nyah had passed one of her Keys to her daughter, as Celeste stood with her, Sondus, and Julian. Sirius fiddled with the Flight Key, concern creasing his face as he watched the sky too. But it wasn't the stars Jaromir realized he was watching, but a distant spec of blue circling the island restlessly, accompanied by the bird-like silhouettes of a flock of skyriders. Talina hadn't unleashed her powers yet, but it was obvious she intended to.

Izell stood next to him, then Neala, Jaromir, and finally Gwendolyn. With Lyana placed on the outside of the circle with the sacrifice, they were all ready for the spell to come.

Jaromir sent up a silent prayer. On the very cusp of his final duty, he prayed for mercy and held Izell's hand all the tighter.

Chapter 40

Izell

The ground began to rumble as full dark descended. She clutched Jaromir's hand while the seconds ticked by, feeling both slower than cold molasses and faster than her racing heartbeat. At any moment, she'd need to release her mate and let him face his fate in Heaven, no matter what it might be.

But first, she had to help another face their end. Lyana came over with the dagger containing Lucia and asked, "How do you want to do this?"

Izell leaned in, watching herself appear in multiple facets of the ruby gemstone. "Can you hear me?" she asked.

The ruby rang out with a hollow *ping*.

She lifted her arm and stripped away the illusion of scales, showing the demonic runes that glowed in lines resembling simmering embers. "When Lyana, Jaromir, or I tell you that it's time, I require that you leave your prison and surrender yourself to the Dark Eye spell as its sacrifice."

Lucia didn't respond or bang on the inside of her prison. The only sign that Izell's words did anything was a burning sensation on her arm as the markings flared. "Our agreement was 'anything' in exchange for me taking Jazrach's spark, and this is the kind of anything I want," she said. Those within earshot nodded their agreement.

After a few more moments, Izell gestured to Lyana, who

returned to waiting outside the circle of Key holders. She was fairly certain there would be no other reply than silence, which was the only response she needed.

Out of nowhere, a swirl of power raced over her head. *"Would you like a better view?"* whispered the last voice she expected. Zalice. She glanced around, but there was nothing, just a puff of wind.

"A better view of what, exactly?" she grunted.

He chuckled. *"The battle. I can link you with one of my skyriders."*

Well, she'd be a fool to say no, but she was still terribly confused as to how one of Faerie's gods was speaking to her while she was on Earth until he spoke up again. *"Nyixa used to be a part of Faerie. This is my territory too."*

She nodded to herself, bracing as she felt his magic settle over her mind's eye. She'd experienced recently how his wind magic lent a better vantage without moving from one spot, though he kept this spell looser so she could see and hear with her own senses or tune out. The skyrider he'd attuned her to was a silky white female who chirped in surprise the first time she noticed the link.

"You will be scouting for Izell. Your first priority is guarding my daughter, but you will listen for Izell and if she needs a better view of what's coming toward the Dark Eye spell," Zalice instructed.

"Okay, Father," the skyrider said, chipper. She swooped around the battlefield so Izell could get a finger on what she was seeing. While she stood in the center of the island, the eastern-most third was useless for fighting, covered as it was in white stone shards. Their forces were expecting demons from the north-west side of the island, forming battle lines as the ground continued to quake.

"Good luck, Izell. The elements are with you," Zalice said before his presence blew away on a stiff breeze.

She refocused on what was directly in front of her, seeing that he meant that more literally as four fae positioned themselves in the cardinal directions a few yards from her circle. "So proud I could cry," she projected to Keegan while pretending to wipe a tear from her cheek. He shot her a quick look, but it no longer held the same meaning. The man he reminded her of was long gone.

Dressed in dark battle armor, Keegan was wreathed in flames as he performed a fourth of the complicated full-body spell work that produced a geas formally titled The Elements' Defense. Theron, Sorsha, and Ash completed the spell with him, summoning a translucent sphere that would repel attackers and magic as long as they stood in place without faltering. The geas was one of endurance; the act of warding off attacks would start wearing on them, and if even one of them stepped out of line, it would fail.

Vidia stood by Keegan's side, ready to defend him, while Queldian paced between Sorsha and Theron. It took Izell a minute to recognize Ash's defender, a sleek horse with a shining coat as dark as the night, fully kitted out in battle armor. Though more unassuming than a dragon, he was Comet, Kalimea's immortal war steed, with enough unicorn blood in his line to know exactly how to fight independently and keep himself alive, no matter the enemy.

But if Comet was here, what was Kalimea riding into battle?

Izell didn't have long to question it, because the next quake had her stumbling. "It's time!" Lyana shouted. The barest glimmer of moonlight glowed on the horizon.

The Key holders linked hands, forming a circle. Fae magic loved its circles, finding power in infinite loops with no defined beginning and end. Nothing happened for a heavy moment, but then Lyana started to speak the language of ancient fae. An undercurrent of power rose from her, and the materials lying on the ground began to stir.

Concentrated sulfur stink rolled in. Olivia gagged, hiding her face in her sleeve. No matter what, they couldn't break the link of magic, so Izell unfocused her attention, seeking out the skyrider she'd been linked to. The white dragon had joined a formation around Talina, electric energy crackling as they watched the earth open into a yawning maw filled with hellfire red.

Demons streamed out, rushing with balls of flame and swinging weapons. But this group in the sky waited until the first winged demon emerged, a single slash of lightning grounding the figure immediately. Thunder muted the sounds of battle below.

Even though she watched from the skyrider's eyes, Izell felt the beads of sweat rolling down her back. Every moment that passed, her allies were dying from the sheer number of enemies rushing at them. She saw only moving specs and flashing lights, but it was enough.

Where was the Unseelie army? The white skyrider seemed to sense Izell's thoughts, glancing around and refocusing her gaze with a raptor's pinpoint accuracy. She scanned the ground like looking through a magnifying glass, able to see the darkness of the demon's eyes. No Unseelie.

Darting to the side, the skyrider focused in and out on a blemish hanging over untouched rock. It grew into a line, spreading and stretching into a sheet of reflective glass. A portal shimmered to life, and on the other side was Kalimea in full battle armor, blowing a curved horn of war. She was astride a white stag constructed from cobwebs of light, his ethereal glow the first thing to pass onto Nyixa's soil.

The moment a delicate hoof touched down, the portal ripped wide open, enough for several fae to ride abreast as the army poured in. Unseelie always announced their presence, and singing was too kind a word for the eerie, screaming melody sung from the throats of fae descended from demonic followers, now carrying gleaming, angel-blessed weaponry.

Izell returned to her senses, but not before she caught a glimpse of something that had the skyriders shrieking. She heard the distant echo of it from her own ears as she shook herself off, watching the slow progress of the new Dark Eye. Metal fused and bent, turning into a huge base to hold the finished globe. Shards of glass circled far over her head, outlines glowing. They rearranged themselves like a massive, invisible hand was rotating and moving the shards with no obvious purpose.

Electricity flashed overhead, and Izell wasn't the only one

turning her gaze skyward. "Talina," Sirius muttered, his palms fused to the spell but tension lining his whole frame.

With a sigh, Izell hopped into her skyrider's mind again, earning an irritated screech from the dragon. Talina had turned into a burst of wind, reemerging several yards from the danger as her dragons circled a demon held aloft on dark, feathered wings.

"I just wanted to say hello." Lucifer spoke nonchalantly, flipping a replacement sword between his hands. His face was a slit of darkness under a full-face helmet, and static already danced over his armor, searching for weaknesses to get to the demon within. "Come back, little blue girl. Your soul is so powerful."

The first streak of light passed by like a falling star. Izell felt some of her tension release, recognizing the flight of an angel falling to Earth. Dozens of streaks followed, and Lucifer tutted, while Talina raised her hands skyward. She must've been waiting for the angels, for from her hands wove black storm clouds, which expanded rapidly to cover the sky.

Skyriders snapped their jaws at Lucifer, holding him back for precious seconds. Only the angels disrupted the demigoddess's spell, sending rippling holes through the clouds which were quickly mended over. The devil scythed through the nearest skyrider in an explosion of feathers, and Talina cried out as she pointed at him. A thick tongue of lightning burst from her storm as it continued to expand on its own, joined by the blasts from several charged skyriders.

Lucifer fell, twitching, like any other person hit by such concentrated power.

"She's going to be okay," she said quietly, returning to herself. All they could see was the falling outline of the slain skyrider, Lucifer too far away to be more than a speck.

The sky rumbled, dark clouds boiling with menace as the battlefield muted to shades of black. Sirius glanced her way, electricity dancing in his ruby eyes. Izell could feel the borrowed energy in him, the excess that Talina now drew from as she smote distant figures with ion blasts. She couldn't help but be impressed with the young demigoddess.

"I hate that she's a target. They're going for her now," he

muttered, his fangs bared. "Hurry up!" The bark was aimed at Lyana, who faltered for a split second.

She started chanting the next part of the spell, which channeled the power of their Keys. Sirius had to quiet down as pain gripped them all, feeling to Izell like needles under every inch of skin. She gritted her teeth but cast a worried glance to Julian and Gwendolyn, knowing this was the most dangerous part for them. While she wore a Key, they *were* Keys. Gwendolyn sagged, while Julian was pale and stoic, his icy blue eyes glowing brighter.

The glass shards rotated faster above, floating inward so they looked like a shattered sphere. Jagged edges pointed toward each other like puzzle pieces, waited to be slotted and fused together permanently.

Izell spotted wings, her eyes widening when she realized it was Lucifer, smoke billowing from fire on his feathers that he completely ignored. He landed atop the geas, shadows wreathing his fist as he punched the translucent shield. It held, but a pained groan echoed from the four fae keeping it up.

"Fuck. Let me fight," Sirius muttered, his expression promising murder as they watched Lucifer hit it again, this time dodging Vidia's claws as she shot herself airborne and swiped at him while avoiding flying glass.

"Patience," Neala said, though she sounded just as furious.

Lucifer raised his fist for a third strike, when a flash of bladed danger swept at him, both of them taking skyward. She'd only caught a glimpse of Lilith, who'd come at him with two massive cleavers, her face and feathers marked with stark white war paint. Just the impression of a hoof remained as the geas held.

Izell released an anxious breath. If the Queen of Lust was here, that meant that she was honoring their agreement, even if she was using it as a path to slaying Lucifer. But Lilith had never flinched from her ultimate goal, and that made them allies... for now.

She listened to where they were at with the spell, feeling the tug on her Key lessen. The pieces of the Dark Eye weren't even close to each other yet, the whole process in need of more power.

She gave her occultarus a nudge with a spark of magic, sending it into the floating center of the floating glass shards.

Lyana took five minutes of painstaking reciting to change energy sources to the golden occultarus. The spell called on its gleaming contents next, which spilled out in ropes of pure elemental power. Heat and light nearly blinded her as she watched piece after piece of glass slot together, edges melting with the sizzle of concentrated fire magic. The base formed first, a pristine curve of superheated, dragon-forged glass.

Her heart dropped with every *clink* of shards finding their place on this new, huge occultarus. She glanced across to Jaromir, who watched the approaching finale with a determined set to his jaw.

She allowed herself a single sob, which corresponded with a crack to her fragile heart. He met her gaze, and his lips formed the words *"love you"* before he prepared to bring the spell to its conclusion with one last, irrevocable phrase.

Chapter 41
Jaromir

He knew his moments could be counted on his fingertips. Lyana was saying the last lines of the spell while holding the dagger containing Lucia aloft. Four multicolored whips of magic coiled out to take it from her, constricting to shatter the blade and turn the ruby into powder. They spread to hold the limbs of the creature that fell from her prison, struggling and hissing.

Due to Izell's pact, Lucia could barely resist as she was drawn toward the center of the forming Dark Eye. But only his sacrifice would end her life permanently and trap her shadowy magic under the sealed glass forever.

Jaromir met Izell's gaze, drawn to her. White hair whipped around her head from the fierce wind pushing from the spell before them. Her face was open, vulnerable—the expression he'd only been able to coax in the dark of night, in those moments when she felt safe to share herself. A thousand glimmering stars danced in her fae eyes. Their mating bond stirred, echoing with heartache.

If she could say one thing to him now, he knew it would be "don't go."

He smiled softly and let his lips form "I love you" since his own heart was so full. It was incredible, the sense of peace dwelling within him as he prepared for his last words. He knew this wasn't truly the end to anything but an era of strife and deception. Life would go on. Incredibly, life would be nurtured by his mate, one of the oldest fae around.

Jaromir coughed out of nowhere, muffling it in his shoulder.

He just hoped the ritual would leave enough of his soul to go back to work at once. Though he didn't understand all of Heaven's rules, surely there would be a period of disarray as an influx of souls arrived from this battle. Plus, the angels here had to be accounted for. He could sneak away through the Veil, returning to his mate and child before anyone noticed.

It could be simple. He doubted it would be *that* simple, but his wishes had wings, and his time had come. Lyana spoke the last words, ones that he'd been warned to listen for. At this point during the original formation, King Oberon had ritually offered himself—mind, body, soul, and magic—to seal the spell permanently. His greatest work, his swan song.

Jaromir drew breath to offer the same with words he'd memorized, all in the ancient language of the fae. Air left him in a pained wheeze. Lyana's last words hung in the air, the Dark Eye nearly complete, save for a few large chunks of glass to complete the top. Lucia's spirit hung over them, still held firmly by lassos of multi-colored magic.

Seconds passed as Jaromir struggled to fill his lungs, but it was like the muscles were suddenly paralyzed. Pained tears filled his eyes. He felt rather than saw Gwendolyn, to his right, shift to face him. "Sorry. It will fade soon," she whispered.

His eyes bulged with disbelief and horror. *Please, don't betray us right now,* he thought. *Not again.* When his sight cleared, he recognized the look of acceptance she wore.

"Truth is, I knew I wouldn't survive this ritual anyway. Cossette shared everything. Live, Jaromir. Your child deserves a father." Her frail hand gave his a squeeze before she belted the phrase meant for him and the air grew heavy around her.

Dark spots winked into sight as he struggled to watch history unfold. Gwendolyn was ripped from his hold by an invisible hand, abruptly breaking up their circle. Something shattered with the sound of tinkling crystal.

Jaromir took an ugly gasp as the stone on the Mending Key burst next, and he realized *all* the Keys were breaking, the force laying everyone flat in the circle. He hit the bare stone hard, losing his hard-fought breath with a groan. At least from this vantage, he saw Gwendolyn's form aloft, face to face with Lucia for the last time.

Magic-fueled wind rushed around them, howling as light enveloped the nephilim, flowing out of her. Still, he saw her embrace the demon, her words a mere whisper. "It always had to be me, old friend. I wish you peace."

He expected venom from Lucia, for her last moments to be as unpleasant as the rest of her existence. Instead, she hugged Gwendolyn back, her response lost to the vortex of the completed Dark Eye. Her body was disintegrating, pulled downward into the glass below in billowing clouds of pure demonic energy.

Gwendolyn was also coming unraveled, dissolving rapidly into particles of light. Soon, all that was left of either of them were their hands, holding on for one final moment, until Lucia was pulled down and Gwendolyn rose, the only thing left of her a shining silhouette with magnificent, feathered wings. And then she was gone, a new hole ripped into Talina's storm clouds.

The last glass piece of the Dark Eye *clinked* into place, sealed closed with one last wave of white-tinged magic. Jaromir pushed his aching body up with a groan, disbelief warring with his consciousness as he coughed and choked to clear his lungs of whatever poison Gwendolyn had slipped him. He recognized her oldest trick: putting it in something he drank.

A hand closed over his shoulder, pulsing magic to help quell his coughing. He looked up at Izell, who embraced him tearfully, holding him nearly as fiercely as he held her. They didn't say anything; they didn't need too. Their bond mixed with heady relief bounced back and forth.

"H-help!" It wasn't until Olivia's panicked voice cut through his awareness that he realized they were still surrounded by people and warring figures. Some, like Neala and Sirius, had rushed off to fight the moment they'd regained their wits. It didn't surprise Jaromir at all.

However, he realized Gwendolyn hadn't given a single soul a warning of what she was going to do. Nyah was a sobbing mess, shaking her head as Adrius and Celeste flanked her with comforting rubs and murmurs. Gabriel stood nearby, watching the sky with a dazzled smile on his face. Which left Jaromir to struggle to his feet and approach Olivia as she knelt over her mate, who lay unconscious where he'd fallen.

She grabbed Jaromir, clutching his shirtfront desperately. "Please, he's not breathing! All the Keys broke, but he *was* a Key..."

"Let the man work, girl," Izell snapped, pulling her off of Jaromir.

He knelt by Julian, checking the other man's vitals with a troubled frown. *"I knew I wouldn't survive this ritual anyway."* Gwendolyn had been the only other living Key, but she'd been much older than healthy, brawny Julian Fairfax. Yet his heartbeat dwindled as the moments passed.

Jaromir reached inside himself desperately, hoping that he'd absorbed some of the Mending Key despite its destruction. There was no thrum within him, no intelligent magic ready to help him heal another. But he didn't come up empty, not when he felt a calm inner warmth and the achingly familiar tingle enter his fingertips.

His Gift. Impossibly, his Gift answered, reading Julian's ills and responding by speeding along his natural healing. The other man took in a deep sigh of air, his heartbeat steadying. "He'll be okay," Jaromir murmured, meeting Olivia's tearstained gaze.

"Thank you," she said, kneeling by her mate's side. "I'll take care of him from here."

He took Izell's hand, about to tell her the good news, when her lips pulled back in a snarl. A dragon's fierce growl rumbled from nearby, Queldian prowling over to put himself between them and two figures that had just landed.

"Just your friendly Lust demons," said Rosier, smiling with bloodstained teeth. He was covered head to toe in demon blood, darkening the white war paint on his face. Lilith leaned on his side, favoring one leg.

Jaromir asked her, "Did you get him?"

Her lips pressed into a fine line. "No. But very soon, I will rule Hell. We came to tell you that we're retreating. The Veil will be stable shortly." She spoke quickly, her amber gaze burning into Jaromir and ignoring the menace of several fae and their familiars aiming spells in her direction. She untied a bundle from her belt, tossing it toward him. "For my friend." With a nod, both demons spread their wings, seeming to disappear once they were in the air.

Queldian beat him to the package wrapped in plain brown paper. The dragon sniffed it over, his solid brow knitting in confusion. "Why'd she call you her friend?" he asked, lifting his head so Jaromir could take it, since it'd apparently passed his inspection.

"Later," Jaromir replied. His fingertips were still tingling, and the sounds of battle were fading from around them. "If the Lust demons are retreating, that must mean they all are..." Which meant he had survivors to tend to. His purpose, finally fulfilled.

Izell and Queldian flanked him, magic and fangs at the ready. But Jaromir wasn't going for the fighting, as the demons were all flooding back through the rift in the ground. He instead walked the bloodstained rock, too sober in the face of death around him to share the good news of his Gift.

Occasionally, he would crouch down, sensing the spark of life in someone mortally injured. It was the Gift at work, knowing where he was needed. He closed many eyes as well. Suddenly aware of how quiet it'd grown between them, he cleared his throat and said, "In the old times, this was part of my duties. To save everyone I could and give the rest some dignity for their service."

"Of course," Izell murmured.

Wings swept in, the glow preceding the angel that landed nearby. "Good evening," Soren said. He was a beacon in the night, shining in all his Archangel splendor. "Perhaps I can make this faster for you."

Spreading his arms, Soren made a lifting motion. A sweep of magic left him in a halo, floating over the ground and into every creature that lay upon it. Demonic corpses turned to dust. Nearby, a glimmering soul left the body of a fallen vampire, and the new angel tested his wings before taking to the sky rapidly.

"This is my job, too." Soren wore a sober expression as he watched more souls take flight. "My friends, consider my shock when I heard about what befell you in Hell. But you have succeeded where you thought you would fail."

"I think it'll hit me soon," Jaromir said, reaching over to link fingers with Izell. They shared a glance, neither smiling yet. There was a lot to be thankful for, such as his life and the successful Dark Eye spell, but soon, he would need to grapple with the quiver of guilt that wove in with his gratitude.

A glowing hand rested on his shoulder. "My people believe that a sacrifice is the noblest of acts," Soren said gently. "Gwendolyn has given you both a priceless gift. Cherish it. I'll take care of this."

It seemed like it was already taken care of, but Jaromir nodded, grateful for the Archangel. He tugged on Izell's hand, taking her away as Soren went to work reviving those still alive.

There was a lot swirling under the surface for him. Gratitude, mostly, but the guilt didn't abate just because of a few kind words, and Jaromir still felt like he needed to do something, prove something, even with their obvious victory. For once, Izell's presence steadied him, her calmer emotions his rock, warm with love through their mating bond.

"Are you sure you still want forever with me?" he asked. He realized he was taking her back to the Dark Eye, the one landmark everyone was bound to return to when the fighting was completely finished.

He also recognized the nerves deep in his chest, the worry that she was waiting for tragedy to part them. "Hey, you stop that," she said. "All those tears and hysterics weren't just for show. This whole time, I thought the executioner was going to part us, one way or another. I *knew* it was coming."

"It was. But not for either of us, it turns out." He finally laughed, because if he didn't, he'd break down. Izell was already crying, but all he felt from her was overwhelming joy.

She threw her arms around him. "We're mates. And we're having a baby, Jaromir! Why can't we have forever?" He spun her around, carrying her now.

"We've already spent half of it apart. I want the rest with you," he said, committing the love in her sparkling eyes to memory forever.

Chapter 42
Izell

The new Dark Eye turned out to be the best rendezvous point around. They spent the better part of an hour watching moonlight gleam over its pristine surface before the united army started milling about.

Izell caught a few shifters talking about scantily clad demon women jumping out of nowhere to ambush the attacking demons from behind. It turned out Lilith really had kept her word. Visiting Hell was one of the best tactical choices they could've made, though it was the kind of decision she would've never seried. No wonder this night ended nothing like what she'd expected.

She and Jaromir sat on a slightly slanted rock together, with her on the side sloping into him. She used it as an excuse to lean her head on his shoulder, occasionally shooting him adoring smiles, like she was surprised to look up and see someone she loved so much. Not everything was wonderful yet, but having them both still here, together, was an excellent start.

They didn't rise until she caught sight of a glowing stag, her breath catching. "Grandfather," she said. King Oberon was little more than a shimmering outline, and she recognized that staying corporeal for so long was taxing, even for the greatest fae to ever live.

"You've done it, my dear. I am so proud of you." His warm

regard washed over her, even though her fingers went through his limned form when she reached for him.

She knew his remaining time was brief and precious, but that was okay. She'd had more time with him than she'd ever dreamed. "It's time for you to rest, isn't it?" she breathed.

"Not quite yet." He stepped forward, his snout applying the most delicate of pressure to her belly. *"Blessings for your babe."*

Just like that, he slipped through her fingers, heading along the row of important faces also gathered under the Dark Eye. He stopped before Nyah, whose nose was still red, but she'd since put on her queenly façade for her shifter people. *"And blessings for your babe as well."* Oberon touched his nose to her rounded form.

The shifter queen startled. "Thank you," she murmured.

"Something tells me you have a lot of mischief to look forward to, between the two children coming," he said with an ethereal laugh.

Nyah seemed to snap out of her stupor more, pointing across the way at Izell. "No, not my baby. Her baby. Have you met Izell?"

"Two's company!" she called back.

If Oberon could smile as a stag, he would. He shook out his head and moved on, heading toward Kalimea, who noticed his path and patted her belly with a hopeful expression. He stopped short of touching her. *"Kalimea, Queen of Faerie. You have brought peace and prosperity to the lands I left behind."* His voice echoed over the watching crowd. Several fae elbowed each other, the Unseelie Army hanging on every word.

"In marrying a Seelie King, you proved that it was possible for Seelie and Unseelie to coexist peacefully. It's all I ever wanted to see in life. I believe, through your leadership, you have changed the fae who used to be one step from demons themselves. Tonight, not only you, but the brave army you've led, have proven that you are friends to humanity."

Izell's breath caught, and she wasn't the only one. Anyone who understood Oberon's curse over the Unseelie knew he'd set the bar to break it impossibly high, saying that they had to prove they were friends to humanity. A hopeful smile crossed her face as her grandfather paused, letting it sink in for everyone.

"I declare that, from this moment forth, there will be no more Unseelie. Faerie will be united once more, with four races to honor the elements who sustain us."

Oberon touched Kalimea's hand, and a burst of magic went up between them, a single flash of light that rolled over the watching crowd in a wave. Awed murmurs followed, but no one was changing physically. Izell wondered if it would take time, but she still grinned as Kalimea covered her mouth with her fingertips. She bent her head to speak with the stag further, private words passing between them.

Kalimea lifted her head after a few minutes and shouted, "Where's Ash?"

Izell moved closer, having an idea of what the Unseelie Queen wanted. Ash walked over to her sister with her head high, even though she was extra pale with fatigue. "Yes?" the other fae asked.

"Tell me the truth," Kalimea said, smiling broadly.

Ash hesitated since this act caused her pain and it wasn't necessarily common knowledge that the Unseelie Princess could speak the truth at all. "You're my sister," she said.

They waited, staring at each other.

Ash slowly started to smile as well. "That didn't hurt," she blurted, followed by an avalanche of facts, all truths that rolled from her tongue easily. The waiting Unseelie army started talking in a murmur of voices, confirming that they, too, could speak the truth.

Kalimea didn't let this drag on for long. She stood straight and gestured over a small group, including Nyah, Izell, and most of the Blood Princes. Standing outside the group were Alex Rehnquist and his mate, plus a few other vampires and angels of rank.

"It's time we go home," Kalimea said, gesturing to the Dark Eye. "With Lady Gwendolyn's passing, all of the standing portals have collapsed. We have to go back to Faerie the old-fashioned way, but our vampire friends will also need to use the Dark Eye to return to their Earth homes."

Nyah bit her lip. "No more quick travel from Faerie to Earth? I was hoping we could rebuild Nyixa, but if we have to choose…"

"There's nothing that says we can't use the Eyes to make that possible. But our people are tired and have earned their rest first," Kalimea answered.

"Then my people will return to Adrun, for now."

"Very well. The first portal will go to vampire lands, though. I'll use the Dark Eye and have one of you direct where the portal lands—since I've heard it was a human Sorceress who broke the last Eye," the Queen of Faerie said. Behind her, Violet's whole face was a deep shade of silver-gray.

Izell turned to Jaromir. "Where do you want to settle?" she asked. They'd never discussed it, not when they were so sure there would be no settling as a couple. If it was just her decision, she'd return to Adrun, the place that had been home for thousands of years. But Jaromir didn't necessarily have a place, not with Nyixa a battle-torn ruin.

"New York," he answered after a short consideration.

She lifted a skeptical brow in return.

"No, really. We can build a home together, learn the modern technology."

"Humans and their boxes," she grumbled.

"And their indoor plumbing, and cars, and the knowledge at their fingertips…" he started, ticking those points off. "Plus, we can always visit Faerie if you don't end up liking it."

She forced herself to actual think about everything Earth had to offer. The technology boxes *did* seem pretty useful, and their books were entertaining. It also wouldn't have to be forever. "I have to admit…I love the idea of a fresh start somewhere new with you," she said.

Just like that, they lined up with the vampire friends when the time came for the Dark Eye to spin up a portal to New York. They ended up saying far too many goodbyes, though. With the shifters heading back to their homeland, that meant that Adrius and Nyah would be going back with them. Sirius would be accompanying Talina, which didn't really surprise her.

"I've got a handsome bard waiting to write a song about this night. We were thinking of seeing Faerie together afterward," Neala said as farewell, an eager smile on her scarred face.

Next to her was Cossette, dressed for combat, solemn as ever. "Sorry to surprise you like that. Zalice said it was a requirement for everything to turn out okay."

"Would it have hurt to warn me?" Izell grumbled but still pulled her into a brief hug.

"Probably," Cossette replied with a hint of cheer.

Before she knew it, she was being shuffled into the group heading for New York, earning more than a few startled looks. No, for once, they weren't looking at her. Queldian paced behind her, lifting his head proudly from all the attention.

"'Scuse me, but how are you planning on hiding a dragon?" Alex asked, raising a brow.

Said dragon spared a fanged grin. "I've been practicing walking on two feet." Confused silence answered him. "With *illusions*, of course. The answer to most everything is magic."

"Of course," the vampire answered, bemused. "I'm so glad to return to a place with no bloody magic."

Izell was just glad to have a chance to settle down.

Epilogue

6 months later

Jaromir

One fine June evening, Jaromir had the kitchen window propped open as he hummed over a sizzling skillet full of eggs and ham, Izell's favorite breakfast. At least for now, because she had a habit of requesting everything from pickles to triple chocolate ice cream upon waking. But he was pretty sure she'd mumbled "omelet" when the alarm clock woke them not long ago.

The shower ran elsewhere in the house while he cooked. It was an important day, but he worried his mate was moving too quickly. As they were on a vampire's nocturnal schedule, the morning sickness attacked her every evening without fail. Thankfully, most days, it was mild, despite the drama she explained her symptoms with.

"Like my stomach is in a cat fight with the baby," was his new favorite Izell-ism.

His phone pinged, and he looked at the message. He was considered an early adopter of technology out of the Ancients, having mostly gotten the hang of it by now. It was from Charlotte, one of the vampires assigned to him and Izell to help them transition to suburban life.

"Bringing you guys a couple visitors. :)" the text read.

He waited for the shower to cut off before calling, "Izell!"

"What?" she called back sharply.

"We're about to have company," he said.

She moaned in denial. "Tell them I died."

Shaking his head, he plated up breakfast and poked his head into their bedroom, where she was tussling with a dress. The seams complained from her rough treatment. "That's a little dramatic, don't you think?" he suggested while rushing over to help her settle the fabric over her body. She'd picked a coppery number with extra folds to compliment her swollen belly.

He held her hips as she tried jabbing her feet into a pair of shoes, before gently pushing her to sit. Kneeling down, he tied them on for her. "It's this half-human baby you gave me," she groused. "We shouldn't have company for three more months. I'm about to resemble a beached whale."

"It's not that bad," he replied.

She started working her hands, settling the usual illusion of scales and fangs over herself. In private, just the two of them, she usually left it off now for him to love her as she was. He had the feeling that she would eventually let her old appearance go but knew intimately how difficult it was to break old habits.

This time, though, she paused before giving herself the tail. "Wait, what kind of company?"

"I didn't ask."

"Why didn't you ask? Should I be a shifter, or a human?" she grumbled.

"Armando and Charlotte are bringing them, so I assume shifter," he said.

She sighed but completed the shifter illusion. "I need to have words with them through the technology box about bringing visitors."

He'd given up correcting her. "Cell phone" was apparently a dumb name for the technology boxes.

"Well, it is midsummer..." Jaromir beamed and offered her a hand up, tucking her to his side. Though they saw their fae friends more often than he expected, via the new Dark Eye, today was the official day when any fae could cross between the two planes. Which meant their visitors could be anyone.

Her tail twitched as she ate. Because of the...*unique* construction of their custom house, the kitchen window overlooked the drive. Anyone looking back would see her as a human, though, because she'd layered enchantments over the whole structure to make it a safe place for her and Queldian to be themselves. She watched the drive like a hawk until a sleek car came zooming to a near-miss of a stop a few inches from their closed garage door.

The car idled while two people got out of the back, before leaving with a friendly beep of its horn. One visitor was wearing a set of royal blue clothes, complete with a foppish hat, and the other was a tall redheaded vampiress who was looking a little softer than the peak muscular shape Jaromir remembered.

He let them in, and Izell eyed Cedric over the rim of her teacup. "Stars above. We get parted for a few months, and you find an even more ridiculous thing to wear."

"Nice to see you too," he practically giggled.

She stood with a little groan, and then it was hugs all around. "C'mon, let me give you the grand tour," Izell said, puffing with pride. She loved their house, as she'd designed it herself. There were few right angles, the house itself as round as possible, with circular windows and wedge-shaped rooms. The only structure that logically would have to be a box—the garage—was detached from the rest. It wasn't like Izell drove anyway.

The living room currently sported a merry fire crackling in the fireplace and Queldian stretched out in front of it like a scaly cat. He blinked lazily at the two visitors. "Is it time yet?" he rumbled.

"A couple more hours," Jaromir answered. They couldn't visit Nyixa until night fell over it. But today was still a big day, and he was glad of a distraction to while away the time as he and Izell settled on the couch, his arm casually around her shoulders. They had a plush setup, with a loveseat for the other couple, which Neala sat upon while Cedric dragged over a cushion to perch on, cross-legged, by her knee.

He released his lute from its carrying case and played a few twanging chords. "So...you might have noticed this." He spread his arms to indicate his blue ensemble. "I'm now, *officially,* a junior member of the historian's guild."

"So official," Izell said, snorting.

"We're actually here to ask a couple questions, if that's okay," Neala said, pushing the brim of her mate's hat down over his face.

"Are you officially a junior historian as well?" Izell asked.

"If you can believe it...yes."

"So, you're *not* working for Sondus anymore."

There was a twinkle in the other woman's reddish eyes. "I didn't say that. He pays well. But we're chronicling your group's trip to Hell and writing a book."

"I wrote you guys a song too," Cedric put in cheerfully.

Neala chuckled. "And there's a song. We've talked to Sondus, Lyana, and Sissaron, but—"

Queldian lifted his head with a soft growl. "Well, then you're missing half the story!"

"What did Lyana say?" Izell grumbled. "She probably didn't tell you the whole truth."

Jaromir cleared his throat. "I just wanted to hear the song," he said, startled by the sudden hostility.

The lyrebird shifter promised the song was almost done, while Neala turned to Izell. "Lyana had nothing but good things to say of you, don't worry." Her scarred mouth framed a smile. "All of them agreed that we should be naming you as our true savior when it comes to averting the apocalypse."

"Our working title for the book is *Rulers of the Night: A Chronicle of Archfae Izell Firebrand's Mission to Hell.*" Cedric made a grand sweep with his hand. "What do you think?"

Izell was blushing fully, though it was hard to tell with her illusion. Jaromir could feel the flash of heat from her as she shifted next to him. "It seems a little much?" she said.

"Eh, we'll figure it out. So, what do you say? Care to tell us what happened in your own words?" Cedric flashed his perfect white smile.

Soon, they were regaling the pair with their side of the story.

Jaromir kept an eye on the time, knowing they had time but that time evaporated quickly in their interest in sharing everything. "Are you two going to Nyixa tonight?" he asked toward the end of their retelling.

"Wouldn't miss it for anything," Neala answered. "We thought we'd hitch a portal with you all."

"One more question, though!" Cedric exclaimed.

"That's fine," Izell answered the other woman. She'd propped her feet up on a pile of cushions at some point and lay back, her eyes lidded. "What's the question?"

"It's for Jaromir, actually. After the Dark Eye was created, we heard that Lilith passed you something before returning to Hell." He leaned forward with bated breath. "What was it?"

A true secret there. Jaromir hesitated. He'd never actually shared the gift with anyone but his mate and her dragon. But it was on the mantle, hiding in plain sight. "I think it would be best if you didn't record this for your chronicle," he hedged. This only seemed to make Cedric's interest keener, so he stood and took the item down, along with the letter that was folded up neatly below it.

The lyrebird shifter put down his pen. "If you say so. I'm dying to know what she gave you, though."

Jaromir handed him the item and sat back down with Izell. "It was this and a letter, wrapped in thick, brown paper. I'll read you what she wrote, because..." He held up the paper, which was blank to anyone but him. A quirk of soul magic, he and Izell had decided. It read:

Dearest Jaromir,

If you are reading this, you've survived the battle. I wasn't sure that any of you would.

I've been thinking about what friendship looks like between two beings on either side of the Veil. Most would say it's impossible, but you and I both have long memories. Maybe one day, we will work together again.

In the meantime, I've decided to tell you the truth about our transference spell. I knew you were desperate when you offered what remained of your angelic light but not desperate enough for what the spell really did to us. You see, you offered me a part of your soul, and I took it. There is only one fair trade for that, and it is a part of my soul. My "spark," as your people call it.

Before you panic, I gave you a little piece of what remains of my angelic core—the Lily you met during the transference. Since I have never killed another with my light, Lily's power can live on in you. Congratulations on receiving your Gift back. Who knows, maybe it'll be more powerful than you remember.

I need you to take the item in this package and keep it. Consider it a souvenir from your time in Hell. Every time I look at it, I'm disgusted. It should have a home elsewhere, where it doesn't stir old memories.

Go prosper in peace. I hope your daughter is as strong as her mother and as steadfast as her father.

Yours,

Lilith

Cedric and Neala exchanged a glance, both of them looking at the item more closely. With every hint of the blade removed, it'd taken Jaromir and Izell a while to figure out what it was, too, but eventually, the cracked crystal pommel gave it away. "It's what remains of Soulcleaver," he supplied. "And I'd prefer if you didn't share that it's in our possession."

The lyrebird shifter yelped, nearly dropping it before his mate swooped in to catch it. "We won't share it," she promised. "Do you think there's more to why she gave it to you than it 'disgusting' her?"

There were multiple theories between him and his little family, but Izell answered with the most likely case. "We assume she doesn't want Lucifer to get it back, so she took the opportunity to make sure someone she trusted on Earth has a hold of it."

Cedric sighed. "Darn it. This is such a juicy secret."

"Then aren't you glad you know it, little bird?" Izell snipped.

"Yes, actually. We're only apprentice historians anyway. Surely they can ignore a couple holes. Like how this guy is back." He hooked a thumb toward Queldian. Since Jaromir hadn't wanted to be here for another couple hours explaining the loophole that'd given the dragon a new body, he just hadn't. They'd said they'd woken up from Hell and he was alive again, just like Sissaron.

A solid mystery was good for history. It got more people interested in it, in Jaromir's opinion.

He checked the time and stirred, glancing toward Izell. "You ready to go?" he murmured.

"Nothing like being fashionably early," she said. With a few waves of her hands, she had a portal open to take them all to Nyixa.

Izell

Well, sort of early. They emerged on Nyixa's beach, where an assortment of shifters was already amassed. The sun was merely a sliver over the ocean, meaning their vampire friends could safely emerge. Those that lived here were just starting to come from the shelters built to save them from the punishing light of day.

She wasn't feeling too sociable today and could no longer blame her dragon. Not when he was alive and flanking her like a protective shadow. Her daughter was doing kick flips in her belly; at least, that's what it felt like. She had no doubt which parent her girl would take after—Jaromir, of course, because she was such an agreeable, static child.

No, unfortunately she had the feeling she'd be raising a mini version of herself. Neither Earth nor Faerie was ready for another Izell, but they were getting one anyway.

She met with her old people, taking the line of well-wishes and even greeting some new babies from others. Access to Faerie had done her people well in some respects. In others...not so much. She took the most direct path to the distinctive pair standing on a patch of scraggly grass, some of the first life that was attempting to grow on Nyixa's battered land.

Adrius and Nyah wore their best. She was in her gilded breastplate, a frothy, multicolored skirt brushing the sand. Her hair was twisted up to support her crown, while his was already a little crooked. His massive hands cradled their newborn, rocking him gently. It took away from the badass "Dragon of Adrun" scaled leather he wore, but that'd never truly been Adrius. The gentle, cooing man soothing his son was the King of Adrun she knew and approved of.

"Are you sure about this?" she asked after greeting them with a formal bow. Appearances were still important, as they were about to make a final decision that affected all their people.

"We're lucky we have the opportunity to do it, Izell," Nyah answered, her chin lifted in stubborn surety.

For this crew of shifters—most of the inhabitants of the Adrun she'd left behind, plus a few new faces who'd either chosen the shifter way or mated into a shifter family—had evacuated their lands for the time being. They were gathered today for a monumental show of magic and a new place to call home.

The gods would be moving Adrun from Faerie to Earth today, rejoining it to Nyixa to make a mega island. It turned out that raising Adrun had made the land unstable, more prone to collapsing back into the ocean than staying afloat in Faerie. That left Adrius and Nyah with a decision: either they could let the island and shifter culture sink for good, or they could reattach it to Nyixa and use the power of the Dark Eye to keep it stable.

For a people that found little acceptance in Faerie, even after everything they'd been through, most wanted to keep their land and culture away from purist fae that called them *mort loci*.

"I, for one, can't wait to have an Adrun-Nyixa," Nyah continued, her words slightly pointed.

"I look forward to Nyixa-Adrun as well," Adrius replied in the same tone.

Izell wet her lips, hiding a grin. "We haven't named the island yet?"

"We have," they said at the same time.

Jaromir coughed a laugh behind her, having caught the tail end of their conversation. He rested a hand gently on her back, and she leaned into him, sharing a brief, adoring look.

"We kept your home too, just in case you wanted to return to it," Nyah said, a hopeful thread in her voice. "It would be just a portal away from your, ah, cylinder home." They'd visited once, with the help of the Dark Eye, to share the news of the Adrun and Nyixa merging and the birth of their child. It sounded like she was still baffled at Izell's design decisions.

"I can definitely see us spending a lot of time there," she assured Nyah. Truth was, she missed that home, as great as it was to have technology boxes and transportation boxes and box stores. "Our girl deserves to see both sides of her culture. Plus...I'm hoping she'll be good friends with Rafe."

The baby in Adrius's hold giggled, like he recognized his name already. She reached for him and, after a small shuffle, cradled him to her chest. Little Gabriel Raphael Fabron already had a mop of blond hair and the sweetest expression, his baby blue eyes fixed on her face in fascination.

"I'm sure they will be! Have you decided on a name for her?" As quickly as she beamed, Nyah's eyes clouded. "Let's see what's holding up the gods, too." She turned away abruptly, heading for the Dark Eye spun up into an open portal, where fae of all kinds came and went.

Nyixa was something of an attraction, half-recovered from its long dip in the ocean and the scene of battle that had destroyed everything that remained, save for the giant occultarus that protected them all. With a stable population incoming, it would surely get rebuilt more quickly.

"Is something wrong?" Izell asked.

Nyah scrubbed at her cheeks. "Sorry. The weirdest things remind me of my mother," she said quietly. "One of our last conversations was about Rafe and how I was naming him in honor of my father."

Well, she hoped the other woman was wearing waterproof makeup. "That's interesting. Because I was going to name my girl in honor of your mother."

Nyah muffled a gasp. "What? Really?" She looked to the sky, trying to fight off some tears.

"Really. Because of her, I get to hold my mate every night and know he's not going anywhere." She started getting teary just watching her friend. "We're pretty sure her name will be Gwyneth Anderon Firebrand. I'm not too sold on that last name, but *someone* doesn't remember his family name."

Jaromir shrugged. "Yours is better, I'm sure. We're thinking of doing the same thing as you, Nyah, giving our girl a nickname."

"Andie," they said together. She laughed a little. They were starting to sound like one of those mated couples that had been together forever, answering questions at the same time and finishing each other's sentences.

Nyah sniffed, smiling broadly. "It's a lovely name. Thank you...for giving her that honor. I'm sure she would try to tell you not to do it, but she deserves to be remembered for what she did for all of us."

They stopped on one of the blank flagstones that had been added, ringing the Dark Eye. Eventually, it would have a decorated courtyard, just like its counterpart in Faerie. Nyah breathed out, regaining her composure in stages. "You know, she didn't warn me or anything, but she knew the spell would signal the end of her life. My last memories of her are shopping and Christmas and...well, the Dark Eye. But I look at it, and I'm happy, because I had more time with her than I thought I would. And she died for what she believed in."

"It's how she always wanted to go," Adrius murmured.

Nyah fanned her face. "And she's with Father, finally."

At that moment, the portal to Faerie rippled, and out flew Talina, wearing a trailing gown that shimmered and danced with the movement of her wings. "Hi hi!" she exclaimed before spotting Nyah and landing in a graceful sweep. "Oh no, what's wrong?" She clasped her hands, glancing over her shoulder as Sirius followed close behind her.

"Nothing!" Nyah said quickly, pulling the blue fae in for a hug. The brothers did much the same for a quick, hearty greeting.

"Where's my junior?" Sirius grinned, taking little Rafe.

Izell exchanged an amused glance with Jaromir. Someone took his uncle role all too seriously, and they had a small bet going for how long it'd take baby fever to spread.

"My father should be along shortly," Talina told them. "He's pretty sure this is going to be no big deal, but it's, like…a really big island. Can we really splish-splash an island into Earth's ocean without any humans noticing?"

"That's what magic is for," Izell quipped.

The demigoddess rolled her eyes. "Yeah, I guess."

As promised, the next person through the portal was the Lord of Storms himself, dressed in his fine, silver-lined tunic, not a hair out of place. He flicked his wrist, and the Dark Eye immediately started to slow, the portal sputtering out to reveal the star-kissed surface of the massive glass orb.

"Good evening." His static-filled voice was warm, despite a stoic expression. "My daughter has told you correctly. I intend to help splish-splash Adrun over here posthaste."

Talina covered her face with a delicate hand.

"As long as you're sure?" he directed the question to Nyah, who nodded. "We can establish a few spells to keep this secret. Cyranos already has something planned regarding mist and currents, last time I checked. And I wanted to try something to keep your more photosensitive friends safe during the day. No one should be denied the warmth of the sun."

Nyah practically vibrated with delight. "That sounds lovely. We can make Adrun-Nyixa a haven for all supernaturals here on Earth."

Adrius opened his mouth to correct her, but Zalice spoke first, "Have you two considered Nyrun or Adixa? You're bound to confuse someone otherwise."

The shifter royals both paused, and while they did, the Lord of Storms turned back to the Dark Eye and raised his palms. It rotated slowly, the smoke within swirling into a tornado of energy. Izell backed up to a safer distance, feeling a little blessed to see this much magical power being exerted. There probably would never be anything quite like a god wielding the largest tool a spell caster could find.

As far as she understood, Raenith was currently standing at the Light Eye, doing much the same thing. Cyranos and Getana were manipulating the water and earth around the island of

Adrun directly so that when it appeared, it was only briefly submerged.

It took hours to make the transfer, but the other island appeared out of the blue when it was finally done. The ground under her feet trembled, juddering as the two islands rammed together, water geysers marking the intersection miles away. The gods made it look easy, though she knew the magic in use was beyond any other.

Zalice straightened, wiping his brow. The shifters cheered down on the beach, several heading for the place where beach met the verdant greenery of the druid-blessed Adrun. Izell scoffed and made a portal to get there quicker, leaving it open for her companions.

Getana was already at the intersection, smoothing and flowing the lands together so there was no ugly scar where the earth rucked up in a chain of mini mountains. She smiled and waved when she spotted Izell. The goddess was wearing summery red hair and a back full of blooming flowers and oak trees woven to resemble leafy wings.

Getana left the work for a moment to step onto the Nyixa side of the new joint island, clucking her tongue. "Oh, this will not do. This land is *so* salty," she said.

Before she could lift her fingers, Izell said, "Sounds like a challenge for your druids."

Getana smiled. "Quite right! I forget I'm not the only one that likes shaping nature. Cyranos is just getting all the water off your new land back there, but we managed to move it over with only a minor earthquake or two. Most of your buildings should be standing with no issue."

For the second time in not too long, Izell hid her amused expression by licking her lips. *No big deal, just a couple earthquakes.* Only a goddess would be so casual about such things. "The palace is okay?" she asked for Nyah, who'd probably faint if it toppled.

"Oh, yes. I made sure that one stayed up. Would be an awful shame if it cracked," Getana said in a merry chirp.

"Cracked? What cracked?" the shifter queen asked, just now coming over after admiring the bulk of Adrun by Earth's starlight.

"Nothing, dear. I'm glad you were patient enough to wait for midsummer. We managed to do this nearly painlessly," Getana answered. "We're going to have a hard time fading back into myth after all this excitement!"

Zalice flashed her a knowing look. "Something tells me you'll be seeing more of her in person," he whispered behind a hand.

"What can I say? We have land! On Earth! And half of these little shifters love me most anyway." The Goddess of Earth was practically beaming, her hands clasped under her chin. "Why wouldn't I come visit?"

He rolled his eyes. "Sense of mystery, sister."

"I sense there's an abandoned peak you can brood on," she sniffed.

Jaromir slanted a disbelieving look at Izell, gesturing to them. She shrugged in return. "Want to see my old home again?"

"I'd love to," he said.

From how the two gods were going on, she had a feeling they wouldn't be missed for a quick side trip. She waved a portal into being and stole her mate away, their shoes hitting soggy earth on the path to her old house. Other than the tang of ocean water, everything was as she remembered. Her little house in the woods, tucked away from prying eyes. Her shoulders loosened to know that there was no one else around, just the man she loved more than anything.

"I've lived here, on my own, for so long. It's not much, but it's mine, and I can't wait to share it with you and Andie," she said, taking his hand. They strode together to the front door. As she opened it, out flowed a steady stream of water, plus a flopping fish. It looked just as surprised to see them, and Izell jumped away with a yelp.

Maybe they should've waited for the God of Water to unflood her home. Either way, she shared a laugh and then a kiss with Jaromir, brushing noses with him as their lips parted.

"One thing's for sure," he said, the look in his eyes pure devotion. "Eternity with you will never be dull."

Izell felt that truth resonate down to her heart. Many wanted a simple life when they settled down, but not her. And through her mating bond, she knew he shared that feeling. "No, eternity with me will be an adventure. Guaranteed."

She sealed that promise with another kiss.

**Want more Blood Legacy? Don't miss...
Dhampir's Wish: Blood Legacy Series Christmas
Special**

Also by Elise Hennessy
Altare World

Are you ready for a high-flying adventure on gryphon-back? Join Sivana as she becomes the first female cadet at the highly competitive Gryphon Rider Academy after the blind gryphon Arimus chooses her as his new rider.

Dragon Riders of Pern meets Song of the Lioness in this YA fantasy series in which a pair of underdogs rewrite what's possible in a formerly all-boys military academy.

- See Gryphon Rider Academy on Amazon -

About the Author

Elise Hennessy is an author of young adult fantasy full of adventure and found family. She holds a master's degree in journalism and enjoys crafting unique stories. When Elise is not busy writing, she's trying to reduce her prodigious TBR list. She lives in Texas with her family and is owned by two cats.

Find out more about her books at: www.elisehennessy.com

Glossary

Adrun: A section of Faerie submerged under the ocean and shrouded in magic to make it impenetrable. Formerly a prison for the cursed Fell. Queen Nyah renamed it from "The Fell Lands" when she and her shifters reclaimed it and eliminated the Fell curse. It is a place of complete darkness that sustains life through druidic magic.

Alchemyst: An incredibly rare sub-distinction of vampire with golden blood. They can create powerful tonics and potions with one drop of their life essence. They are immortal, but lack the superhuman aspects of vampirism and the bloodlust.

Angel: A being of pure light and a denizen of Heaven. All angels are called to uphold and spread a grace, or positive emotion/trait. Can only be permanently killed by another angel or demonic magic.

Blade: A fae skilled with martial magic and a weapon of choice, usually a sword. Traditionally they serve as bodyguards to Sorcerers.

Blood Prince: A title given to the few Fell Hunters that survived the Fell Crisis. They are the first vampires and each started their own unique bloodlines.

The Crossing: Seelie fae can cross The Veil and travel between Earth and Faerie or vice versa during midsummer in a magical process called The Crossing. The only way to otherwise cross between the two worlds is through one of a handful of well-hidden portals.

Demon: A being of pure darkness and a denizen of Hell. The most common demons represent one of the seven sins, though it's possible to find a demon that represents any negative emotion. Can only be permanently killed by another demon or angelic magic.

Deveaux Accords: A set of laws created by the major covens of New York City and enforced by Ancient vampiress Cossette Deveaux. Covens are required to police their members to keep mortals safe.

Dhampir: A half-human, half-vampire by birth.

Drasonii: Literally "dragon-blessed." Members of a fae orchestra with instruments blessed by the four dragon gods of Faerie. The instruments are peerless and capable of conveying the emotions of a song to a listening crowd.

Druid: A fae or shifter that has manifested the virtue of druidism. They maintain the balance of nature through husbandry and control of the elements. It is possible to be both a Sorcerer and have druidism, but a fae or shifter that has both gifts is considered a druid exclusively. A druid in Faerie serves the four gods and the balance of the elements, while a shifter druid in Adrun keeps the land alive in the absence of sunlight.

The Everlasting War: The conflict between angels and

demons. The Veil was created to keep this eternal war away from Earth and Faerie.

Eyes of Worlds: A pair of giant tools that anchor The Veil into place. One was created by the willing sacrifice of an Archangel—it is the Light Eye located in Faerie. The other was created from an unwilling greater demon and became its prison—it was destroyed during the events of *Dream Walker*.

Faerie: A separate world magically linked to Earth. The place of origin for all magic and mythical creatures.

Fell: A fae afflicted with a curse of eternal hunger. The curse was spread from Fell to fae via a bite and was considered incurable. Fell are twisted creatures known for squat, frog-like legs, sharp and interconnected teeth like a bear trap, black veins, and pitch-black eyes. All Fell were banished from Faerie to The Fell Lands (see Adrun). The Fell Crisis or Fell War occurred when the Fell learned they could create portals to Earth during the Dark Ages and began consuming man and beast alike like a black tide of locusts. After their defeat, all records of the Fell were expunged from mortal record to hide the existence of vampires.

Fell Hunter: The first vampires. Soldiers exposed to Fell blood became strong and fast enough to fight Fell in the service to humanity. Though the first Fell Hunters were turned by accident, many were turned on purpose after the phenomenon was studied. In those days, being a vampire was considered a sacrifice for the greater good. Most Fell Hunters died fighting monsters.

Fell Keys: Thirteen in total, referring to a set of rings with gemstones of pure magic. Each one represents one of the schools of fae magic and grants the wearer great power.

Fell Madness: The boogeyman of vampirism. First manifested in Fell Hunters when they consumed too much Fell blood. Fell

Madness gives vampires black veins, a mouthful of sharp teeth, and endless hunger for blood. Very little is known about the affliction because those that manifested it were swiftly executed. In modern day, the affliction can be cured by an Alchemyst's potion.

The Gift: Some vampires manifest the Gift rather than the abilities of their bloodline. They are capable of healing others from even the worst of mortal wounds. The Gift leaves if a vampire uses it to harm or kill others.

Heartsong: The fae version of a lifemate (see below). Every fae has a unique melody that they create when they come of age, which they refer to as a heart's song. Two fae with harmonizing heart's songs are destined to be mates.

Heaven-Hell Accords: A set of rules agreed on between angels and demons as it concerns their interaction with Earth. As the Everlasting War is based off of balance, if a demon is summoned to Earth, an angel is allowed through The Veil to hunt it down. Resurrections of newly created angels or demons is strictly forbidden. Hell attacks, Heaven defends. Demons historically have bent these rules to the breaking point.

Lifemate: A perfect match to a vampire. It is possible to identify a lifemate on sight and many vampires describe the sensation as being as subtle as a punch to the gut. A lifemate is usually a vampire's perfect opposite. It is possible for a vampire to have more than one lifemate, but the phenomenon is exceedingly rare as most vampires don't survive to an advanced age if they lose their first lifemate.

Mort Loci: Translated to "death speaker." A derogatory term for a person with the soul of an animal inside of them. The fae consider such people possessed or cursed. (See shifter below.)

Nephilim: A person with angel parentage, who is capable of wielding light magic. Nephilim are considered extinct in modern day due to The Veil and the Heaven-Hell Accords.

Nyixa Island: A chunk of The Fell Lands that the Fell managed to drag to Earth. It is a relatively large island with the Dark Eye at its center. After the Fell were defeated, vampires made it their seat of power before it was sunk to the bottom of the ocean in a bid to eradicate Fell Madness. It has only resurfaced recently in modern times and is considered inhabitable.

Occultarus: A tool used by Sorcerers to concentrate their magic. Instead of using complicated gestures to summon magic, a Sorcerer can hold an occultarus and cast spells more quickly. An occultarus is a sphere of glass forged by dragon fire and contains concentrated magic within. The Eyes of Worlds were modeled after occultari and are giant versions of them.

Primordial Fae: The very first denizens of Faerie. They were powerful, but unstable, and evolved into the four sub-races of greater fae, split into the four elements of earth, fire, water, and wind. King Oberon is the most notable Primordial.

Seelie Fae: Greater fae who aligned with angels before The Veil separated Faerie from Heaven and Hell. Their tongues are cursed to utter only the truth. While Faerie is at peace now, Seelie and Unseelie have historically been at war along the same lines as their patrons. Their sub-races are terran fae (earth), solar fae (fire), astral fae (water), and aether fae (wind).

Shifter: A fae or human with the soul of an animal within them. While the fae will refer to a shifter as *mort loci* in a derogatory manner, the denizens of Adrun all became shifters as the Fell curse cannot take root in a body with two souls within it. The creation of a shifter is a partnership and the resulting person can appear fully humanoid or gain physical characteristics of their animal side. Some shifters fully give in to the whims of their animal and never return to humanoid form.

Spark: A piece of a demon's soul that can be given to a "willing" person. A spark will slowly corrupt the person's soul until it resembles the same level of darkness as the original demon, twisting their personality in the process. A spark can out-live a demon if they are killed. Powerful demons can "resurrect" by taking over the body of a humanoid afflicted by their spark.

Spellbreaker: A fae skilled in reflecting or mitigating magic. A highly trained Spellbreaker can render a Sorcerer's magic useless.

Sorcerer: Originally a distinction for the rare fae who can control all thirteen schools of magic, this title is also awarded to the sub-class of vampire that has silver blood and the ability to control every school of fae magic. Sorcerers are highly trained and often manifest extra rare abilities called virtues. The five virtues are: true sight, future sight, empathy, druidism, and mediumship.

Unseelie Fae: Greater fae who aligned with demons before The Veil separated Faerie from Heaven and Hell. Their tongues are cursed to utter only lies. While Faerie is at peace now, Seelie and Unseelie have historically been at war along the same lines as their patrons. Their sub-races are curse fae (earth), destruction fae (fire), death fae (water), and blight fae (wind).

Vampire: Descendants of the original Fell Hunters, spread by their cursed blood. The existence of vampires has become a myth to modern mortals as the purpose of vampires has tarnished from war heroes into former mortals trying to avoid their mortal coil. Contrary to popular myth, vampires are not walking corpses; they eat, breathe, and reproduce, though the chance of conception narrows as a vampire ages. Young vampires act a lot like humans with a taste for blood, though as they age they grow more powerful and inhuman. Vampires manifest an aura, which communicate to each other how old and powerful they are.

The Veil: A magical barrier that separates Earth and Faerie from the realms of Heaven and Hell. Anchored in place by the Eyes of Worlds, it's been in place for over a thousand Earth years and prevented the worlds from coming to ruin by being battle-grounds for angels and demons.

Cast of Characters

Modern Day Vampires

Residents of New York City's covens.

Alexander Rehnquist

A vampire nearing his five hundredth year. Master of Coven Rehnquist and skilled shapeshifter. He is bitter rivals with Bryant Collins and lost his first lifemate due to the conflict between their covens. Fate crossed him one night and he ended up partnered with a second lifemate, Violet Reynolds.

Violet Reynolds

Formerly a mortal zookeeper, Violet was exposed to vampirism after Lucia secretly turned her into a kind of vampire that hadn't been seen in a thousand years. She became a silver-blooded Sorceress, learned how to master her magic, and captured Alex's love.

Julian Fairfax

One of the officers of Coven Rehnquist. The only vampire who mysteriously manifests an icy cold aura. He searched for his life-mate for hundreds of years until they were united via Lucia's machinations. He was viciously hunted by Lucia due to him killing her obsession. Possesses the Winter Key.

Olivia Cooper

A struggling mortal actress who was kidnapped to New York. She knows of the vampire world due to her best friend, Charlotte, but was quickly over her head after taking in Violet's blood and turning into an Alchemyst. She developed magical empathy and used it to save her Ancient allies from Jazrach's corruption. Due to her blood and quick thinking, she transformed a portal manifesting a connection between Earth and Hell into one that linked Earth to Adrun instead. Possesses the Shadow Key.

Charlotte Smith

Olivia's best friend and the only dhampir around. She is loyal and protective of her friend, joining Coven Rehnquist when Olivia did. She joins the supernatural police and becomes Armando's patrol partner when Julian retires.

Armando Nizzola

Julian's cousin and a member of the supernatural police. He is Charlotte's lifemate and earns her affection in the Christmas special *Dhampir's Wish*.

Bryant Collins

A bitter rival to Alex and Coven Rehnquist. He owns the telecommunications company Haven and thus members of his coven are referred to as Haveners. He is an Ancient and a religious zealot, believing the Light Key is his by his faith. He allied with Lucia thinking he could finally crush Coven Rehnquist with her might and magic, instead realizing his mistake too late after she got his entire coven killed and sacrificed his wife's heart to power a portal. He now seeks repentance for his misguided ideals.

Kim Cox

Bryant Collins's wife, known for her sadistic personality and enjoyment of torturing others. She is deceased as of *The Winter Key*.

Cossette Deveaux

The Ancient leader of the most powerful coven in New York City. She is an albino and a rare vampire who possesses future sight. She is stuck in the body of a little girl due to the twisted ideals of her vampire master. Due to her unique circumstances, her mind is damaged. She usually acts like a cheerful and sweet girl, but sometimes shows hints of her age as she delivers prophecies of the future.

Ancients

Surviving Fell Hunters whose bloodlines have shaped the vampire world in their absence.

Adrius

King of Adrun

Strongest Fell Hunter and owner of the Shield Key. He fell into a deep pit of depression to be separated from his lifemate, Nyah. Possessed every vampiric ability until he became a shifter by bonding to the spirit of the dragon Zerenth.

Lucia

The first vampire Sorceress. She inherited Jazrach's spark and was slowly driven insane. Nyixa was sunk partially to contain her evil. Upon dying in *Queen's Return,* she was reincarnated as a demon of corruption and now terrorizes her peers as she tries to capture a powerful soul to fulfill the debt of her escape from Hell. Was briefly Queen of Vampires in *Blood Curse.*

Gwendolyn Firetree

A nephilim who represents the grace of duty. Conspired to sink Nyixa in *Blood Curse* to contain Fell Madness and Lucia. She has committed her immortal existence to curbing the damage of old vampires on the brink of Fell Madness by making them mysteriously "disappear."

Sirius

Blood Prince Sirius, the Dawn
Adrius's second-in-command and brother. Was once a kind and
giving man, but emerged from his thousand-year rest bitter, angry,
and unable to fully control the whims of his inner beast. He is a
shapeshifter and possesses the ability to walk in daylight without
harm.

Korin

Blood Prince Korin, the Bane
The gentle giant of the Ancients, a steady and quiet personality.
He is a blood tracker.

Neala

Blood Princess Neala, the Wraith
A mute orphan raised by Gabriel and Gwendolyn. She defied the
odds and survived the Fell Crisis, though she sustained several
terrible wounds that scarred her face and chest. Despite being an
illusionist, she refuses to hide her scars or make herself more
attractive and feminine. Loved and lost her first mate, Marcus
Hartson, to Lucia's machinations.

Elandros

Blood Prince Elandros, the Legion
Squire to Gabriel Legion and also his murderer due to unfortu-
nate circumstances. Possessed the ability to make minor illnesses
and blights. After being blackmailed for the rest of his life by
Lucia, he confessed his crime to Gwendolyn and was forgiven.
Deceased as of *The Winter Key*. His soul was delivered to
Heaven in *Queen's Return*.

Jaromir

Blood Prince Jaromir, the Mender
The doctor of the surviving Ancients. He was in possession of the
Gift until he was briefly afflicted with Fell Madness in *The
Winter Key*. He believes himself incomplete without his Gift.

Cast of Characters

Qin

Blood Prince Qin, the Ascended

He is considered a greedy coward by his peers, as he took a payment from Lucia and went into hiding, never to be seen again.

Taryn

Blood Prince Taryn, the Blade

Lucia's bodyguard due to taking a stage three love potion and being enslaved by his emotions. While he was immediately driven to Fell Madness upon being released from her control, he found his peace and center by becoming a druid as of *Queen's Return.*

Marcus Hartson

A close friend to the Ancients and Neala's former mate. After his mating bond was severed by Lucia, he was poisoned by her cursed blood and grew increasingly insane as the years passed. Died in an honorable duel with his son Julian after he drove the family to the brink of ruin from countless wars with other vampires. Deceased as of *Blood Curse.*

Adrun

A land of shifters and eternal darkness, full of life despite the odds.

Nyah

Queen of Adrun

Banished to the Fell Lands in *Blood Curse* due to Lucia's machinations for her throne. Instead of dying in the desolate land, Nyah used her Alchemyst blood to cure the Fell around her one at a time and establish life with the help of the Spring and Autumn Keys. Once her people discovered they could become shifters to permanently stave off the Fell curse, she was crowned Queen of Adrun and ruled with an empty throne beside her until she was reunited with her lifemate, Adrius. She is a shifter bonded to the greater wolf spirit Night's Howl.

Cast of Characters

Celeste

Princess of Adrun

A shy druid accustomed to taking the form of her beast, the greater fox spirit Swift Spirit. Raised believing her father was a great hero, she helped push him out of his depression so he could achieve his destiny and win back her mother's affections.

Izell Firebrand

Considered to be the oldest fae alive. She is King Oberon's granddaughter and the first Archfae of the astral fae people. She's been through a lot and has learned to keep her true thoughts hidden under a thick layer of cynicism. Bonded to the spirit of her familiar in life, the golden dragon Queldian. She's a distant ancestor to Keegan Firetree, much to his chagrin.

Cedric Applewhite

A half-fae, half-human born in Adrun. He inherited an enchanted lute from his grandfather and became a self-taught musician. He is known for his energy and enthusiasm.

Chandra

Blood Princess Chandra, the Dreamer

The only Ancient locked into the Fell Lands alongside Nyah. She shed her vampirism and bonded to an earth spirit, becoming the head druid of Adrun. She now believes in peace, love, and parties, and gladly helped Taryn escape the grip of his rage.

Caladorn Nightweaver

An astral fae Blade who lost his wife tragically when they were both afflicted by the Fell curse. He surrendered his newborn daughter, Sorsha, to Neala and promised to repay the favor one day. He serves Nyah as her general and has developed an icy façade to endure his immortality alone.

Calinhes Nightweaver

An incredibly powerful Sorcerer who was afflicted with the Fell curse while defending an academy full of fae children. He became the leader of the Fell, crowned the Fell Emperor, and became the reason the Fell came to Earth due to his keen mind and magical prowess surviving the transition. His familiar was Zerenth and the dragon mourned Calinhes's death for an eternity, refusing to believe his master turned into a monster until confronted by the facts. Deceased as of *Blood Curse*.

Faerie
The mythical residents of a secret world.

Orin Lux
King of Faerie
A solar fae who cemented the peace of Faerie by marrying the Unseelie Queen, Kalimea Dread.

Kalimea Dread
Queen of Faerie
A destruction fae said to be soft for an Unseelie due to her efforts to curb homelessness and creation of social welfare programs. She is a forward-thinker amongst a people used to cruelty and callousness from the royals that preceded her.

Talina Evenfall
A circus performer and aether fae who has caught Sirius's eye as a potential lifemate. She is a ballerina who can defy gravity with powerful wind magic. Her familiar is the iridescent pink hummingbird, Gem.

Sorsha Shadestone
An astral fae Sorceress with the true sight ability. She was born in the Fell Lands, but her father gave her to Neala to raise, who adopted her alongside her brother-by-circumstance, Keegan. She is petite, sweet, and still sometimes acts like a teenager when she lets her guard down. Otherwise, she's a diplomat and advisor to King Orin from her position as an Archfae.

Cast of Characters

Keegan Firetree

An astral fae Blade who comes off tight-lipped and reserved. He was adopted by Neala alongside Sorsha and took on his adoptive mother's warrior persona. He is considered to be very powerful due to bonding with a fire dragon as his familiar.

Ashaela Dread

Unseelie Princess

Queen Kalimea's destruction fae half-sister. She is a Spellbreaker and trained assassin who relies heavily on her shadow magic. She is cagy and sarcastic, preferring not to be identified by her titles as she does not want to be the heir to her sister's throne.

Theron Shadestone

A powerful terran fae druid who has earned the title of Arch-druid due to his skill in training young druids. He is standing in for his mate, Sorsha, in her absence from Faerie. His honest and to-the-point personality is already rubbing the rest of the Archfae the wrong way.

Sondus Arus

A spymaster for the royal family. He lost his wings long ago as a punishment from the last Unseelie Queen and thus has very little magic. His quick mind and photographic memory serve him well in his chosen profession.

Lyana Wavecaller

A guardian of one of the last known portals between Earth and Faerie. She is a sea serpent shifter, bonding to the soul of her familiar when he died. Fae society shunned her for her choice to become a *mort loci* and she was forced into a lonely underwater post.

The Trader

A reptilian lesser fae who runs a supernatural pawn shop.

Cast of Characters

Saniya

A wishmaker djinni, freed after millennia of servitude to the Unseelie royal family. Hides away in a remote village and rarely reveals herself.

King Oberon

A Primordial fae who served as the first King of Faerie. He originally welcomed both angels and demons to Faerie before they started infiltrating amongst his people and causing strife. He created The Veil and the Eye of Worlds in a powerful spell that was fueled by his life force. His sacrifice also cursed Seelie and Unseelie alike, but the way he worded the spell suggests that the Unseelie may one day break it by proving they are "friends to humanity."

Other

Soren

A humble man who is Adrius's guardian angel.

Gabriel Legion

In life, a vampire named for the amount of Fell he killed. In death, an angelic soldier whom has returned to Earth to hunt Jazrach. He was the original commander of the Fell Hunters before his untimely death.

Jazrach

A greater demon of corruption whom was unwillingly sacrificed to create the Dark Eye of Worlds. He plotted to escape his prison and eventually stole a living body to wreak havoc and spread his corruption. He is deceased as of *Queen's Return*, but his spark remains...

Getana

Fae goddess of earth.

Raenith
Fae goddess of fire.

Cyranos
Fae god of water.

Zalice
Fae god of wind.